LOOK UNTO THE LAND

A NOVEL

For Sam,
With appreciation and all best wishes!

GEORGE ROLLIE ADAMS

BARN LOFT
PRESS

Look Unto the Land

First Edition

This is a work of fiction. References in the book to historical events, real people, or real places are used fictitiously. Other names, characters, and events are products of the author's imagination, and any resemblance to actual events, places, or persons, living or dead, is entirely coincidental.

Library of Congress Control Number: 2022912734

Publisher's Cataloging-In-Publication Data
(Prepared by Cassidy Cataloguing Services, Inc.)

Names: Adams, George Rollie, author.
Title: Look unto the land : a novel / George Rollie Adams.
Description: First edition. | [Pittsford, New York] : Barn Loft Press, [2022] | Series: Small town race relations
Identifiers: ISBN: 978-1-7333669-6-0 (paperback) | 978-1-7333669-7-7 (hardback) | 978-1-7333669-8-4 (ebook) | LCCN: 2022912734
Subjects: LCSH: Veterans—Indiana—History—20th century—Fiction. | Families—Indiana—History—20th century—Fiction. | Petroleum industry and trade—Arkansas—History—20th century—Fiction. | Oil well drilling—Environmental aspects—Arkansas—Fiction. | Farmers—Arkansas—History— 20th century—Fiction. | Crime—Arkansas—History—20th century—Fiction. | Arkansas—Race relations—History—20th century—Fiction. | Revenge—Fiction. | LCGFT: Historical fiction. | Environmental fiction.
Classification: LCC: PS3601.D3745 L66 2022 | DDC: 813/.6—dc23

BARN LOFT PRESS
Paperback ISBN: 978-1-7333669-6-0
Hardback ISBN: 978-1-7333669-7-7
eBook ISBN: 978-1-7333669-8-4

Cover Photograph Courtesy of Arkansas Museum of Natural Resources
Cover Design by Bruce Gore, Gore Studios, Inc.
Interior Design by Amit Dey
Author Photograph by Amanda Adams

PRINTED IN THE UNITED STATES OF AMERICA

This book is dedicated to:

The memory of Grace Lou Adams Davidson,
who collected the initial batch of local history clippings and
other materials that interested me in this historical topic, and to

The hope that scientific knowledge, rational thinking,
and intelligent policy-making, planning, and conservation
practices will prevail in time to save our planet.

CHAPTER 1

Henry Grant stood stiff-legged and sweat-soaked among dozens of other men jammed into the seats and aisles of passenger cars clacking and swaying along the Missouri Pacific line. More than two hours had passed since the train left Little Rock in stifling July heat and humidity from morning thunderstorms. The travelers were headed for Berrytown and the newest South Arkansas oil field. A place where jobs awaited, and maybe riches for a lucky few. Both promised tonic for the ills of the depression of 1920, still gripping the country after two long years. It wasn't work or hope for fortune that brought Henry, however. He was looking for someone. A man with a debt to pay. One money would not resolve.

In every car, the stink of unwashed bodies and stale tobacco smoke hung in the air amid talk heavy with anticipation and uncertainty. Henry recognized both. He had seen them time and again four years ago in other cramped spaces, aboard ship and in European trenches with men of the American Expeditionary Force.

Not all the other passengers were looking for jobs or chances to sell their wares or launch new ventures. Some were swindlers and con artists looking to hoodwink those who found success by working for it. Some were tourists eager to see the new and exotic. Both the hopeful and the curious came from all over the Midwest and Northeast. All were drawn by near-daily reports of new-found pools in the oil-rich Gulf Coast Plain, their seductiveness magnified by images, real and imagined, of earlier strikes in East Texas and North Louisiana. Places with romantic sounding names like Spindletop, Ranger, Mexia, Burkburnett, and Caddo. Even more tantalizing was a big strike last year at El Dorado, a few miles south of Berrytown. Many of the travelers had squeezed aboard in Little Rock, but most had been en route longer. Henry had first boarded a coach in Indianapolis.

Because the rail line cut a westward arc from Little Rock, the train crossed meandering Scuppernong Creek and entered Union County and Berrytown with the late afternoon sun behind it. As the cars slowed, Henry, a fair-haired and sinewy man of above-average height, bent to look over the heads of seated passengers. Miles back he had given up his bench seat to an older man no longer able to stand. Through lowered windows on his right, Henry saw a new station house still bare of paint and a loading platform teeming with men he assumed were there to meet new arrivals or board coaches for points south.

Most of the waiting bore haggard expressions from a long day of grubbing about for every sort of bounty the country's latest boomtown might offer. Some wore business suits and fedoras or straw boaters and carried carpetbags, leather valises, or tin suitcases. Others—derrick builders, drillers, roughnecks, and roustabouts who traveled back and forth six days a week from more established El Dorado—carried lunch pails or stood empty-handed. Their fedoras, flat caps, cotton shirts, denim overalls, and cord pants were stained black with oil, mud, and grime. None in the crowd wore a policeman's or sheriff's uniform, but some toted pistols. Even a quick scan of the swarm told Henry it would be harder than he had imagined to find the man he sought, though likely easier to make him pay and then move on unhampered.

As the travelers pushed their way toward exit doors, Henry's own pistol—an Army officer's Colt .45 he had walked away with after his discharge and now carried in a side pocket of his khakis—pressed into the man in front of him. If the fellow noticed, he gave no sign. Probably, Henry thought, because he, too, was armed.

While working his way toward the front of the car, Henry leaned over again, looking this time to the other side. Beyond a two-track siding, haphazard piles of wooden crates of every size and description created a maze through which men struggled to steer horse-drawn buggies and wagons pulled by mule teams. Past those lay stacks of lumber, racks of pipe, and mounds of assorted oil-field equipment.

Henry recognized some pieces from having grown up near the huge but now mostly depleted Trenton Oil and Gas Field in central Indiana. Some items resembled tools and machinery he had seen recently in smaller, also declining fields in the southwestern part of the state. He had already searched both areas for the man he sought. Not surprisingly, some pieces were new to him, as high expectations were attracting the newest and best resources available. Newspapers from the *Wall Street Journal* to the *Indianapolis Star* all boldly predicted that Berrytown would become the biggest field yet, surpassing even El Dorado, once the object of similar attention. There, hundreds of wells still supported several refineries even as production began to slow.

Shouting teamsters, whinnying horses, and braying mules amplified the turbulent scene around the train. But neither the commotion nor the stench of animal manure, outhouses, and sulfur from the oil field bothered Henry as he stepped down from the coach. He secured his battered leather valise and blended into the tangled mass. He looked like any ordinary oil-field laborer. Work shirt, sturdy boots, denim jacket slung over one shoulder, and well-worn, floppy fedora pulled low on his forehead. The hat covered a jagged red scar that stretched along a third of his hairline, a souvenir of shrapnel from German artillery in France's Argonne Forest. Despite the visual reminder of his wound, Henry was what many would call a handsome man, but vanity played no role in how he wore the fedora. He wanted to avoid attention that might make it harder to accomplish what he had come to do.

First, he needed food and a place to stay. Then a job, less for the money than a way to blend in while he searched. His meager savings, sufficient to sustain him for a while, nestled in his wallet. He was of two minds about what kind of work to seek. A string of different jobs would allow him to spend enough time in separate locations to nose around without raising suspicion. On the other hand, a job like driving a freight wagon—trucks being of limited use in heavy oil-field mud—would enable him to cover the greatest amount of territory in the least amount of time. Henry knew how to handle a team. As a boy he had done a man's share of work on the family farm. One that no longer bore the Grant name thanks to the man he was looking for, though that wasn't the main reason Henry sought him. The matter ran much deeper.

Henry had also spent a lot of time around horses and mules during the war. In terrain torn up by constant shelling, turned into sucking mud by heavy rains, and littered with unexploded shells and tons of twisted barbed wire and smashed armaments, pack mules had been the only reliable way to get food, ammunition, and other supplies from the rear to men in the trenches. They had helped keep Henry and the doughboys in his company of the 129th Infantry Regiment alive. As he made his way across the loading platform, the teams here reminded him of the army mules' near-constant coming and going, and made his decision for him. He didn't bother asking anyone on the loading platform where to find work. Nor did he waste time looking for someplace where jobs might be posted. Instead, he set out to find the nearest mule yard belonging to a hauling outfit.

Returning from an outhouse behind a row of frame commercial buildings, Mary Dutton, a slender, fair-headed woman in her early thirties, paused outside the roughly cobbled door of her back-room shed to clean her shoes on a board set into the ground for a boot scraper. Oil-field workers and others dirtied the black-and-white tiled floor in the drugstore up front every time they came in. But even though her cousin Eunice Hornbeck made her sweep that floor several times a day, Mary cared less about it than about the uneven plank floor of the windowless enclosure where she lived with her twelve-year-old son, Jimmy.

"Mary! What's taking you so long?" Eunice called, sticking her head through the millwork door separating the drugstore workroom from Mary's and the boy's quarters. "We have customers."

"I'm coming," Mary said, as she crossed the sparsely furnished room. It held two canvas cots set against opposite walls with mosquito netting and a bedsheet hanging alongside each. The worn linens provided the only privacy mother and son enjoyed. A round-top wooden trunk sat at the foot of Mary's cot. A small wood-burning stove, three wooden shipping crates for kitchen cabinets, a makeshift table, two straight chairs, another crate supporting a hand-cranked Singer sewing machine, and a rickety dresser that Eunice had thrown out of her own home a few blocks away completed the furnishings. Wall pegs held a few changes of clothes.

Mary resented her cousin's intrusion, but there was nothing she could do about it. The shed was the only home she and Jimmy had known since shortly after the boy's father was killed in New Mexico in 1916. He had gone there with the Arkansas National Guard to help rid the southwest of the Mexican revolutionary Pancho Villa. Andy Dutton was on the arid US-Mexican border only a few days before a corporal driving one of the six hundred Dodge trucks General John J. Pershing brought along to help with logistics ran over him. The accident snuffed out his life before he served long enough to qualify Mary for a survivor's pension.

Mary paused in front of one of the packing crates and poured water from a flowered pitcher into an unmatched bowl and washed her hands. After drying with a cloth she took from a wall peg, she sighed and walked through the workroom and into the well-appointed store.

Hand-crafted wooden cases displaying patent medicines, cosmetics, notions, and other items behind glass doors extended most of the way along both side walls and rose nearly to the pressed-tin ceiling. Waist-high, glass-top counters stood in front of them, filled with tobacco products, shaving goods, candies, and sundries. A new soda fountain with a marble top and seven wooden stools occupied part of one wall up front. Near the door, a rack held the latest issues of *Saturday Evening Post*, *Ladies Home Journal*, *Argosy*, *The Sporting News*, and *Police Gazette*. A wooden counter with a cash register stood across the back. Behind it, a shelf held Grover Hornbeck's mortar and pestle and other tools he used to mix drugs, both those he dispensed himself and those doctors prescribed. Below the shelf, a locked cabinet held alcohol and small amounts of cocaine and morphine. Under rules from the Harrison Act and Prohibition Amendment, Grover couldn't put them in medicines unless he received a doctor's authorization and made a record of it. Over the whole, two ceiling fans stirred the warm, sticky air.

Eunice, a sturdy woman of early middle age who had a passion for fashionable clothes and used makeup like a house painter with lots of enthusiasm but little skill, finished counting change to a man who left with a small package wrapped in brown paper tied with string. She walked over to Mary, leaned close, and said in a voice only she could hear, "That was the last packet of marijuana, and that man upfront in the blue cap is probably gon' want some too. He's already been in twice this month. We don't have any more made up, and Grover's gon' be out a while longer. So, go back there and put some together. And be quick about it. I'll take care of the other customers."

"You know I don't like doing that, Eunice," Mary whispered. "It's against the law. I've got Jimmy to worry about."

"I told you before. Selling marijuana is not against the law. You worry too much."

"I know selling it isn't, but the way you're getting it is. You're gon' get caught, and we'll all end up in jail."

"Shush."

"I'm not gon' have any more to do with it."

"Yes, you are, 'cause you don't have any choice. I'll put you and that bratty kid of yours out, and you know it. So, go on now."

CHAPTER 2

Henry stepped off the south side of the station platform, waited for a Model T Ford to pass, and crossed El Dorado Avenue, which ran eastward parallel to the railroad tracks before curving back south somewhere down the line, toward its namesake fifteen miles away. Despite its fancy-sounding handle, the avenue was little more than dirt and mud. Henry walked half a block west to a cross street where a crudely lettered sign proclaimed "Broadway," another moniker heavy on hope, though accurate about size. Twice as wide as normal for most any town, Broadway was a sea of mudholes and muck, where horses and mules strained against heavy loads, teamsters yelled and cracked whips, car and truck drivers ground gears in search of traction, and pedestrians waded up to their ankles, risking both dignity and injury to get to the other side. Only men on horseback seemed immune from struggle, their mounts doing the work for them. Both the roadway and the buildings on each side bore streaks of dark sticky film, the result of wells sometimes blowing out and spewing crude high into the air where shifting winds carried it for miles, blackening structures, trees, crops, and laundry hung out to dry.

According to the newspaper reports, Berrytown had grown from a few hundred souls to more than two thousand overnight. As Henry stood on the corner looking up and down Broadway, he thought lumbermen and carpenters might be making out almost as well as men who came for the oil. Only a scattering of buildings, most of them houses, stood to the north toward Scuppernong Creek. But to the south, a dozen or more new, hastily erected frame structures, some one-story and some two-level, stood along the first three blocks, among a handful of still-vacant lots and half a dozen older buildings also made of wood. The blocks in this direction were longer and divided in half by wide alleys. Henry could make out a bank, a hotel, a restaurant, several stores, a post office, a telegraph office, and a combination filling station and auto repair shop, among others. There were no sidewalks, but most buildings had a wooden porch-like walkway covered by a shed roof. Above the shed roofs, hand-lettered signs announced goods and services available inside. Assorted wagons and cars stood randomly next to the walkways, along with a handful of saddle horses awaiting the return of their riders.

Henry knew at once that he had miscalculated by thinking it would be easier to get directions from a teamster making a streetside delivery than from one caught up in the mess back at the train station. But he didn't turn back. He figured an opportunity for inquiry would present itself soon enough, and meanwhile, he may as well learn more about the place he had come to. No matter what job the man he was looking for might have taken here, or how hard he was trying to hide, he was bound to come into town occasionally. He wouldn't be able to stay away from the sort of amusements that boomtowns were known to offer.

Henry started down the east side of the street, staying on the plank walkways as much as possible while keeping an eye out for a freight hauler loading or unloading. He passed a general store, a vacant lot, and the restaurant, which had a line of customers spilling out the door, then crossed an alley and drew up abruptly at the end of the block. He had noticed a snarl-up of some kind from back a ways, but he hadn't been able to make out the cause until now. A wagon with a four-up team of eight mules sat with a front wheel buried nearly to the axle in a huge mudhole, while the mules strained to no avail against their harness. The driver was cursing at them and beating them with his bullwhip, its thin leather cracker popping loud as a pistol shot and raising large welts across their backs. Henry could see that the mules would never be able to move the wagon.

In anger turned to rage, the man threw down his bullwhip, reached under his seat, and climbed off the wagon with an axe handle. Still yelling, he slogged toward the pair of lead mules and began striking them about their heads and shoulders. With that, Henry's plan to avoid attracting attention went up in smoke alongside his temper. His mind flooded with images of mules squealing as German artillery spilled their guts into battlefield mire or blew them into water-filled craters from which no amount of scrambling offered escape.

Henry dropped his jacket and valise, leaped off the walkway into the muck in front of Hornbeck's Drugstore, lunged for the man, and caught his arm just as he raised his weapon to strike another blow. Startled, the assailant turned around and hesitated just enough for Henry to reach up with both hands, jerk away the axe handle, and ram the end of it hard into the fellow's midsection. He fell forward clutching his stomach and surrendering up the sour remnants of his last meal. "You low-life son-of-a-bitch," Henry said, "if I ever see you doing that again, I'll stick that thing down your blooming throat."

Aware now that people were staring at him, Henry looked for the quickest way to get out of sight. He grabbed his jacket and valise and set out east along Seventh Street between the drugstore and a dry goods emporium on the south corner. His head pounded with every step, as it always did when something happened to flood his mind with the sound of exploding shells and the smell of bloated bodies, human and animal, lying unretrievable in no man's land. He knew he should have anticipated something like this happening and steeled himself against it somehow. He had likely ruined any chance of catching on with a hauling outfit. When word of it got around, mule-yard owners would think him either too soft to handle their stock or too quick-tempered to put up with.

Maybe that was just as well. Mule-team drivers were called "mule skinners" for a reason. In the hands of a cruel man, bullwhips could take the hide right off an animal. Henry could understand drivers stinging a mule with a whip when reins and verbal commands failed to control them. He even thought he could put up with being labeled a mule skinner, because to most people it was just another name for driver. But he couldn't stand to see any more mules beaten.

No stores or other businesses fronted onto this portion of Seventh Street. Henry kept to the edge of the roadway, and by the time he cleared the south side of the drugstore and some outbuildings behind it, all he could see ahead were vacant lots and a few houses. He was beginning to think he had erred again, when he heard someone call out, "Hey, Mister, want to buy a paper?" Henry turned and saw a freckle-faced boy he guessed was ten or eleven running toward him, a mop of blond hair flopping and pantlegs of faded bib overalls making swishing noises. He carried a stack of newspapers under one arm.

"Do you always chase down your customers?" Henry asked, amused by the boy's doggedness.

"No, sir," the boy said, coming to a stop. "But I saw what you did back there, and I figured you was new in town and could use a paper. I got to sell as many as I can. We need the money, my momma and me."

"What paper is it, and how much does it cost?"

"It's the *Berrytown Journal*," the boy said. "Just got started up and it's two cents. Only comes out once a week, but it's got all kinds of good stuff in it."

"Got any good advertisements?" Henry asked. He wondered if the paper listed jobs or carried ads that could suggest places for him to search out.

"I don't know if they're good or not, but there's a bunch of them."

"Okay," Henry said. "I'll take one." He set down his valise, fished into a pants pocket, and brought out a coin. "Here's a nickel. You can keep the change if you can tell me where a man can find a cheap room for the night."

"I'm afraid I can't do that, Mister. It ain't that I don't want the extra three cents. It's just there ain't no rooms nowhere. Too many people coming. There's folks sleeping in all sorts of places. Even on people's porches and out in the woods. There's a fellow over at the livery stable—that's up next to the train station—that's got a big tent, and he's renting out cots to shift workers from the drilling rigs. Gets a dollar a shift. Some of them outfits have their own tents, though. Some of the sawmills too. And I hear some of them's got real good grub. There's one right out east of town a ways. You'd probably come on it if you followed the railroad tracks."

"How do you know all that?"

"It ain't hard," the boy said. "I sell the *Arkansas Gazette* mornings and I keep my ears open. Remember good too."

"Well, I'm sure glad you do," Henry said, "and I reckon you better keep the whole nickel."

"Gee, thanks, Mister," the boy said. He turned and ran back toward Broadway.

"Hey!" Henry called after him. "What's your name?"

"Jimmy," the boy shouted over his shoulder.

A few paces farther along on Seventh, Henry turned left up a small, unmarked street leading back to the train station. The corner lot behind the drugstore was vacant. Ahead, a pair of houses stood on the right, and on the left, large letters proclaimed "Big Sally's Place" across the side of a crude, two-story windowless building fronting onto Sumac Alley. A pile of scrap lumber lay in the rear. As Henry drew closer, two women in sleeveless flapper dresses came out the back door and lit cigarettes. One was short, blond, and small-boned but big-bosomed, the other was tall with flaming red hair.

"Hey, honey," called the larger woman. "If you're looking for something, I can show it to you."

"No, thanks," Henry called back. "Maybe some other time." He made her out as several inches above six feet in height, with all her body parts more than plentiful in proportion.

"Name's 'Sally,'" she said, waving. "You be sure and come see me, you hear?"

Henry put up his hand and waved but didn't look back. As he walked, the image of the women smoking stayed with him. He remembered the time his mother caught his twin sister Helen trying a cigarette. That hadn't ended in so amicable a fashion, and he had gotten all the blame, deservedly so, because he had given it to her. He missed his mother and sister every day, and his father as well.

Across the alley, another half block—this one with houses on both sides of the street—brought him back to El Dorado Avenue, where he turned east and soon came upon the cot tent the boy had told him about. Seeing it put him back behind AEF lines in France, receiving treatment in an army field hospital. The enterprising fellow running the place here had gotten hold of two army field hospital tents, each about fourteen-by-sixteen feet, and placed them end to end, creating enough room to sleep up to twenty men at a time. Henry remembered waking up under a similar canvas with his head throbbing and men screaming for more medication. He could still see the overworked doctors and nurses rushing about trying to help them. He hated the thought of spending even a single night here.

There was no opportunity to do so, anyway. A hastily scribbled sign on a board leaning against a tent stake read, "Full up." Two men stood talking near the entrance. They were dressed like the workers he had seen earlier on the station platform. Henry crossed the so-called avenue and approached them. With dusk beginning to fall, he needed to find somewhere to stay soon.

"Hi, fellows," he said, "somebody told me there's a sawmill over east of here a ways. You know anything about it?"

"Yeah," said the taller of the two. "It's about three miles down the tracks there, if they ain't moved it further out. It's one of them peckerwood mills. Only got a few hands and three or four sledding teams. They move around to wherever they can buy timber close to the railroad. You looking for work?"

"Yeah, and a place to stay," Henry said. He switched hands with his valise.

"Well, you might be in luck," the smaller man said. "They're likely short out there right now. One of their hands got killed this afternoon, and another one got fired 'cause of it. Came by here just a little while ago and told us about it. He was mad as hell."

"What happened?"

"We ain't sure, exactly. Guess something got caught in the circle saw. Anyway, it slung out a big slab that hit a fellow in the back of the head. Killed him right where he stood. The one they fired got blamed for it."

"Helluva way to go," the taller man said.

"Yeah, it sure is," Henry agreed, "but I reckon I'll head on out there and take a look."

He told the men he was much obliged and started walking. He didn't figure to work more than a couple of days if he got hired. That would be enough to meet his immediate needs and give him a chance to learn more about the sawmill side of oil-field work, although he didn't think there was much chance the fellow he was hunting would ever take a mill job. It was too risky for Ed Tuttle. Sawing was only one hazard. Felling the trees was another. Back home, Henry had known more than one man who almost chopped off a foot or leg while trimming trees already down.

Tuttle had played on Wabash College's undefeated football team with Henry in 1910, but other than that, he had never been one to court physical harm. Or do anything strenuous he could get out of. This despite being a large man with natural strength. He had done the bare minimum required to stay in the Wabash starting lineup. And Henry remembered he once said he probably never would have been at Wabash if his great-uncle Joseph hadn't been a highly respected president there in the 1890s, and Ed's father hadn't gone around to all the trustees reminding them of everything the old man had accomplished for the school. The only work for hire Tuttle did after college was around Indiana's oil fields, and that was because he was brawny enough to do much of it with relative ease and cunning enough to hide a good amount of shirking. Knowing that, plus finding some newspaper clippings that Tuttle carelessly left behind, made Henry think Berrytown was the most logical place to look for the him. Meanwhile, in his every waking minute, Henry regretted the day he had invited the guy to come home with him for Christmas.

CHAPTER 3

A few miles west of Berrytown, Otis Leatherwood wrapped gnarled hands around his hoe handle, pulled it to his chest, and leaned on it. The blade rested on soil where until a few days ago a promising cotton crop flourished. Otis wore bib overalls over a faded denim shirt and a sweat-stained felt hat, its wide, limp brim drooping over heavy eyebrows and ears too large for stringy gray hair to hide. Thank God, he thought, he had only planted ten acres of the stuff. At least now he wouldn't have to drag his seventy-year-old bones out of bed to try to pick it by himself, what with all would-be hired hands now working in the oil field. All he saw before him was blackened rows of wilting plants and ruined bolls thanks to a second gusher having been brought in only a little way northwest, out toward Louann in southern Ouachita County.

Yesterday up in his hay loft he could make out drilling derricks off in the distance. The darn things were marching toward him like an army of giant praying mantises. He had been told by multiple lease hounds wanting access to his sixty acres that he was sitting on rich oil-bearing formations and if he didn't sign up and let the drillers in, one of these days wells on his neighbors' land would suck the oil right out from under him. Something or other, they said, about oil moving under pressure down there, and a law called "the rule of capture" letting somebody else just take what was rightfully his. The greedy bastards had even sent goddamned doodlebuggers and creekologists out to impress him with their divining rods and fancy boxes filled with wire, springs, and bells to try and prove he could be a rich man. As far as he was concerned, they all—lease hounds, doodlebuggers, creekologists, drillers, the whole bunch—could go straight to hell. If they didn't make one here first.

Otis shifted his weight, took the hoe in one hand with the blade hindmost, and walked across the rest of the ruined field and through a gate into his outer pasture. It, too, bore a black glaze despite the recent rain. He thanked the good Lord that he had enough hay and grain stored away for his milk cow, plow mules, and prize saddle horse, Trixie. Fortunately, too, his barn had shielded much of his garden from the scourge. He continued to Owl Creek, which wound across a corner of his land and through that of his neighbor Isaiah Watson before emptying into Scuppernong Creek.

Black scum lay on the trees and bushes along the creek bed, but there was less film on the water than he feared. He had heard heart-breaking stories about the El Dorado Oil Field to the south. Streams so full of oil that fish, turtles, and frogs couldn't live in them. Squirrels, raccoons, deer, and fox all gone someplace else looking for water to drink. Birds, too, so folks said.

Not many years ago here, wild scuppernong vines were everywhere. Several industrious souls had pocketed good money by cultivating them and making wine from the thick-skinned muscadine grapes they yielded, hence Berrytown's name. Few scuppernong vines remained, but thankfully, mulberry bushes were still plentiful. Normally, mulberry jelly graced many a breakfast table, but there likely wouldn't be enough unsullied berries for more than a few jars of the popular delicacy this year.

Otis wasn't alone in his early-day meandering, and soon he came across Isaiah Watson doing the same. "Morning, Isaiah," Otis greeted him. "Ain't this a mess?"

"Lordy, ain't it, though?" replied Isaiah, a stocky black man a decade or two younger than Otis. He was wearing overalls and a limp straw hat. "Ruined all twenty acres of my cotton."

"Yeah, mine too."

The two men stood silently for a while, each lost in his own thoughts while gazing at the land. Otis leaned on the hoe handle again. Isaiah absentmindedly fingered the oily leaves of a mulberry bush as if confirming its condition. The pair had been neighbors for almost longer than they could remember, farming through good times and bad, each coming to the other's aid when Mother Nature threatened a crop, or some piece of equipment broke, and the other needed a hand. Despite having children who needed her at home, Isaiah's wife Luella had nursed Otis's wife Alma during a long bout of pneumonia that had nearly killed her. And during another later that did.

Nowadays, Otis lived alone in his graying two-story house, the second floor of which he had rarely set foot in since Alma's passing. Their only child Eunice, long ago grown and married, hardly ever looked in on him, and when she did, all she talked about was how much money she and her husband were making in town. Otis guessed that was partly his fault because after Alma died, he struggled just to pull himself out of bed in the morning and didn't pay much attention to Eunice and her needs. Soon it seemed like all she wanted was to get off the farm, which he took to mean get away from him. So, he continued to ignore her. And now, frankly, he dreaded seeing her. Seemed like she was just waiting for him to die so she and her puny husband, whom Otis had pegged from the outset as an untrustworthy man of weak character, could get their hands on his property.

"Mr. Otis," Isaiah asked, breaking the silence and using the customary form of address for blacks speaking to whites, "has that lease man been around to talk to you again?"

"There's been a bunch of them. Do you mean Luther Pike, that fat little turd that wears them checkered suits? He told me you and him had been talking."

"Yes, sir. That's the one."

"Yeah, he's been back. Couple of times. Last time I told the son-of-a-bitch if he came on my property again, I'd shoot him. Sorry, I didn't mean to swear in front of you." Besides being a farmer, Isaiah was also a preacher. Though unschooled in the scripture beyond a lifetime of Bible reading and churchgoing, he pastored the Mt. Tabor New Hope Baptist Church, a small, poor congregation close to town. "He been talking to you again?" Otis asked.

"Yes, sir. He come out again yesterday."

"You ain't listening to that line of bull he's peddling, are you?"

"No, sir," Isaiah, said. He looked down and scraped a shoe around in the dirt. "Well," he added, "I reckon that ain't exactly the whole truth of it. I did let him talk on a bit, and he made this leasing business sound awful good. With all them other wells already messing up near 'bout all there is, I got to wondering how much worse one more could make it."

Otis took off his hat and wiped his forehead with his sleeve. "Isaiah, you and me have been friends how long now? 'Bout twenty years?"

"Yes, sir. Something like that."

"I thought I knew you better. Thought you was too smart to go along with this crap. Thought you loved the land too much to let them idiots get hold of it."

"Well, like I said, looks like they can't hurt it much more. And I got people over at Mt. Tabor what could use a helping hand. If I had me a well, a little oil money would go a long way with them, and the church building too. It's in bad shape, and my people done seen what happened with Reverend Richardson over there in Ouachita County."

Charles Richardson was also a black farmer who spent part of his time doing the Lord's work. A few weeks earlier, a drilling outfit from down at Shreveport, Louisiana, had hit a gusher off to the east, practically in Richardson's backyard, and no more than seven or eight miles from where Otis and Isaiah were standing. Besides setting off the madness now swirling all around Berrytown, it left Richardson and his family unexpectedly holding a potful of money.

Otis put his hat back on and stared at Isaiah, who looked down at his feet again. After a bit, the older man said, "I sure hope you ain't gon' throw in with them bastards, but if you do, you and me are still gon' be friends. I'm not gon' let the sorry sons-a-bitches take that away from us. Let me know what you decide. If you go with them, I'm sure as hell gon' keep a close watch on them." He slid his hand down the hoe handle and turned to go.

"Mr. Otis," Isaiah said, "my boy Robert wants to know is Jimmy gon' be out to your place again anytime soon." Other than Isaiah, about the only people Otis cared to be around anymore were his niece Mary Dutton and her son. Jimmy and Robert, similar in age, had been playing together for years.

Sometimes Jimmy walked the several miles out to visit, and other times Otis brought him out and carried him back to town riding double on Trixie. He did it both because he liked the boy and because he knew it raised Eunice's hackles.

"Yeah, I expect he will. Want me to send him over?" Otis asked, not stopping to look back.

"Yes, sir. That'd be right kind of you," Isaiah called. Then, remembering something from the last time they talked, he added, "Are you still planning to put up a new chicken house?"

"Not very goddamn likely in this mess," Otis replied, still walking. "Sorry about the cussing."

Isaiah shook his head and stepped off toward home.

~

Eunice Hornbeck often didn't get to the drugstore before midmorning. She liked to sleep late and have plenty of time to put herself together. Grover didn't complain about it. He preferred to get his own breakfast. Toast, jam, and coffee instead of stacks of buttery pancakes and thick syrup that Eunice laid out when she cooked. Plus, most of the time she let him do whatever he wanted with her in their bedroom, and that along with her head for business was plenty reason for him to maintain more than a passing acquaintance with pots and pans. Beyond those things, though, he'd as soon not be around her.

It was different with Mary Dutton. She was easy on the eyes, had just the right amount of round in all the right places, and didn't talk much. He didn't know what she was like in the dark behind closed doors, but it wasn't for the lack of wanting and trying. He had to be careful, though. A little tumbling around in that shed in back of the store wouldn't be worth losing what he had up front.

One morning after having already swept the drugstore's tiled floors and polished the counter and every other part of the soda fountain, Mary was shelving a new shipment of Black Draught Laxative and Smith Brothers Cough Drops when a short, muscular man wearing a dusty black suit and carrying a leather Gladstone luggage bag came in and took a stool up front.

Eunice, having only just arrived, was at the cosmetics counter giggling with Sally Boudreau and a short, busty blond named Vera Hudson. Both were dressed like they were ready for an evening out and were all painted up like Eunice, though they had applied their goop with greater flare and a more practiced hand. They came in often, and Eunice liked listening to them gossip about men to whom they sold floor time, as well as services of a more intimate nature, at Sally's dance hall around the corner.

Grover, his pasty face made more so by a white druggist's coat hanging loose over his suit vest and trousers, was at the back counter grinding away at something for a prescription. A man covered with oil-field grime and wearing a bandage over one ear and part of his head was trying to hurry up the mixing so he could get back to work.

Neither Grover nor Eunice seemed to notice the man in the black suit, so Mary put down the box she was holding, smoothed the skirt of her handmade dress, and went to help the fellow. As she approached him, he removed his fedora, revealing thick black hair and piercing gray eyes that gave her a chill. Still holding the hat, he smiled and said, "Good morning," but his greeting didn't soften the disquieting nature of his gaze. When Mary asked if she could help him, he mumbled something about soda fountains being poor substitutes for saloons and ordered a Hires Root Beer. While Mary was mixing the syrup and carbonated water, he placed the fedora on the stool next to him and asked if she would let Mrs. Hornbeck know that Floyd Roper was here.

Having seen him in the store looking at their patent medicine cabinets the day before and not buying anything, and now seeing him with the black case, Mary figured him for a traveling salesman. Until now, however, patent medicine salesmen had always asked for Grover.

CHAPTER 4

With his valise hanging from a rope looped over his shoulder, Henry tromped through muddy soil churned earlier by mule-drawn wagons carrying eight-inch pipe and then dug up and thrown back on itself afterward by scores of men wielding shovels. The sun was well up and he wished he had bought a canteen before leaving Berrytown, or when he passed through El Dorado.

Ahead of him, the line of torn earth stretched in a straight line northward as far as he could see back toward Berrytown. There wasn't another soul in sight. Henry had expected to see mule teams coming and going and other men heading out looking for pipeline jobs. Earlier this morning, when he boarded the "Roughneck Special" that chugged back and forth several times a day between Berrytown and El Dorado, he had thought that walking out to that peckerwood mill last night might prove a lucky break. Now, he wondered if what the foreman there said about work being available on pipelines was right.

The accident back there with the saw had not only killed one of the millhands, it had also ripped up the belt from the steam engine driving it, and the mill had shut down until they could get a new one. The guy in charge, a barrel-chested fellow named Al Jenkins, had been well along toward drowning his troubles in moonshine when Henry arrived. Still, he was sober enough to know he couldn't afford to hire replacements until the mill was ready to start up again. From his perch on the end of the lifeless log carriage, he waved a half-empty Ball jar at Henry and delivered the bad news. But, he said, seeing as how Henry was already out there, and it was getting dark, and they had a couple of empty cots and a big pot of beans boiling, Henry might as well stay the night.

In addition to getting a hot meal and a cot under the stars, Henry had also gotten everything he needed to know about oil-field sawmill operations, and more. Jenkins said there were at least half a dozen other peckerwood outfits scattered around cutting timber, mainly cross ties for new railroad spurs, firewood to feed oil-rig boilers, and boards for drilling platforms, but also beams and braces for wildcatters that didn't have steel derricks. Men had been hurt at some of those other mills as well. Then there was also the Edgar Lumber Company in Wesson, about ten miles southwest of El Dorado. It had a mill so big the company employed its own doctor. That clinched it for Henry. This was way too dangerous a line of work for Ed Tuttle. There was no need to poke around sawmills any further.

But that wasn't all Jenkins had told Henry as they ate then sat around jawboning while the beans settled in their bellies. He said if Henry wanted to find the easiest work anywhere around and get a good wage and a decent place to stay, he ought to go out to where they were laying a big pipeline way over south of town. Some company out of Shreveport was bringing it up from El Dorado. Jenkins hadn't seen it himself, but his cousin Lonnie had. He worked there, and according to him, they had a camp with two big cot houses, all the food a man could eat, and even wash pots to boil your dirty clothes in on Sundays.

Jenkins said Lonnie was something called a "pounder." All he had to do was sit astride long joints of eight-inch pipe and beat on them with two little ballpeen hammers, making a cadence, like on a drum. That helped men out front of Lonnie pull together with big tongs they used to grip the next joint and screw it into a connecting collar. Everyone worked in shifts. Two hours on and two hours off. For that they got six dollars a day. The only thing pipeline workers had to watch out for was snakes.

Except for the vipers, this sounded to Henry more like something Tuttle might go for.

Jenkins had also shared something else that piqued Henry's interest. Right in the middle of telling about the pipeline, Jenkins had asked, "Where're y'all from? I know you ain't from 'round here, and you sure don't talk like all them boys coming up from Texas. You from up North somewheres?"

It was a question Henry had prepared for before leaving Indiana, and he lied without hesitating. "No, my daddy was, though. Came out from Boston to work on Anheuser-Busch's refrigerated rail cars up at St. Louis. Met my momma and stayed on. Guess I just naturally talk a little like him." Henry had read how Anheuser-Busch had its own short-line railroad and built its own refrigerated cars, and he figured bringing up the beer maker would always send the conversation off in another direction. Which it did, this time at least.

"Yeah," Jenkins said. "Goddamn Prohibition. I wish to hell all the rest of them ole Temperance Union biddies had died back when Carrie Nation did. It's a helluva thing a man can't get a drink without sneaking 'round for it."

"It don't look like it's bothering you none," Henry said, motioning toward the Ball jar.

"Oh, there's plenty of good stuff here abouts," Jenkins said, "and you don't have to look hard for it. I just didn't like all the old saloons having to close up. 'Course, you can usually still get a drink in a barrelhouse if they don't think any federal men are hanging 'round, and that's pretty much anytime. I've heard about them fellows, but I ain't never seen one. Seems like they're scarce as hens' teeth. And the law we got 'round here, they don't mind the booze so long's there ain't too much fighting and stuff."

"What's a barrelhouse?" Henry asked.

"That's what everybody calls these new dance halls, specially them out near the drilling camps. I think it's 'cause some of the seats is made outta beer barrels, but I've heard tell of bouncers stuffing drunks in empty ones and rolling them out the door. I don't rightly see how they'd fit them in, but maybe that's why.

"Anyways, that's the reason I asked you about the way you talk. I heard somebody else sounded kinda like you at Big Sally's Place a couple of Saturday nights ago. Big fellow. I asked him where he was from, too, but he didn't say. I got the impression that him and the ones he was drinking with had been working on the pipeline like my cousin, 'cause one of them said something about sleeping out in the boonies and coming all the way up to Berrytown just to see Big Sally. Can't say as I blame them. That gal's something to behold, all that red hair and them big knockers."

Henry knew there were lots of men here from Illinois, Indiana, Ohio, and other northern states. He had been on the train with some of them. Still, Jenkins' story merited checking out. Henry wanted to ask Jenkins what the fellow he had been talking to looked like, but Jenkins liked gabbing too much. He might run into the man again and say something that would spook him.

Twice as Henry walked along playing the sawmill conversation over in his mind, he passed signs of previous camp life. Every now and then he heard the dull, ground-shaking thump of an explosion up ahead somewhere. It boomed like artillery fire, and he struggled between wondering what it was and trying to ignore it.

After a while, he topped a rise in the gently rolling landscape of forest and farmland and saw a large clearing with two good-sized, once-white tents standing off to the right and a jumble of horse-drawn and mule-pulled wagons loaded with pipe and other supplies clogging up the center and left side. The animals stood resting in their harness, heads down, tails swishing at flies and other winged annoyances. A bunch of men, mule skinners Henry assumed, were either milling aimlessly about the snarl-up or sitting around on crates. Beyond the jam, several men were rushing around yelling while others stood idly in clumps. Some distance past them, scores of wide-bottomed bald cypress trees stood like scaly guardians along the swampy banks of a creek flowing across the path of the approaching pipeline. Sunlight glistened off the muddy water. Henry quickened his step and touched his pants pocket for the feel of his pistol.

~

Mary passed Floyd Roper's message on to Eunice and went back to putting up newly arrived patent medicines. Sally and Vera left the store, and Eunice went over to where Roper was sitting. Grover continued filling the prescription for the man with the bandaged head, and neither of them looked up. No one else was in the store. Mary finished her shelving chores and began the never-ending task of cleaning glass cabinet doors and showcase tops. She worked as quietly and as close to Eunice and Roper as she dared without being noticed and shooed away.

Grover and Eunice had built the store well before the oil boom, and most folks in tiny Berrytown had thought them crazy for wasting good money they would never earn back. There being no other pharmacies between El Dorado, seat of Union County to the south, and Camden, seat of Ouachita County to the north, however, Grover had thought the location ideal. Ever since he passed the state exam to become a certified pharmacist, he had dreamed of having the finest drugstore he could afford on money he got from selling a sizeable tract of timber inherited from his father up toward Little Rock. When he met Eunice, working then as a bookkeeper for a drugstore in Camden, and shared his dream with her, she latched onto him immediately as a ticket to better things in life. Until now, Hornbeck's Drugstore had been little more than an overdressed oddity in a small town in the middle of nowhere, but Eunice had proven a creative helpmate, and their little enterprise was well positioned to take every advantage the rapidly growing population offered.

"Hello, Mrs. Hornbeck," Roper said, flashing his best smile as Eunice came behind the soda fountain counter. "I'm Floyd Roper, with Arcadia Pharmaceuticals down in New Orleans. I believe we met when you and your husband attended the American Pharmaceutical Association meeting up at St. Louis a couple of years back."

Eunice was sure she had never met Roper, and she knew she and Grover had never been to St. Louis, or anywhere else for a meeting of the American Pharmaceutical Association, but she saw no reason to admit it.

"Yes, Mr. Roper," she said, striking a just-so posture and clasping her hands together on the countertop. "What can I do for you?" The man's gray eyes locked onto hers, and despite his smile, his stare was like a cloud passing in front of the sun on a cold winter day, dimming the light and stirring a chilling breeze.

"Well," Roper said, "I think it's a matter of what I can do for you, and it's not about this new line of patent medicines." Before Eunice came over, he had removed several bottles and some small, print-covered cartons from his top-opening bag and laid them on the counter for show. "Although," he continued, gesturing toward his little display, "I'd be delighted to take an order for some of these too."

"Oh?" Eunice said, question-like. "And just what is it you think you can do for me?"

"I'll speak frankly, Mrs. Hornbeck." He smiled again and locked his own hands together on the countertop. "I've been in town for a couple of days, and the reason I haven't called on you before now is that I've been observing things and talking to people. You'd be amazed what a person can find out just hanging around over at Big Sally's Place and some of those other barrelhouses. You have any idea what I've learned about y'all's drugstore, other than it's got mighty fancy appointments for a town like this?"

Mary had made out most of what Roper said, and she chanced a glance at Eunice, who didn't notice. Eunice's eyes narrowed and her already round mouth drew into a tighter circle. She was about to speak again, when Roper said, "I know all about how you and Mr. Hornbeck are getting that marijuana you're selling, and I figure if you're willing to do that for peanuts, you'll be willing to do something else kinda like it for real money."

"Mr. Roper," Eunice said, her brow furrowed now. "I don't know what you're talking about. And keep your voice down, will you?"

"Don't worry," Roper said, grinning again. "That fellow back there with his ear all wrapped up can't hear me, and one of us is gon' have to tell Mr. Hornbeck when he gets through. I don't care if Mrs. Dutton there hears either, 'cause she's gon' have to know sooner or later too."

"Mary Dutton don't have anything to do with running this business, Mr. Roper," Eunice said in a loud, agitated whisper.

"No? Well, maybe not, but how come you have her making up packets of marijuana you're buying from that fellow Simpson that's going 'round posing as a tobacco salesman?"

Eunice's knees went weak, and she looked behind her, wishing there were stools on her side of the counter.

Roper went on. "You and I both know it's coming from Mexico, mostly across the Rio Grande, but some up through California. Either way, it's coming across Texas to New Orleans hiding in plain sight on the Southern Pacific. Pretty slick operation all around. I expect you also know it's illegal to grow it in Mexico and it's against the law to buy it and sell it in Texas, don't you?" When Eunice didn't reply, Roper kept talking. "I bet you want to know how I know all that. First off, Simpson works for the same people I do. And second, I've talked to half a dozen folks 'round here who've been buying it from y'all. They know you're the one in charge of it, and they've seen you and Mrs. Dutton both bringing it out of the storeroom."

Eunice looked again at Grover, who was still occupied with his mortar and pestle, and at Mary, who a few seconds before had moved farther back to avoid being told to go to the storeroom for something.

"What is it you want, Mr. Roper?" Eunice asked, her thoughts wavering between trepidation and excitement.

"Mrs. Hornbeck, with all these people coming to Berrytown from all over, and especially all the whores that're gon' flock in here from near-about played-out Texas oil fields and other places, you and your husband are sitting on a goldmine. There's gon' be a bunch of folks looking for cocaine and heroin and morphine that ain't sold in prescriptions, and I can provide it to you. We've got merchant seamen getting it in Europe and Mexico and bringing it into New Orleans in hatbands, petroleum jelly jars, and all sorts of things, even chicken carcasses."

Eunice was now gripping the edge of the counter with both hands. "Let's just suppose for a second that we'd want to have anything to do with that, Mr. Roper, how would anyone know we had the stuff to sell?"

"You just leave that to me, Eunice. You don't mind if I call you 'Eunice,' do you, seeing as how we're gon' be working together on this? I'll plant the word in a couple of the right places, and it'll spread around quick enough."

"Suppose we don't want to get involved?"

"You're already involved, Eunice. Why else do you think I'd be telling you all this? You're breaking the law already. I know you believe the Treasury agents are spread too thin to care about a little operation like yours, and in a way, you're right. But it cuts the other way too. You might say the folks I work for are too big for them. We've got stuff coming up on the railroad through Shreveport to Kansas City and up the Mississippi on riverboats to Memphis and going all over from both those places. So, we know how to work around agents, and we know how to work with them. We know how to keep them away from where we don't want them, and we know how to sic them on where we do. You'll do what I want, or I'll get you shut down before the next gusher comes in."

Mary hadn't been able to hear all that was said, but she had heard enough. Moving quietly to avoid attracting attention, she laid her dusting rag on top of the candy case, eased past Grover in the back, then rushed through the storeroom. She barely made it to her slop jar in the shed before throwing up.

CHAPTER 5

As Henry closed on the pipeline camp, he imagined himself coming face-to-face with Tuttle. An intense tingle spread from the base of his neck across his back and down his arms. Soon he might have the despicable coward in his sights, or even within his grasp. Picking up his pace, he kept his eyes focused ahead, past the wagons, toward the men near the edge of the creek. Toward a point that, although still distant, was already turning his hope of collecting Ed Tuttle's debt into keen anticipation of doing so.

"Hey, bub!" a man called out. "Watch where you're going!" A second later, something jerked Henry around, breaking his single-minded trance and pulling him back into the moment. He almost went down but managed an awkward hop to keep his balance. The rope holding his valise had caught on the unseen end of a pipe sticking farther out than other lengths from the rear of an oddly parked wagon.

"You all right, bub?" the man who had done the shouting asked. He was leaning against the rear wheel of another pipe-bearing wagon, this one facing straight ahead a few feet away. "If you're looking for a job, I expect you've come to the wrong place. Swamp done stopped them cold."

Henry gathered himself and the valise, now sporting another gash in its aging leather, and looked at the man.

He was tall and thin with graying hair under a pushed-back fedora. Once-red suspenders held up his dirty britches, and he gripped a bullwhip in one hand.

"Why is that?" Henry asked.

"They ran into a den of water moccasins. Big sons-a-guns. Size of a man's arm. Bit two fellows right through their boots. One of them's dead. The other one's good as. Caused a helluva ruckus, what with everybody thrashing around and hollering. The fellow running the outfit can't get nobody else to go in the water."

Henry's first thought was that he had come too far to be deprived by a bunch of snakes. He hoped neither of the men who got bit was Tuttle. His second thought was that if Tuttle had signed on here, he might not be around much longer. This would likely set him to looking for some other line of work.

"What makes you think I'm looking for a job?" Henry asked. He shifted his valise to his other shoulder. Then, seeing that this would make it hard for him to get to his pistol, he moved the bag back again.

"'Cause I get around all over where there's digging and drilling and such, and I've seen plenty of fellows like you looking to catch on somewhere. Why else would you be way out here carrying that clumsy bag of yours?"

"Yeah, well," Henry said, "tell me something. How do they lay that pipe through water anyway?"

"I didn't know myself till I got out here this morning and watched them for a while. First thing they do is try to chop out them cypress knees for a path. If they can't chop them out, they blow them out with dynamite. Then they use poles to hold up the pipe joints while they screw them together, then they just lay them on the bottom. Must have a couple hundred men up there. I expect you gon' see some of them hauling ass now, though. Soon as they can get paid off. Come to think on it, I reckon if you ain't scared of getting bit, the boss man probably will have a spot for you."

"Well," Henry said, lying for the second time in two days, "I'm not afraid of snakes. I think I'll just go on up and have a look."

Henry made his way through the remaining parked wagons, most of them hitched to two-up mule teams, and came even with the sleeping tents. The sides were rolled up and he could see row after row of cots, pretty much like what the AEF had used in France. He could also now see a large cook tent. An image of mud-covered doughboys freshly rotated off the front and standing in line for their first hot meal in days flashed before him. He stopped and pressed a fist against the throbbing that sprang across his forehead. The pressure he applied didn't help.

Pushing on, he entered the swirl of disgruntled and angry men at the head of the pipeline. Three huge black, headless water moccasins, each four feet long if an inch, lay where the pipeline left dry ground for wet. Henry wondered how whoever got ahold of them managed to do it. An axe was stuck in a stump nearby, its handle pointing up at a forty-five-degree angle with a man's cap hanging off the end like a symbol of triumph. But if a victory had been gained in the ruckus, it belonged to the snakes. They had caused a work stoppage and heightened fear that wouldn't soon go away.

A burly man in knee-high lace-up boots, apparently the foreman, was yelling at the workers to get back in the water or draw their pay. "I don't give a good goddamn about the snakes," he yelled. "You signed on to do a job. Now get your sorry asses back in there."

"Ain't gon' do it," one man shouted back. "You can get in there yourself. I'm leaving, and I want my pay."

Several other men yelled, "Me too." But one by one, most began wading back into the swamp.

"Get that next wagon up here and get that pipe unloaded!" the foreman shouted. "Anybody wants to quit, go ahead. You can have your pay when I get done here."

Henry moved back toward the camp and over a ways, to the edge of a copse of black gum trees with thick underbrush where he could remain hidden. If Tuttle was here and walked back to the tent area, Henry would see him. Even if Tuttle had grown a beard or otherwise tried to disguise himself, Henry was confident he would recognize him. He had a habit of coming up on his toes with each step except when running. Henry thought he did it as some sort of swagger. In any case, if he wasn't among those quitting and heading back to camp now, Henry could simply wait until the end of the workday and watch for him among the men who stayed. Either way, Henry could avoid taking a job on the pipeline crew himself and having to look for Tuttle during the workday while hoping Tuttle didn't see him first. Plus, Henry wouldn't have to risk getting snake bit here or at some other water obstacle up ahead. Nothing had ever scared him more than snakes, not even German artillery. He had feared them since accidentally picking up a harmless grass snake in an armload of firewood when he was a boy.

While trying to avoid thinking about the possibility of stirring up a timber rattler, Henry sat on the forest floor and took out his .45. As he watched, he wished once more that he had bought a canteen in Berrytown or El Dorado.

~

"I don't think there's really much danger in it," Eunice said in a low voice, as she finished telling Grover about the visit from Floyd Roper. "The man makes my skin crawl, but he's right. I can't remember ever reading anything in the papers about Treasury agents operating anywhere close to here, and anybody that's gon' be buying from us isn't gon' talk. They won't want to risk losing their source."

The two of them stood close together in the back of the store, in the corner opposite the storeroom door. The fellow with the bandaged ear was long gone, no one else had come in, and Mary had not returned from the back. Eunice was nudged up against her husband, one arm around his waist, one breast pressing against him. If anyone came in, she could break away and feign embarrassment. Meanwhile, a little tease might help persuade Grover.

"What about Mary?" Grover asked. He glanced toward the front and reached for Eunice's other breast, but she caught his hand in hers. "From what you've told me," he said, "the woman's already nervous about the marijuana. This might push her over the edge. She might give us away."

Eunice released Grover's hand, touched hers to his chin, and gave him one of her best smiles. "No, if there was to be any trouble, she'd be in it just as deep as us. Besides, we're giving her a place to live and paying her enough to put food on the table and clothes on her and that boy. She's not gon' risk that."

"I don't know, Eunice." Grover tried to grab her hand, but she moved it away. "Fast as the town's growing," he said, "there's gon' be other places she can work, and for a lot better money. And you know she's been taking in sewing. She could probably set up a little shop somewhere."

"She's not gon' do any of that. She tries to, we'll just threaten to kick her out and tell people we caught her stealing out of the cash register."

"What about Otis?" Grover asked. "He might take her in."

"Daddy? Ain't no way. First off, she's too timid to ask him. And second, he's never gon' let another woman in that house of his. Damned old fool. He treats it like some kind of shrine to Momma. Didn't even want me there. You know that."

"Well, maybe. But he's awful partial to Jimmy. That might be enough to change his mind if we boot her out."

"No, I don't think so," Eunice replied. "But I've got an answer for that too. I'll tell him she was using the shed for a whoring den while Jimmy was on the street selling newspapers or out there visiting him. That man ain't set foot in a church in years, but he's straitlaced as they come. I don't care if Mary is his niece. Something like that would ruin her as far as he's concerned."

"All right," Grover said. "Let's do it, but you deal with Roper and her too. You tell her what's gon' happen if she don't play along, and we'll both keep an eye on her."

"Don't worry. I'll handle it."

Grover started to pull his wife close for a kiss, but Eunice patted him on the chest, pushed him away, and said, "Save that for nighttime."

He watched her walk to the front and stare out the windows at the street. She will be happy as a jaybird to have more money, he thought, and so would he, but there might also be another kind of benefit for him. With Mary more over a barrel than she already was, maybe now she would be a little less standoffish toward him. A little more willing to do a special favor for him now and again. Maybe back there in the storeroom when Eunice was busy gossiping with Sally.

CHAPTER 6

Within minutes after Henry settled under the black gum trees, more than a dozen men passed within a few yards of him. All were heading to collect their possessions from the cot tents then wait to get paid. None was Tuttle.

As Henry waited for the sun to sink and for the men who had remained on the pipeline to come by when they were done for the day, he became aware for the first time since arriving in Berrytown that his rage and burning desire for revenge were coloring his reasoning. Badly as he wanted to kill Tuttle—after first beating him senseless if opportunity allowed—he had always intended to make a clean get away. Or at least give himself a chance to. He hadn't figured on dying, either at the hands of others when he acted or the hands of the law afterward. If his twin sister and his parents could have a say in it, they'd want him to stay alive. Of course, they wouldn't want him to kill Tuttle in the first place. At least his sister and mother wouldn't. In any case, he owed them his best effort to survive.

It would be easy to shoot Tuttle from where Henry sat, or to rush out and get closer to him first, but there were only two likely avenues of escape—east or west. He couldn't flee north toward the creek. And the cleared pipeline path south back to El Dorado offered no cover. If he headed east or west, some of the workers might be able to hem him in if they tried, and he didn't want to shoot any of them. None had done him any harm, and most of them likely had families, too, like he once did. He might try sneaking into where Tuttle was sleeping and killing him somehow in the dark of night—either strangling him or cutting his throat—but if that awakened anyone, he would still have the same getaway problem. The longer he sat and waited, the more difficult trying to end Tuttle's sorry life here seemed. At least, Henry decided, if he stayed hidden and watched, he could see whether the degenerate asshole was around, then devise a way to keep track of him until he could get him alone somewhere.

Henry was used to waiting. He had done plenty of it in the army, especially in France. Waiting for orders. Waiting for supplies. Waiting for German shelling to stop. Waiting for AEF shelling to begin. Waiting for the signal to climb out of trenches and crawl under barbed wire. Waiting for medics to patch him up. Waiting for his wounds to heal, only to discover later that some—the ones in his mind—would not. And finally, waiting to return home, only to find it was no longer there as he had known it.

After seeing the Ball jar with Al Jenkins' moonshine, Henry had lain awake much of last night thinking about growing up in rural Grant County, Indiana, named for some pioneering ancestor. And about working in nearby Muncie at the Ball Brothers Manufacturing Company plant for three years after college, instead of going on to law school, because the gas wells on the family farm had played out and he didn't have money for tuition and expenses. And about moving back home afterward to help run the farm. Which he did until his father encouraged him to answer a Selective Service call offering army commissions to college graduates who could pass a qualifying exam. For some it offered a path to a professional career, albeit a risky one.

As the afternoon dragged on and hunger began to court thirst, Henry pushed both away and continued to watch the expanse between the swampy creek bed and the camp. From time to time, a lone pipeline worker returned from the work area. Probably, Henry assumed, after rethinking the likelihood of getting snake bit, or after seeing one in the water. The latter would have been enough to persuade him.

With order restored, mule skinners who had been waiting with their teams began to bring up their wagons and unload cargo with help from members of the pipeline crew. Henry saw that some of the mules in the dozen or so teams seemed well-cared for, while others had open sores on their legs and shoulders. Many of the latter also wore harness that was ill-fitting and in disrepair. In his view, only someone mean or ignorant would treat mules this way. He grew furious and ground his teeth as he fought against the urge to charge out, seize the men driving those teams, and punish them for their ill treatment of the animals.

When, finally, the pipeline foreman blew a whistle to end the workday, the crewmen filed by Henry's hiding place in ones and twos. They were easy to see, and Tuttle wasn't among them. As with sawmills, Henry thought now he could reasonably eliminate pipeline-laying sites as likely places to find the man.

Although Henry had been in Berrytown fewer than forty-eight hours, it seemed longer, and here he was miles from a town, hiding in the bushes, his belly cramping, and night falling. It was time to lie again, probably twice.

Henry eased farther back into the black gum trees, stood on legs wobbly from sitting so long with little movement, and began circling around the camp. Once he had gone far enough back toward El Dorado, he emerged from the forest and walked north again, as though approaching the camp for the first time.

With the sun now below the horizon, kerosene lamps cast dim light on portions of the camp and left others in shadows and near darkness, exactly as he had expected. The place smelled of animal manure, swamp water, and human sweat and waste. Most of the men were either standing in line near the cook tent or already sitting on crates, makeshift benches, or the ground, eating from tin plates. A stew of some kind Henry thought, but one too weak to cover the other odors. Henry guessed that men who had quit and waited for their pay had gotten it and left while he was circling around, for he hadn't passed anyone on his approach.

No one paid him any attention as he stood surveying the scene. He reckoned they were well used to men coming and going. The broad-shouldered foreman was talking to two other men standing in front of a smaller tent out of view until now. Henry walked toward them intending to introduce himself. He had prepared for this moment too. Al Jenkins had never asked his last name back at the sawmill because he had no job for him, but this was different. The foreman needed hands and would want a full name for the payroll ledger.

Before Henry could speak, the man looked up and eyed him for a second before saying, "You looking for a job, fellow, you came to the right place. Six dollars a day and all you can eat morning and night."

"Yes, sir," Henry said, "I am. Name's Smith. Henry Smith." It wasn't at all original, and there were probably more than a few Smiths around, both those who bore the name for real and those who didn't, but Henry thought Smith sounded good with his given name. Most likely no one would give it a second thought anyway. The most important thing was keeping Tuttle from hearing "Henry Grant" somewhere and fleeing the area.

"You ain't scared of snakes, are you?" the foreman asked.

"No, sir," Henry lied again. It was getting easier all the time. "I grew up around them."

"All right, grab yourself an empty cot in one of them tents and get some grub. I'll find you and sign you up when I finish here."

The food had not risen to Jenkins' description of it, but it had been filling enough. And the foreman had paused with Henry only briefly to get his name again, pencil it on a list, and tell him to be up and ready to work at dawn. Henry had lucked out in finding a cot in a corner, and now with all the lights out, he tried to suppress memories of hospital tents and go to sleep amid a cacophony of snoring, low conversation, and occasional cries of, "Watch it," as first one man then another stumbled out to the holes in the ground that passed for latrines.

Dozing in fits and starts, he struggled to separate dreams from conscious thought. Recollections and images of his sister Helen filled both. How inseparable they had been growing up, yet how happy she had been for the chance to attend Indiana State Normal School in Terre Haute while he was at Wabash in Crawfordsville. How joyous their homecomings had been. How they had cried together after college, when they learned that their father's gas royalties had stopped coming and he had secretly mortgaged the farm to continue paying their tuition. And how much she had loved the teaching job she held when Henry left for the army.

Eventually, the sweet memories of those times turned to terrifying images of Helen in some kind of fog, visible one minute and out of sight the next, crying out to him for help, as he sank into some sort of morass, unable even to move as the fog turned black and blocked her out completely. He tried to shout, "No! No!" but the words came out only in some strange, drawn-out guttural way, and she did not return. His yelling awakened him, as it always did, and like always, he wondered if anyone near him had heard.

The man in the cot next to him grunted loudly and turned over, but no one else was stirring. Henry didn't know how long he had slept, but he didn't want to risk going back to sleep. Like all the others, he had slept in his clothes. He rolled off his cot, slipped on his boots, and holding his valise under one arm, crawled quietly under the partially raised tent flap. After quick glances to his left and right, he crossed the few feet between the tent and the tree line and passed into it unseen.

CHAPTER 7

Otis Leatherwood's eyes moved side to side, like Trixie's ears shifting back and forth, as man and mount threaded their way through the tangle of freight wagons, cars, and trucks struggling along Broadway under an already blazing early morning sun. Otis estimated that hundreds more people had poured into Berrytown since he last ventured in. Some strode along with apparent purpose. Others stood in doorways and spilled off the plank walkways in front of buildings. Some of the men wore work clothes. Others wore suits. Otis guessed the former were roustabouts and roughnecks and the rest lease hounds, land speculators, and salesmen. Some of the women wore ordinary dresses, while others sported fancy getups and faces awash in lipstick and rouge. The plainly dressed were likely housewives, store clerks, and secretaries, Otis thought. The rest were clearly ladies of the evening, advertising their wares in broad daylight. He had never much liked coming to town under any circumstances, and the farther he rode today, the more he thought about flies swarming over a manure pile.

He made his way down to Hornbeck's Drugstore, dismounted, and tied Trixie's reins around a post supporting the shed roof. He had come for a bottle of Black Draught, the need for which he blamed on all the craziness that had befallen the once-peaceful community. He had gotten so wound up over it that he could just about spit nails, but his other end was drawn up tighter than a tick's rear.

His condition wasn't helped when Luther Pike emerged from the store right as Otis stepped up onto the walkway. The stocky lease hound's paunch was straining his checkered suit same as the last time Otis saw him. He held a sheaf of papers in one hand and thrust the other out before Otis could get around him. Jimmy Dutton pushed through the door right behind the man.

"Mr. Leatherwood," Pike said, showing a toothy smile. "Good to see you. I was just thinking about swinging by your place again."

Otis ignored Pike's outstretched hand. "You needn't bother, Pike," Otis replied. "I ain't changing my mind." That wasn't all Otis wanted to say, but he didn't want to cuss in front of the boy.

"I just don't want you to miss out," Pike said. "If you don't change your mind pretty soon, that nigger Watson's gon' wind up with money that oughta be yours."

Otis moved closer to the lease hound. "I don't like that word, Pike. Don't be using it around me, or Jimmy here either. Isaiah's a friend of mine, and far as I'm concerned, he's a darn sight better man than you are."

"All right, all right," Pike said, taking a step back. "But you might not know him as well as you think. Tell you what. Why don't you take one of these handbills and think some more about my offer? You ought to buy some shares too. I got so many leases now, I'm selling stock in them." He peeled a sheet off his stack and held it out.

Otis took the paper, stuffed it into a pocket on his bib overalls, and stepped around Pike and into the drugstore without a word. Jimmy followed him.

"Ain't you gon' look at it, Uncle Gramps?" Jimmy asked. Mary had suggested the boy call Otis that because he was the closest thing Jimmy had to a grandparent. Mary's father George, Otis's brother, had been killed in a sawmill accident when Mary was sixteen, and her mother Florence had died from the Spanish flu in 1918. Jimmy's grandparents on the Dutton side were gone, too, or all but. The flu had also killed Andy Dutton's father and left his mother an invalid. She lived with her sister down in Louisiana and Jimmy almost never saw her.

"Yeah, I reckon so," Otis replied. He didn't care what the handbill said, but he pulled it out to humor the boy. There was no one near the magazine stand, so the gray-haired old man and the fair-haired youngster stepped over to it.

The handbill was divided into sections with bold headlines followed by smaller-print promises that anyone buying shares from Pike and Company would get rich: "Gusher or Money Back!" "Gusher Guaranteed!" "You Cannot Lose!" "Now or Never!" The one that grabbed Otis's attention asked, "Am I an Honest Man?" The spiel underneath read, "I absolutely, unequivocally, and without the batting of an eye GUARANTEE you a tremendous, hair-raising, fortune-making, oil-splattering, earth-destroying, monster gusher. There is no more chance of you missing a gusher than there is of my flying to New York tonight and jumping off the Woolworth building tomorrow."

"Damn fool," Otis said, forgetting about not cussing in front of Jimmy. "He's right about one thing, though. Men like him are gon' ruin the land. Ain't no doubt about it. They're already playing hell with it."

"He gave Momma one of those," Jimmy said, "and there's a whole bunch of stuff like that in the *Journal* this week."

"Yeah," Otis said. "Pike's not the only one running around lying and cheating. We better talk to your momma."

~

Isaiah Watson was out back of his barn standing next to his sorghum mill when Otis and Jimmy walked up on him later in the day. "Luella said to come on back," Otis greeted him.

"Whoa!" Isaiah said, jerking around. "You scared me."

"Didn't mean to," Otis said. "Little early to be ruminating 'bout making syrup, ain't it?"

"Yes, sir," Isaiah said. "I just like to come back here to think sometimes. Talk a little with the Good Lord." He looked at his other visitor. "Hey, Mr. Jimmy. How you doing today?" Custom not only required blacks to use "mister" when addressing white men. It also applied to white boys, regardless of age.

"I'm fine," Jimmy said. "I come over to play with Robert. Thought maybe me and him could go fishing or something."

Otis said, "I told him the oil that blew over here the other day probably done killed all the fish anywhere around, but he wants to see for hisself."

"Yeah, I'm afraid you be right. That's one of the things I was talking to Him about," Isaiah said, looking toward the heavens. "I don't like what's happening, but I'm powerful conflicted." He took off his straw hat and fanned himself with it. "Sho' is a hot one, ain't it?" He put the hat back on and said, "Mr. Jimmy, Robert's over yonder pulling weeds outta the garden, what's left of it. You can tell him I said it's all right to go fishing."

"Thanks," Jimmy said, and took off running.

"You be back to my place before dark," Otis called to the boy. Then to Isaiah, "He's staying with me tonight."

Isaiah nodded. "Yes, sir. I know the boy gon' like that."

Otis pulled a plug of honey-sweetened Brown Mule tobacco out of his overalls and extended it to Isaiah. "You want a chaw? It's fresh. Got it in town this morning."

"Mr. Otis, begging your pardon, but you know I don't use that stuff. And you pretty much always let Jimmy walk over here by hisself. I'm wondering if you got something special on your mind."

Otis fished out his pocketknife and took his time opening one of the blades. He cut out a one-inch square of tobacco, carefully refolded the knife, put it back in his pocket, and stuck the chaw in his mouth. After positioning it just so with his tongue, he bit down on it and smushed his lips together. "That's some sweet," he said.

Isaiah waited while his neighbor savored the tobacco.

Otis chewed a bit longer, then leaned to the side and spit. "I saw that fat turd Pike this morning," he said, "and he got me to worrying that you're about to sign up with him."

Isaiah turned toward his mill and stared at it as if seeing it for the first time. It was little more than an open-sided cast-iron box sitting chest high astride two cedar logs sunk like posts into the ground, each anchored to a smaller post with rounds of bailing wire. The box held two vertical cast-iron squeezing cylinders and a spout to drain cane juice into catch buckets. Each cylinder had an interconnecting gear on top. An iron rod rose from one of them. A twenty-foot-long pole was bolted a little off center to the upper end of the rod. The short end of the pole had a blacksmithing anvil chained to it for a counterweight, and the other end was outfitted so a mule could be hitched to it and walk in circles around the mill to turn the cylinders. Isaiah and Otis had fed sorghum stalks into them and boiled and skimmed the juice in an adjacent cooking shed together for many hours over the years.

"Well, sir," he said, still staring at the mill. "He did come by again."

Otis spit another stream of tobacco juice into the dirt. "He was acting like you sold him a lease. You didn't, did you?"

"Ain't sold him one yet, but I ain't gon' lie to you. Me and Luella been talking about it. We can sho' nuff use the money. Our boys could, too, and there's the church like I told you before."

"Aw, Isaiah, no." Otis removed his hat and slapped it against his leg. Isaiah, having not taken his eyes off the mill, flinched. Embarrassed at his friend's discomfort, Otis said, "I'm sorry. Look, don't do it. What good's money gon' do you if you have to live in this oil-slick hell the rest of your life? And think about what happened when that Murphy well blew in over at Norphlet last spring. Fire so high they could see it three counties over, and now they got a four-acre-wide hole in the ground deep enough to swallow up half of Berrytown. I hear tell there's folks coming from all over just to look at it, and they sure as shooting ain't getting no oil out of it. You let them drill here, you might get money, but you also might not get nothing but a hard time."

Isaiah looked at Otis for a moment, glanced at the ground, then turned his back on his friend and stared into the distance, toward the woods standing along the edge of his property.

"Well," Otis asked, "ain't you got nothing else to say?"

Isaiah had plenty he would like to say. He would like to say he knew Otis was right about how the oil boom was hurting the land. More than that, he would like to say how worried he and Luella were for their two oldest boys, William and Samuel, who had gone up North during the war, like thousands of other Southern blacks, looking for work and a chance to make a better life. Gone to Chicago, where after the war dozens of black folks were killed in riots that grew out of tension from overcrowding and a shortage of jobs after the all-black 8th Illinois National Guard and other black veterans returned from Europe looking for opportunities previously denied to them.

Similar things had occurred in more than two dozen other cities in 1919. Isaiah would like to say how scared he and Luella were of something like that happening around here. Surely, he thought, Otis must know that less than three years ago more than two hundred blacks were killed over at Elaine in eastern Arkansas because they were trying to organize for better sharecropping pay. And just last year, angry whites had burned more than thirty-five city blocks of a well-to-do black section of Tulsa, Oklahoma, to the ground after a group of black men foiled an attempted lynching.

Isaiah had read about all these things in the *Chicago Defender*, a black-owned newspaper that William and Samuel took turns mailing to him. Even after reading about the tragic events, he still didn't understand everything that touched them off. He knew, however, that one spark was common to every occurrence. He had seen and experienced the effects of it many times, in many ways. It was simply that a lot of white folks didn't like black folks. There was nothing that Isaiah and Luella having money could do to change that. But if there were any other way that money might help them—maybe enable them to move to some place safer, if one even existed, and if not, then at least to Chicago to be with William and Samuel—they certainly would like to have it, especially for Robert's sake. Isaiah didn't like even thinking about leaving his congregation in Berrytown. It seemed cowardly and selfish, and he had spent many hours on his knees out here talking to Him about it. Still, he couldn't shake his earthly fears and desires. He also couldn't say any of this to his friend. Otis was white. He would never understand.

Chapter 8

Henry dipped his razor into the pan of water and wiped it on the towel he shared with three other men who had slept on the floor of Louise Franklin's covered back porch in El Dorado three nights running. For a dollar a day, each got a dry place to lay their heads, access to the well pump and outhouse, and permission to leave their belongings in their landlady's locked storage room while at work or wherever. Given that El Dorado's population was still hovering at somewhere around forty thousand, compared to four thousand or so when oil was first discovered here almost two years ago, Henry counted himself fortunate to have found lodging of any kind.

He had decided while walking back from the pipeline camp that instead of catching the Roughneck Special right away, he may as well poke about in the county seat for a few days. He still believed Tuttle was in Berrytown, but he would be more confident of it if he made at least some effort to check around El Dorado, like he had done earlier with the oil and gas fields back in Indiana.

The El Dorado field was much larger than the Berrytown field had proven to be so far, but it was slowing down. There was still a lot of drilling and plenty of places for a man to get lost, but a measure of order was starting to set in. That wouldn't appeal to Tuttle. He liked booze and fast women, and it seemed to Henry that the authorities in El Dorado were trying to crack down on both.

One of the other men staying on Mrs. Franklin's porch told him that the police chief had hired a bunch more officers and the county had built a barbed-wire stockade to serve as a jail behind the courthouse. Before that, the fellow said, men taken into custody had been held in leg irons at the railroad depot. A local judge had even ordered all the prostitutes out of town. Some of them had relocated to the boondocks and were working out of barrelhouses that also sold illegal liquor, but the chief and the judge had at least taken some of the edge off things.

There were still a lot of lease hounds scouring the countryside, but the showplace Garrett Hotel, which had been the scene of a lot of the early frenzy, with some men sleeping on cots in hallways and chairs in the lobby, and with others like H. L. Hunt gambling and cutting oil deals night and day, now housed company men in from all over to talk pipelines, rail cars, and refineries as well as land sections and stock shares. The locals had formed something called the Arkansas Independent Oil Producers Association, and there was even talk of an amusement park and a community swimming pool.

During his first day in town, Henry had taken his soiled clothes to one of several small laundries that had opened during the boom, then spent the rest of his time walking around looking in store windows, standing on street corners, and eavesdropping. The second and third days, he rented a horse and rode randomly over the countryside seeing what he could of drilling and other oil-field operations from public roadways. Henry knew lots of folks saw greenbacks when they looked at the chewed up and blackened swarths of land spouting derricks and oil spills, but as the son of a farmer, he tried to imagine the now-gone green trees and crops.

By the end of the third day, Henry had come to two conclusions. The first was that Tuttle might well have come to El Dorado instead of Berrytown. The second was that unless he, Henry, just happened to get lucky, finding the lowlife scoundrel was going to be a lot harder than he had previously thought, and he had no real plan for how to go about it. After lying awake most of his third night on the porch, he decided to stick with his original inclination and concentrate on Berrytown. He also decided that his initial instinct about the kind of job he needed was right. He hoped that with all the boomtown hustle and bustle, he had been wrong to think that the incident with the idiot wielding the axe handle on the day he arrived had stuck in anyone's memory. He had to find a way to get a mule-skinning job so he could go all over the countryside while appearing to fit in.

~

When Otis Leatherwood walked into Hornbeck's Drugstore a little after two in the afternoon, he was taken aback to see there were no customers. At first, he thought the place was deserted. Then he heard feet scuffling and saw movement over in the back corner to his left, where the floor-to-ceiling cabinets stopped short of the rear wall. A woman's voice cried, "No! Stop it!" Something banged against the wall and a loud grunt followed.

A second later, Mary Dutton ran from the darkened recess toward the door to the storeroom, swinging her right arm behind her as if waving something off.

"Mary, what's wrong?" Otis called, walking toward her.

Grover Hornbeck stumbled out of the corner all bent over. He froze when he heard Otis's voice.

Mary stopped too. She brushed one hand quickly over her hair and smoothed her dress with the other. "Uncle Otis," she said, her cheeks flushed, "I didn't hear you come in."

"What's going on?" Otis asked. "You all right?"

"Yes, I'm okay now. We were dusting the cabinets, and a big spider fell on me," she lied. She didn't dare let Otis even suspect Grover was groping her. Otis would slug him for sure. Eunice would find out, blame her, and throw her and Jimmy into the street, and they would have no place to go. She was pretty sure Otis wouldn't take them in. He'd had plenty of opportunity to do so if he wanted to, and she wouldn't ask him. It might turn him away from her and Jimmy entirely. Other than her way-off invalid mother-in-law and Eunice, whom she detested, Otis was the only family she and Jimmy had left, no matter that he kept them more or less at arms-length. And Jimmy loved him.

Otis looked at Grover.

"Women," Grover said, trying to straighten up and attempting a smirk. His eyes spoke something closer to pain or fear, though.

Otis didn't know exactly what had just happened, but he knew what it looked like, and it wasn't dusting shelves. "I need to talk to you for a minute, Mary," he said. "Let's go up front." He started to tell Grover to give them some privacy, but Grover had already turned around and begun fiddling with something on his work shelf.

With no one else in the store, Mary joined Otis near the candy counter. "You sure everything's all right in here?" Otis asked.

"Yes, I'm positive."

Otis decided not to push further. "Okay," he said, removing his floppy hat. "I wanted to talk to you the other day when I brought Jimmy back, but I could see how busy y'all were, what with the town filling up the way it is." He paused and glanced around the store. "What I can't figure right now is why this place is empty. Come to think of it, there ain't many folks on the street either. Anyway, what I wanted was to tell you not to let that Pike fellow talk you into buying any of them phony shares he's peddling. Jimmy told me you had one of his handbills."

Before Mary could reply, Jimmy, overalls-clad and barefoot, burst through the front door gasping for breath. "They're about to hang a colored man down yonder behind the car place!" he said. The combination gasoline station and automobile and truck sales and repair shop stood a long block down Broadway, across Eighth Street on the corner. There was a huge vacant lot in the rear.

"Y'all stay here," Otis said, and rushed out the door. Jimmy went flying out behind him.

"Jimmy, come back!" Mary shouted. She ran after him, but he was already halfway down the block, darting among other people hurrying out of stores and into the street.

~

Henry stood under a shed at Fowler & Son Wagons watching a bank of storm clouds roll in from the southwest and ignoring the sounds of some sort of fracas over east somewhere. Before leaving El Dorado on the noon run of the Roughneck Special, he had discarded his leather valise and culled his possessions so they fit into a new canvas rucksack he could tote any number of ways wherever he went. He had it on his back now, with his pistol still riding in a pants pocket. The grip stuck out some, but he wasn't alone in that.

He was waiting to talk to Fowler or his son about where he might land a mule skinner's job. He had inquired at the livery stable near the depot, but the man in charge there had been in a rage over some fellow in a suit, likely a lease hound, returning a buggy with a horse that was all lathered up and missing a shoe. "Ask at Fowler's," was all the guy would say.

When two gunshots rang out, Henry stepped into the street, looked across Broadway, and saw people crowding into the vacant lot behind Mac's Autos. Everyone at Fowler's ran to join them. Henry followed along more leisurely, crossing the main thoroughfare and walking past the automobile place and half a dozen broken-down Model T's and Chevrolets done-in by roads that even the brand-new Federal Highways Act could not have helped.

When he turned into the vacant lot, Henry saw a large black man standing on the back of a stake-bed REO truck with a noose knotted around his neck and his hands tied behind him. The other end of the rope looped over the limb of a huge oak tree and back to the truck, where it was tied to one of the posts supporting the wooden railings around the flat cargo bed. The REO's engine was idling, and several men stood alongside it with shotguns cradled in their arms, as if they had just returned from a successful deer or duck hunt. Dozens of other people—men, women, and children—were crowded around looking on amid cries of: "Goddamn nigger!" "Get that truck moving!" "Hang the son-of-a-bitch!" The men with guns wore angry scowls, but the fellow behind the wheel, who didn't appear old enough to shave, looked frightened and uncertain.

Despite the summer heat, the black man had on a tattered doughboy jacket faded from brown to near gray. That and the way he stood—his body ramrod straight despite fear writ large in his eyes, open wide and flitting about—reminded Henry of men in the all-black 369th Infantry Regiment that had fought in the Meuse-Argonne offensive and spent more days in the trenches of France than any other American unit. Henry held them in high regard.

"He's a goddamned up-North nigger," a man standing behind Henry said to the fellow next to him. "Ain't even one of ours. Talks smart-ass. I heard him over yonder when they caught him."

Henry turned around and stared at the man. Tall and skinny, he was dressed like an oil-field worker but looked too old for it. "What's he accused of?" Henry asked.

"Raped a little white girl's what they say."

"Who's they?"

"Everybody."

"I heard gunshots. Was he hit?"

"Nah. The fellows was just making him hurry up and get his black ass on the truck."

Henry pinched the bridge of his nose to dull the pain spreading across his forehead. "Where's the law?" he asked.

"You mean ole Constable Burns? Ain't seen him. He's probably hiding somewhere with a jar of shine. If he knows what's good for him, he'll stay wherever he is. We're gon' teach this sorry bastard a lesson."

Henry turned back toward the truck and pushed his way through the crowd to the men with shotguns. He counted eight of them. They were younger than the man Henry had just talked to, and from the way they were dressed, he guessed they were all townspeople—carpenters, mechanics, and store clerks.

"Who's in charge here?" he demanded.

"Who wants to know?" one of the men asked.

Henry ignored the question. "Anybody see him do anything?"

Astounded that anyone would challenge them, one of the men replied without thinking about who was asking, "Girl's momma saw him with his hands on her in a ditch."

"What did the girl say?"

"Ain't nobody asked her," the fellow said, still cradling his shotgun in his arm, barrel toward the ground, like the others. "He had hold of her, her momma seen it, and that's enough. You need to shut up and move on now. This ain't none of your affair."

Henry started to walk away then swung back. When he did, his .45 was pointed at the last man who had spoken. "I think I'll just wait till Constable Burns comes. Why don't one of you go get him? And if that truck moves so much as an inch before that driver shuts off the motor, I'm gon' shoot him, and then I'm gon' shoot a bunch of you."

One of the other men made a move to bring up his shotgun, and Henry turned the pistol on him. "I wouldn't do that, friend," Henry said.

The fellow in the truck killed the engine.

CHAPTER 9

A sudden thunderclap sixty seconds into the standoff behind Mac's Autos sounded like a gunshot and scattered most of the crowd. It also kept the men with shotguns frozen. They had no plan from the outset, and the unexpected appearance of one man challenging them with a .45 automatic left them undecided about what to do next. They had an advantage in numbers, but as much as they wanted to kill a black man, none wanted to die trying. Now they and Henry stood staring at each other as the sky turned darker and rain came down in sheets. The black man remained motionless in the truck bed with the noose still around his neck, water pouring off his bare head in rivulets.

Henry knew he was lucky no one had charged him from behind. Now, he could see in the eyes of the men in front of him that bluster was giving way to fear. "We gon' stand here all day or is one of you gon' go get the constable?" Henry shouted over the downpour.

"I'll go," the truck driver said, climbing out of the cab. "I know where he likes to hang out. It ain't far."

"Good idea," Henry said.

"Yeah, Percy, you yellow dog," said the man who had done most of the talking. "You just go ahead on."

"Keep quiet," Henry said.

He looked at the black man, who now only stared off into the distance. Henry thought about telling one of the men with guns to put his down and go untie the man and remove the noose. He probably hadn't raped anyone, but Henry didn't know that for sure. He was reasonably certain, though, that if he let the man go, two things would happen. The men with guns, or others, would hunt the fellow down and hang him somewhere else. Meanwhile, if the girl's mother persisted with her version of what had happened, the constable or the county sheriff would charge Henry with some crime for interfering.

As they all waited, Henry mentally kicked himself for acting impulsively again and drawing attention, but he knew if he had taken time to think about it, he would still have done what he did. The guy who back at Mrs. Franklin's had told him about the new El Dorado lockup had also told him about a mob burning a black man named Lawrence alive there a few years ago, after he "talked back" to a white man who pushed him off a sidewalk. Gunfire had been exchanged, some other white man had been killed, the sheriff had been shot in the foot, and angry whites had destroyed a black-owned barber shop and store. After that, they had gone after Lawrence.

Henry figured this thing wouldn't end well either, regardless of what happened after the constable showed up. Even if he got the man off the truck, people would still be riled. The guys with guns might go after the accused again somewhere later. Tongues would wag in any case, and Tuttle might learn Henry was in town and run. In Henry's mind, however, what Tuttle had done was even worse than what was alleged here. This only made Henry more determined to catch up to him. Meanwhile, he couldn't walk away and let the mob have its way.

The deluge not only soaked onlookers who had remained in the vicinity after the initial thunderclap, it dampened their taste for blood, and one by one they started drifting away. Dirt in the vacant lot began turning to mud, and water ran in little streams to puddles that covered the soles of Henry's and the others' shoes.

"You nigger-loving son-of-a-bitch," one of the men said, regaining some of his nerve.

"Shut up," Henry ordered.

Except for the rain, time seemed to stand still. Even the few bystanders who had managed to find partial shelter under the overhang of the roof on Mac's building now began clearing out.

~

Otis and Mary had been unable to catch up with Jimmy before he wiggled his way to the front of the crowd around the REO. They were still looking for him when the lightning struck and loosed the downpour, and they stood their ground as others rushed past them for cover.

"Oh, God," Mary cried, "please let him be safe."

"He's here somewhere," Otis said. "I'll keep looking. You go back to the corner and watch in case he gets by me. If you get him, take him on back to the store. I'll catch up."

Soon, Otis didn't see anyone left in the lot except Henry, the man on the truck, his captors, and a handful of other men. Otis watched them for a moment then headed back toward the drugstore hoping to see the boy and his mother there, or somewhere on the way. He found them standing under the shed at the entrance, dripping wet and shivering from wind the storm had kicked up. Mary was fussing at Jimmy about putting himself in danger the way he had.

"Why ain't you inside?" Otis asked them.

"We were watching for you, Uncle Gramps," Jimmy said. "Did you see that man with the pistol? Momma and me did. I was just gon' tell her about selling him a newspaper."

"When was that, Jimmy?" Mary asked.

"A few days ago. He asked me where he could find a cheap place to stay."

"Did he say anything else?"

"No, ma'am."

"He probably just come here," Otis said. "Anyway, he's got grit. I'll say that for him." He opened the door. "Come on, now. Let's get inside."

Before following Jimmy through the door, Mary looked back down the street toward Mac's Autos.

Rain was still beating down when Percy returned with the constable. Burns was tall, wide, and aggravated. Water ran off the brim of his hat, and his body strained against his extra-large bib overalls. A worn leather belt helped rein in his gut and held a holstered pistol. From what the fellow in the crowd had said about Burns earlier, Henry had expected a doddering old guy about halfway looped. The constable didn't move very well, but he was not old, and if he had been drinking, it didn't show.

"What the hell's going on here?" he asked after he lumbered across the lot and planted himself near the rear axle of the truck. "Talk to me, Elbert," he said to one of the men holding shotguns.

The man nearest Burns started to speak, and Burns cut him off. "No, on second thought, just shut the hell up. Percy done told me y'all think this boy raped a white girl. Any of y'all see it?"

"No," the man on the end said, "but . . ."

"Anybody else see it?" Burns interrupted.

"No," the man on the end said again, "but her momma said . . ."

"Where's her momma?"

"She run off somewhere with the girl."

"What's her name?"

"Ida Johnson. She lives . . ."

"I know where she lives," Burns cut him off again and turned to Henry. "And who the devil are you? I ain't seen you 'round here before."

"Just a man that didn't want to see somebody hung without a trial," Henry said.

"You got a name?"

"Yes, sir. Henry Smith," he said, sticking with the alias.

"All right, Henry Smith, and all the rest of you jaybirds, I'm gon' count to three, and when I get there, here's what's gon' happen. You boys with the shotguns are gon' shuck them shells on the ground, and Smith, you're gon' take the clip outta that pistol and put both of them in your pocket. All y'all be real slow about it."

Once everyone was disarmed, Burns looked up at the black man. "What's your name, boy?"

"Sir, it's Levi Birdsong."

"Well, Levi, Percy here is gon' climb up there and take that rope off you, and then I want you to sit down real easy like, and me and him and Mr. Smith there are gon' take you up to the township building."

All but one of the bystanders who had lingered now gave up their vigil and went looking for someplace dry. One man watched until the truck got moving, then started on foot for the township building.

Rain continued coming down by the bucketfuls.

CHAPTER 10

Scores of gawkers stood under walkway sheds watching the REO slip and slide up muddy Broadway with the cargo of constable, accused rapist, and armed stranger who had dared to interrupt the lynching. Constable Burns rode up front with Percy as he fought the bucking steering wheel and clumsy gears. Henry and Levi Birdsong sat silently on the floor in back, partially hidden by the wooden side planks. No one except the man who had followed the REO out of the vacant lot tagged along all the way to the township building. Not even the eight men who had been forced to empty their shotguns into the waterlogged vacant lot. Armed now only with anger, embarrassment, and determination to see Levi Birdsong strung up by and by, some of them had gone in search of dry ammunition. The others had gone looking for Ida Johnson and her daughter.

All the way to the township building, Henry wondered how safe the accused man would be while awaiting trial, and how much all of this would hurt his chances of finding Ed Tuttle. The REO crossed El Dorado Avenue and the railroad tracks, turned west for half a block, then pulled right, into an alley, and stopped alongside a rapidly thrown up frame building fronting onto Fourth Street. Behind the unpainted structure, three men stood chained to trees with nothing between them and the rain except the clothes and hats they were wearing.

"Ain't got no jail," Burns said to Henry, when the truck came to a stop and the bulky lawman climbed out, breathing hard from the exertion. "We just leave them out here thinking about their evil deeds till the justice of the peace turns them loose or sends them off to the county sheriff. Help Percy there get him down and bring him inside first, though, so we can set down some whys and wherefores and keep his honor happy."

Henry, still wondering how to get himself untangled from the matter, did as he was directed. The little party went up a couple of board steps and through a narrow door into the yet unpartitioned building. A beat-up wooden desk and a few chairs occupied one corner. In the center a thin middle-aged woman of medium height stood with her arms draped over the front of a miniature version of herself. They had been standing there long enough for water dripping from their dark hair and flowered dresses to form small puddles on the bare wood floor.

"Mr. Burns," the woman said, looking at the constable. "I'm Ida Johnson and this is my daughter Rosa."

The little girl looked at the black man and smiled. Henry saw it and glanced at Levi Birdsong. He stood erect, shoulders back, arms at his side, like before on the truck bed, and stared straight ahead. With his faded doughboy jacket, he looked almost as if he were at military attention.

"I know who you are," Burns said to the woman. "I'm glad you're here. Saves me from having to look you up."

"I'm afraid I made a terrible mistake," Mrs. Johnson said, now gripping her daughter's shoulders. "I saw that colored boy pulling on Rosa's arm, and she was crying, and I thought he was hurting her, and I grabbed her and run home. I was scared he might hurt me too. First white man I passed, I told him, 'That Negro back there attacked my little girl.' When we got home, Rosa told me she'd been running and skipping on the road, and she fell into the ditch, and the colored boy only stopped to help her up. I knew there'd be trouble, so we come over here as quick as we could."

Henry looked again at Birdsong. He didn't move except to close his eyes for several seconds.

The constable breathed in deeply, then let it out with a huge sigh, as if tiring of the whole business. "Who'd you say that to?" he asked, balling up his fists and resting them against his worn belt, elbows sticking out.

"I don't know," Mrs. Johnson replied. "I was so scared I didn't notice anything when we went past him except he was white."

"You do know, don't you, that a mob just about lynched this boy?" Burns asked.

"I didn't till you just said it, but I figured something like that might happen. That's why I come. I don't care much for coloreds, but I don't want to see nobody hurt for something they didn't do."

"Well, that's good," Burns said. "But if it hadn't been for Mr. Smith here, this boy would be dead now, and we'd have a murder on our hands and Lord knows what else. You best think about that and get your facts straight before you holler wolf again. Now, I got to figure out some way to keep him alive till word gets around that he didn't do nothing. If anybody asks you anything about this, you be sure you tell them the right of it. You hear?"

"Yes, sir," Mrs. Johnson said, and turned to go without so much as a peek at Birdsong. As she and Rosa stepped through the front door, however, the little girl looked back and waved.

It didn't take Burns long to do his figuring. He told Percy to go find as many of the eight would-be lynchers as he could, set them straight on what had really happened with the girl, and tell them the constable said they had better get their rear ends in gear and spread the word double time or there'd be hell to pay. Then he told Henry he could leave and that he, Burns, would keep Levi Birdsong in the township building and stay with him the rest of the afternoon in case any of the hotheads decided to come looking for him.

"And Mr. Smith," Burns said, "you stay outta trouble. That gun you're toting is a state misdemeanor. I don't try to enforce it 'cause there's so damn many fellows walking 'round with them, but if you shoot somebody, it'll go hard with you in court."

"Yes, sir," Henry said. "I'll remember that." Then to Birdsong, "Good luck to you, big fellow."

"Yes, sir. Thank you, sir," Birdsong said, and saluted.

~

By the time Henry stepped out the front door of the township building, the rain had let up some, but he was already well past soaked. The clouds made it appear as though dusk was coming early, and he stood on the small stoop looking up and down Fourth Street, trying to think where he could find a place to dry out and spend the night. The cot tent that the newsboy had pointed him to a few days earlier was only about three blocks east, back across Broadway past the train station, and although he knew it was probably full up, he decided he may as well look there first and try to hold off the memories it sparked. He had managed to do that well enough at the pipeline camp, though that tent had been larger.

He hadn't gone three paces when he heard someone behind him call out, "Mr. Smith, sir? Can I talk to you, sir?"

Henry turned around and watched as a small, wiry black man with coffee-colored skin and short hair with flecks of gray approached him holding a wet, floppy-brimmed hat with both hands. He sported a thin, neatly trimmed moustache and had a mule skinner's whip tied to a rope belt that he didn't need to hold up his bib overalls.

"Yeah, okay," Henry said. "But how do you know my name?"

"I heard you say it to Constable Burns back yonder when them men was about to hang my cousin."

"That's your cousin in there?" Henry asked, motioning toward the door behind him. "You don't look anything like him."

"Well, we ain't close cousins or nothing like that," the little man said, tugging at his hat as if it were an accordion, "but we're sho' nuff cousins. Way back yonder somewhere when we was all living in Alabama, his part of the family went off up to New York, and my part came over here. Anyways, I know you don't care nothing about all that, and you ain't got time for it either. I just want to thank you for saving him. I know he ain't out of the woods yet, but least ways them men didn't hang him, and I sho' do appreciate what you done."

"You always talk this much?" Henry asked, amazed by the outpouring and relieved that it was a black man who had called out to him and not a white man waiting to chew him out, or attempt worse, for his interference.

"No, sir," the little man said. Then he shook his head and went on, "Well, yes sir, I reckon I do, 'cause lots of folks say I'm always running on. But I don't like to talk about no private stuff. This right here's just something special. Anyway, my name's Calvin. Calvin Birdsong. Like I said, I sho' do thank you, and if there's anything I can ever do for you, you just ask me. I been 'round here a long time, and just about everybody knows me. Well, except for them what's come to town new and all."

Henry looked the man over again. "I'm pleased to meet you, Calvin. My name's Henry."

"Yes, sir, Mr. Smith. I heard that too."

"You can call me 'Henry.'"

"Yes, sir, Mr. Henry. I'll do that."

"Okay, Calvin, there actually might be something you can help me with. But first, you need to know that your cousin's gon' be free to go soon as the constable gets word to all those guys that were trying to hang him and let them know that the little girl said all Levi did was help her up after she fell down running."

"Praise the Lord!" Calvin said. He rocked back and forth from his waist a few times then whispered, as if in prayer, "Thank you, Jesus."

"Calvin," Henry said, "I see you've got a mule skinner's whip there. Are you a driver?"

"Yes, sir, I am. I reckon I'm about the best there is in these parts."

Henry grinned. "Well," he said, "seeing as how you're so good at it and just about everybody knows you, would you happen to know a mule yard where another fellow that's handy with mules can catch on?"

"Yes, sir, I expect I do. You ain't talking about yourself, are you?"

"Yeah, I am."

"Well, sir, you just come on, then."

~

"Y'all are getting the floor all wet!" Eunice wailed. Having returned to the drugstore moments before the downpour, she was standing midway back in the center, hands on hips, glaring at her father, Mary, and Jimmy. Despite having little use for the old man, she turned a little green anytime she saw him with her cousin and the boy. She had recognized for some time that Otis cared more about them than he did his own flesh and blood, and it would be just like the old coot to leave his land to them. She knew she needed to be nice to him if she didn't want that to happen, but every time she tried, she remembered the way he ignored her after her mother died. Truth was, she hated him, and she knew that he knew it. "Mary, get a mop and clean this floor up," she ordered. "And be quick about it."

"We ain't done talking," Otis said, his eyes narrowing and the furrows across his forehead deepening. "Y'all mop every time somebody comes in outta the weather, or is it just after certain folks?" He gestured at a spate of muddy footprints left by customers who had come and gone since the rain started.

"It's all right," Mary said. She put her hand out as if to touch Otis's forearm but drew it back. "It's my job." She glared at Eunice then patted Jimmy on the shoulder and said, "Tell your Uncle Gramps good-bye and go on to the back."

Otis told them both, "So long," and stood watching as they walked through the store. "Remember what I said about them handbills," he called after them. When they were gone, he turned to his daughter. "Eunice, you ought not talk to Mary like that in front of the boy."

He left without giving Eunice a chance to reply. But she hadn't heard him anyway. She hadn't even given a second thought to Mary's saying, 'Uncle Gramps,' something that would normally have set her on edge. Instead, she stood puzzling over Otis's comment about handbills.

CHAPTER 11

"You never drove nothing bigger than a two-up?" Wilbur Moss asked. He followed his question by spitting a stream of brown slime within two feet of Henry's boots. A sixtyish white man not much bigger than Calvin Birdsong, Moss had a sweat-stained derby hat on his bald head, a blacksmith's apron over his pants and dirty-white union suit, and a lump of snuff in his lower lip. The three men were standing in front of a large wooden barn, one of two sitting next to each other in Moss's mule yard just off the road to Camden, near Scuppernong Creek and the Ouachita County line. The barns, several sheds opposite them, and three large corrals in back were enclosed by wire fencing. Between the compound and the road, half a dozen wagons of various types sat in a ragged line, as if awaiting teams and drivers. Except for Calvin, Moss, two men unloading hay, and another trimming hooves in one of the sheds, the place seemed deserted, almost as if floundering. A slew of hoof and wagon tracks told otherwise, however.

"No, but I've been around horses and mules all my life," Henry said, "and I figure I can learn easy enough." Not only had he never driven anything bigger than a two-up team, he had never driven a team that large. But he figured driving four mules couldn't be much different than driving a pair. So, he lied again, though he preferred to think of it as merely a misrepresentation.

"I can teach him," Calvin said. He had already told Moss how Henry saved his cousin and how Elbert Krebs was one of the men trying to hang him. Because Calvin listened almost as much as he talked, he knew that mentioning Krebs would get Moss's attention. Krebs was married to the man's sister, and they had a houseful of kids they couldn't feed and clothe properly because Krebs kept gambling away what little money he earned from his ramshackle farm and few odd jobs. Far as Moss knew, the man had never even attempted to catch on as a roustabout on one of the drilling rigs. Moss figured he was simply too lazy. A man didn't need any special training to fetch tools, pipe, and other stuff for the roughnecks and drillers who did the main work on rigs. In sympathy for his nieces and nephews, Moss had hired the man once himself, but that hadn't lasted a week before Moss caught him beating a horse. Hungry kids or not, Moss wouldn't tolerate cruelty to his animals.

"That all you got?" Moss asked.

"Yep, I reckon it is," Henry said, "except I can't stand to see animals whipped. I saw them suffer too much in the war. If you expect your drivers to be rough with your stock, then I don't want to work for you."

"Calvin here tell you to say that?" Moss asked, grinning. He stuck out a dirty, calloused hand. "I reckon you'll do. Lord knows, fast as oil men are rolling in here, just like they done down at El Dorado, I sho' can use more skinners. But I tell you this. If I ever catch you hurting any of my stock, I'm gon' be upside your head like a peckerwood on a sweet gum tree. Pay's six dollars a day, and that's six days a week before sunup till after sundown, or long as it takes to get every one of them mules fed and took proper care of."

"You won't have to worry about me, Mr. Moss," Henry said.

"Just call me 'Moss.' Everybody does. Reckon 'Wilbur' don't sit very easy on the tongue." Moss spit again and asked, "So, you was in the army, huh?"

"Yes, sir. With the AEF."

"Yeah, I figured. My nephew was, too, only he didn't come home. You an officer?"

"Yes, sir."

"I figured that too. You got the look. You got a place to stay?"

"No, sir. I was planning to ask at that cot house over by the depot."

"They ain't had no room over there for days. You can bed down in one of the hay lofts till you can find a place. Reckon I don't have to tell you not to take no kerosene lamps up there. Or do no smoking anywhere 'round here."

"No, sir."

"All right," Moss said. "We'll start you off working in the yard tomorrow, and then we'll put you on a two-up. Now, I got work to do. Calvin here will show you 'round. You're lucky I let him off today to see to his sick momma."

"Two-up mules or horses?" Henry asked.

"Mules," Moss said. "Only horses we got is saddle horses. Mules is better for hauling. Some people think they're stubborn. But that ain't it. They're just smarter than horses. They learn quick. They ain't gon' wade into something they don't think they can get out of. They don't eat too much and get the colic, and if they get loose, they don't run off too far.

You got to treat them right, though. You beat on them, and you're 'gon have a devil of a time working them. You do right by them, and they'll follow you 'round just like a puppy dog."

After Moss left Henry and Calvin to get on with other business, Calvin said, "That man sho' took to you. I ain't never seen him talk so much to a new man. He ain't never offered to let nobody sleep in one of the barns neither."

With the rain having fallen off to a few light pockets and the sun trying to break through the remaining clouds, Mary had let Jimmy go off to watch town folks trying to cope with the muck the storm left behind, and she had almost finished cleaning the drugstore floor. Eunice, still pondering Otis's remark about the handbills, was in the back making a show of wiping display cases. Each was pretending to ignore the other when Floyd Roper came in with Sally Boudreau. The short, muscular man in his black suit with his boxy leather case and the tall, red-haired, buxom woman in a low-cut lime-green dress with matching umbrella would have made an unlikely couple anywhere. But seeing them together was especially startling for Mary and Eunice, who had no idea they knew each other.

"Good afternoon, ladies," Roper said, as the pair walked past Mary toward the rear. He glanced around the store, confirmed that there were no customers, and said, "We've brought your new merchandise." He placed his Gladstone bag on the back counter and said, "Let me show you what we've got for you."

Mary busied herself near the soda fountain, but Eunice moved around behind the work counter. She looked at the case, then at Sally, who smiled, and then at Roper. He was smiling, too, but his cold, gray eyes sent a different sort of message.

"It's what we talked about," he said, as if Eunice hadn't grasped what he meant by 'merchandise.'"

She knew there were no customers, but she scanned the store anyway. She had expected Roper to show up at some point with the things they had discussed, but not this soon, and not with Sally Boudreau in tow. Eunice wondered how much she knew. Roper had said he would get the word out to interested parties that certain illegal substances could be had at the drugstore. However, seeing proof of his promise standing before her was unsettling, even though she counted Sally as a friend.

"Where's Mr. Hornbeck?" Roper asked, his hands resting on the top of the Gladstone, ready to open it.

"He's in the back," Eunice said. "I'll get him."

Roper turned to Mary, who remained near the soda fountain. She was squeezing her broom handle so hard her knuckles were turning white. "Come on back, Mary. You've got to see this too. By the way, you don't mind me calling you by your first name, do you, seeing as how we're gon' be working together?" Mary didn't answer or move. "I sure hope not," Roper said, grinning. Then the smile faded and his gaze narrowed. "Come on, Mary. Now!"

Mary looked at Sally, who stared back blankly. Eunice emerged from the workroom with Grover trailing behind, and said, "Mary, I heard Mr. Roper call you. Get on back here." Mary slammed her broom against the tile floor and walked away leaving it where it lay. Eunice scowled at her but didn't say anything more.

When everyone had gathered around, Roper looked up front again, double-checking that no one else had come into the store. Then he opened his case, took out several cartons of patent medicines, and set them aside. Next, he removed a wooden box that fit snugly into the bottom of the Gladstone. He put the case on the floor, set the box on the counter, and removed the lid. "I'm not gon' take everything out," he said. "I just want to point out what everything is. If anybody walks in, I'll put the lid back on and we'll start talking about that hanging y'all almost had down yonder a little while ago."

"What's Big Sally got to do with this?" Grover asked, the worry in his voice plain to all. "Why's she here?"

"She's 'gon be your first customer," Roper said. He reached up and put his arm around her shoulder, and she shrugged it off. "Her girls are 'gon be regulars," he said, "and she's 'gon help me get the word out to other folks."

"How do we know we can trust her to keep her mouth shut if Treasury agents come poking around?" Grover asked, glancing at Eunice.

Roper answered before Eunice could speak. "Don't be stupid, man. If she talked, she'd lose her supply, and she could probably be prosecuted too."

Eunice was growing impatient. "Show us what all this is," she said, "and let's hurry up and get it out of sight."

"Okay, I've brought you some morphine you won't have to report like you do when you get it legally. And there're some Tiemann hypodermic kits in here like you probably used to sell before Harrison. They ain't against the law by themselves, but you need to keep them out of sight with the rest of this stuff. If you put them out on display, everybody's gon' be pretty sure you're selling more morphine than you're putting in prescriptions. There's also a good supply of cocaine and heroin in here for snorting. That's the little bottles on the end. Clear ones are cocaine. Brown ones are heroin. And here's a price list for everything." He took a folded paper from his coat pocket and handed it to Eunice.

"I'll be back every couple of weeks to take inventory, collect the proceeds, give you your cut, and refresh the supply. You try cheating me and my people, or you lose anything, it's like I told you before. We know how to get Treasury agents to look where we want them to and how to stay out of their way at the same time. We can get y'all shut down and locked up before you know what's hit you. And in case you ain't heard, Congress has got a new law now that raises the ante on Harrison violations to a $5,000 fine and ten years in the pen.

"So, your buyers are gon' come in here and ask you on the sly for Crescent City Powders, and you're gon' ask them which kind, and they're gon' tell you, "Plain" for morphine, "Clear" for cocaine, and "Brown" for heroin. Then you're gon' wrap whichever it is in that brown paper you've got over there and take their money. Simple as that. Somebody happens to overhear and ask you what Crescent City Powders are, all you got to do is tell them it's an extra-high-strength laxative for people who ain't gone in a month."

CHAPTER 12

Before Roper and Sally left the drugstore, she bought one of the Tiemann hypodermic kits and some morphine, and Roper insisted that Mary handle the transaction. "Just so we can be sure you're gon' keep your mouth shut," he said. "We're all witnesses; you're selling illegal Crescent City Powders. You're in this deep as we are."

As soon as Mary handed Sally the string-tied package, she pushed past Eunice toward the workroom door and her living quarters in the shed. Her broom remained where she left it.

Roper started to call her back, but Eunice said, "Let her go. She'll be fine."

~

After Roper and Sally left, Eunice and Grover decided it would be best to keep their new merchandise in the workroom. When a customer requested Crescent City Powders, one of them, or Mary, could say, "Yes, I believe we have some in the back," ask what kind the customer wanted, then say, "All right, let me go look." Whoever was doing the clerking could also do the wrapping back there too.

Grover kept an eye on things up front while Eunice went to find a good spot for the wooden box. When she entered the workroom, she half-way expected to hear sobbing coming from the shed despite Mary's fit of temper with the broom. Eunice stood for a few moments listening, and hearing nothing, she set the box on a workbench, tiptoed to the door into Mary's quarters, and put her ear to it. Still hearing nothing, she placed her hand gently on the doorknob, turned it slowly, and cracked the door just enough to peer inside. She didn't worry about making noise. She kept the hinges well-oiled specifically for occasions when, to her mind, she needed, as landlady, "to check on the condition of my property."

Even absent sobbing, Eunice expected to see Mary lying or sitting somewhere with her face buried in her hands. Instead, Mary was kneeling on the floor in front of her round-top trunk.

Eunice could only see the trunk from the side, but she already had a good idea of what was in it because she had opened it and briefly lifted the tray out one day when Mary was away. On that occasion Eunice had sent Mary on an errand. To be certain she had not returned through the rear entrance and Jimmy wasn't there either, Eunice had knocked on the door, pushed it open, and called out before entering.

Thinking now that maybe the trunk held something of interest she had missed, or that Mary had added something new, Eunice watched as Mary took out the tray and set it down beside her. It held her sewing materials, an empty wallet that had belonged to her father, some doilies her mother had crocheted, a bundle of letters that Andy Dutton had written to her before his fatal accident in New Mexico, and a few other small items Eunice had noted before. The only new thing now was what appeared to be an advertising handbill of some sort. Eunice couldn't see what it was for.

Mary then removed a few articles of winter clothing and set those on top of the tray. Eunice had glimpsed those previously, too, and was about to close the door and return to the wooden box holding the drugs, when Mary reached deep into the trunk and pulled out a thin board that was the same width and length of the trunk and covered with the same flowered paper that lined the inner walls. Mary set it aside too. Then she lifted out a quilt that Eunice had never seen before.

As far as Eunice could tell, nothing about the quilt seemed unusual, and she wondered why it had been hidden. She supposed Mary could have put it under the false bottom simply because the space was available. If that were the case, however, she puzzled why Mary had not pushed the false bottom to the floor of the trunk and put the quilt on top of it. Perhaps, Eunice decided, the sides of the trunk had some sort of built-in rails that wouldn't allow the thing to go all the way down.

By now, Eunice's calves and shoulders were starting to cramp from scrunching down to get the best view. She started to rise and was about to ease the door shut, when she heard Mary begin to cry. Ignoring the growing pain in her legs, Eunice continued to watch.

~

Mary held the quilt almost reverently as she sat back on her heels, laid it in her lap, and ran her fingers over it. She prized it most among the few things she still had from a time long past, when she dared to dream of a better life. Presently, she pulled it to her chest, buried her face in it, and let it soak up tears she made no effort to hold back. It wasn't fear about the drugs that unleashed the flow. It was the way she and Jimmy had to live. It was the overwhelming loss in so few years of everyone close to her except her son. And it was her endless worry about what lay ahead for them, especially for Jimmy. He helped her with the ordinary chores of daily living, worked at selling newspapers and sometimes running errands for people, had friends among town kids, liked visiting his great uncle and playing with the little Negro boy that lived on the next farm over, and seemed happy enough. But she wanted him to have a bigger and cleaner place to live, better clothes, and a mother who had more time for him. She had cried plenty when her own mother passed and again at the news of her husband's death but never since then. She tried hard not to feel sorry for herself and to keep up a cheerful front for Jimmy. But right now, giving in to her sadness seemed easier than fighting it.

After a bit, Mary wiped her eyes with the backs of her hands and rested the quilt on the edge of the trunk. She ran her fingers over the cloth once more, feeling the texture of the fabrics and the stitches her mother had made binding together pieces cut from flower sacks and clothing no longer wearable. The coverlet wouldn't have won any prizes in a county fair. But to Mary it couldn't have been more beautiful. Florence Dutton never liked sewing and learned to do it only because farm women had to know how to make clothes for themselves and their families. She started piecing the quilt together when Mary was a child, but the stitching went slowly. So painfully slow, in fact, that Florence often left it untouched for months at a time. After a long while, she decided to hold onto it and give it to Mary as a wedding present.

Mary remembered the day she received it as if it were yesterday. "It's the simplest sort of a Nine Patch," her mother had said, "but every stitch in it was put there with love for you and hope that you will have a long and happy life."

The quilt had seven horizontal rows and five vertical rows of one-foot-square blocks separated from each other by four-inch-wide strips made from irregular lengths of fabric stitched end to end. Similar strips ran along each of the quilt's four outer edges. The blocks alternated between ones that were solid and ones that were composed of nine smaller blocks of various types of cloth sewn together. The result was a mishmash of prints and all the colors of the rainbow. It looked even more unusual because Florence had decoratively quilted only the solid blocks—except for those on the four corners, which she had also left unquilted. Almost anyone other than Mary would have thought the quilt common at best, possibly even ugly. But she adored every inch of it, even the stiff and ungainly corners that contained so much stuffing her mother couldn't have quilted them even if she had tried. These were intended, her mother explained, to help hold the quilt in place when spread over a bed untucked.

Florence had not been totally truthful in that regard. The four corners held more than ordinary cotton batting. They held her hope. They held a gamble she hid from her husband. And they held her faith that if she were right, then sometime somewhere Mary would discover her secret and benefit from it.

Mary's father George had been part owner of a small sawmill and fancied himself something of an authority in matters of business. When Mary was born in 1892, George, inspired by his new-found responsibilities of fatherhood and an article he read about Cornelius Vanderbilt in *Munsey's Magazine*, had bought some shares of stock in the Pullman Car Company and set them aside for his daughter's future.

Unfortunately, the next year the country plunged into economic panic. The crisis stemmed from multiple causes, including a drop in commodity prices and an over-supply of silver, but the most visible cause was over-expansion of railroads. Banks failed. Shipping, railroad, and related companies lost business. And stock values plummeted. Early in 1894, after the Pullman Car Company cut workers' wages to near-starvation levels, they went on strike with support from the American Railway Union and its socialist president, Eugene V. Debs. In more than two dozen states, union members refused to handle trains with Pullman cars, and rail traffic came to a near standstill across the country.

In George's view, causing something this catastrophic was about as low as a man could sink. It didn't matter that the union represented the workers, not the company. He thought the strike hurt too many people, and he didn't want anything to do with what he called "the whole damn mess." Over time, he grew so enraged that he told Florence to destroy the Pullman stock certificates. He said they were worthless, he didn't want them in the house, and he didn't want to touch them. Said they would probably jinx the sawmill. Later, after a sawdust fire destroyed the mill and left the family barely scraping by on their small farm until he found work in someone else's mill, George said he wasn't surprised. He said he knew something like that was bound to happen.

Meanwhile, lacking George's fixation, Florence figured the railroads would bounce back someday and the certificates would be worth something. Besides, she thought the embossed documents were too pretty to tear up or burn. So, she sewed them inside four oilcloth packets she made to waterproof them and then sewed one of the packets into each corner of the quilt she was making for Mary. Florence put an extra layer of cotton batting around each packet to hide at least some of their stiffness and was careful not to puncture them as she completed the quilt.

In the years afterward, every time anything was said about railroads within George's hearing, he went into a rant. Before the mill burned, he even refused to saw crossties for routine railroad maintenance, claiming that he had enough business without dealing with them. Florence never mentioned the certificates to him. After a while, she rarely thought of them, and she never told Mary about them, not even when she knew she was likely dying from the Spanish flu. Before Florence's doctor put her in quarantine, her congested and swollen lungs were hemorrhaging, and she was drowning in her own blood and couldn't speak.

Mary had never questioned her mother's explanation about the odd design of the quilt. That was partly because, given her mother's ineptness as a quilter, Mary had not grown up around many quilts and had no real basis for judging them. And it was partly because despite prizing the quilt, Mary had never used it. She was already pregnant when she married, and she knew her mother would be disappointed in her and hurt when the baby came only six months after the nuptials. Using it on her wedding bed didn't seem right somehow. But she held onto it because her mother had made it for her, and she loved her mother even more for it.

After a while, recalling good times in the past with Florence and George helped Mary push aside some of her sorrow about the present. She smiled, caressed the quilt again, and picked up the handbill lying in the trunk tray. She remembered her uncle's warning, but she also knew he despised everything about the oil boom, from the sudden influx of people to the noise and commotion and the mess that gushers made. She knew, too, that Luther Pike wasn't the only man speculating and dealing in oil stocks. She had seen their ads in the *Berrytown Journal* and heard people talking about them in the drugstore—firms like the Mike Lyvers Syndicate, the Pat Marr Company, the Strong Oil Corporation, and the Rica Oil Company, among others. She had heard men bragging about buying stock from all of them, and she had seen families—not a lot, but some—go from barely scraping by to being able to trade their wagons for automobiles and their farms for homes in Camden, Little Rock, and other cities after wells came in on their property, or when shares they had bought paid off. She had only to look out the drugstore windows every day to see the promise of better times coming true. She saw hundreds of new faces arriving in Berrytown every week, and she watched the chaotic dance that unfolded on Broadway every day as increasing numbers of vehicles of every sort and size vied for right of way.

"Now or Never!" Above all else she had heard, and above every other headline on the Luther Pike handbill, that one loomed largest to Mary. "Now or Never!" She had been pinching her scarce pennies for months and months trying to scrape together enough money for a better place for her and Jimmy to live. She never really believed she would succeed, but she knew she had to keep trying. Now, however, with the boom in full force and housing the scarcest commodity of all, her dream seemed doomed for the foreseeable future, and maybe forever. Doomed, that is, unless she risked everything and got lucky. Maybe she would fare better with oil than her daddy had with Pullman. She checked Luther Pike's handbill for the particulars of how to invest with him. Uncle Otis didn't need to know.

Eunice watched Mary put the quilt back in the false bottom of the trunk, study the handbill again, lay it back on the tray, then return it to the round-top and close the lid. Mary didn't get up immediately, but Eunice didn't want to chance spying any longer. She closed the door between the workroom and the shed and, gritting her teeth, managed to pull herself erect without a sound, her curiosity overriding the pain in her legs and shoulders.

CHAPTER 13

Henry swatted another mosquito and shifted his weight on the wagon seat for the fourth time. Having left the Missouri Pacific rail siding more than two hours ago with a wagonload of dirt-moving fresnos ticketed to an oil pit contractor out east, near the Standard Umpsted settlement, he had been waiting under a scorching sun to get across Scuppernong Creek for most of the time since. Dozens of teams hauling lumber, pipe, drill bits, and other supplies to the oil field, or returning to town to pick up more of the same, were bunched up on both sides of the creek waiting to cross the only bridge. The narrow timber-and-board span sat low over the water and had no railings. Haulers had learned the hard way that trying to get two wagon teams across at the same time was a recipe for disaster. A passel of them had gone over the side, their mules braying helplessly, their wagon beds splitting open, and their loads sinking into the water and muck.

Calvin had said to expect delays. He had also said be glad the ground had dried out some since the big thunderstorm. Still, several wagons were bogged down along the road on both sides of the bridge, while other drivers, Henry among them, were trying to pull around them. The result, besides the bottleneck, was a lot of shouting, cussing, and near fistfights.

Using up daylight sitting on his backside was not getting Henry any closer to Ed Tuttle, but he still thought this job was probably his best chance of finding the man. This despite a slow start even before today. After Moss had found out Henry didn't know how to use a bullwhip, he had shaken his head as if to say, "Yeah, I should've known." Then he had let fly a string of slime-laden four-letter words and kept Henry working in the mule yard for three days instead of one, taking pointers from Calvin when he was around, and other times walking back into the woods to practice snapping at tree limbs and bushes.

"A driver's got to know how to use one of these things when he needs to," Moss had said, "but don't you ever come back here with the hide split on one of my animals. You do, and I'm gon' show you how it feels." This was the second time the little man had made a big threat, and Henry suspected Moss wouldn't be afraid at least to try to make good on both.

Despite Moss's outsize declarations, however, Henry knew he was getting special treatment. Besides no other new hires being allowed to sleep in one of the barns, none got paid to learn on the job. He believed his good fortune was because of Calvin and wondered why. He had seen Moss's dander rise when Calvin mentioned Elbert Krebs's role in the attempted lynching, but that didn't account for the friendly manner Moss displayed toward Calvin when he introduced Henry, or afterward when Henry saw them together around the yard. Moss hadn't said anything about Henry's carrying a pistol either, though surely, he must have noticed. Pondering all this while waiting at the bridge jam provided no answers.

When it was Henry's turn to pass over, his two-up team of one black and three brown mules took him across the muddy planks into Ouachita County without any special urging. The mules were happy to be on the move too.

Within a few miles Henry entered a landscape that sparked memories of battle-scarred fields in France and sent pulsating pain to both sides of his head. Unable to let go of the mules' reins and press his fingers against his temples, he scrunched his eyes and tried to will the throbbing away.

Where forests of trees had once stood, now there were forests of derricks. Only a few decaying tree trunks rose here and there from the oil-soaked soil, dying sentinels stripped bare of bark and limbs by crude spewed from gushers. All other trees had been cut for derrick timbers, or to feed the ravenous boilers making steam to power the drilling.

Some derricks stood close to each other, while others stood well apart. The separated ones were newer. In their haste to suck up as much oil as possible from every pool they found, oil companies and their drillers were bringing the black gold out of the ground faster than they could store it or get it to refineries. To slow things down, try to control waste, and prevent derrick fires from jumping to other wells and wiping out entire sections of a field, the Arkansas Conservation Department had recently directed that all new wells be at least two hundred feet from lease lines and four hundred feet apart. That was helping, but not much. Which is why Henry was hauling fresnos.

Drillers were turning the fast-flowing oil into earthen pits to hold it until wood or steel storage tanks could be built or enough pipelines laid to transport it to tank cars on railroad sidings or, in some instances, directly to refineries. In the race to beat out competitors, developers didn't worry a lot about how much of the stuff sank back into the ground, or what would happen if someone got careless with a match, or if heavy rains eroded pit walls and crude ran into creeks and bottoms.

Formally branded "Fresno Scrapers" when invented to dig irrigation ditches in California, the fresnos Henry was hauling were key to this temporary but dangerous strategy. In the hands of experienced crews, they could move huge volumes of earth. They had been used extensively in building the Panama Canal, and Henry had seen them used in the army. Roughly the width of a pair or a two-up team of horses or mules needed to pull them, they resembled sections of smooth culvert pipe sliced in half horizontally and turned up on edge, with runners welded to each end, the lower lip filed sharp, and a handle welded to the back so that a driver walking behind could tilt the blade to get the best digging angle. Their presence spoke tomes about the scale of the Berrytown field.

Perched above his load of fresnos, Henry soon found that the main road into Standard Umpsted—where earlier, sawmill tycoon Sidney Ulmpsted had bought in the big Richardson well, and where now, he had thousands more acres under development—was barely distinguishable from dozens of side roads heading into various parts of the jumble of drilling rigs, boiler houses, oil pits, and makeshift worker camps.

Just as derricks dominated the skyline, finished pits commanded Henry's view of the ground. Ranging up to three hundred yards on a side, they formed a series of black lakes dotting the landscape almost to the horizon. With excavated dirt piled along the edges like levees, most had a storage depth of ten to twelve feet. As Henry drove past them, he saw six- and eight-inch pipes from more than a dozen wells spewing thousands of barrels of sour-smelling, high-viscosity "heavy" crude into them.

In the remaining available space, crews were at work digging more of the giant holes. First, two-horse plow teams broke up the ground. Then, fresno teams scraped up the loosened soil and moved it to the outer rims. Nearly all the pit diggers were black men, and Levi Birdsong was supposedly somewhere among them, doing some sort of roustabout toting job that Calvin had finagled for him. Most of the men had been brought in from Texas by pit contractors who originally employed them in oil fields there. In addition to those on site here, others worked in the growing development out west of Berrytown, past Otis Leatherwood's farm toward Louann. There were more than two hundred of them altogether, and they had their own camp a little north of Berrytown in southern Ouachita County, complete with a general store and two barrelhouses. Locals called it "Lone Star Hill."

After following Moss's directions as best he could and stopping twice to ask for more, as well as to see if he could spot Tuttle somewhere, Henry reached the pit site he was looking for. He helped with the unloading and was soon back at the bridge over Scuppernong Creek waiting in line to cross.

As Henry sat, reins in hand and mosquitos buzzing around him again, he thought more about Levi Birdsong, having kept an eye out for him among the pit crews. Henry had been curious about the man from the first time he saw him, and after a couple of days working with Calvin, Henry asked him if Levi had served in the 369th. Calvin said he had and was surprised Henry knew about the regiment. Henry said of course he did. He had fought alongside it from the Meuse-Argonne offensive right through to the Armistice. He knew the unit had originally been the 15th New York National Guard, was known up there as the Harlem Hellfighters, and had been decorated by the French government.

When Calvin didn't offer anything more, Henry figured he was being cautious because he was black and Henry was white. But Levi's manner seemed like something beyond a black man's normal deference to a white man, so Henry pressed Calvin further. He asked if Levi had been hurt in the war and how he came to be in Arkansas. Calvin said he'd been wounded, but no one in the family knew how exactly, or where it happened. Levi often had bad headaches and had trouble remembering things. He also tended to treat all white men like they were army officers. Henry assumed this was probably because in the 369th, all the officers were white, like in most black units. Calvin said Levi was harmless as a puppy unless someone said something about his uniform jacket, then watch out. After name-calling and street fights involving dozens of black veterans touched off a deadly riot in New York City a few years back, Levi's family had sent him down here, where they thought he would be safer.

Henry knew about that riot. As well as ones that happened in Chicago, Washington, and elsewhere after two hundred thousand black veterans like Levi returned from Europe no longer willing to settle for second-class citizenship, then clashed with whites who were caught up in bad economic times and egged on by a resurgent Ku Klux Klan and others peddling fear of blacks, Bolsheviks, Catholics, foreigners, and anyone different from them. Still, Henry couldn't help smiling when he recalled what Calvin said next. It was not in the least a laughing matter; it was a deadly serious one. But

Henry liked that Calvin was bold enough, and comfortable enough with him, to say it.

"Begging your pardon and all, Mr. Henry," Calvin had said, "but I don't know what Levi's people was thinking. I believe they's as touched in the head as he is."

~

For days after watching Mary with her quilt and the handbill, Eunice Hornbeck could think of little else except getting back into Mary's trunk and taking a closer look. Several times she sent Mary out of the drugstore on made-up errands when Jimmy was out selling newspapers. Each time either more customers came into the store than Grover could handle alone, or he went off somewhere leaving her to tend the place by herself. She became so anxious about it all, and so irritated with Grover, that she wouldn't even let him fondle her in bed, let alone use her to shine his stubby manhood. When he quit trying, that upset her still more. So much so that she then tried to seduce him in ways she had only heard Sally and Vera talk about. When he told her, "Stop trying to act like a whore because you're not equipped for it," she cried herself to sleep three nights running.

Meanwhile, in the store, they growled at each other over every little thing. But both of them, and Mary as well, did everything possible to be precise and discreet every time one of Sally's girls, or anyone else, asked for Crescent City Powders. And that was happening more and more.

CHAPTER 14

By mid-August, geologists and others in the know were starting to think the Berrytown field might be larger than the El Dorado field. Oil men of every stripe, from promoters to roughnecks and all in between, continued arriving in the little town, some alone and some with wives and children. After them came more storekeepers, more tradesmen, more schemers, more prostitutes. And more of all types of machinery, tools, equipment, extra parts, and everyday items people needed to do all the things they had come for. It was said that every rail siding in every community of any size south of Little Rock was jammed with boxcars and flatcars loaded with freight slated for Berrytown.

Oil-field supply outfits built warehouses wherever they could find space along El Dorado Avenue and the rail line both east and west of Broadway. One enterprising new arrival came with enough money already in hand to set up a bus line running twice daily from Berrytown to El Dorado and Camden. Like the Roughneck Special, it served men laboring to get oil out of the ground and those seeking to profit from it without ever dirtying their hands in it. Another newcomer started building a movie house ambitiously named the "American Theater" and began looking for musicians to accompany the silent pictures he planned to bring in. Two local men opened new eating establishments. Some folks called them "restaurants," but they were so hastily thrown up that only the food fit that notion. However, they reduced the long wait time at the only other eating place for a while, until even more folks flooded in to grab their share of riches under the Berrytown rainbow.

This was a nightmare for Otis Leatherwood, who now not only hated coming to town more than ever, but also was getting near-daily visits from lease hounds—Luther Pike in particular. Having talked with Isaiah Watson again when Jimmy Dutton came out for another visit, Otis knew the same thing was happening with his neighbor, and he feared Isaiah would cave any day now. As if that were not enough, some fellow wearing fancy knee-length, lace-up boots and driving a big yellow touring car with "Packard" plastered in gold-colored script across the front came out to Otis's house and said his company was thinking about building a pipeline that would cross Otis's land and he would like to look it over.

Otis's response was simple and to the point: "The hell you say! Get your sorry ass off my property and don't come back unless you want a belly full of buckshot."

The flourish of activity proved a boon for Otis's daughter and her husband, though. So much so that their good fortune continued even after another newcomer opened a competing drugstore a block south of them on the other side of Broadway. Eunice and Grover stayed so busy with customers that they no longer had time to fight during business hours, although Eunice remained no less interested in getting into Mary's trunk. Their forced foray into illegal drug sales kept pace, too, and when Floyd Roper showed up with a new supply, he was pleased to see that he had been successful in getting the word out.

Eunice liked that Sally Boudreau popped in every day or two with a new girl and always had a juicy story to tell. Vera Hudson remained Eunice's favorite after Sally, however, because despite having a quick wit and a flair for makeup, she had what Eunice considered sad eyes. Eunice normally didn't give two cents what anyone else thought, or for that matter, what they did, unless it affected her. But for some reason, she thought that behind Vera's façade of big smiles, big bosoms, and flashy clothes, she was deeply unhappy, and that worried Eunice. She recognized that caring about Vera was unusual for her, but she didn't spend any time trying to understand it. She just let it be what it was and enjoyed both women's company when they came to the store. Other than that, she never saw them. That was a choice she made for reputation and business; it wasn't because she objected personally to what they did for a living. Truth be told, she sometimes wondered what it would be like to be them, Grover being such a wimp, and men all the time fawning over them like no one other than Grover had ever done to her.

For Wilbur Moss, the rapid influx meant more hauling contracts, and for Henry it meant not having to learn to drive a four-up team of eight mules, never mind a ten-up or fourteen-up. There were plenty of hauling jobs for two-ups, a relief to Moss, Calvin, and Henry, all. Henry admired the skill of the men, mostly black, who drove the ten-ups and fourteen-ups, but he was glad he didn't have to learn to do it. Teams that large took four skinners each, with three men spaced out astride certain mules from the lead animal on back to guide different sections of the team in unison as they performed the ballet required to make sweeping turns around curves and corners. Because those teams pulled enormous steam boilers and other huge loads, they bogged down more often and covered less ground than smaller teams. Working with one of them would have slowed Henry's search for Ed Tuttle and limited his options once he sighted the man.

Things picked up in different ways for others in the community. With no jail to hold offenders, Constable Burns didn't bother much about fistfights and public drunkenness, or even about where those with booze got hold of it, Prohibition notwithstanding. He was mildly concerned about reports of hijackings occurring with increasing frequency when oil-field workers, mule skinners, or others got caught traveling alone at night in the boonies, but seeing as how his jurisdiction didn't extend very far out of town and he tired easily from his excessive weight, he tended mostly to put those out of mind.

Burns also didn't worry himself about increasing prostitution and gambling connected to barrelhouses, or about new ways Big Sally and her colleagues came up with to advertise their services to newcomers. A good number of the women lived in rented rooms in houses along Broadway north of the railroad tracks and took to lounging on porches and hailing men passing by at all hours of the day and night. Others began renting saddle horses and riding out to work camps to offer their services on site. Still others partnered with professional gamblers and bootleggers who built barrelhouses near the larger camps. The most notorious such establishments were several miles northeast, in a settlement that came to be known as "Blackjack Hill," and not due to the card games. Also, every so often, weather and road conditions permitting, Sally and some of her associates put on the most alluring attire they dared wear in public and paraded up and down Broadway twirling parasols and calling out greetings to everyone in sight, men and women alike.

Some in Berrytown found the women's public strutting amusing. Others did not. Despite its small size when the boom started, Berrytown had two white peoples' churches, one Methodist and one Baptist. Their ministers now preached harder than they ever had about adultery, fornication, gambling, booze, and sin in general. The church women prayed and gossiped about all of those. A handful of men talked about the need to "get rid of bad elements," but so far, none had the will or means to do anything about their concerns.

Henry observed this rapid change from walking into town every evening and standing in line to buy a hot meal, and from his perch atop his two-up wagon, sometimes sitting on the spring seat and sometimes sitting on the loads themselves. After more than two weeks of driving, he hadn't come across any sign of Ed Tuttle, nor even found an opportunity to talk discreetly to anyone who might have seen him. He was, however, noticing a lot of new mule skinners and teams that were not part of Wilbur Moss's operation. When Henry mentioned this to Calvin Birdsong in passing one morning before they left the yard, Calvin told him he had heard that two men from Kansas City had set up a new hauling operation out southwest of town somewhere and were bringing in hundreds of mules from Missouri. With good animals selling for up to three hundred dollars each, this was a huge investment, and Henry wondered out loud if Moss might be concerned about the competition.

Calvin grinned and said, "Mr. Moss? Nah, he's got too good a thing going to worry about no bunch of Missouri mules. They ain't gon' bother him a lick."

Before Henry could ask why, another driver, new to the yard, interrupted with a hitching question, and Calvin walked away with him, leaving Henry puzzling over his meaning.

~

Mules being intensely loyal, Moss allowed his drivers to use the same animals every day if feasible. He believed they worked better that way. Soon, Henry and his team—Jake, Ben, Lon, and Sam—formed a bond that surprised even Moss. Skinners wiped their animals down and fed them each evening and curried and brushed them again each morning before harnessing them, and even when he came off a long day tired, dirty, and hungry, Henry enjoyed making his team comfortable.

Moss also insisted that all barn and corral areas be kept as mudhole free and dry as circumstances would allow. Mules already spent way too much time wading and standing in water and oil-field mud and slime. If allowed to accumulate on their lower legs, it would eat away the skin and leave them crippled. So, Henry also spent time, along with others at the yard, draining and filling holes and spreading sand when they could get it.

Despite such care, Jake and Sam each developed a painful thrush infection in one of their frogs, the fleshy area at the back of the hoof that cushions weight and aids blood flow. Because Moss had run out of iodine and copper sulfate, either of which would cure them, and because all his other animals and drivers were out on runs, he sent Henry to Hornbeck's Drugstore for a new supply. Until Jake and

Sam healed, Moss said Henry could drive another team whenever possible, and otherwise there were countless other chores he could help with. Henry didn't like losing even one day that he could be looking for Tuttle, but having grown more curious about Moss's operation, he welcomed the chance to look further around the yard, this time with more wary eyes.

CHAPTER 15

"Momma, Momma," Jimmy Dutton said, yanking on Mary's sleeve.

"Shh, not now, Jimmy," Mary whispered. "I'll talk to you later."

She hated putting Jimmy off, but she had just sold a package of plain Crescent City Powders to one of Sally Boudreau's friends and was heading up front to help other customers. Even after several weeks with no Treasury agents coming around, handling the stuff still made her jumpy, and the last thing she wanted right now was hearing Eunice fuss about Jimmy being underfoot when there were customers in the store.

Jimmy shifted the stack of *Arkansas Gazette* papers he was cradling under one arm and tugged on her sleeve again. "But Momma," he whispered, "that's him. That's the man that stopped the hanging." He pointed toward two men standing in front of the patent medicine counter. Both were wearing dirty khaki pants, denim work shirts, and felt hats. "He's the one with his hat pulled down," Jimmy said. "I saw him outside before he came in."

Mary glanced toward the men, then mouthed, "Okay," to Jimmy and gave him a back-handed wave out of the store. He started to speak to the man on this way out but thought better of it and left quietly and unnoticed.

Since the incident that stormy day behind Mac's Autos, Mary had thought several times about the stranger who faced down a bunch of shotgun-toting white men hot to hang a black man. She had heard about lynchings over the years, but never about anyone stepping in to stop one. She didn't know many "colored people," as she called them, but she deplored the way most whites treated them and the racial violence that had erupted in so many places across the country in recent years. Headlines about it in the newspapers on the drugstore's magazine rack had haunted her dreams for weeks after each incident.

Beyond that, though, having lost her father to a snapped chain in someone else's sawmill and her husband in a truck crash during a military campaign in a remote wilderness hundreds of miles from Arkansas, she hated violence of any kind—even when she had to knee Grover Hornbeck to keep him off her.

Andy Dutton had enlisted in the National Guard for some romantic notion he had about serving the greater good, and as his wife, she had supported his decision. However, that only made losing him hurt worse. Later, although she believed she understood why America entered World War I, she grieved for soldiers who died in it, for those that returned from it with missing limbs and shell shock, and for families who surrendered loved ones to it.

She liked that the man up front stopped the hanging that day in Berrytown, and based on things she had heard, she guessed he couldn't have done it any other way. Still, his method bothered her, especially now that he was standing a few feet away and she could see the gun he was carrying. Despite all that, for reasons unclear to her, she was intrigued by him, and had been from that day in the thunderstorm, even though she hadn't seen him clearly then. She disliked the feeling.

With Grover at the soda fountain and Eunice helping two women with cosmetics, Mary walked behind the patent medicine counter and asked, "Who's next, please?"

Neither man spoke until Henry looked at the other fellow, who shrugged his shoulders and said, "I guess I am."

Mary glanced at Henry to confirm, then froze as his eyes widened and he stared at her so intensely that she found it difficult to look away. His mouth opened and closed as if he wanted to say something then thought better of it. Color drained from his face, and they stood in awkward silence until, after a long moment, he muttered, "Yes, he is," and turned away.

Puzzled and a little frightened, Mary found what the other man wanted then carried it to the rear, wrapped it, and took his money. After closing the register, she stared at Henry's profile before returning to the patent medicine counter. He had his back to it now, and as she watched, he removed his hat, swiped at his forehead with a bandanna, and replaced the hat in a swift and practiced move that allowed her only a quick glimpse underneath it. This was enough, though, for her to see the jagged scar just beneath his hairline, and she wondered how he had gotten it. It could have been in an oil-field accident somewhere, she supposed. But given how he stopped the lynching, and that he was going about armed, she doubted that was the case.

When Mary took her original place behind the counter, Henry swung toward her but kept his gaze below her eyes. He rested his fingers on the edge of the glass top, and said,

"I'm sorry if I startled you. I didn't mean to. It's just that for a second there, I mistook you for someone else."

"Sure, okay," Mary said, her head tilted, trying to see under the brim of his hat. She had noticed earlier that his eyes were blue, like hers for the most part, and in the split second he had his hat off, she saw that his hair was a deep honey color, also like hers.

"What can I get for you?" she asked, then added, "My name's Mary Dutton, by the way."

"Henry Smith," he said, giving his alias without looking up or offering his hand. "I need two of the biggest bottles of iodine you have and three bottles of copper sulfate." Then sensing her curiosity about the order, he added, "It's for mules. I work for Wilbur Moss."

"All right," Mary said. She pulled the items from the glass-doored cabinet behind her and took them to the cash register table. Henry followed her back and watched her wrap his purchases, but never looked up at her face. When she finished, he paid her, took the package, mumbled, "Thank you," and walked out of the store. Mary's eyes followed him through the front door and lingered on him when he stopped on the wooden walkway. As she watched him squeeze his temples with his free hand, she wondered why in the world she had told him her name, and chided herself for doing so.

When Henry returned to the mule yard, he doctored Jake and Sam, put the extra bottles in a medicine box in one of the storerooms, and threw himself into the rest of his chores. At one point Moss said something about how furiously Henry was shoveling manure, and he said he was trying to work soreness out of his shoulder. Moss's only response was to grunt and spit.

When quitting time came and Henry was certain everyone had left the yard, he went to the small corner recess he had carved out in the hayloft of the back barn, using a few odd boards from a pile behind it. Seated on a pallet he had made of straw and empty feed sacks, he opened his rucksack of meager belongings. From it, he took a double-cell lantern he had bought at one of the general stores and a string-tied package of crackers and cheese he had purchased two days ago to carry with him on long hauls. After only a couple of bites, he set the package aside and rubbed his temples with the heels of his hands, trying again to stop the pounding that had been with him all day. Failing, he reached for the rucksack again and took out a photograph wrapped in oilcloth.

His hands shook as he peeled off the waterproof cover and looked at the four faces peering back at him—a man, a woman, a boy, and a girl, all smiling and full of life when the picture was taken a dozen years ago. His father, his mother, himself, and his twin sister Helen, before he left them and went off to Wabash College. Before he brought Ed Tuttle home for Christmas and introduced him to Helen. When all four of them, instead of only one, was alive. Henry brushed his fingers over the picture, as if in doing so he could somehow feel their faces, or they could sense his touch and know how much he loved them still.

Looking at them and remembering good times always brought a measure of relief from the heartbreak he carried with him every day, but it also always intensified his loathing for Ed Tuttle. Henry had never really liked Tuttle when they were football teammates, but he hadn't particularly disliked him either. That Christmas, when Tuttle was going to be alone for the holidays and Henry felt badly about it, he never imagined that Helen would fall for the guy. Although her doing so was unexpected, it didn't seem especially troubling at the time. Then, in the spring, Tuttle abruptly dropped out of college and went to work as a gofer in the southeastern Indiana oil and gas fields. He kept popping up to Terre Haute to see Helen at normal school, though, and in time they married and settled in Marion, where Helen found a teaching position she loved. Tuttle worked at a series of dead-end jobs before catching on at the Ball jar factory in nearby Muncie. He lived alone there until Helen finished out the school year, quit her job, and joined him.

They were still in Muncie when Henry entered the army and shipped out to France. He didn't know if he would live to return, but he certainly didn't expect that if he did, everyone else in the photograph would be dead or nearly so.

Not long after Henry arrived in Europe, his father died of a heart attack, and Helen and Tuttle moved onto the family farm to take care of it and Henry's mother. Tuttle had neither the ability nor the stomach for the hard work required to keep the place going, however. He let it run down while squandering their little income on booze and gambling, instead of paying down the mortgage that Henry's and Helen's father had taken out to pay for college. When Helen refused to sleep with Tuttle any longer, he raped her repeatedly. And when she became pregnant and pleaded with Tuttle once again to tend to his responsibilities, he flew into a rage and beat her to death with a fireplace poker while her mother, lying ill in an adjoining room, listened helplessly to her screams. By the time a neighboring farmer happened by hours later, Tuttle had fled. Law enforcement authorities never caught up with him.

Henry was on a troop ship crossing the Atlantic when the murder occurred. Following his discharge at Fort Dix in New Jersey, he returned home not only to find his beloved twin and her unborn baby dead, but his mother in failing health from lingering effects of the Spanish flu and the trauma of hearing Helen beg for her life. For the next two years, while plagued with nightmares of men and animals screaming in pain amid ear-shattering explosions, Henry divided his time between caring for his mother, trying to save the farm, and waiting for the authorities to apprehend Tuttle. When his mother died in the fall of 1921 and the bank foreclosed on the mortgage a month later, the last of everything Henry had once held dear was gone. The life he had known before the war was completely shattered, and he blamed it all on Tuttle. From that point forward, Henry lived for one thing only. Find Ed Tuttle and kill him.

After a few days of flailing about early on in Berrytown, Henry now had a plan and a regular means of searching the area without arousing suspicion. He also still had the story of the sawmill foreman, who had run across someone fitting Tuttle's description in Big Sally's Place. Having become comfortable in the role of mule skinner, Henry intended soon to start frequenting barrelhouses and chancing to catch Tuttle in one of them.

And then today happened. For a moment when he glimpsed Mary Dutton's eyes at the drugstore and saw how her dark sandy hair framed them, it was almost like seeing Helen standing there. Mary was even the same height as Helen. In all the hours and minutes since seeing Mary, Henry hadn't been able to stop thinking about his sister and wondering about the woman who resembled her.

CHAPTER 16

It was bad enough, Eunice thought, that someone else had the gall to build a second drugstore in Berrytown, but it was nothing short of criminal that they had to go and build it in spitting distance of Hornbeck's. At least, she reasoned, it didn't enjoy the lucrative sideline that she and Grover had going. Roper had assured them they would remain Berrytown's sole source, and by now, any concern Eunice had initially about getting caught had given way to excitement about being daring and about her and Grover having more money in their pockets. Selling Crescent City Powders had become as routine as selling ice cream, Moon Pies, and St. Joseph Aspirin.

Still, any sale that Compton's Drugs and Notions made was one that Hornbeck's didn't. And who knew what different products they might bring in? Under the guise of welcoming the owners to town, Eunice had walked over to see their furnishings and shelf stock on the first day they opened their doors to customers. She didn't want to go again, however, for fear of looking afraid of competition. So, every now and then, she had Mary go there to buy something Hornbeck's didn't carry—a particular magazine, a distinctive brand of thread for her occasional seamstress work, a new corn plaster, or some little thing Compton's advertised in the *Berrytown Journal*.

During one of Mary's forced shopping excursions, Eunice, unable to hold off any longer, took a chance on getting a quick look at Mary's quilt and the paper she had been so engrossed in the day Roper delivered the first batch of Cresent City Powders. After giving Grover a made-up excuse about checking on inventory in the back room, Eunice hurried to the doorway connecting it to the shed. She was pretty sure that Jimmy wasn't around anywhere, but she cracked the door a tad to check before entering.

Once inside Mary's and Jimmy's living quarters, Eunice went directly to the trunk. The first thing she saw when she opened it was the Luther Pike handbill. She gave it a quick once over and was surprised she hadn't seen one floating around town somewhere. She was also surprised that Mary, who had no money, had any interest in it. Thinking that maybe Mary had somehow managed to put away a little nest egg somewhere, Eunice made a mental note to come back and poke around some more another time. Now, though, she hurriedly removed the remaining contents above the trunk's false bottom, lifted it, and took out the quilt.

Having never sewn anything, Eunice knew nothing about quilts, other than that her mother, Alma Leatherwood, had made several. Eunice had slept under them during winters before leaving the family farm. The few quilts she and Grover owned had been passed down from his mother, and Eunice rarely put them out, preferring store-bought blankets instead. She didn't care for the mishmash of material and colors in Mary's quilt, but she liked the checkerboard pattern of squares with nine little squares inside some of them. She guessed that if she had time to spread it out and step back from it, the thing would do well enough to use in a pinch if a body had little else to keep warm with.

Having satisfied her curiosity, Eunice returned the quilt to the bottom of the trunk and put everything else back the way she found it, as best she could recall. Then she slipped back into the workroom thinking about Luther Pike.

~

For several days after going to Hornbeck's, Henry thought of little else except his dead sister and getting another look at the woman in the drugstore. He was so distracted that when he returned his rig to the mule yard in the evenings and wiped down and fed his team, he could scarcely remember where he had gone during the day. He simply followed orders and directions from Moss and took little note of his surroundings. Often, he didn't even watch for Tuttle.

Then one dawn when Henry was harnessing his team, Jake accidentally stepped on Henry's foot. Henry pushed Jake off his dented boot then hopped around on one leg cussing. The big brown mule lowered his head and tilted his ears back. Having grown up around draft animals, Henry knew that, unlike with horses, this was a mule's way of showing affection. It also seemed as if Jake were apologizing, and this stilled Henry where he stood. Here was a mule responding in the moment to Henry, while Henry had been plodding aimlessly from one sunrise to the next doing nothing but dithering around about Tuttle and Mary Dutton. He was wasting time.

The next morning, Henry cornered Moss and said he had strained his back while taking part of his load of derrick timbers off his wagon, hauling the rest across a muddy creek where the bridge was out, then unloading those and coming back for the rest, hauling them over, and reloading the first batch. He had done no such thing, but he knew Moss would believe him because, according to Calvin, most drivers had to do it occasionally to avoid getting helplessly stuck.

"Hurts like the devil," Henry said. "I need to get some Mentholatum Ointment before I head out again." Moss, who was preoccupied at the time with a man trying to sell him an unwanted team of oxen that was blocking access to the Camden road, waved Henry away with a gesture he took to mean, "Okay, go ahead."

As Henry walked along Broadway toward Hornbeck's, his heart raced and stomach bile rose to his throat. He began to question what he was doing, and why. Maybe he had only imagined that Mary Dutton looked like Helen. But if she did, what then? Would seeing her again lessen the agony of having lost a part of himself he missed every day? And what if it only worsened his pain?

He knew he had behaved oddly when he saw Mary before, possibly even startled her, and he didn't want to do that again. Perhaps he could get a good enough look at her today by keeping to the sidewalk and peering through one of the store windows unnoticed. That way, whether she looked like Helen or not, he could walk away without disturbing her.

If she did look like Helen, seeing her would be like glimpsing his sister one last time. Painful or not, it would give him a measure of the closure he missed when she was laid to rest while he was returning home from Europe. He might even feel, if only for a moment, some degree of the almost unfathomable bond that only twins share. If nothing else, amid the heartbreak of being unable to see, touch, or talk with his sister, maybe he could find a measure of solace in knowing that someone in her likeness was still walking the face of the earth. He could hold that image, as well as memories of Helen, in his mind and his heart and never lay eyes on Mary Dutton again. In the future, when he needed anything from a drugstore, he would go to the new one he had heard about.

Also, no matter how Mary appeared to him this second time, after seeing her, he would redouble his efforts to find Tuttle. Henry wanted now more than ever to stand over his dying body, watch his life ebb away, and have the satisfaction of knowing his worthless soul was descending into Hell.

Despite all the ruminating, rationalizing, thinking, and rethinking, when Henry reached the front door of Hornbeck's, he couldn't resist going inside. His curiosity propelled him so forcefully that he never even glanced through the windows. Crossing the threshold, he told himself he wouldn't stammer and look away this time. But he wouldn't linger either. He would greet Mary politely and avoid staring but take enough time to see her clearly. Then he would buy the ointment like he told Moss he was going to, and leave, never to return.

Once inside, Henry saw that Mary and another woman, older and stouter, whom he remembered from his first time in the store, and a man, whom he took to be the pharmacist, were busy attending to the needs of more than a dozen housewives, laborers, and men whose rumpled suits exposed them as lease hounds and lawyers. Mary was behind the notions counter on the right. Henry edged over to the magazine rack nearby, picked up a copy of the *Saturday Evening Post*, and pretended to scan its pages while glancing up as often as he dared without drawing attention.

Mary gave no sign of noticing him as she and the other woman moved about helping customers. The pharmacist remained busy behind the rear counter. At first, watching Mary was so much like watching his sister that Henry almost forgot to breathe. As he had seen before, Mary was about the same height as Helen and had similar hair and dimples. But Helen had been lean and athletic, and Mary was not. Henry and Helen had been so inseparable growing up that she tried almost every sport and stunt he did and walked with what he teasingly called a "tomboy gait." Mary moved more gracefully. Purposeful yet fluid and smooth. Henry liked it. He also liked the way she tilted her head as she listened to customers tell what they wanted to buy. And he liked her voice, soft and lilting. Lower pitched than Helen's.

Henry stopped leafing through the magazine and stood staring. The longer he watched, the more differences he saw. When Mary demonstrated a spring-loaded measuring tape, she couldn't extend her left arm all the way. He wondered if she had broken her elbow sometime, and how. He saw, too, that although she had blue eyes like Helen, one was partly hazel, the lower half greenish brown with a splash of yellow. He liked how this made her look mysterious, even mischievous.

Something new began pulling at him now, a kind of longing he had not experienced since before the war. His gaze wandered to Mary's breasts, full under her loosely cut dress. He thought her lovely and alluring. Before he lifted his eyes, she turned toward him, as if sensing his stare. Embarrassed that she saw him looking, he jerked his head back to his magazine, his face growing warm. When he looked up again seconds later, she had turned back to her customer.

Unprepared for what he had seen and felt, he put the magazine down, walked to the front door, pushed it open, and headed down the street toward Compton's. He didn't see Mary come to the front of the store, step outside, and watch him walk away.

CHAPTER 17

Each morning for weeks Otis Leatherwood had been climbing off the cot in his makeshift room behind the kitchen madder than one of his setting hens after he chased her off her nest to get her eggs. He couldn't find peace anywhere anymore.

Before oil fever turned everything around him upside down, he had loved rising by sunup, listening to birds sing, seeing sunlight glisten on dew-laden grass, smelling his barnyard and animals, and feeling his boots land on well-trodden farm paths or sink into newly turned soil.

Those pleasures were now mostly things of the past, ruined by the breeze-driven stink of raw petroleum flowing into earthen holding pits near and far, and by unwanted gas burning atop vent pipes because the oil men didn't know what else to do with it. Ruined by the black, sticky droplets that fell on everything like rain every time a gusher came in and the wind blew in his direction. Ruined by the mushrooming number of people crowding into his world and all the noise, accoutrements, and human failings they brought with them. Ruined by worry that his neighbor and long-time friend Isaiah Watson was on the verge of succumbing to the same temptation of potential riches as every other landowner who now had one or more noisy derricks or worthless dry holes where once stood cotton, corn, and orchards, or timber that was home to deer, squirrels, racoons, and other of the Good Lord's critters. Ruined by the black-green film that now floated, sometimes several inches thick, on streams from which he and others once pulled bream, perch, and catfish for food and sport. Ruined by sensing that all he had worked for his entire life was doomed and he would never get it back, just as he could never get back his beloved Alma.

For a long time after Alma passed, Otis's grief had run so deep that he ignored the small daily pleasures that until recently he had begun to enjoy again, just as for years he had ignored his and Alma's only child Eunice to the point of driving her away with indifference. He had never much missed Eunice, though, what with all the high-minded ways she had taken on even before she met up with her shifty husband and his inherited money, so he had never tried to patch things up. Otis knew he had wronged her, and he wasn't proud of it, but he believed she had wronged him in much the same way as he grew old alone. Thus, he had been content to consider the score settled with no need to write any more pages in their book of life.

At some point—he didn't know quite when—Otis had finally managed to dig far enough out of his grief to resurrect and savor his memories of Alma and the things they had once done together. Her photograph, taken of the two of them not long after they wed, was the first thing he saw every morning and the last thing he saw every night. When his chores permitted, he spent a little time every day sipping morning coffee or late-night moonshine while sitting in a rocker on his front porch and talking out loud to Alma as if she were there in the flesh instead of only in his mind.

For the past several weeks, however, he had been so irritated by all the hullabaloo around him that he couldn't clear his head enough to enjoy such moments. But today, perhaps because he knew he was reaching his tolerable limit of frustration and misery, he had willed himself up even earlier than usual, brewed a pot of coffee, taken a cup onto the porch, and watched the sun come up, its rays managing to light Berrytown's eastern sky in changing shades of pink, red, yellow, and orange even through the oil-laden haze. "Ain't it beautiful?" he observed to Alma.

Then he heard it. A screeching, ear-piercing wail, like a wounded goose or stuck pig. Only it wasn't coming from an animal. It was coming from the same yellow ragtop Packard that the pipeline fellow with the fancy knee-length, lace-up boots had been driving the day he showed up out of the blue spouting some nonsense about building a pipeline across Otis's land, and whom Otis had run off with the threat of buckshot. The blamed fool was barreling up Otis's access road so fast Otis feared he would crash into the house.

Instead of waiting to find out, Otis hustled inside for his over-under .12-gauge shotgun, determined to make good on his threat. By the time he returned, the Packard had skidded to a stop, and not one, but two men were getting out. One was the pipeline guy. The other was Constable Amos Burns, who rocked the Packard side to side as he lowered his considerable mass off the running board.

Otis ignored the constable and shouted to the fellow with the fancy boots, "I told you if you come 'round here again, I was gon' shoot your sorry ass, and now I aim to do it!" He shifted his feet on the weathered porch, raised the gun from waist level, and set the stock against his shoulder.

"Hold it, Otis!" Constable Burns yelled, puffing toward the front steps.

"What the Sam Hill are you doing here, Amos?" Otis yelled back.

"Put that gun down, you damn fool," Burns shouted, "before you hurt somebody!" He lumbered to a stop at the bottom of the steps, shoved his hat back, and wiped his forehead with the back of his hand.

"You didn't say what you're doing here with that son-of-a-bitch," Otis said. He kept the gun pointed toward the pipeline fellow.

"For one thing, I'm here to keep you from shooting him."

"That ain't something you can do, Amos, and if y'all don't get the hell off my property, I'm liable to shoot both of you. Now, git! I mean what I say!"

"You ain't gon' shoot nobody," Burns said. "You know dang well if you do, some judge will fry your butt quicker than spit."

Otis shifted his weapon left and fired the top barrel. Glass hadn't stopped falling out of the Packard windshield before the pipeline fellow was back behind the steering wheel trying to restart the engine.

Burns took a step back. "Goddamn it, Otis!" he said.

"I got another barrel, Amos, and you've got about half a second to finish telling me what you're doing here."

"I brung you a court paper," Burns said, reaching into the front of his overalls.

"If it's got anything to do with that jackass, I ain't interested in it."

Burns started to speak again, but Otis beat him to it. "You got any idea what that thieving bastard's up to? He wants to put one of them pipelines across my farm."

"I know," Burns said. "That's what this paper's about. It says he has the right. It's the law. Them idiots up there in the legislature have done give the pipelines eminent domain. Means they can put them lines anywhere they want to."

Otis fired again. His second shot whizzed by Burns's left hand and took out the right front headlight of the Packard. Before the stunned constable could say anything else, Otis popped out the two empty shells and shoved in two more. Having flooded the big Packard's twin-six engine in his haste to get away, the pipeline fellow sat jerking the steering wheel and grinding away on the starter, succeeding only in running down the battery.

"All right, Otis," Burns said, moving forward again and putting one foot on the bottom step. "That's enough. I know you ain't gon' shoot me, so I'm coming up there. You ain't got no choice but to take this paper. County sheriff down at El Dorado asked me to bring it to you."

Otis fired two more shots. The first took out the other Packard headlight and the second shattered a portion of the bottom porch step. "Okay," he said, loading up again, "if you ain't done shit yourself, come on up here, but tell that fellow he better stay right where he is."

"I think he knows that already," Burns said, and struggled on up the steps onto the porch.

Otis lowered his gun. "Damnit, Amos," he said, assuming a friendlier tone with the man he'd known for years. "This ain't right, and you know it. These goddamned leeches don't care about nothing but that slime they're bringing up and the almighty dollar. They're ruining the land..."

"You don't have to tell me, Otis," Burns interrupted. "I got eyes. And I'm sorry as I can be about this here paper, but I ain't got no say in it, and you don't neither."

"Well, I sure as hell ain't gon' take it lying down. You're right, I ain't gon' shoot nobody, but I'm gon' fight it somehow.

Somebody's got to stand up to these blockheads. Might as well be me. Maybe I'll get me a lawyer if there's one ain't already bought off." He leaned the shotgun against the wall, walked over to the side end of the porch, and stared off into the distance.

"That's part of the problem," Burns said, joining him. "All the lawyers is chin-deep in this crap. The politicians up at Little Rock too. Look, the pipeline company has to pay you for however much land they take. It ain't gon' amount to much, and it sure as hell ain't gon' pay for all the noise and disruption, but you can use it to pay for what you did to that automobile. You do that, and I'll see they don't press no charges against you. That's the best I can do for you."

"Yeah, I know ain't none of this your fault, Amos, and I appreciate about the car, but you and him better figure out some way to get that thing off my land right now. I kinda liked beating up on it, and I got a whole other pocketful of shells."

"I don't know nothing about operating one of them things," Burns said, "but that fellow's already got a wagonload of surveying stuff headed out here. Maybe the mule skinner can hook his team to the car somehow and pull it back out to the public road at least."

"He's got what coming?"

"Surveying stuff is all I know. Yeager there, that's his name, Milo Yeager, told me most landowners south of you have been following the law and cooperating with him, and his people have already figured out the route pretty much right up to your property line. They were scared to get any closer, though, without them papers. You shook him up pretty good last time he was out here."

"Yeah, well, maybe I ain't done with him yet."

CHAPTER 18

Never in his life had Henry been as befuddled as on the morning he walked out of Hornbeck's Drugstore without saying a word to Mary Dutton. A few things had flummoxed him momentarily on the gridiron, and many more on the battlefield. But in those situations, Henry had been forced to make quick decisions and move forward. After turning tail when Mary caught him staring at her, he had not only been surprised and confused, but also embarrassed and afraid, and all those emotions had stuck with him. What must she have thought about his staring at her? And about his abrupt departure? And why did he care? He had done what he'd set out to do, which was find out whether Mary resembled Helen.

But while Mary favored Helen, she differed from her so much that when Henry looked back on that morning, he found himself thinking more about Mary than about Helen. He hadn't anticipated this, and he wasn't sure what, if anything, he wanted to do about it. The longer he ruminated about it, however, the more he wanted to see her again, but now, unlike before, not because she reminded him of his sister. He found himself thinking more about the simple pleasures of a woman's company than he had at any time before the war. There had been little opportunity for it in France, and none when he returned home after the fighting only to find everyone and everything he held dear either dead or ruined, or near it. As soon as he learned what Ed Tuttle had done to Helen, he had vowed right then to make him pay, and from the moment the bank took away the farm, getting that revenge had been the only thing that mattered to him. He still wanted it, but it was no longer the primary thing spinning around in his head as he drove his mule team during the day or lay in his barn loft corner at night.

A few days after the drugstore debacle, Henry was visioning Mary while hauling a load of surveying and camping equipment west out of Berrytown. The honey color of her hair, the allure of her eyes, the way her dimples deepened and framed her mouth when she smiled. He was seeing all of these in his mind when he failed to spot the righthand turnoff that Moss said led to the Otis Leatherwood farm. Being good and faithful mules, Jake, Ben, Lon, and Sam plodded straight ahead when there was no "Gee" or tug on the reins to tell them to turn. A little later, Henry, confused now about where he was, but gambling that he had made the first turn and knowing that soon after it he had to bear left, called out, "Haw." And the mules headed left down yet another wrong road, going even farther away from the Leatherwood place.

Henry didn't know he was lost until farmland gave way to forest, and by that time he didn't see any place to turn around, even though this road, like the main one he had been on, showed signs of heavy traffic despite there being none now. With no other choice, he kept going. Shortly, he came to a clearing at the edge of a creek and saw he wasn't the only one with a roadway predicament. A near-truck-sized, oblong iron boiler, so heavy it must have required at least a fourteen-up team to move it, lay belly-up off to the side. Henry figured it had been left there some time ago when whoever was hauling it couldn't get it across the creek. What those haulers or someone else had managed to do, though, was cave in a portion of the log-and-board bridge, which seemed a likely reason why Henry hadn't seen anyone else in a while.

Downstream of the bridge a few yards, a Model T Ford carrying a woman and two young children, who were all but hidden among luggage and household goods piled in the back and tied onto the running boards and fenders, was stuck up to its axles in the middle of the creek. The woman was behind the steering wheel revving the engine, and a man in oil-field garb was standing with his back to the rear of the vehicle, leaning against it and trying to push it forward but succeeding only in getting himself covered in mud. When he saw Henry and his team approaching, he gave up his shoving, took off his hat, and waved like a halleluiah preacher greeting a bunch of sinners rushing forward to answer his call. The woman, unaware that the man had stopped pushing, kept her hand on the throttle, and mud and water continued spewing all over the man.

"Turn it off, Sarah, turn it off!" the fellow yelled as he sloshed toward the near shore. "Boy, am I glad to see you," he called to Henry, while running his hand through thick white hair streaked with mud. "Name's Pete Taylor. Folks call me 'Cotton.' You think you could give us a hand here? We sho' do need it. I figured 'cause the water's not that deep, we could just drive around the bridge, but as you can see, we didn't get far."

"Yeah, sure. Be glad to help," Henry said, remaining on the wagon. "I've already messed up my run. Took a wrong turn back there somewhere. Where're you folks headed?"

"Over southwest of someplace called Louann. A buddy wrote me about it. Said they're opening up some new tracts 'round there. I'm a roughneck, and we just come up from Texas."

"Yeah," Henry said. "They're pushing a new pipeline out that way. Going all the way to Stephens, way I hear it. If that don't work out for you, there's plenty of drilling over east of Berrytown too. We've got to get you out of that water first, though."

"I ain't got no chains," Cotton said, "but I've got rope."

"We'll take the chains off my load," Henry said, climbing down.

Over the next half hour, Henry and Cotton managed to jerry-rig a hitch to the front axle of the Ford, and Jake, Ben, Lon, and Sam pulled it into the road on the other side of the creek without the need to remove any Taylors or Taylor possessions. After waiting long enough for Cotton to help his wife and daughters Ruth and Nell out of the car and introduce them, Henry said quick hellos and hurried back across the creek to retie his load and hitch the mules back to the wagon. Before Sarah stepped back into the Model T, she called, "Come out and see us sometime. We're gon' have a tent house, and I'm a good cook. I'll make you a pie."

It was late afternoon before Henry found his way to the Leatherwood farm after stopping twice on the main road to ask directions. Once there, he was soon sorry he hadn't just headed back into town and told Moss he had gotten so thoroughly lost he had never been able to find the place. Uncertain where to leave his cargo because his only instructions were "somewhere between the road and the house," Henry stopped his team short of the big, yellow touring car sitting in the yard with both doors open. Two men dressed in overalls sat in rocking chairs on the front porch holding Ball jars half full of clear liquid Henry doubted was water. One, a gray-haired older man that Henry assumed was Otis Leatherwood, cradled a shotgun across his lap. The other, a younger man whose bulk spilled out between the seat and arms of his chair, had a pistol resting on one knee. Henry recognized him as Constable Amos Burns. He also recognized signs that both men had probably already emptied at least one other Ball jar. He got down off the wagon, walked toward them, saw the mess someone had made of the Packard, and stopped.

"'Bout damned time you showed up," Otis said. "It's near 'bout dark."

"Yes, sir, I'm sorry about that," Henry said. "Where should I unload this stuff?"

"You ain't gon' unload it," Otis said, getting up and grabbing a porch post to steady himself as his shotgun fell to the floor. "You're gon' unhitch that team and pull that big yellow pile of crap out to the road and leave it sitting there. Then you're gon' hitch back up and haul whatever it is you've got on that wagon back to wherever it was you got it. Ain't nobody gon' put no pipeline across my land. I don't care what the law says.

"You're gon' take this big turkey stinking up my porch back to where he came from too. And another thing: If you happen to see the idiot that was driving that pile of junk wandering 'round out there somewhere, don't pick him up. His name is "Dagger" or "Bagger," or something like that, but you'll recognize him 'cause he's wearing a pair of prissy boots laced clear up to his pecker."

Henry didn't want to go back without leaving his load, but neither did he see any potential benefit from arguing with a half-drunk old man who had a shotgun and may have already gotten the town constable on his side by out-drinking him. So, Henry said, "Yes, sir," and began walking away. When he got even with the Packard, he turned back toward the old man. "You do this?" Henry asked.

"You damn right, I did," Otis said. "You want to make something of it?"

"No, sir," Henry said, grinning and heading for his team. "Just thought I'd ask."

"Wait a minute, boy. Don't I know you?"

Henry paused and looked back at the old man again. "No, sir, I don't think so. I'm new around here."

"Yeah, I do." Otis said. "You're the fellow that saved that colored boy from getting hung down there behind Mac's Autos that day. Damned good thing you done."

"Yes, sir. I was just glad the constable there showed up when he did. If you want me to take him back to town, you best do something to sober him up while I take care of the car."

"Yeah, reckon I better," Otis said, and almost tripped over his shotgun as he moved toward his plastered drinking partner. After catching himself on another porch post, he punched Burns on the shoulder, and shouted, "Wake up, you old turd! Help's here."

Henry unhitched his mules from the wagon and hooked them up to an automobile for the second time that day. After prying a board off one of the crates he was hauling and jamming it between spokes of the Packard's steering wheel and down to the floorboard, he managed to drag the wounded vehicle in a straight enough line to get it within a few feet of the public road. Once he hitched the team back to the wagon, he and Otis hefted a mumbling Amos Burns headfirst into the foot well in front of the seat.

As the mules got underway with Henry's feet planted on the constable's backside, Otis called out, "What's your name, boy?"

"Henry, sir. It's Henry Smith."

"Smith, huh? Well, Henry whoever you are, don't bring that crap out here again. I won't be so hospitable next time."

Henry waved without looking back. He knew Moss would be furious with him, but he didn't believe the little man's anger would last long, and he couldn't help chuckling about Mr. Leatherwood. The old man had spunk. Well before Henry got back to town, though, his thoughts returned to what got him lost in the morning.

CHAPTER 19

"Well, how about that?" Eunice Hornbeck said, coming around the cosmetics counter to embrace Vera Hudson as Sally Boudreau looked on with a noticeable lack of enthusiasm. "When's the big day?"

As usual, even on a weekday afternoon, Vera and Sally were decked out in colorful, low-cut dresses of sheer crêpe-Georgette to show off their wares. In addition to being fond of both women and always enjoying chatting with them, not to mention selling them and their lady-of-the-evening friends Crescent City Powders along with cosmetics and toiletries, Eunice, in her fashionable ankle-length skirts, pleated blouses, and occasional sleeveless jackets sometimes envied them for their carefree style and the way men looked at them. She, of course, would never dress like them. It would be bad for business. Every woman in Berrytown not working in a barrelhouse would take their trade to Compton's, and she didn't want to lose even a penny's worth. Nothing moved Eunice like money. Ever since she found Luther Pike's handbill in Mary's trunk and looked him up, she had been sure she would soon have lots more of it, but she still loved selling merchandise.

"It's way too soon, if you ask me," Sally said. "She ain't known the fellow but a couple of weeks. Anyway, we're gon' miss her. She's about the most popular girl I have. Every man that comes in asks for her first."

"Me and Roy—that's his name, Roy Long—ain't set no wedding date," Vera said. "We've got a going-away date, though." She smiled and shrugged her shoulders just so. "He said there ain't no use getting in a hurry. He's a driller, a real good one he says, so I'm lucky. We're leaving Sunday. Gon' get us a tent house up at that new field close to Stephens and get married after he's brought in some wells up there. That's when everybody's gon' want to hire him, and he'll have lots of money."

Sally rolled her eyes and shook her head. "I told her the only thing that man wants is somebody to hide his sausage for free till he decides to move on somewhere, but she's bound and determined. So, I reckon we're gon' have to give her a sendoff Saturday night. You're welcome to join us if you can get away from Grover for a while. I know he won't come."

"He won't let me come either," Eunice said, using her husband as an excuse to keep from taking a chance on being seen in a barrelhouse, even though the idea of one excited her. "But I'm gon' send over a little something for the tent house." She didn't have to think twice about what that would be.

Jimmy turned over and hid his face in the thin, lumpy pillow on his cot. He had grown accustomed to the constant rat-a-tat sounds that the needle of his mother's Singer made as she cranked it with one hand while guiding whatever she was sewing with the other. But hard as he tried, he couldn't block out the light from the single, naked bulb hanging over the center of the room.

Lately, Mary had kept it on well into the early morning hours while working on a growing pile of sewing she was taking in from women coming to the back door of the shed at night after supper, sometimes more than twice a week. When Jimmy had asked her how they knew to do that, she said, "Women share things with each other, but don't you be mentioning nothing about it to Cousin Eunice. She wouldn't like it." Jimmy said he thought Cousin Eunice already knew about the sewing. Mary said she did, but not how much there was of it the past few weeks. Which was why Mary had agreed to make Ozella Gordon, the Methodist preacher's wife, and her eleven-year-old daughter Elizabeth two additional skirts in exchange for an old trunk Mrs. Gordon had sitting on her back porch one Sunday when Mary went over after church to take measurements. Jimmy asked why, if women talked among themselves about his mother's sewing, they didn't talk to Cousin Eunice about it. Mary said they all knew if they did, Eunice would fuss and carry on and try to talk them out of coming. When the boy asked why Eunice would do that, Mary said it was because her late nights were likely driving up Eunice's electric bill. She didn't want to tell him it was because Eunice was jealous that Otis seemed to care more about his niece than about his daughter. That wasn't something to share with a twelve-year-old, especially one already worried whether his selling newspapers on street corners and running errands for tips were helping out enough.

"Darn that man, anyway," Mary said under her breath, then hoped Jimmy hadn't heard. She had let a fold at the bottom of Mrs. Gordon's skirt slide while thinking about Henry Smith then sewed half the hem the wrong length instead of paying attention to what she was doing. There was something about him that kept gnawing at her. Something about the way he had looked at her—once like he knew her and later like he hadn't seen her at all that first time. And both times, he had almost literally run away from her. Why was that? And what was the story behind the scar he seemed to be hiding on his forehead? Was he trying to keep someone from recognizing him, or did he think it distracted from his appearance? Didn't he know he was handsome despite it? And why was she even thinking about how he looked and if he would come around again? She had enough on her mind already, what with worrying about getting caught selling marijuana and Crescent City Powders, getting this extra sewing done so she would have enough money to invest with Luther Pike, and trying to keep Grover's hands off her. He had cornered her again this morning and grabbed her bottom.

After waiting two days for the right opportunity, Eunice decided to take a chance while a crowd occupied Mary at the soda fountain and a line of customers awaited Grover's attention at the prescription counter. There were other customers in the store, and she might miss a sale or two and maybe even get yelled at by Grover, but she couldn't delay any longer. While helping a man looking for an alternative to Durham cigarette papers, she told him she thought they had some Prince Albert papers in the back, and if he wished, she would go look. When the man said he did, she walked calmly to the rear of the store, went into the storeroom, closed that door, then rushed to the doorway into the shed.

Without even cracking the shed door first to make sure Jimmy was not inside—she had seen him going off somewhere with another boy a little earlier—Eunice threw it open, hurried to the trunk at the foot of Mary's cot, and raised the lid. Working as quickly as possible, she removed the tray, fished her hands down the sides to the false bottom, and lifted it and set it aside, leaving the items that were resting on it mostly undisturbed. Relieved to see Mary's quilt still there, she pulled it out, tossed it toward the door, and replaced all the other contents of the trunk.

After she closed the lid, she grabbed up the quilt in both arms, ran for the door, and only then noticed that now there was a second trunk, this one at the foot of Jimmy's cot. She knew she would lay awake all night wondering what was in it, but there was no time to check it now. Back inside the storeroom, she put the quilt in an empty box that had once held soda fountain supplies, gambling that neither Mary nor Grover would discover it there until she could take it home that evening wrapped in fabric she had bought down the street a few days before and also hidden in the storeroom.

If Grover asked what was in the package, she would tell him it was material for new curtains she planned to get someone other than Mary to make for her sometime soon, and he would likely never ask her about it again. She wasn't worried about Mary missing the quilt and questioning her about it. Mary would be afraid to do that, but if she did, feigned offense and firm denial would probably end the conversation.

When Eunice returned to the front, Mary and Grover were still busy at the soda fountain and the prescription counter, respectively. Neither seemed to have noticed her absence.

"I'm sorry, sir," she said to the man she had been waiting on, "we are out of Prince Albert papers at the moment. Do you want some of the Durham brand?"

CHAPTER 20

On the evening that Henry returned to the mule yard well after dark with his wagon still loaded and told about the dust-up at Otis Leatherwood's place, Moss hadn't seemed angry or surprised. He said he had known Otis for years and knew he wouldn't like seeing pipeline stuff appear on his doorstep and would likely kick up a fuss. When Henry asked why Moss hadn't warned him, he said he knew Milo Yeager and Amos Burns were going out there first, so he figured they would have the old man settled down by the time Henry got there. Besides, Moss said, he had been busy with other things that morning. He said he reckoned Yeager would let him know when he wanted to try making the delivery again and maybe he would have Calvin take it. Said Calvin knew the old man too.

Henry and Moss had talked behind the barn closest to the road, the one in which Moss had an office of sorts. Henry had glimpsed Moss through the center aisle while pulling into the yard, stopped the team, and hustled to the rear to tell what happened. Now, looking back on the brief conversation before going to sleep the next night, Henry wondered, as he had at the time, why the failed delivery hadn't bothered Moss more. Sure, the load would get out there sooner or later and Moss would collect a freighting charge on it, but that would be at the cost of some other job that had to be postponed or given up altogether. Plus, Yeager might bellyache about it around town, which could cost Moss other jobs. It seemed to Henry almost like Moss had been in a hurry to get rid of him, as if he didn't want him in that part of the yard. Henry had never been back there before, not even when he first came to work for Moss, or when Jake and Sam had thrush and he had done chores around the barns for a couple of days. As near as Henry could recall, the area behind that barn looked the same as the one behind the barn where he now lay on his sleeping pallet.

Ever since Calvin had told him Moss wasn't worried about competing with the big outfit bringing in Missouri mules because he had "too good a thing going," Henry had wondered if Calvin meant something more than hauling freight. Henry had never found a good time to ask Calvin more about it, however, without putting him on the spot or raising suspicions that might end up costing Henry his job if Calvin mentioned it to Moss.

As a result, Henry had been intending to poke around the yard more closely when it seemed safe. Having now learned the usual pattern of comings and goings, he decided that this was as good a time as any. He didn't know how many mule skinners worked for Moss, but from what he saw when most everyone was harnessing and hitching up every morning, he guessed there were forty or more. Other than Calvin, he had avoided getting acquainted with any of them. Evenings, they returned from their freighting runs at different times, then did their brushing, feeding, and such as quickly as possible and scattered. Aside from one recent hire, Henry was almost always the only person in the yard after supper time.

The exception stemmed from Moss's mistaken idea of security. As more and more people poured into Berrytown, crime was keeping pace, and then some. Aside from prostitution and moonshining, which until recently upstanding citizens had been mostly ignoring for lack of concern and any real means to deal with them, hijacking topped the list of felonies. Men on back streets and country roads on payday or leaving barrelhouses during early morning hours any day, especially across the county line in Blackjack Hill, made easy targets. But there was plenty of property theft too.

Having taken note, Moss had hired H.W. Epperson—a skinny, often out-of-work second cousin on his mother's side—as nightwatchman. Once H.W. saw that Moss never checked on him, he was usually asleep with a Ball jar before the cicadas and tree frogs even hit full stride. Coming back evenings from supper in one or another of Berrytown's cafés, Henry had seen H.W. often enough to know he favored the tool shed near the mule yard entrance. Presumably, he thought any potential thieves would have to pass right by him and be easy to catch. Never mind that unless they came early, he probably wouldn't see or hear them.

To avoid any chance of someone seeing a strange light, Henry left his battery-powered lantern behind when he climbed out of his loft. Before heading to the other barn, he looked in on H.W. After finding the would-be nightwatchman sleeping peacefully, Henry crossed the yard, and moved quietly along the side of the front barn, being careful not to alarm the saddle horses inside. He wasn't concerned about mules. All were in the corrals on the far side of the yard, and mules didn't spook easily anyway.

The moon provided enough light to see that the only thing different back of this barn was a fence gate large enough for a wagon to pass through. Tracks showed it had been used but not as often as the gate out front. For what, though? Henry had never seen a wagon back here, but he hadn't been looking for one either.

The double back doors of the barn were standing open for air circulation like those on the front, and on both ends of the barn where Henry slept. When he went through them, he discovered something else he had not seen before. The two barns pretty much mirrored each other, but the storage room at the rear of this barn had a padlock on it. The only other locked room Henry had seen on the place was Moss's office up front. Clearly there was something here that Moss didn't want seen or messed with. Henry squinted through moon-lit cracks in the wall and wooden door. Straw was strewn about the floor and several beat-up wooden crates about two-feet square were stacked in one corner.

Little concerned now about H.W. waking up and roaming about, Henry looked around some more before walking back to the other barn and returning to his loft. As he thought about what he had seen, about what Moss said regarding Calvin's knowing Otis Leatherwood, about the amount of moonshine that Otis and Constable Burns appeared to have consumed after Otis shot up the Packard, and about H.W.'s nightly habit, it wasn't hard to imagine what Wilbur Moss's "too good a thing" was. In addition to his regular business, the feisty little mule handler was almost certainly hauling liquid freight. Or, at least, having Calvin do it for him.

Henry wondered if any other of Moss's mule skinners were also transporting it, and where Moss was getting it. Was he making it himself somewhere? That didn't seem likely unless he was going off during the day sometime. He was always around mornings and evenings, and it would be impossible to make the stuff on Sundays alone.

It was an interesting puzzle, but Henry didn't care whether Moss was only hauling, or both making and hauling. He had seen enough to know that plenty of other folks around the oil fields were also trying to fill the stimulant void created by Prohibition; he just didn't want to get caught up in it. He knew from what Al Jenkins had said that first night back at the peckerwood sawmill and from reading newspapers left lying around in cafés that federal agents, though spread thin, were trying to crack down on both the moonshiners making the stuff and the bootleggers transporting it. In most places, county sheriffs were working at it too. Like Jenkins, Henry hadn't seen much evidence of their success around Berrytown, but that didn't mean they weren't looking.

The more he pondered all this, the more he wondered if maybe Ed Tuttle had gotten involved at some level somewhere. Maybe, Henry thought, he should take a risk and talk with Calvin. See if he knew anything potentially helpful he was willing to share.

There was one more thing too. Barrelhouses. Henry had only looked in a couple so far. He guessed he should check out some more, even though he had about decided that the chances of catching Tuttle in one of those were somewhere between slim and none, and certainly not as good as the possibility of discovering where the man was working. Wherever that was, he had to be there six days a week every week. Going to a barrelhouse was an arbitrary, sometime thing based on a whim.

That is, unless Tuttle had a favorite hangout he returned to again and again. That thought alone made it impossible to consider giving up completely on barrelhouses. Back that first night in town, Jenkins had said something about seeing a big man that talked kind of like Henry at Big Sally's Place and that he and the fellows he was with had made a special trip from El Dorado to see her. Having seen Sally himself soon after getting off the train from Indiana, Henry could easily imagine Tuttle doing that. So, he decided to spend a few evenings there and see if Tuttle turned up.

CHAPTER 21

Eunice and Grover almost never shared a noon meal anymore, except on Sundays, when the drugstore was closed. They had so much business now that one of them always stayed in the store while the other went to a café or, usually, home for a sandwich or leftovers from the night before. This way they didn't have to worry about leaving Mary to deal with Crescent City Powders customers alone. She handled them well enough, but knowing that selling illegal drugs made her skittish, they didn't trust her to be there by herself. Especially if Floyd Roper showed up to check on them or freshen their inventory, or worse, in the unlikely event that one or more federal agents came snooping around.

All night and the next morning after stealing Mary's quilt and sneaking it home wrapped in fabric with plans to tell Grover, should he ask, that she was having new curtains made, Eunice patted herself on the back for thinking of a way to hurt Mary without her finding out about it for a likely long while and then not knowing who to blame for it. Maybe she would blame Jimmy. That would be amusing to see. Eunice also congratulated herself for thinking of a way to get the quilt out of Berrytown so there was no chance Mary could ever get it back. There was one thing Eunice had not resolved, however, and by around ten o'clock she was worrying about it so much that she was making mistakes around the store—dropping things, not wrapping purchases properly, and giving incorrect change.

Shortly before noon, Grover, concerned not about Eunice but about the effect this untidiness was having on his nerves and might have on business, suggested that she go home to eat and stay there long enough to pull herself together. He didn't ask what was causing this behavior because he didn't really care so long as she took care of it. Probably some kind of female thing he guessed.

When Eunice smiled and said, "Honey, I could just kiss you," he was so stunned, he nearly dropped the large-size bottle of Mrs. Winslow's Soothing Syrup he was wrapping for an anxious mother with two small children in tow. He didn't know he had just solved Eunice's problem.

Moments later, while she was in the back room getting her purse, she cut a long piece of string and tore off a long sheet of wrapping paper from one of the spare rolls there. She folded the string and paper together and stuffed them into her handbag. She would have plenty of time to get home, wrap the quilt like it was a package from the store, and walk it to Big Sally's Place. She didn't like the idea of going there, but she would go to the back door, where there was the least chance of anyone seeing her, and if anyone asked, she would say she was delivering a special order of ladies' products. That would shut up whoever dared to inquire. The icing on the cake was not having to explain to Grover why she was gone longer than usual.

~

Sally Boudreau was heading through the kitchen for a backyard smoke when one of her black cleaning women handed her an envelope with her name printed on it and a large package wrapped in brown paper tied with double string around all four sides. "Who brought this?" she asked the cleaning woman, who was already dipping her mop back into a bucket of soapy water.

"That lady from the drugstore 'round the corner," the woman said. "One's married to the man over there."

"Did she say anything? Ask you to tell me anything?"

"No, ma'am. She was in a right smart hurry."

"All right, thank you," Sally said.

She tore open the envelope and read the note inside: "I can't make the celebration for Vera, but I would like her to have this for her trousseau. Ask her not to say who gave it to her, however. Someone we both know would not approve. I know she will understand. Your friend and Vera's, E."

Curious, Sally took the package upstairs to her quarters and opened it. "Good Heavens!" she said out loud. "That woman ain't got no taste at all." Chuckling, she wrapped the quilt back, thinking all the while that Vera would never use it.

Henry walked into Big Sally's Place a little before nine o'clock. It was Saturday night, and the barrelhouse was packed. Sally and all the other barrelhouse operators, those in town as well as those near the big work camps, laid out their welcome mats every night. But Saturday was special. It was payday. Roustabouts, roughnecks, drillers, loggers, mule skinners, pipeline workers, and more—men who had no family ties and men who had them but ignored them—washed off as much oil-field crud as time and circumstances allowed and set out to put their long work weeks out of mind, if only for a little while.

A cloud of cigar and cigarette smoke floated near the pressed tin ceiling. Along one side, men lined a bar made of flooring planks. Some sat on stools that had seen better days in other joints in other boomtowns long played out. Other men stood between them, some facing the bar and calling loudly for more drinks, and some facing the room, ogling and grabbing at Sally's girls. Other men sat at tables scattered around the other sides of the room, some drinking, talking, and playing cards and some so full of hooch they didn't know where they were, or care.

In one corner, a man on a low platform banged away at an upright piano, laboring along with a guitar player and a fiddler to churn out the latest Charleston and Foxtrot tunes. Having the right instruments and hitting the right notes didn't matter as much as being loud and keeping up a rhythm.

Four bits got a fellow a six-ounce glass of moonshine. Two bits bought a two-minute tussle with one of the barrelhouse girls on the dancefloor in the middle of the room. Both prices were higher than in some speakeasies in big cities, but here money flowed with the oil.

Some things for sale in Big Sally's Place had no posted price. The cost to take one of the women up the stairs in the back was negotiable depending on what the customer wanted, how badly he wanted it, and how much time it involved.

Once inside, Henry's ongoing concern that Tuttle might spot him first somewhere and flee southern Arkansas ratchetted up. That could well happen with a crowd like the one tonight. Henry knew there was at least one back door, and there might be others. There was a better than even chance, however, that Henry, as the hunter, would see his prey first.

Henry stood for a few moments just inside the door scanning the room, then stepped to the left, placed one foot against the wall, leaned back, and slipped his right hand into his pants pocket to his .45. Just another oil-field hand arrived too late to find a table or a place at the bar. From here he could see anyone entering or leaving by the main entrance, and possibly also by the one rear door he knew about. All along, he had cared more about killing Tuttle than about getting away with it, but he had always figured he would get the man alone somehow, do what he needed to do, then slip away. That might not be possible inside Big Sally's, but if Tuttle was here and Henry saw him first, Henry could step outside, wait for him, and follow him to someplace suitable for a confrontation or blind assault. On the other hand, if Tuttle saw him first and tried to run, Henry would have to chase after him to avoid shooting someone else and to give himself a chance to escape after doing Tuttle in.

As Henry looked slowly from one face to another around the room, the possibility of finally having a chance to shoot the man seemed more real than ever before. More, even, than when Henry had thought Tuttle might be with the pipeline crew down near El Dorado and had watched for him there among men struggling in swampy waters full of cypress knees and water moccasins. Henry had killed in battle, and although he had later regretted it, he had considered it his duty then and afterward. But he had never known any of those men.

This was going to be different, and as he thought about it, with the long-awaited opportunity maybe only minutes away, new images arose alongside those of his father, mother, and sister—especially Helen—that he had been turning over and over in his mind for months as he plotted revenge. Now, crowding in alongside them, as if in a dream, here was Levi Birdsong, standing in the back of a truck, a rope around his neck, with angry men ready to take his life for an imagined offense based on the color of his skin. And here was Mary Dutton, who reminded him so much of Helen, yet was different in ways that aroused emotions he didn't know he had. What would have happened to Levi if Henry had found and killed Tuttle before that day behind Mac's Autos? Would those men have gone ahead with the lynching? And what about Mary? If Henry killed Tuttle now and couldn't get away with it, he would never see her again. Was he prepared to live with that? Or what if he killed Tuttle and did get away with it but Mary found out about it later somehow, what then?

"Hey, fellow, you okay?" Sally asked, shaking Henry's shoulder, and startling him.

"Huh?"

"Are you all right? We don't mind drunks in here. In fact, we encourage it. But folks ain't used to having somebody stand in the door, get in their faces when they come in, and be muttering about machine guns, snakes, and ropes."

"Was I talking out loud?" Henry asked. He was sweating and had moved away from the wall and back into the doorway. "I guess I must've just got caught up thinking about something. I'm not drunk."

"I reckon you sure did," Sally said, looking at him more closely now. "I ain't seen you in here before, but I know you from someplace. Where was that?"

"I don't believe you do, ma'am," Henry said, thinking now to pull his hat down and lower his head.

"Well, hon, maybe not. I don't recall that scar you're trying to hide, but I don't usually forget a handsome face when I see one. And you're one good-looking man, scar or no scar. You want to come upstairs with me, I'll do you for free."

"Maybe some other time," Henry said, trying to back out the door.

"That's it," Sally said. "You told me that once before. You was walking up the street one day when I was out back with Vera smoking."

"Yes, ma'am, if you say so," Henry replied. And he was gone.

CHAPTER 22

For many in Berrytown, Sunday morning was different from other mornings. It was a day free from work except for chores at home. Most people who had lived in Berrytown before the boom went to church—whites to the Baptist or the Methodist church in town and blacks to Rev. Isaiah Watson's Mt. Tabor New Hope Baptist Church out in the country, or the church that Rev. Charles Richardson had pastored over in Ouachita County before oil was discovered on his land. After church, most of those folks spent time with family members. Some visited around in the community. And sometimes, a few—the braver ones and the more curious—took the opportunity to drive about and view the changes to their town, grown now to several thousand inhabitants and more than three times as many buildings as before the first well blew in. Some of the newcomers spent their Sundays in much the same way as the long-time residents. Some only rested up for the coming week. And some nursed the effects of their Saturday night exertions or found ways to repeat them.

For still others in Berrytown, Sunday morning was like every other. Drillers and others operating rigs with wells nearing completion had to keep the drill bits turning to bring the wells in safely. Men responsible for the gas flares burning off unwanted gas and for guarding the massive oil pits against acts of vandalism or carelessness with cigarettes and matches had to stay alert. At least some mule skinners had to tend stock in mule yards. And some men, alone or with families in tow—men like Cotton Taylor, whom Henry had pulled out of a creek and who was now settled with Sarah and their children out near Louann—used the time to relocate to different jobs or search for better places to live.

Vera Hudson and her intended, Roy Long, had planned to be among those on the move Sunday morning after her last night at Big Sally's Place. But they didn't start for their new tent house in Stephens until midafternoon. In the several weeks since Sally opened her doors, the seductive smile, blond curls, and curves that Vera liked to show off in sheer flapper dresses, and which had drawn Roy's attention, had also drawn a lot of regulars to her upstairs bed. A good number of them were in Big Sally's Place the night Henry went there, after word spread that Vera was leaving. And they all wanted to give her a personal sendoff, alone. Not wanting to disappoint, she accommodated one after another until Sally called a halt at three a.m., offered free drinks on the house, and lifted a toast to the happy couple. Only, Roy, a lanky Texan not given to idle conversation, didn't hear it. Nor was he happy. He had sat drinking alone in a corner and watching a steady flow of Vera's guests up and down the stairs, until he passed out.

Unable to shake him awake, Sally finally tossed a pitcher of water on him around two p.m. Sunday afternoon. Roy sat up, looked about to get his bearings, let loose a few cuss words, then staggered to his feet and went sullen. Sally told him Vera was almost finished packing and they needed to go so she,

Sally, could get things squared away for the night crowd. Like all the other barrelhouses, she kept her place open seven days a week. She said she had a new girl coming in to take Vera's place and needed Vera's room. She handed Roy a glass of hooch, and he gulped it down and headed upstairs. Without a word to Vera, he grabbed her carpetbag and the old, rawhide-covered Sears travel trunk Sally had given her, pushed past her into the hallway, and stomped down the stairs with his bride-to-be trailing after him.

Vera gave Sally a quick hug and followed her betrothed out the back door and waited beside the fancy Chevrolet V-8 touring car he had borrowed in Stephens, after promising to pay double for repairs if he damaged the vehicle in any way. The car was four years old but still a beauty and not anything any friend of Roy's would have been driving had the fellow not won it in a poker game with a liquored-up lease hound. Roy tossed the carpetbag and the trunk onto the rear seat, climbed in, started the engine, and waited for Vera to join him. She stared at him for a moment, then opened the passenger side door, got in, and slammed it extra hard. Roy glared back at her and roared out of the lot as fast as he could gear up the powerful Chevy engine.

As they bounced over rough dirt roads toward Louann and the turn off to Stephens, neither spoke until Vera, peeved and bored, leaned back in her seat and planted her new black patent leather shoes against the dashboard, her spikey heels resting on the polished mahogany.

"Get your goddamned feet down, woman, before you scratch the wood!" Roy shouted. When Vera ignored him, Roy reached over and smashed his arm downward across her knees, which resulted in precisely what he feared. Her shoes left ugly scratches across the gleaming panel as her feet slid to the floor. "Goddamned your whoring soul!" Roy yelled. "Now, look what you did!"

"You ain't got no call to talk to me like that," Vera said. "What I do ain't never bothered you before."

"You ain't never tried to screw the whole damn town right in my face before neither."

"I told you yesterday was my last day, didn't I? You should've stayed away from Big Sally's till this morning."

Roy hit the steering wheel with his fist, then stared straight ahead for a while. Vera kept her feet on the floor and her mouth shut. Then, without warning, Roy veered off the road, skidded to a stop, exited the driver's seat, and climbed into the back. Fearing the worst, Vera ducked her head and leaned into the passenger side trying to open her door.

"Goddamn it!" Roy yelled. He grabbed her carpetbag with one hand and her trunk with the other and tossed them as far from the car as he could sling them. The carpetbag sailed into a copse of trees, and the trunk hit a wheel rut and bounced into a blackberry thicket.

"What the hell are you doing?" Vera yelled. "Them's my clothes and presents! That pretty quilt Eunice Hornbeck gave me is in that trunk!"

Roy climbed out of the rear, got back under the steering wheel, and headed for Louann and beyond.

With Vera yelling, "Go back and get my stuff!" until she was hoarse, Roy kept driving. In a bit, he said, without taking his eyes off the road, "When I get you to Stephens, I'm gon' burn them things you're wearing, I'm gon' get you some new clothes, I'm gon' remind you what a real man is, and I don't ever want to hear nothing else about no Berrytown, no Big

Sally, and no Elouise Cornsack or whatever the hell her name is. You mention one of them just once, and I'll beat your ass till it ain't no good for sitting, screwing, or anything else."

Isaiah Watson rapped a second time on Otis Leatherwood's porch steps. Ordinarily, no black man would dare approach a white man's front door. He would go to the back in keeping with custom. But between Otis and Isaiah, some things were different.

"Mr. Otis, you in there?" Isaiah called, the use of "mister" not being one of the traditions put aside. He had on his black preaching suit, and his son Robert stood at his side.

Presently, Otis opened his screen door and stepped out onto the porch. One strap of his overalls was unhooked, and he had several newspapers under one arm. "Afternoon, Isaiah," he said. "Is anything wrong? I thought y'all was always in church all day on Sunday." He laid the papers on his rocking chair.

"We are, but Robert figured Jimmy was out here with you. Said he saw him walking down the road and kept begging me to let him come over. Seeing as how school's 'bout to start up and all, and they won't be seeing each other much for a spell, I said we'd come find out, and if you didn't mind, he could play for a little while."

"Yeah, sure. Jimmy's out in the barn doing something or other. Robert, you can just go on back there and find him. He'll be glad to see you."

Robert looked up at his father, got a nod of approval, and dashed around the corner of the house. Isaiah shouted a reminder, likely unheard, to come home for church before the sun got down to fist-high over the west pasture. Otis said not to worry, he would see to it.

"Catching up on your reading, are you, Mr. Otis?" Isaiah asked, gesturing toward the newspapers.

"Something like that, I guess. I been saving them, and I was just going back over some stuff about where all the drilling's been done and the leases been sold. You and me are near 'bout surrounded if you add up what's already done to what seems likely. But I guess you know that. Reckon I told you before."

"Yes, sir, I know it."

"You ain't already sold out, have you?"

"No, sir. Me and Luella's still talking and praying on it." Not wanting to get into another conversation on the pros and cons of leasing their land, Isaiah changed the subject. "You ain't shot no more Packards, have you? I declare, when I come running over here that afternoon to see what all the fuss was, I expected just about anything but that. Luella near 'bout died laughing when I told her 'bout it."

"Yeah, well," Otis said, "that fool Yeager's lucky I didn't shoot him. Why don't you come on up here and sit a spell?"

"Thank you just the same," Isaiah said, relieved to have a graceful way to leave. "I got to get on back and see to my reverend duties."

~

"Hey, Jimmy, where are you?" Robert asked, standing in the open door of the dimly lit barn and trying to see through all the dust swirling in the sunlight coming in over his shoulder.

"I'm in here," Jimmy answered, stepping down from a floored storage room into the center aisle of dirt turned to powder by countless animal hooves. His hair, shirt, and overalls were covered with the stuff. "Come help me."

Robert hurried through the door. "Help you do what?"

"I'm looking for buckets that Uncle Gramps won't miss. I'm gon' make me and Momma some money. You could make some too. Come on." Jimmy stepped back into the storage room and Robert followed.

"How you gon' do that?" Robert asked.

"I'm gon' fill up them buckets with oil," Jimmy said, pointing to three rusty milk buckets sitting beside the door, "and I'm gon' sell it."

Robert picked up one of the buckets, turned it over, looked at the bottom, and put it back. "Where you 'gon get oil?" he asked.

"I'm gon' get it off Owl Creek over yonder," Jimmy said. "Some days there's two or three inches of oil floating on top of the water, and I'm gon' skim it off with that thing I made over there and sell it to this man I heard talking to another fellow 'bout it in town. He comes by one of my newspaper corners all the time."

Jimmy picked up his homemade tool and handed it to Robert. "See here? You can make you one. It's just a lard bucket lid nailed to an old hoe handle I found. You drag it along the top of the creek, and when you pull it out, the water runs out through them holes I punched, and the oil sticks to the lid. Then you tap the lid against a bucket and the oil slides off into it. That's all there is to it. I bet we can get a nickel, or maybe even a dime, a bucket for it."

"How're we gon' get the oil to the man's that's gon' buy it?" Robert asked.

"I ain't figured that out yet, but I bet if he knows we have it, he'll come get it. I heard him say that over near Standard Umpsted there's six or eight inches of oil floating on creeks and folks are stringing wire across them and tying boards to the wire, catching oil by the barrelful, and selling it to refineries. I don't know how to do that yet, but I'm figuring on learning that too. Only, we can't let Uncle Gramps know 'cause he don't like nothing that's got anything to do with oil. If he finds out, he'll have a fit."

"You mean he'll tan your hide, don't you?" Robert said.

"Or worse. Look, why don't you see if you can find some buckets at your house, make you a skimmer, and let's meet Wednesday afternoon over there where we fished last summer."

"Okay. I guess I can do that."

"Shake on it?" Jimmy asked, sticking out a dirty mitt.

"Shake on it," Robert said, taking his friend's hand.

CHAPTER 23

If he hadn't been distracted by knowing his route would take him by Hornbeck's Drugstore, Henry might have been laughing when he pulled away from the Missouri Pacific depot on Monday morning and headed south on Broadway. Mac Furston, chunky owner of Mac's Autos, had come walking into Moss's mule yard a little after sunrise, face flushed, puffing hard from exertion and humiliation. The teasing he was about to get would last for weeks. He had several crates of parts coming in from the regional Ford distributor in St. Louis, and both of his Model T delivery trucks had broken down. One needed a new carburetor, the other a new radiator, and Mac had neither. Meanwhile, half a dozen customer vehicles awaited a variety of other items that Mac had ordered earlier and which had come in on the train, and he had no way to get the shipment to his shop.

Moss enjoyed Mac's predicament and discomfort. "Yes, sir," he said, after regaining his composure from nearly choking on his snuff from laughing so hard, "what you need is some good mules. They don't take no tires, no gas, or no spark plugs."

By chance, Henry was at that moment passing the two men with his harnessed team, taking them to a waiting wagon.

"Hey, Henry," Moss called. "Before you go to that sawmill job, help ole Mac here. "Them mechanical horses of his are off their feed today."

~

Henry had spent all day Sunday and much of the night thinking about his visit to Big Sally's Place and replaying all the things that had run through his mind that night. Now he was about to drive his team past Hornbeck's, within a few feet of where Mary probably was standing. His pulse quickened and a shudder slid down his back. Without really thinking it through, he pulled his team over to the right side of the street, leaped down, and tied the lead rein to a hitching post. That wouldn't stop Jake, Ben, Lon, and Sam if something spooked them, but Henry knew that was unlikely. He ducked around and through cars, trucks, and other teams heading up and down the street, eager to apologize to Mary Dutton for acting so strange the last time he saw her and running out of the store the way he did.

With no firm idea of what he would say once he got across the street, he opened the door, stepped inside, and saw her wiping the mirror behind the ice cream fountain. She was wearing a low-waisted blue-and-white polka-dot dress that he knew matched the blue in her eyes. Glimpsing movement through the mirror, she looked up, saw him, and smiled. That did nothing to settle his nerves, but it drew him across the room, nevertheless.

Without noticing whether anyone else was in the store, he removed his hat and said, "Good morning, Mary, I was passing by, and I wanted to stop in and apologize to you for my behavior the last time I was here."

"Oh," she said, turning around and looking by reflex at his scar, and then into his eyes, "what was it that you did?"

Henry shifted his hat from one hand to the other. "You don't know?" he asked.

"No, I don't think so," she said, her smile spreading to her eyes. "Why don't you tell me." She put down the cleaning rag and rested her hands on the front counter, one on top of the other.

"I was staring at you, and when you caught me at it, I just up and left."

"So, that's why you ran out," she said. "I thought maybe you didn't like what you were seeing."

Henry wondered if he had heard right. "What?" he stammered.

"I thought maybe you saw something you didn't like."

"Oh, I liked it all right," Henry said, thinking now that maybe he hadn't offended her after all. Maybe she liked his looking at her. He was trying to think what to say next, when he felt, more than heard, someone walking up behind him.

"Hey there, handsome," Sally Boudreau said, as Henry looked up at her in the mirror. "I saw you over here with this pretty lady, and I thought, 'He must've got tired of talking to hisself.'" Sally turned to Mary, whose smile faded to a look of puzzlement. "He put on quite a show in my place Saturday night, standing in my door mumbling about machine guns, dead mules, ropes, and all sorts of stuff. Scaring people."

Henry stood speechless. He wished he hadn't come into the store. He figured Mary Dutton would now take him for some kind of inarticulate degenerate and never speak to him again.

Pleased at rattling Henry and, she hoped, mortifying Mary, whom she knew Eunice didn't like, Sally patted Henry's shoulder and walked away saying, "Come back and see me again some time. I've got some new girls coming in." At the door, she paused, looked toward the back of the store, and waved goodbye to Eunice, who had heard the entire exchange.

Henry turned back to Mary, read questions in her eyes, and said, "I'm sorry. I know how that sounded, but that's not me. It's really not."

Mary started to say something, but before she got a word out, Henry lowered his head, put his hat back on, stepped back, and raised his hands, palms out. "Look, I really am sorry. I better go." He glanced at her once more, saw her put her hands together over her mouth, and left the store chagrined a third time.

~

When Henry pulled into the yard at the end of the day, Moss was waiting for him and flagged him down in front of his barn office. Henry rolled to a stop thinking about what he knew was locked up way in back.

"Milo Yeager's ready for us to haul pipeline stuff out to Otis Leatherwood's place again," Moss said. "There's two wagonloads this time. I'm sending you and Calvin out there together."

"Is Yeager going out first to make sure that old man's changed his mind, and he's not gon' be shooting at anybody this time?" Henry asked.

"Yes and no," Moss said. "Yeager's going, and he's gon' have the county sheriff and a couple of deputies with him. I don't imagine Otis has got religion about the pipeline, but he ain't gon' want to go to jail either. If you and Calvin leave from Yeager's warehouse about noon, that ought to give Sheriff Lindsay time to talk sense into Otis before y'all get there."

"I hope so," Henry said, lifting his reins again, "I kinda like the old bird. Wouldn't want to see him get hurt or locked up."

Things didn't start as Milo Yeager planned on Tuesday. With his big yellow Packard still missing both headlights—he was furious that the replacements he ordered were apparently stuck on a rail siding somewhere—he had set out with the sheriff and three deputies in plenty of time to get out to the Leatherwood farm well before the wagons. What Yeager failed to plan for, however, was a flat tire. Despite his little army of law officers, he didn't relish confronting Otis Leatherwood again and got so lost in his thoughts that he didn't pay attention to the road. About half a mile from the Leatherwood farm, he ran over an oil well drill bit that had fallen off a truck or wagon earlier, and it shredded the front right tire of the Packard.

The touring car had a twin V-6 engine, a nickel-plated radiator shell, and leather upholstery, but what it didn't have was a spare tire mounted on a rim. Changing the flat required getting the damaged tire off the rim, sealing the holes in the inner tube with glue and patches, putting the patched tube inside the spare, getting the spare onto the front rim, and airing it up with a hand pump. Yeager had no idea how to do any of that. All three deputies were sure they did, but that only complicated matters, as each had a different idea of how to begin. Only when Sheriff Herbert Lindsay, a burly fellow with a natural scowl, stopped their arguing did they succeed. It was then that they discovered that the right rear tire had also been punctured and was also flat. The tire itself wasn't badly damaged, but they had no more inner tube patches. The five of them—Lindsay and the deputies carrying rifles and Yeager plodding along behind—were on foot when Henry and Calvin caught up with them.

Neither Henry nor Calvin was happy to see them, and neither was comfortable as they drove their teams up Otis's access road with armed men sitting on their wagons and another possibly awaiting them. Henry was worried the old man would get himself shot. As feared, when Otis came into view, he was standing at the top of his front steps, shotgun in hand, aiming right at the wagons. He had spotted the broken-down Packard while inspecting a side field and had plenty of time to get to the house and get prepared.

"Hey, Sheriff," Otis said calmly when the wagons came to a stop, "I see that bastard brought in the big dogs this time."

"Mr. Leatherwood," Sheriff Lindsay said, "I've got some papers here."

"I know about your damned papers. And you know what you can do with them."

"We don't want no trouble," the sheriff said, "but if you give us any, we're gon' have to take you into custody." He and the deputies remained where they were on the wagons, but all four had their rifles trained on Otis. Henry and Calvin sat watching, hoping there wouldn't be any shooting. They and their mules would be in the line of fire.

"Well," Otis said, lowering his weapon. "I ain't aiming to go to no jail. You got the upper hand right now, but I ain't gon' have no goddamned pipeline on my land either. If I can't stop it one way, I'll stop it another one."

CHAPTER 24

Even without Otis Leatherwood holding up Milo Yeager's surveying plans for a few days, the new pipeline inching toward Louann and Stephens lagged far behind need. As in other fields around Berrytown, oil was spewing out of the ground faster than rail cars and existing pipelines could transport it to refineries. Several storage tanks had been built and others were under construction, but earthen pits remained the quickest solution to capturing the new crude. Producers ordered up more dirt men from Texas and more fresnos from the J. D. Adams and Company factory in Indianapolis. With all the rail freight coming into South Arkansas, delays and mistakes remained commonplace, and the fresnos ticketed for Louann stayed on the Missouri Pacific rail car carrying them until the train pulling it stopped in Berrytown. Wilbur Moss, constantly on the hunt for new business, was at the depot Tuesday afternoon when the fresnos were unloaded and the flummoxed stationmaster couldn't find any space on the next two trains going back the other way.

"I'm sending you fellows out together again tomorrow," Moss told Henry and Calvin that evening. "Got some digging equipment going to the Skelly oil leases over in Louann. Y'all can wave at Otis when you pass by his place. Just be careful you don't get shot at," he said, grinning.

When Henry was ready to leave the mule yard the next morning, Calvin was still hitching up his team and told Henry he would catch up with him at the depot. Later, when they were loading the fresnos, Henry noticed Calvin had a wooden crate underneath his spring seat. It looked identical to those Henry had seen through a crack in the locked door to the back storage room in the barn where Otis had his office. Calvin didn't mention it and Henry decided not to ask him about it right then.

Jimmy Dutton had managed to sneak his crude oil skimmer and four buckets out of his Uncle Gramps's barn and hide them out back in a row of trees before returning to town on Sunday afternoon. With more time in which to operate, Robert Watson had managed to get away with five buckets. When the boys met up as planned just after noon on Wednesday, Robert wondered if maybe they had gone overboard. He especially wished he had left his mother's egg-gathering bucket at home.

"I was just thinking," he said to Jimmy, as they hurried through the woods on the back side of Otis's farm, "It's gon' be hard to carry all these when we get them filled up."

"We ain't gon' bring them back, silly. We're gon' take them over to the road two at a time and hide them somehow till I can tell that fellow where they are, and he can come get them."

"How you know he'll do that?"

"Well, I don't for sure. But it sounded like he goes around to where folks are skimming and picks up what they've got. Let's just get them filled up, and I'll talk to him the next time I see him."

When the boys got to the creek, they discovered another problem with their plan. They knew the bank would be muddy in most places and they would get it on their clothes, which wasn't unusual for two kids running around a farm with a creek cutting across a corner of it. Now they saw that as the creek had flowed along, rising and falling after each rain, oil had also washed up on the banks. Not much, but enough that the two young entrepreneurs couldn't avoid getting it on their clothes too. They studied about that for a while, then Jimmy said, "We can wash it off in the horse trough behind the barn. Then we'll clean out the trough and fill it up again."

"What're we gon' use for soap?" Robert asked.

"You worry too much," Jimmy said, dropping his buckets and skimmer and starting to take off his shoes and roll up his pants legs.

"Okay," Robert said, and followed his friend's example.

The boys soon discovered that while their system for skimming worked, it was a time-consuming effort. They were having fun, though, and they didn't notice that they were getting almost as much oil on their clothes as in their buckets.

Calvin took the lead as he and Henry left the crowded Missouri Pacific depot and headed west with the crated fresno scrapers that had mistakenly been left on the train when it stopped in Louann the day before. With fall approaching, the weather had been cooler in recent days. It was even more so today, thanks to a southwesterly breeze strong enough to ruffle the mules' close-clipped manes. Henry was thinking less about the weather than about the crate under Calvin's seat. Maybe it wasn't moonshine, and maybe Calvin would tell him about it later. Or maybe there would be a good opportunity to ask about it.

As the wagons passed a point opposite the township building, visible to Henry's right over on Fourth Street across the railroad tracks, he recalled how Calvin approached him outside the building weeks back while Constable Burns was holding the little man's cousin Levi temporarily for his own protection. Calvin had said back at the depot that the oil pit crew for which Levi was a gofer had moved from Standard Umpsted east of Berrytown over to the growing Louann field. So, maybe today Henry would see him again. He thought often of the gentle man who had returned from war, like him, nursing demons others didn't see.

Henry's and Calvin's route, given to Moss by the Missouri Pacific stationmaster, who apparently got it from whoever was ramrodding the digging operations, took them through the middle of Louann. Though much smaller than Berrytown, the little community was also on the rise, with several new buildings going up and oil men and townspeople rushing about with determination showing on their faces and in their strides.

Calvin, with Henry trailing, turned left on the far edge of town and pulled in beside one of the new buildings nearing completion. Henry, not having anticipated this stop, pulled his team alongside Calvin's. No signage indicated the purpose of the building, but its lack of windows, plus what Henry had glimpsed through the doorless front entry as he drove around it, spoke barrelhouse. Without a word to Henry, Calvin dismounted, knocked on the side door, and spoke to someone Henry couldn't see. Then he returned to his wagon, lifted the crate from under his spring seat, and set it just inside the door. After a moment, he went to one of his rear mules, patted its rump, walked up to its shoulder, and appeared to adjust its collar. Then he climbed back on the wagon. He looked over at Henry and said, "Glassware. Mr. Moss was waiting till he had something else coming out here."

Henry let it pass. There would be a better time.

When Henry and Calvin emerged from the canopy of trees over the alley where they had stopped, and turned onto the road going south, the sky to the southwest was growing darker. The clouds were moving eastward, but Henry thought they would likely pass below the oil field. Soon the terrain began to take on the same stark and unsettling appearance of the Standard Umpsted field where Henry had delivered his first fresnos, and where he had returned numerous times. Oil derricks dominated the horizon, though under the new Arkansas conservation law, these were built far enough from each other to reduce the likelihood of fire leaping from rig to rig and destroying an entire field. The few remaining trees stood leafless and black like the soil around them, and great earthen pits, some more than ten acres in size, held hundreds of thousands of gallons of oil awaiting the new pipeline, or snail-paced transport by barrels to tank cars on the Louann rail siding. The morning breeze had become a steady wind, and the rotten-egg stench of sulfur was so strong it burned Henry's eyes and throat. He came upon it nearly every day somewhere, but he had never gotten used to it in any amount.

Heavily rutted dirt tracks crisscrossed the former farmland and forest creating a maze that Calvin and Henry threaded toward the southernmost producing wells, where additional pits were being dug. Other wagon teams and some trucks traversed the paths, too, moving everything from derrick timbers and planks to drill bits and casing pipe. Occasionally, Henry and Calvin had to pull over or wait at a crossroads for others to pass. Even with the waiting, Henry didn't think about looking around for Tuttle out here, nor did he think about Mary Dutton. He was too busy with his team and load.

He did, however, notice a cloud of black smoke billow up a half mile or so beyond them and grow rapidly. Within minutes, men all around him—mule skinners, roustabouts, roughnecks, drillers—saw it too. Oil was burning somewhere, lots of it. Most men working on derricks anywhere close ran toward it with shovels. Many had spent the better part of their lives moving from one oil boom town to the next, and almost all knew about the legendary Spindletop fire that burned through more than one hundred fifty derricks near Beaumont, Texas, in 1903. Even with wells drilled farther apart here, an uncontained fire could still destroy dozens of wells and consume the oil in as many storage pits. Potentially, it could even burn through the entire field, catch nearby oil-slicked creeks on fire, and travel along them for miles, possibly reaching other groups of wells and pits.

Freight haulers who were heading out of the Louann field bunched up in their haste to escape, leaving those heading in, like Henry and Calvin, no place to go. At Moss's insistence, all his skinners carried shovels lashed to the sides of their wagons for digging out when stuck in mud. Both men grabbed theirs and joined the rush toward the fire. There was little chance their teams would run away on the clogged road. There was no place they could go. And if the fire were not put out, they might not survive.

When Henry and Calvin arrived at the source of the smoke and flames, they saw that oil in one of the pits was burning, and men were shoveling frantically at both the near and far ends. Someone, probably the driller from the nearest derrick, was directing arriving men to one or the other end. He pointed Henry and Calvin to the near one.

There, barrel after barrel of oil that earlier had been flowing from a well into the pit through a six-inch pipe resting precariously on top of the pit bank was now spewing onto the ground. Between the pit and the well, a used gate valve made to operate either fully closed or fully open had been left partly closed, causing the sealing seat to separate. When roughnecks attempted to repair it, another used gate valve, this one closer to the well, also ruptured, resulting in chaos. While the drilling crew worked to bring things under control, the gushing oil plowed an open ditch toward the pit bank. By tragic coincidence something or someone—a spark from a tool or a worker stupidly sneaking a cigarette—had ignited the acres of oil in the pit. If flames jumped the pit bank and caught the oil in the ditch on fire, it would act as a fuse straight to the wellhead, causing an explosion that would touch off other pits and wells. All who came to help were risking their lives to bank dirt on the crude-filled ditch.

At the far end of the pit, other men worked with equal vigor to patch a breach in the bank there. For several days oil had been leaking into a small creek and going wherever the water took it. Only now, with the oil in the pit burning, was anyone showing concern. If fire in the pit reached the break and caught up the oil in the creek, it would burn for as long and as far as there was enough oil to sustain it. It would also burn anything soaked in oil on its banks and the banks of other streams linked to it.

CHAPTER 25

After a couple of hours, men working at the near end of the compromised pit succeeded in covering the ditch and ending the immediate threat. Then as many men as working room would allow moved to the far end to help with the breach in the pit bank. Henry and Calvin, tired, dirty, and relieved to have escaped a dangerous situation, went on to their delivery site, unloaded, and headed back to the mule yard. The pit continued to burn, its black smoke visible now as far away as Berrytown.

Once Henry and Calvin got back through Louann, fatigue and familiar ground lowered both alertness and the need for it. As they neared the turnoff for Otis Leatherwood's farm, Henry didn't pay much attention the first time he glimpsed rapid movement at the far edge of an open field to his left. Then he saw it again. With all the fallout from gushers and with oil floating on area streams, Henry doubted he was seeing deer. As Jake, Ben, Lon, and Sam plodded on, he watched through breaks among trees and bushes beside the road. When he finally got a good look, he shouted at Calvin and pointed. Two naked boys who appeared to be about ten or twelve, one white and one black, were darting in and out of the tree line on the other side of the field and racing parallel to the road toward the next field over. Each had a bundle tucked under one arm like a football.

"Looks like Reverend Watson's boy and Mr. Otis's nephew," Calvin called back, loudly enough to be heard over the groaning wagons and the mules' clomping hooves. "Robert and Mr. Jimmy."

"Wonder what they've been up to?" Henry replied.

"I don't have no idea," Calvin said, "but I'm pretty sure I know what's gon' happen to Robert if the Reverend catches him like that."

"Yeah, well," Henry said, grinning, "I don't expect it's gon' sit well with Otis, either. I didn't know that boy was Otis's nephew. I bought a newspaper from him the first day I came to town."

"Yeah," Calvin said. "I've seen him out there on the street corner lots of times. His mother's Miz Dutton that works in Hornbeck's Drugstore."

~

Jimmy reached the corn crib back of Otis Leatherwood's barn ahead of Robert and plopped down on the ground behind one of the log beams holding up the slant-walled structure. Robert landed behind another.

"We took off our clothes for nothing," Robert complained. He slapped his rolled-up pants with his shirt and shoes inside. "I got scratches all over me, and I bet that fire wasn't within five miles of us, I don't care how much smoke there was."

"You don't know that," Jimmy said, setting his stinking bundle on the ground beside him. "Them oil fires spread fast when they get on a creek. I heard men talking about them in town. Anyway, if you didn't think we was in danger, why'd you run so fast?"

"Same reason you did, I reckon. Just wasn't taking no chance."

"You gon' wear them clothes home," Jimmy asked, "or do you want to try to wash them?"

"You said we could wash them in the horse trough."

"Yeah, but we ain't got no soap."

"You knowed that right from the start, didn't you? And you said not to worry about it. You got any idea what my daddy's gon' do to me?"

"Whup you, I reckon," Jimmy said.

"That ain't likely the half of it. What you reckon Mr. Otis's gon' do to you?"

"I don't know. He ain't never laid a hand on me, but then I ain't never give him cause before now."

"What about your momma?"

"She ain't never whipped me, neither, but she's got a way of making me feel real bad when I get into stuff. I don't know. I sure wish I never had heard anything about oil skimming."

"Yeah," Robert said, starting to put on his oil-soaked clothes. "I wish you ain't neither."

~

"It'd likely be a pretty sunrise again this morning, if it wasn't for that goldarned smoke still hanging 'round," Otis said. He was sitting on his front porch drinking coffee and talking to Alma again. "I'm not crazy," he told her. "I know you're not here, but I like to feel like you are, and somehow I think you hear me."

He fell silent for a time, then said, "I just keep thinking about Jimmy. That was sure some dumb stunt he pulled. Really scared his momma when I took him to town and told her what happened. Needs his butt blistered, but it ain't up to me to do it. And she won't do it either. She don't have it in her. Fine woman, though."

Otis looked over at the vacant rocking chair that matched his. "Yeah, I reckon you're right. Jimmy didn't do anything I wouldn't have done." He chuckled, took another sip of his coffee, and set it on the little stool at his side. He had made it for Alma to put her sewing basket on when she did needlework on the porch. When he looked up Isaiah Watson was walking up his access road.

"Morning, Isaiah," Otis called, when his neighbor was close enough. "Come sit a spell."

"Morning, Mr. Otis. Thank you, sir," Isaiah said. He took off his hat, came as far as the top step and, keeping one foot on it, sat down on the porch and leaned against one of the posts holding up the roof.

"If you come over about what the boys did," Otis said, "I'm sorry Jimmy got Robert into that. The boy's only my nephew, and I can't give him a whipping, but I gave him a good talking to. Wish I could make it up to you some way."

"Ain't no need," Isaiah said. "Mr. Jimmy ain't responsible for what Robert did. That boy made up his own mind to go off over there and get hisself in that mess, and he's gon' need a pillow to sit on for a while to help him remember it wasn't no good idea. Anyways, that ain't why I come."

Otis stiffened and a frown came over his face. "Is this something I don't want to hear?"

"Yes, sir," Isaiah said. He noticed he was squeezing his hat with both fists and shifted it to one hand. "It is. Me and Luella has decided. I don't like what's happening all around us, but there ain't nothing I see that I can do to stop it. I've prayed to the Good Lord till I've near 'bout rubbed all the skin off my knees. I reckon He's got some sort of plan I just don't understand, except I know it's unfolding right in front of me. All I can come up with is that me and Luella is somehow meant to be part of it. Feels like it's a way we can help our boys have better than we did. I'm just sorry to disappoint you, Mr. Otis. You've been a mighty good friend and neighbor to us."

Otis took a deep breath, squinched his eyes, and exhaled slowly through his nose, as if resigning himself to a reality he had hoped wouldn't come even though he expected it. "Did you sign up with that snake Luther Pike?"

"No, sir. We gon' sign up with Mr. W. G. Skelly's company. It's the one that's doing all those wells over at Louann."

"You mean that bunch that started the fire that could've roasted our boys and, as it was, sent them running through the woods scared half to death and naked as jaybirds."

"Mr. Otis, I ..."

"Ain't no need to say anything else, Isaiah. I understand. I don't like it. But I understand. You have to do what you think's best for you and your family. Like I told you once before, this ain't gon' keep us from being friends. I'm just glad you didn't sign with Luther Pike. That man's nothing but a crook, or my name's not Otis Leatherwood."

"Thank you, Mr. Otis," Isaiah said, standing to leave. He couldn't think of anything more to say.

Otis got to his feet as well. "I hope this works out for you the way you want, Isaiah, but I got to tell you, I'm not gon' give in to these bastards, begging your Reverend's pardon. I'm gon' fight every way I can think of."

"What you got in mind, Mr. Otis? Seems like to me they done already won everything."

"I ain't ready to say yet. Some of it you'll hear about. Some of it you probably don't want to know."

CHAPTER 26

Mary raked scrambled eggs off an iron skillet onto Jimmy's plate, next to a freshly cooked sausage patty and a biscuit left over from the day before.

He felt her staring at him and looked up. "Momma," he said, "I'm really sorry. I didn't mean to scare you."

She pushed eggs onto her own plate, put the skillet on the trivet she used for her iron, and sat down across from him at their makeshift table in the shed. "You know you and Robert could have been killed, don't you?"

"Yes, ma'am. But we didn't think about that till we saw that black smoke. I just wanted to make some more money to help out."

Mary looked at him across the table. A boy without a father, growing up too fast in a town getting more dangerous and challenging every day, even for adults. "Eat your breakfast before it gets cold."

Jimmy picked up his fork, plunged it into his eggs, then paused and asked, "Are you still mad at me, Momma?"

Mary lifted her own fork, then put it down. "I'm sorry I shook you like I did when Uncle Gramps brought you home. That was wrong. But I'm not very happy with you," she said. "I can tell you that. I'm glad you wanted to make more money for us, but we don't need it bad enough for you to risk getting hurt, or worse. You've got to promise me you won't do something like that again."

"I promise, Momma. I won't."

Mary grasped her fork again. "I think some more chores might help you remember. I finished Mrs. Gordon's and Elizabeth's skirts, and after you sell all your newspapers, I want you to take them over there. Then get the axe and chop all that firewood Uncle Gramps brought us. Not enough for just a day or two. Do all of it. And stack it proper against the back wall. I'll think up something else for you tomorrow."

"Okay, Momma."

"Eat."

Henry paid for his meatloaf and potatoes at Nesbit's Café and stepped outside into a stiff evening breeze and distant rumbles of thunder. There wasn't a star in sight. Without light from the gas flares burning in the distance and flashes of lightning way off somewhere, the sky would have been pitch black. He could almost smell rain coming as he walked back to the mule yard. Tomorrow would likely be nasty. Moss had him slated to deliver rail freight to Berrytown stores. Henry preferred loads that took him into the oil fields. Even the near-about-everyday backups at creek crossings were less aggravating than jam-ups on Broadway, where ox teams and fourteen-up mule teams pulling heavy oil-field steam boilers vied with smaller mule teams, automobiles, trucks, and horse-and-buggy rigs for passage.

The plank walkways in front of stores were equally crowded, especially evenings. They overflowed with men going to or coming from supper or going in and out of pool halls and the general stores that stayed open late even on weeknights to catch their business. Henry had read a *Berrytown Journal* estimate that the population had swelled to more than ten thousand. He believed it. He walked in the rutted street to avoid being jostled, and his thoughts returned to the matter that occupied him all through supper.

He had never considered that Mary Dutton might be married. When he first saw her, what struck him was how much she looked like his sister. Once he began noticing the ways they differed, he found himself thinking more and more about Mary and less and less about Helen. He also didn't think as frequently about Ed Tuttle, often forgetting to keep an eye out for him while making freight runs. Now, learning that Mary was married was disappointing, and he was even more embarrassed about his bumbling behavior around her.

By the time he got back to the mule yard, Henry had decided that the only way to put his chagrin behind him and regain his focus on Tuttle was to go back to Hornbeck's and tell the woman he regretted making an ass of himself, though not exactly in those words.

"Neither snow, nor rain, nor heat, nor gloom of night stays these courageous couriers from the swift completion of their appointed rounds."

As Henry hitched Jake, Ben, Lon, and Sam in a driving rain, the famous line about mounted messengers from Herodotus's history of the Persian Wars played over and over in his mind, like some sort of involuntary chant to help him ignore the chilling water running under his rain slicker and down the back of his neck. The quotation was one of the few things he remembered from his Greek and Roman history at Wabash College. Along with how some famous architectural firm had chiseled it on the outside of the New York City post office building. He had said it over and over in the trenches with the AEF, both because it buoyed him somehow and because he admired the men and mules who ferried messages, supplies, and the wounded between the front and the rear. Henry had not become a mule skinner because he cared anything about the job itself, other than how the mobility of it supported his reason for coming to Berrytown. But he had come to like some parts of the work, especially the dogged strength and faithful obedience of his mule team despite the animals' reputation, undeserved he thought, for stubbornness. The longer he remained here and the longer he drove for Moss, the stronger the connections between past and present seemed to him.

Mule-yard mud, squished and churned by dozens of teams leaving within a narrow window of time, was already at the top of his wheel rims when Henry got underway. Mornings were always busy around the Missouri Pacific depot sidings and in front of oil-field supply warehouses on side streets. Tempers always flared. Cussing and shouting were commonplace. Fisticuffs were not unusual. But all were worse on days like this.

Henry finally managed to get away from the railroad depot and onto Broadway around mid-morning. Because there were no alleys suitable for wagon teams to go behind stores, all deliveries were made through the front doors. Henry planned to drive down the west side of the street, deliver to stores on his right, circle a block a few side streets down, and come back up the east side of Broadway. He had two crates for Hornbeck's Drugstore on that side, and as he was loading them at the depot, he decided he might as well use that stop as an opportunity to speak to Mary Dutton and apologize for acting like a sap.

He barely managed to pull onto Broadway, however, before becoming hopelessly bogged down. The rain was now coming down in sheets, and Berrytown's main drag, worn down by weeks and months of heavy traffic, had water flowing in from every side street, creating a giant bog. All up and down the four main blocks, motor vehicles and wagons had sunk up to their axles. Mules stood drenched and knee deep in the muck, unable to move their loads and imprisoned in their harnesses. Some mule skinners left their stranded teams and sought shelter under packed store sheds, some sat helpless and motionless on their wagons, and some stood beside their lead animals trying to urge them on even though they had no real path forward.

Henry sat for a few minutes pressing his temples as images of men and mules in muddy French battlefields crowded in alongside the scene in front of him. Then he climbed off his wagon and slogged his way to each of his mules and patted their necks and rubbed their noses. He wished there was more he could do for them but there was not. Somehow, some way, something would have to happen down the street to unclog the jam. Maybe dig some drainage ditches and remove some of the teams from their loads to create space for maneuvering. It would help if the rain would let up.

While he waited for things to get organized, he decided to wade across Broadway, walk down to Hornbeck's at the corner of Seventh Street, and try to catch Mary Dutton now. If a bunch of folks were crowding into the store to get out of the rain, this would not be a good time, but there was no harm in checking.

CHAPTER 27

Rain aside, the morning had not begun well for Eunice and Grover Hornbeck either. The day before, a man wearing a wrinkled mail-order brown suit and vest, white shirt, narrow black tie, and brown fedora with the brim turned down all around had come into the store twice. Once he stayed much longer than a typical customer, and once he left after talking briefly with Mary.

The first time was shortly before noon. He stood at the newspaper and magazine rack alternately flipping through magazines and glancing around as if he were either expecting someone or looking for someone. Eunice noticed that he sometimes picked up a magazine without even looking to see which one he was grabbing. Twice he leafed through one a second time, as if he hadn't already handled it. After a while, he left without buying anything.

The second time was around two o'clock, shortly after Sally Boudreau came in to buy a headache remedy. As she and Eunice stood chatting at the patent medicine counter, the man walked up the center aisle near them and paused for a moment or two, staring at something in the cabinets across from them. Then he went back up front to the soda fountain and ordered a soft drink from Mary. When she served it, he asked her something Eunice didn't hear, and they talked for a moment. When Sally left, the man watched her go, and once she was out of sight, he placed a quarter on the counter and left heading in the same direction.

Eunice went straight off to Mary and asked what the man had said. Mary told her he asked if a lot of traveling salesmen came into the store. She thought it was a strange question, seeing as how the whole country seemed to run on the stamina and glad-handing ability of such men to connect folks with things they needed, wanted, or could be talked into. There were almost as many of them as there were different kinds of things for people to buy. Mary said she told him, "Yes, of course," and then he asked her if they got a lot of salesmen from New Orleans.

"I said we did," Mary told Eunice. "Then he said he had heard New Orleans was an interesting place. I told him I guessed it was, and right after that was when he got up and left."

If Mary made any connection between the man's questions and Crescent City Powders, she didn't let on. Eunice, on the other hand, did and fretted about it the rest of the afternoon and all through supper. Finally, not wanting to believe the worst, she convinced herself that the man's visit only meant that agents from the Treasury Department's Narcotics Division were snooping around. It didn't necessarily mean they were actively investigating Hornbeck's. She told Grover that agents probably made routine visits to all pharmacies.

Grover, however, figured they were good as caught. He said the fellow was probably scoping out the store for some kind of raid, like the newspapers said authorities made on speakeasies all the time up North. When their arguing spilled into the bedroom and Grover told Eunice this was all her fault, she snatched up a pillow and blanket and slept in another room.

Sleep did not resolve their disagreement. They were still mad at each other the next morning during the rainstorm.

By the time Henry sloshed through mud and water up over his boots and got to the other side of the street, he had begun to think that stopping in Hornbeck's might not be a good idea. He wasn't the only stranded mule skinner or truck and automobile driver who had abandoned their means of conveyance for shelter under one of the building sheds or in one of the stores. The drugstore would likely be crowded and there would be no chance to speak to Mary Dutton. Plus, he would track up the place and leave a mess for someone to clean up, most likely Mary from what he had seen before. But, he guessed, the place would be plenty dirty whether he went there or not. So, having come this far, he continued threading his way along the plank walkways through knots of dripping-wet men talking, smoking, and spitting as they waited, hoping the deluge would soon let up.

When Henry reached the drugstore, he paused to peer through the window before opening the door. There were more than a dozen people inside, all of whom, except for the Hornbecks and Mary, were working men having come in out of the rain. Mary was standing behind the soda fountain counter with her back to customers, and as she turned to serve one of the men seated there, she glanced up and met Henry's gaze for a split second before carrying on with what she was doing. Henry didn't know if she recognized him, but whether she did or not, and regardless of the crowd, he decided he wouldn't leave without at least speaking to her. And apologizing as planned if he found a private enough moment, though that appeared unlikely.

Stepping inside, Henry saw that the Hornbecks were helping customers in the back of the store and Jimmy was about halfway up the center aisle sweeping. Henry assumed the Fall school term hadn't started, and the boy had been pressed into service to help deal with what the downpour brought.

Henry spotted a vacant stool at the far end of the counter and headed for it. Before he reached it, a man entered the store behind him and shouted, "There you are, you thieving son-of-a-bitch! Give it back!"

As everyone turned toward the speaker, a beefy fellow sitting near the middle of the counter slapped his hand on the marble top, stood up, spun around, and said, "I told you, I ain't got it. Now, leave me alone or I'm gon' tear your goddamned head off."

The first man, slight of build with water running off his poncho onto the muddy floor, glared at the larger man for a second or two. Then he calmly reached under his poncho, came out with a pistol, and fired two shots. The big man fell back against the counter and slid to the floor, a dark red stain spreading across the front of his damp wool coat.

Eunice let out a piercing scream. Most of the other startled onlookers, including Mary, didn't speak or move. Henry turned his back on the shooter, stepped toward Jimmy, took hold of him, then faced front again, keeping the boy behind him. Two other men, having heard the shots, came in from the walkway. Propelled by curiosity rather than intent to interfere, they froze when they came face-to-face with the drawn gun.

"He stole my wallet!" the man with the pistol said. "Look in his side pocket. He's got it, I tell you." He backed up a step and looked all around, his weapon following his eyes. They lighted on Henry. "You do it," the fellow commanded. Henry remained still, holding Jimmy tight. "Do it now, or I'll shoot you too!"

"Tell you what," Henry said. "You put that gun on the counter, and you and me will both look. How about it?"

"Ain't no way," the man said, and began waving the gun around, pointing it at first one person then another.

A bearded fellow on the stool next to the man who was shot said, "I'll do it." Without waiting for a reply, he bent over the victim, who was no longer breathing, and went through his coat pockets. Seconds later, still kneeling, he held up a wallet.

"That's mine," the slight man with the gun said. "I told you he had it. Toss it here."

"How do we know it's yours and not his?" the bearded man asked.

A third shot tore a hole in the bottom of the Hornbecks' new soda counter. Eunice screamed again. The shooter yelled, "That's how! Now, toss it!" He caught the wallet in his free hand and ran untouched out the door and south toward Eighth Street, past men who only gawked at him. It was the fourth shooting in the last ten days; they were no longer a novelty.

Henry took his hands off Jimmy and pressed his temples, as pain spread upward and across his forehead. Mary ran around the counter and gathered the boy in her arms. "Jimmy, Jimmy," she said, "Oh, my god. Are you all right?"

Embarrassed by his mother's reaction, Jimmy pulled away from her, then looked up, saw that she was trembling, and embraced her. "Don't cry, Momma, everything's okay. This here man saved me."

"I didn't really do anything, Jimmy," Henry said, as Jimmy and his mother looked over at him, "but I'm glad you're all right." He nodded toward the front, "I sure hate you folks had to see that."

"You most certainly did save him," Mary said. Jimmy stepped back from his mother, but she kept her arm around his shoulder. "He could have been shot, and you could have too. How is it you know his name?"

"Jimmy told me the first day I came to town. I bought a newspaper from him. I didn't know he was your son, though, till just the other day. Someone who knows your uncle told me."

Henry looked around and saw that no one was paying the three of them any attention. Some of the men in the store had left to avoid further entanglement in the shooting. All the others except Grover had gathered around the dead guy and were talking about who he was and who would go for Constable Burns.

Eunice walked up to the front door and locked it, as if doing so would prevent any further trouble, then began yelling at her husband. "Don't just stand there, Grover. Do something! Go get Randolph!" Randolph Ingramhoff, whose last name no one could pronounce, was the town's undertaker. He was also as slow as his name was long, and unable to keep up with demand. Everyone knew the rickety building he used for a morgue on the southern edge of town was filled with unburied bodies, some dead from natural causes, others from oil-field accidents, and not a few from killings. Folks could smell it from a distance.

With everyone else in the store arguing about what to do next, Henry saw his opportunity. "Mrs. Dutton," he said, ignoring the circumstances and his headache, "I know this is not the best time, but I need to tell you I'm sorry for acting so strange every time I come in here. I must seem like an idiot, but the thing is the first time I saw you, you reminded me an awful lot of my late twin sister. I was near about speechless. Now I know you don't look near as much like her as I first thought. Not that you're not a fine-looking woman like she was. You are." Thinking maybe he shouldn't have mentioned her looks, with her being married and all, he blushed. "I hope it's all right my saying that. I don't mean any disrespect. And that thing the other day with Big Sally, I'm not someone that frequents barrelhouses. I was looking for somebody that night, and I was blocking her front door. That's why she remembered me. I hope you will forgive me and just forget all those other times I was in here."

Mary started to say something but Henry interrupted.

"I'm pleased to have met you, and I'm glad to have met Jimmy here too. He sure seems like a fine boy. You and his daddy must be real proud of him."

Mary started to speak again, but Henry beat her to it once more. "I see somebody's got Constable Burns already. He must've been somewhere close. Anyway, looks like he's got plenty of help to get things cleaned up over there, so I'll just get on out of the way."

"Mr. Smith," Mary said, impulse becoming words before she could stop them, "I'm not married. Jimmy's father was killed in the National Guard." She looked away as soon as she said it.

Henry's first reaction was surprise that she remembered the name he had given earlier, even if it was the most common in the English-speaking world. His second was happiness she was single. His third was guilt about his second. "Yes, ma'am," he said, blushing again. "I'm very sorry." He nodded slightly, put his thumb and forefinger to the brim of his hat in a tipping gesture and walked away.

"Come back again sometime, Henry," Mary called.

She remembers my first name, too, he thought. "Thanks, I'll do that," he said without turning around. He was afraid for her to see the broad smile spreading across his face. Afraid he was reading too much into what she said. Afraid he would look silly. He knew, however, that he would do like she said.

CHAPTER 28

Otis Leatherwood spread the wrinkled, irregular-shaped pages on his kitchen table and, with his stub of a pencil in hand, began reading them again from the beginning. He had spent hours filling them with words. Then he had erased some words and written others in place of them, marked through still others and drawn arrows to newly added ones, and scratched out whole sentences and paragraphs and composed substitutes.

All this after an uncomfortable and irritating train trip to Little Rock and back. Sitting on the way up packed like a sardine amid men talking and smelling of oil. And standing shoulder to shoulder much of the time on the way back with drummers, speculators, roughnecks, drillers, and others, so that the few female passengers could sit.

Once he had all the words and sentences set down the way he wanted them, he planned to copy them over again to make sure the person he was taking them to could read his scrawl. He had already prepared the blank pages. Like with the first ones, he had used a kitchen knife to cut them from brown wrapping paper Alma had saved, folded, and stored under the bench seat of a hall tree that he had splurged on and ordered for her when she went on and on about it after seeing it in a Sears, Roebuck catalog. It was something they didn't need, but she had loved it, and now every time he put his hat on one of the hooks, or lifted it from one, in his mind he was handing it to Alma or taking it from her. As he read, he felt like she was looking over his shoulder. He hoped she liked what she was seeing.

SAVE THE LAND! DON'T KILL TOMORROW!

Here today and gone tomorrow. I reckon you have all heard somebody say that sometime or other. Well, now we're living it. We're killing the land, and if we don't stop it, we ain't going to have no tomorrow.

The WE I mean is EVERYBODY who is either poking holes in the land and wasting what's under it or ruining what's on top of it, and EVERYBODY who's sitting idly by while them that's doing it keeps on at it. That covers just about EVERYBODY in Berrytown and South Arkansas, including them that has always lived here and them that is Johnny come lately.

I know the oil men and oil companies doing all the well drilling ain't going to listen to this old farmer, but it might be in their best interest down the road if they did. And it would be in the best interest of everybody else too. That's because what I'm about to tell you is based on what you can see for yourselves and on what real geologists say, not on what them lease hounds running all over the place trying to get their hands on other people's land and hard-earned money tell you.

Let's take what we can all see. You don't have to look far. There is stinking, slimy oil that's spilled all over just about everything around us. It's not just killing crops and things that grow wild like berries and such as that. It's settling into the ground, and anybody that has ever farmed can tell you that there's thousands of acres all around us where ain't nobody going to be able to grow crops ever again, at least not in the lifetime of anybody reading this now. That spilled oil is killing tomorrow. And all of us that are doing anything that helps the oil men get it out of the ground in the first place is killing tomorrow too.

Look at the creeks and the woods. Has anybody caught many fish or shot much game lately? There's oil sitting on top of the water in near about every creek anywhere around, and it's all over the trees and bushes and the ground anywhere near where there's oil wells. It's ruined what wild game needs to live on. So, the game animals are about all gone. I wonder when they will ever come back. They might never.

Now let's take what we can't all see. I went up to Little Rock and talked to geologists that work for the state in the Bureau of Mines, Manufactures, and Agriculture, and what I found out is that the producers and drillers don't really know a lot about what they're doing. I reckon most of the oil men know that's the case, but they don't care long as they're making money. But the rest of us ought to know it too.

It boils down to this. There's lots of different kinds of rock formations that have oil in them, and what the oil men don't know about them is a lot more than what they do know. The different formations have different amounts of gas and saltwater in them, and that makes a difference in how the oil comes out of the ground and what comes out with it.

These different formations are at different depths under the ground. They may be at one depth in Louann and another depth in Norphlet and so on. The drillers are supposed to take core samples every so often so they know what it's like where the bottoms of their holes are as they're going along, but they're in such a rush to get money that they don't take samples like they're supposed to. They have these new-fangled rotary bits that eat through the rock in a hurry, and that's all they care about.

This is why they get all these blowouts, and it's why you see all the flares in the oil fields. They're burning off gas that's escaping because the drilling went too fast and too deep and hit pockets of gas instead of oil. Gas that's escaping like that and being burned off can't push oil out of the ground, so there's a lot of oil being left down there. I'm told that because of this, the oil companies will never be able to get even half of it.

If you think about that, you can see the oil companies are wasting half of the oil because they can't get it out of the ground because they don't go at it right. And they're wasting half of what they do get out because they can't hold onto it and take care of it once it's out because they don't have enough safe places to keep it. This is ruining the land and killing tomorrow.

The thing is, we still have time to make different choices. The oil men do and the rest of us do too.

If the world really needs all this oil to make cars, trucks, and ships go, like I keep reading about, I reckon there ain't no way people are going to stop trying to get it. What they can do, though, is slow down and be smarter about how they are getting it and storing it. That way the oil men would make more money in the long run, and the rest of us would have a better place to live than we are going to have because of greed and stupid ways of doing things.

I guess I don't blame nobody for leasing out their land in order to make a little money, or a lot of it. Times have been hard. But I'm not going to lease to the oil men, and I hope other people won't either if they don't have to in order to keep a roof over their heads and food in their bellies. Instead of just thinking about all the places we can go and all the things we can get with oil money, we need to worry about whether there will be any farmland, and woods, and fresh water, and plants, and animals left for us to live on down the road whether we have oil money or not.

If you don't want to believe me about what can happen, then look at what the Bible says. You got to remember the land ain't really ours. In Psalms it says, "THE EARTH IS THE LORD'S, AND THE FULNESS THEREOF, AND THEY THAT DWELL THEREIN." That means everything is His, us humans and the animals and the plants too. Every living thing. All of them like I done said. Look in Isaiah and see what happened when a man didn't take care of the vineyard that God gave him and just let it go to ruin. God got mad and tore it up the rest of the way. There wasn't anything left. Then the Lord told him, "LOOK UNTO THE LAND, BEHOLD DARKNESS AND SORROW, AND THE LIGHT IS DARKENED IN THE HEAVENS THEREOF." That's what's going to happen to us if we don't take care of what God gave us. We are going to look unto the land, and there ain't going to be nothing left. Seems like it's already started to happen. There's already lots of days like that around Berrytown. Just look around, and you can see. WE need to STOP THIS NOW.

Please, let's save the land! Don't kill tomorrow!

Otis Leatherwood

Nathan Collier, graying owner-editor of the weekly *Berrytown Journal*, laid the rumpled pages on his desk, raised the green visor he was wearing, and leaned back in his wooden swivel chair. He studied the face of his visitor for a moment, then hooked his thumbs in his vest pockets, and said, "Mr. Leatherwood, you know dang well I can't print this. It's not news. It's just your opinion."

Otis, standing in front of Collier's desk with his hat still on, uncrossed his arms from his bib overalls, picked up the pages, and looked at them for a long minute. Then he tossed them back and asked, "Why not? You put your opinion in the paper all the time."

"That's different. I own the paper. I'm the editor. I'm supposed to print my opinion about things. That's what editors do. They help readers understand what's going on."

"Well, what do you think I'm trying to do? This is things people 'round here need to know."

"I'm sorry," Collier said. "It's not the same thing."

"I don't know why not," Otis said. "But, alright, then print it like a letter to the editor. You're always putting them in. Church ladies complaining about prostitutes. Store owners complaining about shoplifters and pickpockets. All kinds of crap."

"You didn't write it like a letter to the editor. You wrote it more like a news article."

"That's 'cause it is one. It's stuff folks ought to know."

Collier shrugged his shoulders, and the two men stared at each other, Otis waiting for a response and Collier waiting for Otis to leave.

"Okay," Otis said, "I'll change it to a letter to the editor. That good enough for you?"

Collier sat upright in his chair. He looked down the long narrow room that served as his office and printing shop, past his assistant editor and clerk working on the other side of a room-dividing balustrade, and toward the front door, as if trying to will Otis Leatherwood through it. Two presses, one for the newspaper and one for small contract jobs filled the space behind him. Shelves lined the walls, holding folded back issues of the *Journal*, cardboard filing boxes, and cartons of paper for stationery orders and the like. Above them, exposed wooden beams supported the second-floor apartment where Collier lived. Before coming to Berrytown, he had worked on newspapers in several other towns, once even in Little Rock, and he had long dreamed of having his own paper. The boom in Berrytown had given him the chance. He was making money but was deep in debt for the building and equipment. He was smart enough to know that the old man standing in front of him was right, but the only thing keeping the newspaper in the black on a weekly basis was advertising revenue from lease hounds, oil-field supply houses, and the oil companies themselves.

"Mr. Leatherwood," Collier said, "You don't know what you're asking. I still couldn't print that as a letter to the editor."

Otis's chin dropped to his chest. He was tired of arguing. When he raised his head, he said, "Yeah, I know. You're afraid to print it. And I know why as well as you do. So, let's do this. You're in the business of selling ads. Sell me one. Run this as an advertisement." He pointed to the pages on Collier's desk. "Put a big black border on it like you do on some of them oil company and lease hound ads. The ones that's promising to make fortunes for suckers overnight. You know them things are full of lies, but you run them anyway. If anybody gives you any guff about mine, you can say, 'It's just business, like them oil stock ads.'"

"Even if I could do that, Mr. Leatherwood, I doubt you could afford it."

"Try me. Give me a price for four issues. Make it big enough so folks will see it."

"Eighth of a page, four times, that's forty dollars. You got that kind of money lying around? I know your cotton crop was ruined and you're not leasing out any land. Says here you went up to Little Rock. That must have set you back some."

"I'll get the money. Don't you worry none about that. You just get the ad all set up."

"It needs some editing. It's got all sorts of grammatical mistakes in it."

"Don't you change a goddammed word. I got it just like I want it."

"Who helped you?"

"Nobody."

"Come on, Mr. Leatherwood. I'm not sure why, but you don't strike me as a church-going man. Where'd you get this stuff from the Bible?"

"My Alma read the Bible to me just about every night long as she lived. I listened 'cause I loved the sound of her voice."

~

Otis had ridden into town on his ten-year-old black mare, which he had raised from a foal. He stepped down from the walkway in front of the newspaper, went over to her, put one hand on her soft muzzle and the other under her chin, and said, "Trixie, old girl, I know you're not gon' understand, but I ain't got no choice." He patted her neck, mounted up, and rode to Moss's mule yard.

When he got there, Wilbur Moss was coming out of his front barn carrying a block of livestock salt. He set it on a sled with two others then looked up and saw Otis riding toward him. "Morning, Otis, you old scalawag, what brings you here?" he asked.

"I need to sell my horse. Saddle too. Right now."

CHAPTER 29

Otis was on his trip when the big storm hit and the shooting occurred in Hornbeck's. When he got back, after spending the weekend in the state capital because he needed more time there, he had gone straight home and started working on his piece for the newspaper. He had heard about the shooting as soon as his train pulled into the depot, however. Now, after leaving Moss's place and making a return visit to Nathan Collier's office, he stopped by the drugstore to see how Mary and Jimmy were doing before he walked home.

The boy was nowhere in sight, and Mary, as well as Eunice and Grover, were with customers when Otis walked in. He went over to the newspaper and magazine rack and immediately thought he should have made Collier give him the latest issue of the Berrytown paper. After all, he was going to be a sizeable advertiser, for a few weeks anyway. He picked up a copy from the rack and saw that the lead story was about the murder that happened only a few feet from where he was standing.

A companion story looked back at several other shootings and three stabbings that had happened in recent weeks and told about two railroad workers pulling a near-about petrified body out of a tank car they were cleaning. Apparently one or more hijackers had waylaid a man, taken his wallet, crushed his skull, and tossed him into a then-empty car to hide the evidence. Workers at the transfer station had filled the car with crude, and the tanker had made its way to a refinery in El Dorado, been emptied, and returned with the body still inside.

A third story told about plans a group of businessmen were making to get Berrytown incorporated, elect a mayor, and establish a police force to bring some measure of order and public safety. They were now casting about for potential candidates for mayor and police chief, the former to be elected and the latter appointed.

"'Bout damned time," Otis said to himself.

"Time for what, Uncle Otis?" Mary asked, walking up to him.

"Time for somebody to do something to clean up things 'round here, get rid of some of these crooks and rowdies. It's getting to the point where hard-working honest folks ain't safe no more. I heard about the shooting in here. You and Jimmy all right?"

Mary looked away from him, her thoughts torn between his concern for her safety and her bigger worry that her forced association with Crescent City Powders would somehow ensnare her in efforts to clean up the town. An image of the man who had come in recently wearing the brown suit and asking about New Orleans flashed through her mind.

"Yes," she said, weakly. "Jimmy's back in school and he has that to distract him. I just try not to think about it. It's kind of hard, though, with that man's blood still staining the floor over there. I have to admit I get a little scared every time some stranger comes in, or we get a whole bunch of customers."

Otis had hoped his dropping by to see Mary would somehow prove helpful or reassuring, but his question about whether she and Jimmy were okay only set her to worrying more about their safety and overall circumstances. With the boom going on, she could probably find work someplace other than the drugstore, but if she tried that, Eunice would make them move out of the shed, and they would have no place to go. Berrytown had become so crowded that now people were renting space under porches, as well as on them, and more and more were sleeping out in the open in the woods.

More than once, Mary had reconsidered asking Otis if she and Jimmy could go live with him, but she knew he had never stopped grieving over her Aunt Alma's death and had left entire rooms undisturbed since burying her. Jimmy had told Mary several times about his Uncle Gramps reminding him not to go upstairs when he was visiting. Otis would never take them in, and even if he did, it would be difficult if not impossible to get back and forth every day to work in town.

After turning all this over in her mind the rest of the day after Otis left, and then through supper with Jimmy, she waited until he was asleep then went to the trunk at the foot of her cot. She had no one she could talk to about their predicament, no one to tell her things would be all right, no one to hold her and wipe away the tears welling up in her eyes. She wanted to take out the quilt Florence Leatherwood had made, drape it around her shoulders, and remember a time when her mother's touch could make bad things go away, if only for a while.

Mary knelt on the floor, opened the barrel-like trunk lid, and picked up the colorful stock certificate lying on top of the tray. An inch-wide floral engraving, orange in color, decorated each border of the stiff, cream-colored paper. "Luther Pike

Oil Company" in old English lettering sprawled horizontally across the upper one-third, the name framed by dark-gray lines depicting a long, narrow, partially unrolled scroll. Above the name, a derrick gushing oil made clear the promise of the seller and dream of the buyer. Below the name of the company, lines of legalese identified the seller and buyer. An embossed orange seal and Pike's signature, along with that of his company's secretary, proclaimed that the transaction represented by the certificate was legal. Mary owned seven shares, purchased for ten dollars each, in the Luther Pike Oil Company. She had invested almost every penny she had saved over the last three years.

Under the certificate was Luther Pike's handbill, and Mary glanced at the guarantee it made of "a tremendous, hair-raising, fortune-making, oil-splattering, earth-destroying, monster gusher." She had decided days earlier that this was her only chance to get out from under Eunice Hornbeck's thumb. At present, however, it gave her little comfort.

Mary set the tray aside, removed the items above the false bottom, lifted out the panel in anticipation of taking the quilt into her arms, then gasped for breath. She sat motionless for a moment. Then, despite seeing that the secret compartment was empty and the quilt gone, she reached into the trunk and felt around the sides to confirm that her eyes weren't deceiving her.

Her next impulse was to shout at Jimmy, wake him up, and ask if he took the quilt, but that passed as quickly as it came. She didn't believe he would ever take something that didn't belong to him, and certainly not something he knew his mother prized. Unless, she thought, he took it to sell to help support them. She dismissed that idea just as quickly, however. He wouldn't do that without her permission.

There was only one way the quilt could be gone and everything else in the trunk be exactly as she had left it: Eunice must have taken it. And there could be only one reason why: to hurt her. "You bitch!" she exclaimed loudly without thinking about Jimmy lying asleep a few feet away. She looked over at him, and when he didn't move, she folded her arms along the top edge of the open trunk, and laid her head on them. Underneath, where once lay a gift her mother had labored over for so many hours that it became almost a part of her, there was now only a painful emptiness.

~

If Jimmy heard his mother cuss and woke up, he never said anything about it. Mary spent much of the next two days trying to decide whether to confront Eunice about the quilt. There was no way to raise the matter without appearing to accuse her of stealing. And whether she had taken the quilt or not, she would surely be angry and either threaten to put Mary and Jimmy out of the shed or try to do it. However, Mary now reasoned, if Eunice did either, Mary could threaten to tell the authorities that Eunice and Grover were selling marijuana and Crescent City Powders and had forced her to help them. Mary was afraid to actually do that, but if Eunice thought she might, then maybe she wouldn't dare to order her tenants out. Plus, Eunice and Grover needed her in the store. Who else could they get to help them without giving up the illegal drug sales? The answer was no one, except at much greater risk to themselves. After a while, Mary concluded that although Eunice would get angry and fuss and fume, she couldn't do anything that would make things much worse for than they already were.

The next morning, when Eunice was in early for once, Grover was filling prescriptions left from the day before, and they were all preparing to open the store, Mary followed Eunice when she went into the back room to get something.

"Eunice," Mary said, closing the door and remaining in front of it, "someone took a quilt out of one of my trunks. Do you know anything about it?"

The question jolted Eunice, who had her back to Mary while taking a box of tobacco products off a shelf. She had never thought about Mary having nerve enough to confront her. She turned around, set the box on a work bench, and smiled, taking time to think what to say.

"Mary, dear," Eunice said, after straightening the front of her low-waisted dress, "as a matter of fact, I do know about it. I needed something for a gift, in a hurry. I knew you sewed, and I figured you might have something lying around already made up that I could use. So, I went looking, and that old quilt, ugly as it was, seemed good enough, so I took it. Frankly, I didn't think you'd miss it. If you think it was worth anything, I'll gladly pay you for it."

The direct and condescending nature of Eunice's reply didn't surprise Mary. What did surprise her was the boldness of her own response, forced from heart to voice by years of pent-up emotions—fear, anger, and desperation.

"I don't want your money, Eunice," Mary said. She had no intention of giving Eunice the satisfaction of knowing what the quilt really meant to her. "I don't even want an apology, which you're not capable of anyway. I want my quilt back, and if I don't get it, I'm going to the authorities about you and Grover selling illegal drugs. I'll tell them you blackmailed me into helping you, and I'll testify to that in court. You'll both go to jail, but I won't." As soon as the words poured out, Mary's knees went weak, but she held steady, bracing herself against the door.

Color drained from Eunice's face, but she didn't back down. "I don't have the quilt, Mary. I gave it to Sally Boudreau to give to Vera Hudson for a wedding gift. I didn't figure a prostitute would care much about how it looked as long as it kept her and her husband warm this winter, assuming she's able to hold onto him that long." She paused and grinned. "You know, I can't figure out why a man would marry a woman like that. She must be awful good in bed. Wouldn't you think?"

Mary knew now that she wasn't going to get the upper hand over her cousin, but she didn't give up. "If you want to stay out of jail, you need to go find Vera, wherever she is, and get my quilt back."

"I don't have any idea where she is," Eunice lied, "but if you want a quilt that some whore's been sleeping under, or doing whatever on, then you're welcome to go look for her yourself. But I'm not gon' do anything, and I don't expect you will either. So, why don't you just be a good little girl and go on back to work." With that, Eunice, nudged Mary aside and went back to the sales floor.

Mary stood for a long time in the storeroom, fists clinched and teeth grinding. There had to be a way out. There just had to.

CHAPTER 30

Calvin Birdsong found Henry bent over, using a pick and stiff brush to clean dried mud and matted straw out of Jake's hooves while the big mule munched on hay from a rack in the back corral. It had been a long day, and all the other drivers had finished their evening chores and left the yard.

"I've got something for you," Calvin said. "Been hauling it 'round all day looking to catch up with you."

Henry gently lowered Jake's left back leg, straightened up, and stretched his back. Calvin held out a burlap bag with the top twisted several times and a string tied around it.

"It's gon' be getting colder nights," he said, "and me and Levi figured you could use this, sleeping up in that loft like you do."

Henry laid the pick and brush on top of a corral post, wiped his hands on his khaki pants, and took the sack. He could see it held something soft and bulky. Henry figured Levi must have found an abandoned blanket in one of the fresnoes camps. If so, it wasn't anything he needed. He hadn't told anyone, as there had been no reason to, but he had made additional improvements to his sleeping corner—two small wooden crates to hold a few personal items and two changes of clothes, a rickety wooden chair he found alongside a road after it fell off someone's overloaded vehicle, and a couple of blankets he had bought at one of the general stores. He didn't need anything more.

Henry removed the string, let the sack twist open, and looked inside. "A quilt," he said, reaching in and holding it with one hand and letting the sack drop to the ground. He could tell that the material in it wasn't new. Knowing that Calvin lived with his mother, Henry figured she had made it some time back. Even though he didn't need it, he didn't want to say so and hurt Calvin's feelings, or worse, his mother's. Henry's mother had made quilts, too, and this one was plain by comparison, but he was not about to say that either. "This is nice, Calvin. Did your mother make it?"

"No sir, Mr. Henry. Truth is, Levi found it a while back. It was in an old trunk in a blackberry thicket beside the road over close to Louann. Levi was walking home and stopped to pick him a mess of berries and near 'bout fell over it. Varmints had done ate all the rawhide off the outside of the trunk and started gnawing holes in it, but he toted the thing all the way home anyway. I think it reminded him of the army somehow. Anyway, this here quilt was in it all wrapped up in brown paper."

"Well, I sure do appreciate it, Calvin, but can't y'all use it?"

"No sir, Momma's been making quilts for years, and we've got plenty. We want you to have it." Calvin didn't tell Henry what his mother had said about the quilt when they opened the trunk and found it full of fancy women's undergarments and dance hall dresses: "Y'all can just get rid of all this stuff, including that quilt. I ain't gon' have nothing in this house that come from some white folks' whorehouse."

Henry didn't know what he would do with the thing, but he told Calvin to be sure and thank his mother and Levi. While

Calvin held the sack open for Henry to slip the quilt back inside, Henry decided that with no one else around, this was a good time to ask Calvin about his suspicions regarding Moss's bootlegging activities.

"Say, Calvin, remember when you told me Moss didn't need to worry about that big new Missouri mule yard operation taking business away from him? Something about his having 'too good a thing going'? You want to tell me some more about that? I've already got an idea, 'cause I've seen what he's got locked up over there in the back of the first barn, and I don't believe that story you told me about delivering glasses to that place in Louann. I saw you hiding money in one of your mules' collars when you came out."

Calvin stepped back, tilted his head to one side, and held his hands waist high, palms up. "Now, Mr. Henry, why you want to go and ask me a thing like that. You know I can't talk about Mr. Moss's private business. It ain't just that I work for him. He's been good to me, and he trusts me, and I don't want to get him in no trouble. No, sir, please. I can't do that."

Jake looked around and nuzzled Henry's back, begging for more hay, but Henry ignored him. "I don't want to cause trouble for either one of you, Calvin. I just want to know what's going on. I don't plan to tell anybody about it or do anything about it. I'm just curious. I see moonshine all over the place, and it's pretty clear that Moss is running it and you're helping him. But there's got to be a lot more people involved too. First time I looked, there weren't many crates back there. Last time seemed like there was enough to fill half the glasses in Berrytown."

"Aw, now, Mr. Henry," Calvin said, shaking his head, "why you have to go and ask me all this. I thought you and me was friends, as much as a black man and a white man can be. We could both get bad hurt."

The last thing Calvin said only heightened Henry's interest. There must be something sizeable going on. Henry hadn't thought much at all about Ed Tuttle in a while, especially not since the last time he talked to Mary Dutton. But he had never put the man fully out of mind, and a large-scale moonshining and bootlegging operation was just the sort of thing that would attract Tuttle's attention if he knew about it.

Henry didn't reply. He waited to see if Calvin would say anything more.

"Mr. Henry, please. I'm begging you." Calvin was wringing his hands now. "Mr. Moss ain't making no shine. Somebody brings it to him, and I take it where he tells me. I don't know how he knows where that's supposed to be. He just says it and I do it. Sometimes a couple of other fellows that don't work here comes and picks up some too. Please don't ask me no more. I don't know nothing else about it."

"I've got just one more question. Why did you hide money in the mule collar?"

"So if anybody tried to hijack me or any law stopped me, I wouldn't have any money on me. I got a little slit cut in the side of it. Wouldn't nobody ever think to look there."

"If the law caught you with a crate of shine, you'd be in just as much trouble."

"Yes, sir. I reckon I would far as the law's concerned, but I wouldn't be out somebody else's money."

"All right," Henry said, still holding the sack with the quilt. He reached for the pick and brush, then took hold of Jake's bridle rope and said, "Don't worry. I'm not gon' tell anybody."

Like Isaiah did when he came over to talk, Otis knocked on his neighbor's front porch. It was early in the morning, and Luella Watson opened the front door and stood wiping her hands on her apron.

"Good morning, Mr. Otis," she said. "Isaiah just went out to the barn. He'll be glad to see you."

"Morning, Luella," Otis said, taking off his hat. "He told me y'all have decided to lease. I reckon you know I'm against all this, but I hope for your sake it works out the way you want. I'm not gon' help it along, but I understand how you need it. Y'all have been good neighbors to me, and I won't ever forget all you did for my Alma when she was sick."

"Isaiah and me appreciate that, Mr. Otis."

Otis motioned his hat toward her, plopped it back on his mop of gray hair, and headed for the barn. He found Isaiah in a stall settling under his Guernsey milk cow with a stool and pail.

"Morning, Isaiah," Otis said. "Don't get up. I just come over to tell you what I've done and wish you well."

Isaiah stood up anyway. He would never stay seated in the presence of a standing white man, not even one he had known as long as Otis. "Morning, Mr. Otis," he said, holding the stool in one hand and the pail in the other. "What can I do for you this fine day?"

"Go on about your milking, Isaiah," Otis said. He watched as Isaiah sat down again and began squirting milk, the streams making tinny sounds against the side of the pail. It was a comforting, rewarding sound that both men had experienced and appreciated nearly every day of their adult lives. "Like I just told Luella, I come over to tell you what I've done and say that even though I'm still against all this leasing and drilling business, I understand y'all are doing what you think you have to, and I hope it works out for you the way you need it to. I might get in the way of it some, but if I do, it ain't nothing personal, and I need you to know that."

Isaiah stopped milking and looked up. "What're you talking about, Mr. Otis? What have you done, or what are you about to do?"

Otis clasped his hands together inside the bib of his overalls and said, "You asked me that once before, Isaiah, and I still can't say much, except one thing, 'cause I ain't real sure. What I can tell you is I've taken out a big ad in the newspaper saying what I think all this drilling and such is doing to the land and asking people not to do any more leasing. I want you to know it ain't got nothing to do with you. I also got to tell you that when they start drilling on your land, if they need to come across mine anytime to get to yours, I ain't gon' make it easy for them. I hope you understand I can't just sit by and watch them do something I don't think is right."

"You done already told me that, Mr. Otis," Isaiah responded, "but you don't owe me no explanation." He got up and held out his hand. There wasn't another white man anywhere to whom he would have dared offer a handshake. "We been friends too long, and we done talked this oil mess near 'bout to death anyway. If there's anything me and Luella can do for you, you just let me know. We'll be glad to help."

"As a matter of fact, Isaiah," Otis said, taking Isaiah's hand, "I got to butcher a hog pretty soon, and I could use some company and another strong back. I'll give you half of it."

"You got yourself a deal," Isaiah said, squeezing Otis's hand.

CHAPTER 31

On Thursday morning, the week after the shooting in Hornbeck's, Henry drew an in-town route again. This time, instead of starting at the northern end of Broadway and working his way down the west side, he went from the depot to the south end of town and started from there, working his way up the east side first. He didn't want to put off talking to Mary Dutton again any longer than necessary, and he didn't want to chance missing her at noon time.

The likelihood of seeing her put him in a good mood. He turned onto Eighth Street and pulled into the rear of Mac's Autos to drop off two shipping crates. When the skinny fellow who signed for them asked Henry what he was chuckling about, he said, "Oh, I was just thinking about delivering fuel pumps for automobiles in a wagon powered by four mules running on hay."

The fellow was not amused. "If mule skinners like you didn't keep the streets all tore up," he said, "there'd be a lot more cars and trucks on them."

"You ever stop to think," Henry asked, still in good spirits, "if it wasn't for guys like me and the ones we deliver to out on the wells and all, guys like you might not have jobs?"

"I guess you've got a point there, mister. I ain't ever thought about it like that."

"Yep," Henry said, climbing back on his wagon, "there're some days, though, I'm not sure whether we're making progress or messing up more than we'll ever be able to fix."

After stops at the new telegraph office and a just-opened grocery store, Henry halted his team in front of Hornbeck's even though he didn't have a delivery for it. He hoped there wouldn't be any customers so he could talk to Mary privately, but she and both Hornbecks were helping people, and others were waiting. Henry watched what the customers were buying and looked around for something no one else seemed interested in. He spotted it in one end of the patent medicine cabinet then moved to the center of the store.

After waiting until Mary finished with a customer and was ready for the next one, he stepped forward and said, "Good morning, Mrs. Dutton. Do you have any St. Joseph's Worm Syrup?"

"Yes, Mr. Smith," she said, smiling, curiosity registering in her voice. "We don't get many requests for that, but I believe we have a bottle. Follow me, please." She went behind the counter in front of the patent medicine cabinet, and he walked to the front of it. Mary opened a cabinet door, took out the bottle of worm syrup, and set it on the counter.

Before she could speak, Henry said quickly, "I don't really need that stuff, Mary, although I intend to pay for it. I just wanted a chance to ask you something. If I promise to wash off this oil-field grime, will you go with me to supper and a movie Saturday night?" He didn't know why people in Berrytown called their evening meal "supper" instead of "dinner," but he figured he had better follow custom. "That new American Theater up the street is showing *Robin Hood* with Douglas Fairbanks, and they've got a big new organ.

One of Moss's men delivered it a few days ago. I reckon they gave up on violins and horns and such. Anyway, you can bring Jimmy if you'd like to. I'm guessing you wouldn't want to leave him by himself."

Aware now that he hadn't removed his hat, like he had planned on doing when he came in, Henry yanked it off, mussing his hair and exposing the scar on his forehead. Having seen earlier that he seemed self-conscious about the keloid, Mary kept her eyes on his. He blushed anyway and said, "We can eat at Ralph's Café. It's not fancy, but the food is about the best around."

"Okay, Henry Smith. We'd like that, and Ralph's Café would be fine," Mary said, her eyes sparkling and her dimples widening as she smiled. "Jimmy and I will meet you there."

She said "meet you" with such finality that Henry didn't argue. He was delighted she agreed to go. Maybe, he thought, her wanting to meet him at the restaurant was only her being cautious about him, which wasn't unreasonable, given all the lawlessness in Berrytown. But if she was concerned for her safety, then why, he wondered, would she not want an escort. The answer to that could wait until a later time. He had the one he really wanted, and after they agreed on a time, he left wearing a grin that lasted all day.

~

Otis knew everyone would believe he did this, but no one would be able to prove it. Still, if he did it before his newspaper ad appeared the first time, things might point a little less obviously to him and maybe cause Milo Yeager and his pipeline folks to wring their hands a little harder. Without using the actual word, Otis had written about how stupid oil men were in his estimation. And here, less than two hundred yards away, sitting practically in his front yard, was a perfect example.

For a couple of weeks, Yeager and several helpers, all wearing the same kind of fancy high-laced boots, had been striding back and forth across Otis's farm plotting the course of the pipeline they said was going all the way to Louann and probably on to Stephens. At the same time, others in Yeager's outfit had been accumulating stacks of pipe and piles of other supplies in wooden crates just off the main road. Otis saw it all from his front porch every morning and every evening, and from muleback or from his wagon every time he went into town. It was a growing eyesore and constant reminder of the cesspool of ruination into which oil had thrust him and everything around him that he prized. The same circumstance applied to everyone else within miles around whether they would admit it or not.

Sometimes, however, when a person least expects it, things simply fall into place. Tonight was one of those times. There was dynamite in one of the crates out front. Otis had ridden by when some of Wilbur Moss's mule skinners, Calvin Birdsong among them, were unloading it, handling it gingerly like it was already aging and sweating nitro into the straw packing material. There was also darkness. This was the dimmest night of the month. Not only was the moon in a waning crescent phase, but clouds loomed low in the sky.

Even though there was no one else anywhere close around—that dumb Yeager having not gotten around to posting guards, apparently figuring the court order for the right of way was all he needed to protect his stuff—Otis followed his usual evening routine: chores, supper, coffee on the front porch, early bedtime, then lights out. At one a.m., he slipped out his back door wearing a denim jacket over his overalls and carrying a crowbar, a ball of twine, a pocketknife, a flashlight with a scrap of cloth tied around the end to dim the beam, an empty burlap sack, another filled with straw, strips of burlap, and matches.

He heard one of his hogs rooting around, but the only other sound came from his boots landing in dew on the grass. He didn't own a dog, and Isaiah Watson lived too far away for his dogs to detect anything yet, unless they were roaming around for some reason or other. But even if they were, and started barking, Isaiah wasn't likely to get up and check on them. If someone passed along the road, that person might spot Otis, but it was unlikely that anyone would be out here this time of night in the middle of the week.

Otis took his time and worked carefully once he reached the pipeline staging area. He pried open the box of dynamite and put as many of the eight-inch sticks as he felt he could safely carry into the empty burlap bag, twisted it shut, and tied it off with twine. Then he placed the top back on the crate and carried the bag back up his access road, past his house and barn, and some one hundred fifty yards farther. There, among a stand of fruit trees on the fenced-off site of a dwelling razed before his time, he put the bag in a basket he had made years before from strips of white oak, removed two thick boards among several covering the dry hole of an old water well, picked up a rope he had left there with the basket before supper, tied the rope to the handle of the basket, and lowered the basket carefully into the hole until it rested gently on the bottom. He tied the end of the rope around one of the boards he had removed and slid both back over the well. That done, he covered the boards with half a cord of wood he had cut from nuisance saplings on the old home site a few weeks back and not gotten around to hauling up to his house to split for firewood. Otis didn't know if he would ever want to use this dynamite, but it was there if he did, so long as he used it before too much of the nitroglycerin leaked out of the sorbent material inside the sticks and made them too unstable to handle. He reckoned that if he didn't use it, then sometime down the road he would have to figure a way to detonate it so it didn't accidentally injure someone coming along after him.

Back at the staging area, Otis opened a box labeled "Detonator Caps," took out several one at a time, rolled each up in a burlap strip, and packed them in straw in his second sack. After cutting several lengths of fuse cord from the same crate, he put the remainder into the bag, tied it off, and carried it up to his barn. There, in his feed room, he removed three floorboards, put the sack in an empty wooden nail keg, replaced the keg lid, and lowered the keg into a hole he had dug that afternoon. He put some of the dirt he had saved around the keg, pushed the rest into the center aisle, used a rake to mix it into the powdery soil there, put the floorboards back in place, and scattered spilled feed over them before heading back to the piles of pipeline supplies. He wasn't exactly comfortable with that hiding place even though he didn't believe anyone would find it, so he planned to move the caps to another location sometime later.

Otis had a rudimentary knowledge of dynamite from having used it twice to blow up tree stumps, and he figured he didn't need many sticks to wreak enough havoc to slow Yeager down a bit. Beyond that, Otis didn't really expect what he was about to do would change things much. What all this came down to, he reckoned, was that he didn't like a bunch of oil men getting rich without regard for how they were affecting other people, and he wanted to give at least some of them a taste of his own misery, if only for a little while. And he didn't want to hurt anyone else in the process.

There were three pyramid-like stacks of six-inch pipe and about three dozen crates of other stuff out front. Otis put two sticks of dynamite on the ground between the two center lengths of pipe in each stack and one on each side of the pile of crates. He didn't know whether the blast he set off would detonate the remaining sticks, so he carried them, in their crate, to a small depression in one of his adjoining fields where they would be visible from the road later, assuming they didn't go off.

Otis put a detonating cap linked to fuse cord under the edge of each of the eight sticks and connected those cords to another one and ran it up the access road toward his house as far as it would reach. It dawned on him then that anyone investigating the explosion would likely see a burn trail leading right to him, but he wasn't going to back out now. He checked to make sure he had collected all his tools, then he knelt down, lit the fuse, and ran toward the back of his house as fast as his septuagenarian legs would carry him. He got there just in time to throw himself behind the stone casing of his current water well before the blast.

He had halfway expected to blow the windows out of his house, on the front side at least, but although the blast was louder than he anticipated, the force of it went down and up with relatively little push outward. He felt the shock wave, but his house and other structures appeared undamaged from what he could see. His livestock were stressed, though, and let him know about it with their snorting, braying, and wailing.

He got up, went inside, and lit two lamps, like he normally might if awakened by some kind of disturbance. Then he went through the house, picked up his shotgun from the front hall, also like he normally would, and went onto the front porch.

What was left of the wooden crates was on fire, and light from the blaze showed lengths of pipe lying in a jumble crossways of each other, some bent crooked and some split open on one end. The dynamite he had moved into the field was undetonated as far as he could determine from the porch.

After admiring his handiwork for a few moments, Otis went inside, brewed a pot of coffee, and took a cup back onto the porch to wait for whoever and whatever was coming.

CHAPTER 32

Remnants of the wooden crates were still burning when Isaiah Watson, having cut across fields in the dark, stumbled into Otis's front yard breathing hard.

"Praise God!" Isaiah said, when he saw Otis sitting on the porch uninjured. "I was afraid I was gon' find you bad hurt." He had on overalls over a night shirt. One shoulder strap hung unfastened.

"I'm fine, Isaiah," Otis said. "Come on up here, and I'll get you a cup of coffee."

"You know I can't come up there, Mr. Otis. You bound to have a bunch of white people out here pretty quick. They likely gon' be het up enough as it is." He looked around at the fire and the pipe lying all cockeyed. "Don't tell me you went and done what it looks like."

"Okay, I won't tell you. Like I said the other day, there's some things you're better off not knowing. I'm glad you come over, though. I got something I meant to bring you the other day."

Otis went inside and came back with an envelope in his hand. He went down the steps and handed it to Isaiah. "I've made out a will. Had one of them shifty new lawyers in town draw it up all legal and proper, fellow name of Davis. He's got a copy and I want you to hold onto one for me. I don't know if I can trust Davis to do the right thing with it if something happens to me, but I know I can trust you to give this copy to the main beneficiary and tell anybody who asks you that I gave it to you on this here day to hold onto. I also know you won't open it and read it till I'm dead."

Isaiah looked in Otis's eyes for a moment then took the envelope. "Now I know you done this," Isaiah said, gesturing behind him. "And you're right, I don't want to know nothing about it or what else you got in mind. You already got yourself in a heap of trouble."

"Maybe, maybe not," Otis said. "Anyway, right now I'm planning on butchering a hog Monday morning if you can help me then."

"I'll be here at sunup. I hope you are too."

~

Explosions occurred often enough around Berrytown—wells blowing in, stumps being dynamited, and more—that after a while, most people ignored them, especially during daylight hours. Nighttime was another matter. Otis's big boom attracted enough attention that by daybreak he had callers.

Milo Yeager stopped his yellow Packard next to what was left of his pipeline supplies and got out with two other men. They walked around a bit then stood with their hands on their hips looking up at Otis's house. A fourth man remained in the front passenger seat. Yeager went around and talked to him, then everyone climbed back aboard. Yeager steered the Packard, its headlights still missing, up Otis's access road and stopped well short of the porch. Otis saw then that the fourth man was Amos Burns. The portly constable hauled himself out of the car and trudged up to the porch. Yeager and the other two men remained in the vehicle.

"You boys are up and around awful early, ain't you, Amos?" Otis asked. "What can I do for you?"

"You can tell me what the hell happened out yonder," Burns said.

Otis took a sip of coffee and rested the cup on his knee. "Well, there was some kind of explosion. Sure made a mess. Scared my stock near out of their hides. I expect my cow won't give milk for a month."

"I can see that, you dadblamed old goat. You're the one did it, ain't you?"

"Now, Amos, is that how you do your job? Go 'round accusing folks of doing stuff when you ain't got no reason to? You ain't got no jurisdiction out here, anyway."

"I got plenty of reason, Otis, and you know it. You told Yeager you was gon' stop his pipeline one way or another." Burns took off his hat, beat it against one leg like it was dusty and put it back on his head. "But you're right, I ain't got no authority here. Sheriff Linsday has, though, and I reckon he's gon' be out here pretty soon. I came with Yeager mainly to keep you from shooting at him again."

"Well," Otis said, "I'm not gon' shoot the bastard unless he starts shooting at me. I guess I ought to feel sorry for him, seeing how stupid he was, leaving all that stuff just sitting out there with nobody watching it. You tell him there's a half-full crate of his dynamite just over that rise in my field yonder. Tell him I need him to get it off my property before somebody comes along and sets it off for fun or something."

Burns looked where Otis was pointing. "How do you know it's out there? I'm pretty sure you can't see it from that porch any more than I can from down here."

"I saw it this morning. You think I didn't come out and look around when that crap blew up?"

"I'll tell you what I think. I think you blew that stuff up, and I think Sheriff Lindsay's gon' come out here and haul your ass off to jail."

Otis got up and walked to the edge of the porch. "Lindsay can come on out here if he wants to, but he ain't gon' find nothing that says I did this. Now, why don't you and ole priss boots out there just go on back to town and leave me alone."

Burns shook his head, walked back to the Packard, and hoisted himself in. "Turn this thing around and let's go," he said to Yeager.

"That's it?" Yeager yelled. "That's all you're gon' do?"

"Yeah, you knucklehead." Burns said. "Ain't nobody ever gon' find out who did this."

Yeager turned the car around, drove back down the access road, and stopped near the rubble. The two men in the back got out and headed across Otis's field toward where Burns was pointing.

After Hornbeck's closed Saturday evening, Mary stood behind her hanging bedsheet fumbling with the buttons on her blouse and trying to ignore the queasiness in her stomach. What had she been thinking when she accepted Henry Smith's invitation to supper and a movie? She knew nothing about him except he was good looking and seemed charming in a shy sort of way. He carried a gun, and two of the few times she had seen him were occasions of violence. There was also that thing about her reminding him of his sister. He said that wasn't why he wanted to see her, but still, it was a bit unsettling.

Then there was that "Charity Girl" thing she had read about in magazines on the newsstand and not thought about before she said yes. Single women who worked as clerks and secretaries in northern cities, especially during the Great War, and allowed men to buy them food and tickets to events, were often accused of taking charity in return for sexual favors. Even labeled prostitutes. What if people here, including Mrs. Gordon and other women who brought her sewing, thought that about her simply because she accepted supper and a movie from one of the new men in town? Plus, she had heard some church ladies complaining in the drugstore about what they called "animal dances"—the Charleston, Fox Trot, Shimmy, and others they considered vulgar. She wasn't going dancing with Henry, but what if, despite what he told her about that one time in Big Sally's, he turned out to be the sort of man who hung out in barrelhouses?

"Momma, come on," Jimmy said. He was sitting on the side of his cot. Getting dressed for him had only been a matter of washing his face and putting on a clean shirt. "We'll be late."

And that was another thing. Bringing Jimmy along. He was a good boy, but he would be bored silly, except at the movie, which wouldn't be over until well past his bedtime. She didn't want to leave him home by himself, though.

~

Henry thought he would never get the oil stink washed off in the make-shift cold-water shower he had set up outside the fence near one of the back corral watering troughs. He hadn't asked permission to do it, but Moss hadn't said anything about it, probably because some of the other drivers were using it occasionally too.

Mary Dutton had smiled and said yes when Henry asked her to go to supper and a movie, but now he wondered if she would really show up, and if she did, what they would talk about, especially with her son present. Was it even fair of him to have invited her? He hadn't even told her his real name. She was likely to ask him where he was from. Was he going to lie about that too? What if she asked him if he'd been in the war? That seemed likely since she mentioned that her husband had been killed in the National Guard. His time in the army wasn't anything he wanted to talk about. What could he say in response that would be appropriate and not rude?

"There you are," Henry called, emerging from the edge of a bunch of folks milling around in front of Ralph's Café, some leaving it, some trying to decide whether to get in line, some trying to break in line, and some simply loitering. He waved at Mary and Jimmy. They were in front of Hornbeck's, coming up the plank walkway. "Looks like we're gon' have to wait a while to get in," he said, walking toward them. "I didn't know whether to get a place in line or stand out here and watch for you."

"Good evening to you, too, Mr. Smith," Mary said, grinning. Her dark wool coat was open, its belt tied loosely in front. Beneath it she had on a white square-necked blouse and black pleated skirt.

Distracted by her appearance and the glint in her eyes, Henry struggled with what to say. "I'm sorry. I was worrying about the lines. Allow me to start over. Good evening to you, too, Mrs. Dutton and Mr. Jimmy. May I say that you both look stunning." He grimaced, wondering if his choice of words seemed too forward.

"We thank you, sir," Mary said, smiling at both the compliment and the way Henry put it.

"Momma made that blouse and skirt," Jimmy said, trying to get in on the conversation. "She's real good at sewing." He looked up at her admiringly.

Mary blushed. "Sometimes boys talk when they should be listening. But he's right, I did." She was glad Jimmy hadn't told how the coat she was wearing once belonged to her mother and how she trimmed the bottom to make it a fashionable length and used the pieces to make a new wide collar. "But since he brought up clothes," she said, "let me apologize for not wearing a hat. I don't own one."

Henry glanced down at his denim jacket and his khaki shirt and pants. "No need," he said. "Look at me. I don't own anything but work clothes."

"You look fine, Henry Smith," Mary said, looping her bad arm in his. "Maybe we better get in line."

~

"The movie was great, wasn't it, Momma?" Jimmy asked, as he and Mary walked around the corner of Broadway and Seventh Street to get to their shed behind the drugstore. Henry had wanted to walk them home. He said that's what gentlemen do. But Mary insisted that she and Jimmy didn't need escorting, and Henry didn't press her. Looking back, she remembered that he had never said where he lived either.

"Yes, Jimmy, it was. I'm glad you liked it," Mary said.

"Henry's a lot like Robin Hood, ain't he, Momma?"

"How's that?"

"Don't you remember, Momma? Henry stopped them men from hanging that Negro, and he saved me from getting shot that day in the store. He's brave."

"I remember, Jimmy."

"He knows Uncle Gramps too. You didn't know that, did you?"

"No, but Henry's job takes him all over. He meets all sorts of folks." She wondered why Henry hadn't mentioned Otis's newspaper ad. Maybe he hadn't seen it, but it seemed like just about everyone else had, and was talking about it.

Mother and son turned off Seventh Street and reached the back door of the shed. "I'm glad you had a good time, Jimmy," Mary said, unlocking the door, "but I think we've had enough talk about Mr. Smith. It's way past time to get to sleep."

After they made their nightly preparations, Mary lay on her cot worrying about Jimmy getting too fascinated with Henry and whether she had done the right thing seeing him. She wondered why in the world she had told him so much about where she grew up and about her husband Andy. Those were private things, and here she had told them to someone who was practically a total stranger. And he had not told her much about himself at all, other than he had grown up on a farm in the Midwest and been in the army during the war. He hadn't even said where in the Midwest, and she had been reluctant to ask. She sensed he didn't want her to know. That had seemed odd at the time, and looking back on it now, she decided he must be hiding something. Which was scary to think about, although it was also intriguing. He had talked a lot about mules, however. An awful lot. Remembering how passionate he seemed about them brought a smile to her face.

~

Henry lay on his pallet in the barn going over the same things that had gnawed on him all the way back from the movie theater. How stupid he had acted when Mary and Jimmy arrived at Ralph's Café. How they had to wait a long time to get inside. How much Mary had shared about her early life and how little about her current one, and how hard it was for him to keep from telling her things about himself that might give away who he was and why he had come to Berrytown. He wished he had persisted about walking her home. Even though she insisted that she and Jimmy go alone, not going with them seemed wrong. If something had happened to them after he left them, he would never forgive himself. He should at least have followed them discreetly to make sure no harm came to them. Clearly, she didn't want him to know where they lived, and he wondered why. Was she hiding something? Or was she only being cautious about someone she hardly knew?

Henry also wondered how to interpret her response as they said goodnight. When he asked her if she would like to do this again sometime, her words seemed deliberately vague: "Thank you for asking. Jimmy and I had a really good time." Henry wasn't convinced they did, but he knew he had.

CHAPTER 33

After a restless night, Henry woke up on Sunday morning with a different kind of social engagement to keep. While delivering rotary bits and other equipment to a new drill site near Louann the week before, he had run into Cotton Taylor, whose family and Model T he had pulled out of a creek after getting lost trying to find Otis Leatherwood's place the first time. Following up on Sarah Taylor's parting declaration that she would bake a pie for Henry if he would come to dinner sometime, Cotton had insisted that he come today.

There were now so many people in and around Berrytown, both in Union County and in Ouachita County, and living quarters were in such short supply, that the three railroads serving the area—the Missouri Pacific, the Rock Island, and the El Dorado & Wesson—ran multiple passenger trains, sometimes with up to a dozen cars each, back and forth between not only El Dorado and Berrytown, but also to places southwest of Berrytown like Wesson and Cargile, southeast like Norphlet, and west like Griffin, Louann, and Kirkland. The Missouri Pacific ran two trains a day westward even on Sunday because drilling and well tending never ceased.

Henry saw and heard trains every day and was thinking about them broadly as he walked to the station. Railroads across the country were just coming out of another contentious labor dispute, worse than anything since the Pullman car workers' strike of 1894. The newspapers had been full of it. This time it had been repair and maintenance workers going on strike. When conductors, brakemen, and engineers refused to respect the shop workers' picket lines, frayed nerves produced so many violent clashes that the governors of several states in the North and Midwest called out the National Guard to restore order. With tensions now eased, trains were running again everywhere, not just in oil country. Even the Pullman Car Company, so devastated by the previous round of railroad labor trouble, was building on the enormous financial turnaround it had begun a few years back. In addition to Pullman cars, it was manufacturing thousands of automobile bodies for Packard Motors. Probably, Henry mused, Pullman built the body of the Packard that Otis Leatherwood shot up.

Remembering that day put a smile on Henry's face as he reached the Missouri Pacific platform moments before the train for Louann pulled in, steam from its lowering engine pressure warming the chilled air. Like every morning, men carrying metal pails and hinged boxes filled with biscuits, sausages, sandwiches, and such stood in clusters, killing time smoking, spitting, and talking, likely spinning lies as much as sharing truths. Henry boarded with a bulky package wrapped in newsprint tied with string saved from feed sacks. Several women with children got aboard, too, as well as a few men who had come in from outlying camps and spent Saturday night at Big Sally's, one of Berrytown's pool halls, or one of several other establishments happy to separate them from their weekly wages.

Cotton was waiting for Henry at the Louann depot, hat in hand with his thick white hair fluttering in the morning breeze. They greeted each other and shortly gave up trying to talk as Cotton's Model T bounced them around on a deeply rutted road to a campsite about a mile and a half southwest of town. Henry held his package with both hands so it wouldn't shake out of the open-sided vehicle.

Several good-sized tents and a few tent houses sat haphazardly in a copse of partially denuded hickory and oak trees thinned out for space and firewood. The ground was black with fallout from wells that had blown in not far away, and there wasn't a bush or a blade of grass, or even a weed, in sight. Cast iron wash pots, two feet and more in diameter, sat on squat legs or hung from iron rods near each dwelling, and wire clothes lines stretched between some trees. The air bore the sour smell of sulfur. Henry had passed many such camps all around Berrytown over the last few months. They were primitive, but better than what many newcomers found themselves settling for.

Cotton pulled up next to an eight-by-twelve-foot dwelling consisting of a raised plank floor with wooden sideboards three feet high and a canvas tent above that. A tin stove pipe stuck up through an open flap in the center of the peaked roof.

"Welcome to our home," Cotton said, as he killed the engine.

Henry got out and stood with his package under one arm. "So this is where you live," he said, awkwardly. "How is it?"

Before Cotton could answer, Sarah Taylor, an angular woman of medium height stepped through a pulled-back flap at the near end of the tent house. She was wearing a housedress and a feed-sack apron, and she pushed a strand of brown hair away from her face as she walked over to the men.

"I'm so glad Cotton persuaded you to come," she said. "Our girls still talk about how your mules pulled us out of that creek, and I've baked a sweet potato pie just for you." She stuck out her arm for a handshake, and called, "Nell, Ruth, come say hello to Mr. Smith."

The girls, who looked to be about four and six, appeared in the doorway, jumped to the ground, and ran to their mother, stopping short of Henry. He greeted them and wished he had brought some sort of gift for them. Both grinned and said, "Hi, Mr. Smith," in voices so quiet he could barely hear them.

"Come on inside," Sarah said. "It'll be a little crowded, but we'll manage."

She turned to enter, and Cotton touched Henry on the elbow and said, "Please, go ahead. I'll bring the girls."

Henry did as he was asked, his eyes darting around the single room as he stepped through the doorway. A cast-iron stove sat in the middle of the floor. Wires suspended from the cross bar holding up the tent kept the four-inch tin stove pipe from touching the sides of the flap hole above. About ten inches above the stove, the pipe seemed to pass through a metal cylinder measuring about a foot-and-a-half by ten inches. It was mounted with the long side parallel to the flat stove top and had a door in the end. Henry hadn't seen anything like it before.

A full-size mattress sat on a raised board platform at the far end of the room. Several suitcases were stacked at one end, and a rocking chair sat in front of them. Two short pallets rested on a smaller platform along the wall on one side of the stove. A large flat-top trunk stood end-to-end with the platform. Bunched mosquito netting hung from the cross pole near each platform, tied back with string to nails in the wall boards. Opposite the working side of the stove, four wooden crates, stacked two on two, held kitchen ware and cooking supplies. A small table and two straight chairs stood between the stove and the entrance. Another crate in a front corner held a large porcelain bowl. Henry guessed it served both as a wash basin and dish sink.

Sarah went at once to tend to pots on top of the stove, and Nell and Ruth rushed to the back and plopped onto what obviously was their parents' bed. Each of them had a handmade rag doll there. The bed was covered with a quilt Henry could tell was made from feed and flour sacks. A similar quilt was doubled over the two pallets on the smaller platform.

"I hope you don't mind if it's a little cramped when we eat," Cotton said, "but food out here tastes better if we eat inside where we can shut out some of the smell. We're borrowing another chair from a neighbor, and I'm just gon' step out and fetch it. The girls don't need chairs. They sit on their pallets to eat. Have a seat there, and I'll be right back." He paused in the doorway. "Sarah, tell Henry about that new oven we just got from Sears, Roebuck."

Henry sat down at the table and held his package on his lap.

Sarah looked around at him. "I hope you like sweet potato pie," she said. "I got some potatoes off a peddler that came through here a couple of days ago. Traded a flour-sack apron for them. I've got a little table-top sewing machine that comes in its own little wooden case, and I make up aprons from sacks and scraps and use them to barter for stuff. It's right smart fun."

Henry looked at the stack of suitcases, trying to pick out the one with the sewing machine.

"Traded with another peddler for this chicken," Sarah said. "We're gon' have chicken and dumplings, by the way. I've been looking forward to cooking on the stove and baking at the same time. This barrel-looking thing above the burners is my new oven. Cotton ordered it for me first thing when we got here. It's got one barrel inside another one, and the heat from the stove goes up the pipe and around the little barrel and heats up the inside of it before going on out the chimney. Ain't that just the smartest thing you ever saw?"

"Yes, I reckon it is," Henry said, being polite.

Cotton came back with the extra chair, and Sarah ordered him and Henry outside so she could finish getting dinner on the table. Henry put his package on the floor next to the door and followed Cotton outside. They stood around the car talking about automobiles for a few minutes until Sarah called them back inside.

During dinner, Henry asked Cotton about his work and where they had lived before, and Cotton talked about all the places they had set up housekeeping in Texas and Louisiana, going where the latest oil finds led them. Henry told stories about things he had seen around different parts of the Berrytown field while driving for Moss. Cotton's curiosity about those other drilling operations kept him and Sarah from asking Henry many personal questions, and Henry deflected those that did arise. Cotton said they were thinking about moving on to Oklahoma sometime early next year, then went on about it for a long while. The same buddy who had encouraged him to come to Berrytown had already gone to Tonkawa, up in Indian country well northwest of Tulsa, and written that it was the place to be. Sarah never said how she regarded moving around so much, and Henry didn't ask. He noticed, though, that the couple and their girls seemed happy, and this made him think about his family when he was a kid running around in knickers.

Henry almost forgot about his package until it was time to leave for the train station and return trip to Berrytown. He handed it to Sarah. “From looking around here, I’m guessing you don’t need this, but I wanted to bring you something to thank you for dinner. This was given to me, and I thought it deserved a better home.”

Having already cleared the table, Sarah laid the package on it, untied the string, and pulled back the newspapers. “Oh, my! What a lovely quilt,” she said, unfolding it. Henry watched as she ran her fingers over it. “Do you know what it’s called?” she asked.

“No, I don’t know much about quilts. I was around them a lot as a kid, but I wasn’t interested in them. Like I said, someone gave me this one, but I’ve never used it. I prefer blankets.”

“It’s called a Nine Patch,” Sarah said, continuing to unfold it. “It’s unusual, though, ‘cause the corners are stuffed so full of batting they’re all stiff. Anyway, I like it. We don’t need it right now, but we sure do thank you. A body can’t ever tell what might happen down the road. We might need it for a little Cotton sometime.”

CHAPTER 34

"You're sleeping somewhere else tonight, Grover," Eunice Hornbeck said, tossing a pillow and a blanket toward him late Sunday evening. "I don't want you near me. You worry like somebody that's got one foot in the grave, and I'm tired of it. That Treasury man hasn't come back since that one time, and he's not going to. I already told you Floyd Roper agreed with me when he brought that new inventory Monday. The man that talked to Mary was just making a routine visit."

Eunice started for bed then came back into the living room, where they had been arguing since finishing supper. Grover was sitting in a flat-armed wooden rocking chair fiddling with a briar pipe and a can of tobacco he had brought home from the store the day before. Newspapers lay scattered on the floor around him, the blanket and pillow now covering some of them.

"And put that pipe away," Eunice added. "You don't smoke."

"I'm gon' start," Grover said. He held up the can as if seeing it for the first time. "I like the way this Half and Half smells. It's sweet. One of the fellows was smoking it at the meeting yesterday."

"That's another thing," Eunice said, hands folded across her chest, staring down at her husband. "Why'd you let them talk you into serving as a delegate to the county? If Judge Kimbrew approves that committee petition, we're gon' end up with a police force in place of Constable Burns, and Roper's not gon' like that. You shouldn't even have signed the darned thing."

"I had to sign it, Eunice." Grover managed to get some tobacco into the pipe and started tramping it down with his forefinger. "All the other merchants did. It wouldn't have looked good if I didn't. Besides, there's a lot of benefits to getting Berrytown incorporated. We'll have a mayor, and we'll have a council that can levy taxes to fix up the streets, maybe even get some street lighting."

"Yeah, and we'll have police. You're already worrying about Treasury agents catching us selling illegal drugs. What if the federal men get the police to help watch us?"

"I don't think the Treasury men operate that way," Grover said. "There's nothing like that in anything I've read about them in the papers." He struck a match and attempted to light the pipe.

"Grover, do you hear yourself? One minute you're sure we're gon' end up in jail, and the next minute you're 'Mr. Upstanding Citizen' thinking about how much better life's gon' be if the town's incorporated. You're afraid of Treasury agents, but you don't mind a bunch of police running around. Even if they didn't tip off the federal men about us, they'd still probably scare away customers. You're not making any sense."

Having failed on his first attempt, Grover struck another match and tried again to ignite the Half and Half. Again, he failed. He looked around to see if Eunice was still standing there glaring at him. She was.

"Well, I don't care what you think," Grover said. "I'm going with the committee to see the judge. And if he approves the petition, then there'll be an election to see if people who've lived here long enough to vote approve it, and if they do, then we'll be a real town."

"Yeah, and how many people is that? Less than a hundred that're old enough to vote, I bet."

"Maybe, but it'll still be legal, and the town council can tax everybody. Do you know how many folks are living here now? It's at least ten thousand. Probably more."

"And we'll be taxed too. Have you thought about that? I swear, Grover, sometimes I don't know why I ever married you! I'm going to bed."

When the door slammed behind her, Grover struck another match, and this time he succeeded in lighting the pipe. He took a long draw, blew out the smoke, and launched into a bout of coughing. When he stopped, he said loud enough for Eunice to hear, "I'm beginning to get the idea you did it for my money."

A second later, glass shattered against the other side of the bedroom door.

~

Dawn was breaking, but the sun was still not visible in the eastern sky when Isaiah Watson arrived at Otis Leatherwood's place on Monday morning. Isaiah could see the old farmer clearly out behind his barn, however. Under a huge black walnut tree, a fire was going beneath a lidless, new fifty-five-gallon drum sitting on top of two double rows of bricks laid side to side and stacked four high. Two buckets stood on the ground a few feet back from the drum. Isaiah assumed it was filled with water. Several feet above the top of the drum, a pulley was tied to a tree limb big as a man's thigh. A three-foot-long wooden singletree, used normally for hitching a mule or horse to a plow to balance the pull, hung from the pulley on a rope long enough to reach around the trunk of the walnut tree several times. A few feet from the drum, Otis was on his knees nailing boards across two small pine logs to make a low platform about five feet square.

"Morning, Mr. Otis," Isaiah said, walking toward him. Skipping the usual additional pleasantries, he asked, "Where'd you get the drum?"

Otis stopped hammering and looked up at his visitor. "Morning to you, too, neighbor. If you have to know, I stole it. Figured it was time I got something useful outa all this oil mess."

The comment left Isaiah speechless for a moment. He hooked his hands into the top of his bib overalls. "Aw, Mr. Otis, you joshing me, ain't you? You didn't go and get yourself in more trouble, did you?"

"Wasn't no trouble," Otis said. "When I come in on the train the other day, I saw a bunch of these sitting way over behind the depot, and the next evening I just drove my wagon over there and helped myself to one. Like I said, I figured I was owed."

"Oh, my," Isaiah said. "I just don't know what the good Lord's gon' do with you. It's already taking me an extra half hour of praying every night just trying to get Him to even think about letting you through the pearly gates."

Otis laid down his hammer and stood up. "Isaiah, if I had known you was spending that much time talking to Him about me, I would've got a drum for you too. Come on, help me with the hog. I done got him penned up. I figure he weighs near onto two hundred fifty pounds."

Otis walked over to the pen, shot the hog in his forehead, and cut his jugular to drain his blood. When the bleeding stopped, the two men dragged the hog over to the drum of hot water. They used a knife to expose the tendons in the hind legs, slipped the iron hooks on each end of the singletree into the tendons, hoisted the carcass up, and lowered it into the scalding water to loosen the hair on the hide.

When Otis thought they had waited long enough, but not so long that the hair would set to the hide and never come off, they pulled the hog out, maneuvered it onto the platform and began scraping the hair off using knives with dull blades so that they didn't cut into the carcass. They had to dunk it one more time and then splash boiling water over places where they had missed hair the first time around.

Once they had all the hair off, they strung the carcass up again, removed the head and were getting ready to remove the innards, when Union County Sheriff Herbert Lindsay, having walked upon them unheard, said, "That's a good-looking porker you've got there, Mr. Leatherwood."

Startled, Otis jerked back his slitting knife, turned around, looked Lindsay over for a long minute, and noted his badge and the gun belt pulled around his girth. Then, remembering him from his last visit, Otis asked, "You make a habit of sneaking up on folks, do you, Sheriff? You near 'bout made me ruin this hog. I almost cut into the gut sack. You do know that would've spoiled the meat, don't you?"

Isaiah, who had been holding the carcass still for Otis, wanted no part of an argument between two white men, especially when one of them was a sheriff. He eased over to the walnut tree out of Lindsay's line of sight.

"You mean like you ruined Mr. Yeager's pipeline supplies?" the sheriff asked.

Otis lowered the knife. "I'm not sure I know what you're talking about, Sheriff. You accusing me of something?"

"Mr. Yeager thinks you're the one that set off the dynamite. I think you are, too, 'cause you as much as threatened to do something like that last time I was out here." Lindsay slipped his thumbs into his belt and waited for Otis's response, but Otis didn't say anything. The sheriff looked toward Isaiah. "You, there, nigger," Lindsay said, "come out here where I can see you good."

Isaiah removed his straw hat and stepped out beside the hanging carcass.

"Sheriff," Otis said, "this is Reverend Isaiah Watson. He's my neighbor and my friend, and you ain't got no cause to be talking to him like that. You can apologize right now, or you can get your sorry ass off my property."

Lindsay took a step toward Otis and said, "Mr. Leatherwood, you're the one better think about how he's talking. You're in trouble enough already, and if I want to call that black son-of-a-bitch a 'nigger,' I'll damn well do it." The sheriff looked back at Isaiah. "Boy, you know anything about the explosion that blew up them pipeline supplies?"

"No, sir, Sheriff, I don't," Isaiah said.

"Figures," the sheriff said. "How much of that hog is he giving you to keep your mouth shut?"

"I'm giving him half of it for helping me butcher it," Otis said, still holding the slitting knife, "and if you don't get outta our way and let us get on with it, we ain't gon' be able to get done. I already told Constable Burns all I got to say about the explosion, so you just as well leave me be."

"I'm gon' have to look around before I leave. You don't mind that, do you?"

"You can look all you want so long as you stay outta my house and don't bother my stock."

Lindsay crossed his arms over his chest. "You know I can get a search warrant for the house, don't you?"

"Well, if you do, you better bring some help when you come back, 'cause I ain't letting you in there. It's just like my Alma left it when she passed, and I ain't gon' have nobody tracking through it." With that, Otis turned back to the carcass and began gutting it.

The sheriff, unaccustomed to being challenged like that by anyone, stared at Otis's back for a few seconds, then stalked off toward the barn.

"Mr. Otis, you sure you ought to be talking to him like that?" Isaiah asked, when the sheriff was out of earshot.

"He ain't gon' find nothing, and he ain't gon' do nothing," Otis said. "I'm just sorry about how he talked to you."

"That ain't nothing new, Mr. Otis. Ain't nothing new at all. Stuff like that's why me and Luella want to leave. I just got a feeling that things are gon' get worse. All these new people coming in, white and colored both, and all these barrelhouses and prostitutes, black and white. Moonshine all over the place just like there wasn't no law against it. All kinds of money floating around. Everything all tore up like you been saying. It's got folks all het up. They're almost like one of them sticks of dynamite you say you don't know nothing about."

CHAPTER 35

Each weekday morning during the third week of October, like every other forenoon, Jimmy Dutton stood on first one corner of Broadway and then another hawking the *Arkansas Gazette* before school. He also hawked it Saturdays and Sundays, along with the *Berrytown Journal*.

This week, Jimmy's job was harder than usual, but he was enjoying it more. He was earning extra money advertising the Alexander P. Whitlock Show, a traveling carnival out of Denison, Texas, boasting rides, games, sideshows, and a twelve-piece brass band. An advance man for the outfit had spotted Jimmy soon after getting off the train one morning and hired him on the spot.

Like always, Jimmy called out newspaper headlines between sales. Only, now he added news of the carnival and passed out handbills at the same time. Juggling it all was a challenge, but he was getting twenty-five cents a day for the extra work and hoping his mother would allow him to spend some of it on rides and games.

"More gushers in Norphlet! Yankees win World Series! Carnival coming to Berrytown!" he cried, holding up a single newspaper in one hand while keeping the other arm wrapped around the rest, along with the handbills. "More gushers in Norphlet! Yankees win World Series! Carnival coming to Berrytown!"

Jimmy knew that new wells at Norphlet, six miles southeast of Berrytown, would bring more people to the area, and that it was important. He also knew that after setting a new Major League home run record by hitting 59 round-trippers, Babe Ruth had led John McGraw's New York Yankees to a second consecutive World Series victory over Miller Huggins' New York Giants. As one customer exclaimed, that was "the bees' knees." But it was the carnival story that interested Jimmy most. It was coming the very next weekend, and there was even going to be a daredevil lady motorcyclist riding in something called a "motordrome."

Despite Jimmy's shouted sales pitches, however, neither paper carried the two most important pieces of local news outside oil leasing and drilling.

The entire week was a time of organizing in Berrytown, even though most residents were unaware of it. Most were too busy keeping themselves fed and housed, while others were spending whatever off hours they had in barrelhouses, pool halls, theaters, and back rooms playing cards and shooting craps.

Those who were doing the organizing fell into two groups. Both believed they were doing what they were for the good of the entire town. Each wanted to improve what they called "public safety."They had widely different ideas about what that meant and how to go about it, though.

The first group included the committee of community leaders—mostly businessmen like Grover Hornbeck, but also the Baptist and Methodist ministers—who had petitioned the county judge for permission to incorporate Berrytown. This group also included the hundred or so residents who had lived there long enough to be eligible to vote and had done so, approving incorporation by three to one. These organizers had scheduled an election for mayor and town council, but so far, they had not found anyone willing to run for the higher office.

The second group of organizers was larger by half, numbering more than one hundred fifty. They had also gotten up a petition, but theirs had gone to Little Rock, to the state headquarters of the Ku Klux Klan. Like the other group's petition to incorporate the town, this group's petition was also approved. It secured a charter for a Berrytown Klavern of the KKK. These organizers' only problem was waiting for all the Klan paraphernalia they ordered to arrive.

Time seemed to drag on for both groups.

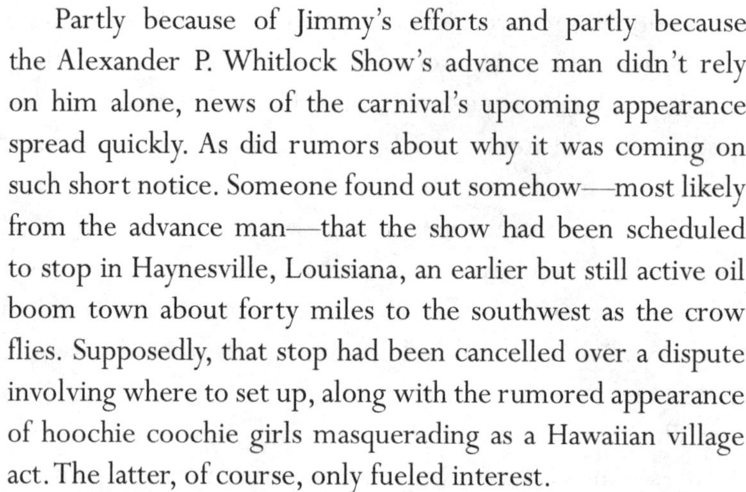

Partly because of Jimmy's efforts and partly because the Alexander P. Whitlock Show's advance man didn't rely on him alone, news of the carnival's upcoming appearance spread quickly. As did rumors about why it was coming on such short notice. Someone found out somehow—most likely from the advance man—that the show had been scheduled to stop in Haynesville, Louisiana, an earlier but still active oil boom town about forty miles to the southwest as the crow flies. Supposedly, that stop had been cancelled over a dispute involving where to set up, along with the rumored appearance of hoochie coochie girls masquerading as a Hawaiian village act. The latter, of course, only fueled interest.

Henry Grant, alias Henry Smith, overheard some of Wilbur Moss's other mule skinners talking about the carnival then saw a handbill that one of them tacked up on the front barn. "Coming! Coming! Coming!" screamed the banner headline across the top. After thinking about it all the next day as he alternately navigated narrow roads and sat waiting to cross crowded creek and branch bridges over toward Norphlet, Henry decided that the show was a good excuse to try to see Mary Dutton again.

That evening after he finished tending to his team, Henry told Moss he needed to stop by one of the drugstores for some tonic before making a freight run the next day.

"Hornbeck's?" Moss asked.

"Yeah, it's the best one," Henry said.

"I figured. But you don't look to me like you need any tonic, lessen it's the kind you get from talking to a pretty woman that's selling it. Ain't that 'bout the size of it?"

"What makes you say that?" Henry asked, afraid that Moss would assign him to a route that didn't leave enough time to swing by the store.

"Just a hunch. I know who clerks at that place, and you've been acting a little discombobulated lately. Women will do that to you."

~

"Step right up, gents and boys! Knock over the bottles and win a prize for your lady! Three throws for a dime! Three chances to win!" the grifter called. "You don't have to be Babe Ruth! Anybody can do it! Three balls for ten cents! Step right up!"

Henry, Mary, and Jimmy stood near the back of a dozen or so onlookers watching player after player try the game and fail. A row of five sets of what looked like painted milk bottles sat on a low plank bench about ten feet back from the open end of a dirty, three-sided tent. Each set of bottles formed a pyramid, one bottle balancing on top of two others. One bottle, and sometimes two, would fall from thrown balls, but almost never three.

Mary and Jimmy were each eating a stick of cotton candy, a first for both. "I bet none of them fellows ever played baseball," Jimmy said between melting mouthfuls. "I bet I can do it. Can I try, Momma?"

He looked up at Henry. "Me and Robert Watson have played lots. We made us a ball out of some wore-out socks, and his daddy cut us a limb and whittled it for a bat. Can I, Momma? You said I could spend fifty cents however I wanted."

"You'd rather spend a dime on that than on a ride?" Mary asked. Henry watched as she laid her hand lovingly on Jimmy's shoulder then brushed a bit of string sugar off one side of her mouth. These simple acts done so tenderly in the first instance and so unselfconsciously in the second tugged at his heart.

"I want to win one of them bird statues for our room," Jimmy said.

"I don't know, Jimmy. It looks really hard," Mary said, trying to talk him out of it instead of flat out refusing his request.

"Mary," Henry said, turning so that only she could see him wink, "I was thinking about giving those bottles a shot myself, but on second thought, since Jimmy's an experienced ball player, would you mind if I hired him to have a go at it for me?"

Mary's smile was worth many times more than the dime Henry was about to lose. He fished in his pocket for ten cents, and by the time he came up with it, Jimmy had finished his cotton candy and was wearing a huge grin.

"Take your time and aim for that open space just below the top bottle, right between the tops of the other two," Henry said, handing Jimmy the money. As the boy walked over to the grifter, a skinny fellow wearing a flat cap and a faded apron with deep pockets, Henry told Mary, "He won't win unless the grifter lets him in order to suck in more players. If you'd like, I'll explain that to him when he comes back. It's not quite as serious a come down as learning there's no Santa Claus."

Mary, who had on the same coat, blouse, and skirt she wore when they went to Ralph's for supper, watched Jimmy walk away, then smiled and said, "Yes, I'd appreciate that. He needs to know some people are like that."

Henry nodded and forced himself not to keep staring into her sparkling eyes. Mary had seemed pleased when he invited her and Jimmy to go to the carnival. But similar to their last evening together, she had insisted that instead of calling for her and Jimmy where they lived, Henry meet them in front of the drugstore. Henry wondered if she lived in the building, but didn't ask. At least her agreeing to go with him dented the concern he formed at the end of their first evening together, when he thought she might not want to see him again.

Tonight, he had met them outside Hornbeck's as she requested. She complimented the new flat hat he had bought for the occasion, and if she noticed he wasn't carrying his pistol, she didn't say anything about it. Before hiding it well away from his sleeping corner in the back barn, he had debated about bringing it, and now he thought perhaps he should have. Not in case he spotted Tuttle but because as much fun as carnivals could be, they also offered plenty of opportunities for rowdiness in a town full of people ready to cut loose, whether to celebrate success or drown disappointment.

Henry, Mary, and Jimmy had walked along with a swelling crowd of oil-field workers and townspeople—men, women, and children—a block down Broadway and across it to the carnival site, two large vacant lots some distance beyond Fowler & Son Wagons. Well before coming in sight of the show, they saw the glow of its generator-powered electric lights and heard the brass band playing John Philip Sousa's "The Thunderer" march and Irving Berlin's "Alexander's Ragtime Band," some words to which Henry and Mary knew, "Come on along, come on along, let me take you by the hand."The music put a spring in their steps, and when Henry offered his arm to Mary and she took it, his lingering reservations about the end of their first evening together floated away on notes from trumpets and trombones.

Now, Mary and Henry looked on as Jimmy paid his dime, took three clothbound balls the size of grapefruit from the grifter, and watched the man demonstrate winning by downing three painted bottles on one end of the shelf with one powerful heave. The ball bounced off the rear wall of the tent. Jimmy looked back at his mother, grinned, then turned around and whiffed on a toss that seemed almost to float past the center set of bottles, missing completely. Jimmy's shoulders fell as he watched the ball roll to a stop in the grass not far behind the bench.

"That's all right, Jimmy," Mary called. "Try another one."

Jimmy gripped the second ball, which felt softer in his hand than the one he and Robert had made, and took aim at the next set of bottles to the right. This time he knocked the top bottle to the ground but the other two didn't move. He studied the next set over then threw a strike that hit the bottle on the lower left dead on and toppled both it and the one above it. The bottle on the lower right didn't budge. He turned to his mother and Henry, shrugged, and walked back to them.

"It's harder than I thought," he said. "I didn't expect those balls to be so soft and light."

"Yeah," Henry said, glancing at Mary then looking at Jimmy, "the ball that fellow used was a lot heavier than the one he gave you. That's just one way the game is rigged. There're at least two more. Sometimes they put sand in one of the bottles so there's no chance of it falling, and sometimes they set one of the lower bottles a little closer to the front of the shelf than the other one so it will absorb the energy of the throw. That usually leaves the other lower one standing. Basically, it's cheating."

"Wow! How did you know that?" Jimmy asked. "And why didn't you tell me?"

"I didn't tell you because it's just something a fellow has to experience for himself, like I did once. I learned some of it, though, from a guy who was in the army with me. He'd worked around carnivals some. Anyway, all these games are rigged some way or other. Over there at the dart toss, the grifter—that's the cheat that's running the game—only blows the balloons up about a third of the way so they're not stretched thin and easy to bust. Then he uses a really sharp dart to demonstrate and gives the players ones that don't have much point at all. Sometimes those work, but most times they don't. They just bounce off. Same thing, almost, with the shooting gallery. The grifter gets your attention with a gun that has a good sight and most of the time gives you one with bent sites. And in that ring toss game, the grifter uses one size hoop to demonstrate and gives you smaller ones."

"I don't think I want to play any more of these," Jimmy said. "Can we go on the Ferris wheel now?"

Mary mouthed, "Thank you," to Henry, then patted Jimmy on the shoulder again and said, "I think that's a great idea. Let's go."

The Ferris wheel stood at the back end of the carnival so that anyone who wanted to ride it had to walk past all the games and sideshows. As Henry, Mary, and Jimmy made their way deeper into the carnival grounds, the noise of the crowd and the cacophony of sounds from the sideshow barkers, the motordrome, and the four-stroke gasoline engines powering the rides occasionally made conversation difficult. When the three broke into an open space, Mary looked at Henry again, smiled, and said, "We can skip the hula dancers too."

"I had no doubt," Henry said, pleased with Mary's teasing.

"But not the motordrome and the hot dogs," Jimmy said.

CHAPTER 36

While the Berrytown incorporating committee scurried about trying to persuade someone they trusted to run for mayor, the governor, whose family had come from Union County, appointed an old acquaintance, a man newly flush with oil lease money, to serve temporarily. He quit after a week of dealing with all the formalities of putting together an administration and trying to meet demands people were making for all sorts of things they had previously been doing without but now considered urgent—paved streets, a police force, better equipment for the volunteer fire brigade. The list went on. "I don't need the aggravation," the fellow said, and he wasn't the only one. Neither his replacement nor the replacement's replacement, both also newly well off and close to the governor, lasted much longer. But it was enough time for the committee to persuade Thaddeus Nalls, the twenty-five-year-old son of the local postmaster, to move back home from Little Rock, where he had been working as an accountant, accept the job on a temporary basis, and run uncontested for the office.

~

With the political machinery now looking like it would come together, and the Ku Kluxers still awaiting their regalia, everyone else in Berrytown went about life more or less as usual.

In Henry's case, it was less. At the end of their night at the carnival, Mary had allowed him to walk her and Jimmy back to Hornbeck's. Although now comfortable enough to tell him that she and Jimmy lived in back of the store, she had still insisted on saying goodnight on the front walkway. This time, she was clear about having enjoyed herself and being open to seeing him again. And he seized the opportunity, forgetting for the moment that Jimmy was standing there with them.

"I have an idea," Henry said. "Do you know who Billy Sunday is?"

"Yes, of course," she said. "He's that traveling revival preacher who used to be a baseball player."

"Right. He played up in Chicago and Pittsburgh. He's gon' be in El Dorado all next week. I don't know how you feel about religion. I'm sort of 'take it or leave it' myself, but the newspapers and magazines say he's a spellbinding speaker and puts on a good show. How'd you feel about going to hear him next Sunday? Just to see what all the fuss is about."

"I guess I'm about as religious as the next person," Mary said. "We go to the Methodist church when we go. Mostly because I take in sewing from Mrs. Gordon, the minister's wife there. Anyway, I think it might be interesting to see Billy Sunday. I don't think Jimmy would care for it, though."

Jimmy, who had been listening, said, "Momma, I can stay home by myself. Why don't you go?"

Mary looked down at Jimmy. "You're a big boy, Jimmy, and very responsible, but I just wouldn't feel right leaving you alone." She shifted her gaze upward. "Henry can understand that, can't you Henry?"

Before Henry could respond, Jimmy said, "Okay, I can go out to Uncle Gramps's house."

"Jimmy, we've talked about that before," Mary said. "It's not safe for you out there now, what with all the trouble over that pipeline. Even Uncle Gramps says so."

"Aw, Momma."

"No means no, Jimmy," Mary said, her tone firmer now.

"Well, maybe I could stay with Mrs. Gordon," Jimmy said. "Every time you send me over there with sewing she says we need to come eat Sunday dinner with her sometime. She says she makes good pies, and I know that's true 'cause I've smelled them cooking."

"Her daughterEvelyn doesn't have anything to do with this sudden interest in Mrs. Gordon's pies, does it?" Mary asked, smiling.

"Aw, Momma," Jimmy said again, embarrassed but not denying his mother's intuition, and the matter was settled.

~

All the following week, as Henry hauled freight southeast to Norphlet, west to Louann, and wherever else Moss sent him, he replayed that evening over and over in his mind—Mary's arm looped into his, her dimples when she brushed away the bit of cotton candy, the way she teased him and Jimmy, the admiring glances he caught other men casting her way. And especially the quick goodnight peck on the cheek she reached up and gave him as she turned to walk around the corner of the drugstore, Jimmy having gone on ahead.

He thought about Ed Tuttle again now, too, and all the man had taken away from him, including the ordinary everyday interactions he could never again have with his mother and sister, little things like the warm moments he had shared with Mary on Saturday night. He looked back, too, at how rage had clouded his judgement when he decided to come looking for the man. He was glad he had come. Otherwise, he wouldn't have met Mary. But what a fool he had been to think he could ever find Tuttle. The possibility hadn't seemed daunting at first. Now, he knew he probably would never see him again. Tuttle might not even have come to Berrytown, or he could have come for a while then moved on, just as Cotton Taylor was apparently thinking of doing with his family. Any thought or reminder of Tuttle still stirred anger and despair about what had been and might still be if Tuttle had not come into his life. By contrast, any thought of Mary brought pleasure and wonder about what could be. As Henry considered whether to let go of the past and embrace the present, his head said one thing and his heart another.

~

While Henry was hauling freight, taking care of his mules, mulling over what had brought him to Berrytown, and thinking about Mary, she was spending most of her time fending off Grover Hornbeck's roving hands, trying to install padlocks on her two trunks, and continuing to worry about what would happen to her and Jimmy if Treasury agents found out about the Crescent City Powders passing through the store.

The man in the brown suit had been in again. This time he had talked to Eunice. Mary couldn't hear the conversation, and Eunice didn't share anything about it with her, nor did Mary ask about it. She did, however, see Eunice and Grover having a heated conversation afterward and hear Eunice shout something about stopping his worrying. No matter what Eunice thought, learning that Grover was concerned made Mary more anxious. Only in the evenings, when she was with

Jimmy and later in bed when she lay awake thinking about Henry, was she able to escape her dread of arrest someday.

Otis Leatherwood had spent most of the previous week finishing up his hog butchering. Using salt mixed with a little pepper and sorghum, he had rubbed down the ham, shoulders, and middling meat—both his share and Isaiah's—and stored it in wooden boxes on shelves in his mud-chinked, log smokehouse. He had not had to worry with other parts of the animal. Isaiah and his wife Luella had taken the meat trimmed from the choice cuts along with some of the fat to grind into sausage to share. They had also taken the intestines to clean and use for sausage casings and cook into chitterlings, the head to make scrapple, and the ribs to can. Otis had teased Isaiah about the need to make all that if he planned to get rich on oil and move off somewhere, and Isaiah had said preserved food could travel too.

Otis planned on using this week to get rid of some of the smoked ham and bacon left over from the previous hog he butchered. He took some into town to Mary and Jimmy and loaded the rest into his wagon and set off to peddle it in the oil camps nearest him to the west toward Louann. He harbored some hope that someday he might earn enough money to buy back his beloved horse Trixie from Wilbur Moss, but in his heart, he knew that was unlikely. Chiefly, he hated letting food go to waste. He also hated doing anything that might help any dad-blamed soul killing the land, but he knew there would be wives and children out there who could use it. It wasn't their fault that their husbands and daddies were ignorant or didn't care about all the damage they were doing.

He followed the main road to Louann for a while, then turned onto one of several service lanes leading toward clumps of oil derricks. The smell of oil and the sight of limbless trees standing in pools of slimy runoff sickened him, but he pushed on until he came to a camp of small, unpainted frame houses put up by whatever oil company was befouling this particular section of land, along with some tent houses and a variety of smaller tents. Children playing on the blackened dirt spotted him first, and when one of the mothers came out and he announced his purpose, others gathered around. His wagon was empty in no time. He hadn't counted on feeling as much sympathy as he did these folks, but after seeing their living conditions, he had practically given away his extra meat, selling it for pennies on the dollar. He left the camp angrier than ever at oil men and mad at himself for caring about their families.

He had also not counted on encountering any oil-field workers, or on anyone recognizing him or confronting him about the ad he was running in the *Berrytown Journal*. But as he was exiting the service lane back onto the main Berrytown-Louann road, a man shouted at him from an REO pickup truck, "There's the son-of-a-bitch now! Hey, you! Stop!"

The truck skidded to a halt in front of Otis's team, leaving him slight room to maneuver around it. Three men who looked like roustabouts or roughnecks jumped out and ran menacingly toward him. "You goddamned crazy old bastard!" one of them yelled, "You need to learn how to mind your own business. Who the hell do you think you are trying to ruin our jobs?"

While not necessarily expecting any such trouble, Otis had come prepared. "Whoa there!" he called to his mules, bringing them to a halt. He wrapped his reins around the break handle sticking up over the wagon bed on his right, then reached under the seat and brought out his shotgun. "I'm the fellow that's gon' blow your sorry asses all to hell if you don't get that goddamned truck out of my way pretty damn quick," he said, bringing the butt end of the gun stock to his shoulder.

"There's nothing more fun than watching a bunch of rats run," Otis said to himself moments later after he managed to pull onto the main road. He guessed he should have let things go with just yelling back, and not shot out that front tire too. The sheriff or somebody would likely be around to see him again.

CHAPTER 37

Clad in his flat cap, new white shirt, and clean khakis and denim jacket, Henry walked briskly down the east side of Broadway to meet Mary in front of Hornbeck's. He was so eager to look good for her that for the last two days he had worn two of his three work shirts, one over the other, to stay warm in the increasingly cool weather while the other one and his jacket were at the new laundry back of the Upton Hotel.

He was two doors from the drugstore when Mary came around the corner of Seventh Street. She had on the same coat and black skirt she had worn to the carnival, but her blouse was blue this time, like her eyes, with small vertical pleats on each side of tiny white buttons set close together.

They greeted each other with broad smiles, neither needing words to express their pleasure in seeing each other. Henry held out his arm, and Mary hooked her stiffened elbow into it. He put his other hand on her forearm, and they started in lockstep for the Missouri Pacific depot to catch the train. They walked a full block leaning into each other before either spoke. Then they talked nonstop. By the time they boarded the train, Henry knew Jimmy was safely settled in with the Gordons until late afternoon and Mary had made the blouse she was wearing. She told him only after he complimented it and asked if she had sewn it, like the one last week.

Henry hadn't anticipated the train being packed. He said he guessed the white Baptist and Methodist ministers in Berrytown were preaching to mostly empty pews today. The ride down to El Dorado was too noisy for much more conversation. He and Mary were relieved to step into the sunlight at the county seat and join others, all dressed in their Sunday-go-to-meeting best, walking a quarter mile or so southwest of the business section to the revival site.

In an area cleared for development but still lacking improvements, a near-circus-size canvas tent rose skyward amid haphazardly parked automobiles, wagons, and buggies. Notes from a trombone version of "When the Saints Go Marching In" drifted through open tent flaps. Several men wearing black suits and ties walked among the arriving crowd alternately hawking pamphlets containing some of Billy Sunday's sermons and urging people to go in and find a seat.

"Looks a lot like the carnival, doesn't it?" Henry remarked, as he and Mary reached the entrance.

"Sure does," she said. "I can't wait to see what the service is like."

The tent was cavernous. Straw and sawdust had been spread liberally on the ground. This being the first of three services planned for this Lord's Day, the combination smelled fresh and was soft underfoot. Based on large assemblies he had experienced in the army, Henry estimated the tent could hold about five hundred people, possibly more. It was a small number, however, compared to Billy Sunday's usual crowds in bigger towns and different facilities as described in newspaper accounts. In the back of the tent, wide planks had been laid across bales of hay for seating. In the front, volunteers from local churches had brought in wooden folding chairs and pushed them as close together as possible. Beyond the chairs, a low platform large enough for a choir of thirty or so also supported a large pulpit with low wings. Henry and Mary found seats near the center aisle in the rear of the front section.

The trombone player, a handsome, well-dressed fellow of middle age with a thick shock of dark hair, stood beside the pulpit, playing the same song over and over as people continued filing in and finding places to sit. Henry recognized him from newspaper pictures. He was Homer Rodeheaver, Billy Sunday's choir director and chief soloist. Well known in his own right, he had several top-selling gospel recordings to his credit and ran a large music publishing house up in Chicago. Behind him, choir members, also volunteers from local churches, were lining up on low risers. A piano sat on the platform off to the right of the pulpit with a pianist waiting to play.

When Rodeheaver decided the tent was full, he signaled to the pianist, cradled the trombone in one arm, lifted the other, and still facing the audience, began leading the choir in singing "The Unclouded Day." His rich baritone voice carried above all the others.

> Oh, they tell me of a home far beyond the sky,
>
> Oh, they tell me of a home far away,
>
> Oh, they tell me of a home where no storm clouds rise,
>
> Oh, they tell me of an unclouded day.

The blended voices on the platform and the sweet, round tones from the piano, combined with the fast pace of the popular hymn, soon had the entire audience, Henry and Mary included, on their feet smiling and clapping in time. "Shall We Gather at the River" and half a dozen other songs followed, with Rodeheaver urging the audience to join in.

When he judged that no further warmup was needed, he swung his free arm in a circle, then raised it higher, palm out, to signal quiet. When the audience took his cue, Rodeheaver shouted, "Ladies and Gentlemen, here is Billy Sunday!"

The trim sixty-year-old former Chicago Cubs and Pittsburgh Pirates outfielder came running out of the wings and bounded onto the stage with the same athleticism that enabled him to steal two-hundred forty-six bases in the eight years he played professional baseball before becoming an evangelist. He was wearing a sharply creased suit cut in the latest style, a white shirt with cufflinks, a silk tie with a diamond stickpin, and black shoes polished to a mirror sheen. Instead of going behind the pulpit, he stood in front of it.

"Folks," Sunday said, his square jaw jutting out and his boyish face turning into a frown, "I'm here 'cause of sin. I'm here 'cause you people in South Arkansas have got an overdose of it. You've got more sin than just about any place on the face of this earth, and I know, 'cause I've been preaching all over creation for half a lifetime. In places bigger than this and in places littler than this. I tell you right now if you don't repent and change your ways, you're gon' burn in hell hotter than any fire all this oil you've got can make."

From that beginning, he tore into gambling, dancing, and liquor of all kinds. No form of them was too small to qualify, and he went on at length about each.

He hit on church women playing euchre at home and on men gambling at poker in back rooms.

He jumped on dancing hardest of all. “It’s simply a hugging match set to music,” he railed. “It’s a sexual love feast. It’s the major cause of prostitution.”

Of liquor, he said, “Prohibition hasn’t stopped men from making booze and ruining their lives and the lives of others with it. I tell you right now, I’m gon’ fight it till hell freezes over, and then I’m gon’ put on ice skates and fight it some more.” What he didn’t tell was that he had a well-stocked wine cellar at home.

As he talked, he paced around both sides of the pulpit. Without pausing, he yanked off his suit coat and threw it on the floor. He wasn’t worried about wrinkling it or getting it dirty. His listeners didn’t know it, but he traveled with a large wardrobe and changed clothes between each service. At one point he began running up and down the aisle and sliding on his knees in the sawdust and straw to punctuate his points.

Henry looked around to see how people were reacting. They were hanging on every word, Mary included. She flinched, as did others, when Sunday ran full out back to the platform and jumped up on top of the pulpit. He jerked his diamond stick pin out of his tie, pulled off the neck piece, and tossed it to the floor.

“I’ve got a word or two to say about evolution too,” he shouted, while fixing the pin to his shirt. “There ain’t no such thing. When scholarship says one thing and the Bible says another, scholarship can go to hell. If I had a million dollars, I’d give $999,999 of it to the church and $1 to education. Ain’t no monkey ever said his prayers at night. If you believe your great, great granddaddy was a monkey, then you take your daddy and go to Hell with him, but leave me out! I came from a different bunch altogether, thank God!”

Sunday went on from there to lambast labor unions, socialists, and immigrants. "Beware of organizers and foreigners. I believe the ten million aliens in this country who have been content to seek fortune under the protecting folds of the Stars and Stripes, but who refuse to be assimilated, should be made to kiss the American flag or go back to the lands from which they came," he said.

Eventually, he began to wind down, and after returning to the sins of gambling, dancing, and drinking for a few more observations and declarations, he brought his sermon to a close. "I have just two more things to say. Some people tell me a revival is only temporary. Well, so is a bath, but it does you good. Some also say to me, 'Bill, you rub the fur the wrong way.' I do not! Let the cats turn around!"

Rodeheaver then took turns with Sunday urging listeners to come down front and repent, or as Sunday put it, "Walk the sawdust trail for Jesus. Do it now." At this point in most Protestant services, ministers relied on quiet hymns like "Softly and Tenderly Jesus Is Calling," but Billy Sunday had Rodeheaver lead the choir and congregation in singing "Onward Christian Soldiers." Now that he had people stirred up, he wanted a closing song with pizzaz to get them moving, not something that might lull them to sleep.

Henry looked at Mary and asked, "Are you thinking what I'm thinking?"

"This is a good time to beat the rush?"

"Right. Before they pass the collection buckets."

Mary and Henry begged people's pardons as they sidestepped their way down their row. Once in the aisle, they headed for the exit. Outside, they made their way through bystanders who had been unable to get into the tent. Then they dodged more men in black suits hawking sermon pamphlets, along with copies of Billy Sunday's book *Love Stories of the Bible* and Elijah P. Brown's best-selling biography of the fiery preacher, *The Real Billy Sunday*.

"He's everything you said about him, and more," Mary said, when they cleared the hubbub.

"Yeah, he's for sure a showman. And he's stirring up a lot more than the Holy Spirit."

"What do you mean?" Mary asked.

"You want to get something to eat?" Henry asked, deflecting the question. He needed time to think what to say to her.

"That would be nice. I'm hungry," she said, letting his reluctance to answer her question slide.

Henry didn't know if cafés and restaurants in El Dorado opened on Sundays, but he figured that with the population having swelled with oil men, there must be someplace serving food.

CHAPTER 38

After standing in line for a while, Henry and Mary took a booth in Larry's Diner on the corner of Main and Washington Streets, across from the red brick Union County courthouse, already slated for a marble replacement paid for with tax proceeds from the oil boom. The diner was long and narrow with booths along one wall, a counter and stools along the other, and slow-turning fans hanging from a white pressed tin ceiling. The menu was sparse but the smells from the kitchen in back promised good eats. They ordered Larry's special—homemade meatloaf with mashed potatoes and gravy. Coffee to drink and apple pie for dessert.

"Henry," Mary asked after the waiter jotted down what they wanted and picked up the menus, "what did you mean back there about Billy Sunday stirring up more than the Holy Spirit?"

"It's nothing," he said. "Sometimes I talk when I ought to keep my mouth shut." He looked down at his hands in his lap then up at Mary, smiled weakly, and shrugged.

She clasped her hands together and rested them on the table. "I think you're pretty good at keeping your mouth shut, Henry Smith. In all the times we've been together, you've hardly said much at all about what you did before you came to Berrytown or how you feel about anything except your job."

She paused, then said, “Well, you have told me a little about your sister and how much you still miss her. Come on. Please. I want to know you better. Tell me what you meant back there about Billy Sunday.”

Henry liked her prodding. He wanted to know her better too. But he couldn’t tell her who he really was or why he had come to Berrytown. Even though he had almost given up on finding Ed Tuttle, or even wanting to, he was still reluctant to risk giving himself away. More importantly, he worried that Mary wouldn’t have anything to do with him if he told her. At the same time, he didn’t want to lie. If he did and she found out, that would sour her on him as well. He had turned all this over in his mind many times, always without finding a way out, and he rolled it all over again now, as seconds ticked away in silence. If he wanted to keep seeing her, and he did, probably more than she knew, he had to share more than he had so far but keep deflecting at the same time.

“Well,” Henry said, leaning forward and folding his hands on top of the table, "those things I heard Billy Sunday saying today are pretty much the same as what's been quoted in the newspapers. But listening to him say them and seeing him while he’s doing it is different than just reading about it. I don’t have any problem with him preaching against prostitution, booze, and gambling, although I do like a good beer and a game of cards now and then. But I think he’s way overboard about dancing.

“What I really don’t like, though, is the way he seems to hate everybody that moves here from some other country. That and labor unions. He just lumps them into one big pot with communists and socialists—which I think he hates especially because Eugene Debs and Emma Goldman have jumped on him the same way he's gone after them. I read that Debs called him a 'buffoon,' and Goldman called him a 'clown.' I don't care much for either one of them, but what I do like about them is that, at least as far as I can see, they're for the little fellow. Billy says he's all for what he calls 'dinner-pail Americans,' but he pals around with the likes of John D. Rockefeller and says working people would be better off sitting in church getting close to God than walking picket lines trying to get better wages to feed their families. I don't agree with that. He also takes things that are complicated and tries to make them seem like a simple matter of black and white. Plays on people's fears. I don't like that either."

"That was a mouthful, Henry Smith. I don't know how you were able to hold all that in."

Henry shrugged. "I guess I wasn't. I'm sorry."

"No," Mary said. "It's all right." She reached over and touched his clasped hands then resettled hers on the table. "I know who Eugene Debs is, but who's Emma Goldman?"

"She's an anarchist. Hates authority of all kinds. Opposed the draft before the war. But she supports workers' right to organize and strike."

"Oh," Mary said. She shifted her gaze from Henry and looked toward the front door.

"Did I say something wrong?" Henry asked. "I didn't mean to get carried away."

"No, not really. I used to hear my daddy talk about Eugene Debs. When he led that big railroad worker's strike back in the 90's, Daddy lost a lot of money in Pullman Car Company stock. He never stopped talking about it. He hated the man."

"The papers say Pullman has come back now."

"Maybe, but Daddy was so mad at the time he told Momma to throw away his stock certificates. Said he never wanted to see them again."

"Huh. That's too bad."

Mary sighed, then nodded and brushed her hand against her temple, as though she felt a strand of hair was out of place. She started to say something, but the waiter arrived with their food, and they spent a couple of minutes arranging napkins and tableware.

"You read a lot don't you, Henry?" Mary asked after they had both taken a bite.

"Habit," he said.

"Where did you get it?"

"Get what?'

"Get the habit of reading so much."

"College," Henry said, before he could stop himself. He knew as soon as he said it that he had opened another line of questioning he would rather not have gotten into.

"You've never said anything about college. Where was it?"

"Wabash, up in Indiana," he said, as memories, good and bad, flooded his mind. "I really liked it. You ever read *Ben-Hur*?"

"No, but I know about it."

"Well, General Lew Wallace wrote it, along with a bunch of other things, and he lived in Crawfordsville—that's where the college is—and he built a writing studio in back of his house. Almost as big, too, least ways how I remember it. Real fancy brick building with lots of plants all around. One of my professors took us there. What I remember most about it is meeting Lew Wallace's wife, Susan Wallace, and then reading her book *The Land of the Pueblos*. The general was governor of New Mexico Territory for a while, and she was an amateur archeologist. The book is probably something your Uncle Otis would like."

"You know my uncle that well?" Mary asked, puzzled.

"Let's just say I've run into him a couple of times. And I've read that ad he's been running in the *Berrytown Journal*."

"I guess you know folks are laughing at him about it."

"Yeah," Henry said, "but I think he's right. I see the wasted oil and ruined land every day. It's a lot like what happened in the Southwest back when the Spaniards came and took the Indians' land and made them work in silver mines. The Spaniards were so greedy and ignorant they only took out the ore that was easiest to mine and left ninety percent of it covered up underground where nobody could really get to it. They also worked thousands of Indians and burros to death and near about destroyed the way the Indians lived."

"Is that why you beat that mule skinner with an ax handle the first day you got to town? It made you think about the burros?"

"You know about that?" Henry asked, hoping he wouldn't have to get into the main reason the mule skinner's actions upset him so much.

"Jimmy told me. He saw it."

"And you still went to supper with me?" Henry asked. "When I finally got around to asking you?" he added, smiling.

"Well, by then I also knew about you stopping that hanging, so it seemed like you had a strong sense of right and wrong." They ate in silence for a bit, then Mary added, "To be honest, though, I'm a little bit nervous with you all the time having that gun in your pocket."

Color rose in Henry's cheeks. "I didn't realize it was that obvious."

"Come on, Henry. I'm not a schoolgirl. I see enough men toting guns, I can spot them pretty easy."

"Well, there you go," Henry said, latching onto a way to dodge the truth. "Seems like every Tom, Dick, and Harry is walking around with one, so it makes sense to carry one for protection. You saw what happened in the drugstore that day."

"Yes, and I still have nightmares about it. So, is that the only reason you carry it?"

"That and habit," Henry said, and knew at once that he had said too much again.

Mary put down her knife and fork. "Habit again, huh? Where'd you get this one?"

"France," he said. "You knew I was in the army. I figured you guessed I'd been in the war." He looked into her eyes and knew that she had. He also knew she had him so mesmerized she could get him to tell her just about anything. "I was an officer. We carried them all the time. I got used to it."

"Yeah," she said, "I thought so. Is that where you got the scar on your head?"

Henry blushed again. He couldn't keep from it when he was around her. "It is, but I'd rather not talk about it."

Mary returned to her utensils. "That's okay," she said. "But you need to stop trying to cover it up all the time. You're still a very handsome man, you know."

Henry felt his face warming again and made two quick decisions. He was going to get them seats in a jitney for their return trip to Berrytown, even if it did cost an outrageous ten dollars a ticket. It would be bumpier but quieter. And when he said goodbye to Mary, he was going to kiss her, and not a little peck either, whether it was daylight or dark and no matter who might see it, even Jimmy.

CHAPTER 39

"Damn it!" Otis Leatherwood shouted a split second before the bucket struck his thigh. Milk splashed onto his overalls and spilled into the dark earth beneath them, ending his brief morning respite.

The rotten-egg smell of sulfur blowing in from the oil fields on morning and evening breezes rankled him every day, but most times when he was in his barn feeding and cleaning up after his livestock, he could almost forget that the world as he had known it was crashing down around him. He loved the sights, sounds, and smells that surrounded him when he shut himself inside the old structure. The weathered wood sheeting and heavy overhead beams he'd carefully set in place years earlier. The loft floor creaking now and again in a never-ending process of settling. The wooden door latches that made a light, mellow thud when he opened and closed them. The mingled sweetness of hay, dryness of dust, and sharpness of manure. And the animals. Musky smelling if they had come in out of the rain and fresh if they had been in the sun all day, at least when the odor of sulfur hadn't settled onto their coats.

Despite his long friendship with Isaiah Watson, Otis had never been much of a churchgoer, or even one for praying, especially since God, if he existed at all, had let Alma die.

The closest he ever came to thinking there was some sort of divine creator was when he walked his fields as green shoots rose from the soil in the spring, or when he was in the barn with the reassuring warmth of his animals around him. The former pleasure was gone, ruined by other men's greed and carelessness, but the latter remained, at least for now.

Both the reality of his losses and the cause of them hit Otis smack in the face every time he walked out of the barn. This morning, they struck him with such intensity that when he went to slam his fist against his leg, he forgot he was carrying the milk pail.

For the first time, over the horizon on Isaiah's place, Otis could see an oil derrick rising above a drilling platform. He knew if the drillers hit oil, other derricks would follow. He tried to tell himself he was at least happy his friend might soon get something he wanted badly for good reasons. He had even made a point of telling Isaiah that more than once. But it was a hard sell to himself, particularly given the ugly gouge the advancing pipeline was making across his own farm.

Otis knew no one was taking his pleading in the *Berrytown Journal* seriously. Only a couple of folks had said anything negative to him about it, but when in town, he had seen their looks and heard the snide remarks they made under their breath when they thought he couldn't hear them. They were fools, he thought. He guessed he had known all along that a few scathing words from an old farmer wouldn't stop the craziness, but he was glad he hadn't kept still and done nothing. He missed his horse Trixie the way he was going to miss Isaiah when he moved, but he didn't regret giving her another home and spending the proceeds to make his point.

He knew in his gut that he was right and people would see it someday. By then, of course, it would likely be too late. He needed to do something more to make them listen.

"You remember me telling you about seeing somebody that talked like you?" Al Jenkins asked, as he handed Henry a signed delivery slip. "I seen him again the other night over at Big Sally's like before. He was drunk 'n a skunk, but he was sure running his mouth. I swear, listening to you now is just like listening to him. How you sound, I mean, not what you're saying."

The Missouri Pacific was laying yet another siding to keep up with the clamor for freight and passenger services in Berrytown, and with other communities nearby growing quickly as well, all kinds of timber products were in high demand. Not even stuff brought in from the big Edgar Lumber Company in Wesson and the even larger Union Sawmill Company in Huttig over to the southeast could keep up with orders. This was a boon for the smaller peckerwood mills especially, and Henry had been dispatched to the one operated by Jenkins, to pick up a load of crossties.

Henry recalled how Jenkins had given him supper and a place to sleep his first night in Berrytown, but he was surprised that Jenkins remembered him. He was even more surprised when Jenkins brought up the other fellow he had mentioned that evening, saying Henry talked like him. Henry didn't think he talked much differently from loads of others who had flooded into the area from places outside the South, and Jenkins was the only person who had ever remarked on it.

Henry thought he had put Ed Tuttle behind him, but hearing this again piqued his curiosity. "I remember," Henry said, as he climbed onto his wagon, his loading done. "You thought maybe he worked on a pipeline down around El Dorado somewhere."

"Yeah, but he's over in Ouachita County someplace now, working in a barrelhouse. Guess he can't drink where he works, or maybe he just likes Big Sally's place. Sounded like he's got mixed up with the Klan somehow. Kept saying something about a big to-do coming up."

"Huh. You remember what he looked like?" Henry had been in Berrytown long enough now without finding Tuttle, and his interest in the man had waned so much, that even though he continued calling himself "Smith," he no longer worried much about possibly giving himself away.

"Not really," the barrel-chested mill operator said, "I was pretty juiced too. He's taller than you, and he walks kinda peculiar like. Raises way up on his toes every time he takes a step. I remember 'cause he left before I did, and he was falling all over the place. We was all laughing at him but he didn't even notice. That sound like somebody you know?"

"Sounds like it could be a lot of folks," Henry said. Recalling what Jenkins had said about water moccasins and pipeline work the first time they had talked, and how, sure enough, they turned up in bunches right after that, Henry said, "You watch out for rattlesnakes, and I'll see you sometime." He released his brake, flicked his reins over the backs of his mules, and said, "Come on, boys. Get up now."

Heading back, Henry wished he hadn't run into Jenkins. He hadn't wanted to think any more about Ed Tuttle. However, there was a good chance it was Tuttle that Jenkins had seen, and that was enough to dredge up all the pain and suffering the man had caused. All the way into town, Henry tried to hold back his rising anger and resurging desire for revenge.

After a late supper of ham and eggs in one of Berrytown's hastily thrown up new cafés, Henry lay on his barn loft pallet recalling what he knew about the Ku Klux Klan from back in Indiana and trying to mesh it with what he knew about Tuttle and the things he had heard and seen about the Klan here over the last few months.

He knew how former Confederates had established the Klan after the Civil War to keep newly freed slaves under white control with all sorts of scare tactics from cross burnings to lynchings. He knew how, after Congress had passed a series of laws in the early 1870s to enforce the Fourteenth and Fifteenth Amendments making freedmen citizens and giving them the right to vote, the Klan had largely dissolved into several splinter groups and lost much of its clout. He knew how after W. D. Griffin's three-hour movie *Birth of a Nation* appeared all over the country in 1915, painting Negroes as ignorant and dangerous and Klansmen as heroic saviors of the white race, an Alabama physician named William Joesph Simmons had reorganized the Klan in Georgia and taken it national. And he knew how a Texan named D. C. Stephenson had shown up in Indiana about that same time, independently organized the Klan there, made it the largest statewide KKK operation in the country, and begun taking a vice-grip hold on state politics.

Henry had thought about the new Klan quite a lot after fighting alongside the all-black 369th Infantry Regiment in France. They had fought for democratic order abroad while the KKK was trying to curtail their own rights back home.

The attempted lynching of Levi Birdsong brought it all back to mind. And now here it was again, this time potentially in connection with Ed Tuttle. Henry thought the Klan was exactly the kind of thing that would appeal to the man, giving him permission to be mean and get praised for it.

With a charter in place from the state Klan headquarters, the Berrytown Klavern had stepped up its recruiting activities in recent days using posters and letters of invitation to certain citizens—tradesmen, farmers, bankers, lawyers, preachers, and oil company executives among them—citing the fraternal benefits of membership and the Klan's opposition to all sorts of things it deemed "ills of society," including liquor, gambling, prostitution, and foreigners. The letters, but not the posters, also called out the threat that the Klan thought black men posed to white womanhood. For an entry fee of ten dollars, the purchase of a robe and accompanying regalia for six dollars and fifty cents more, and annual dues of five dollars, a man could be inducted, made privy to secret signs, passwords, and ceremonies, and have the opportunity to buy authentic Klan crosses, rings, and even broaches for the women in their lives—not unlike the Order of the Elks, or even to some extent the Masons.

Henry despised the whole mess, but he gave credit to Simmons for one thing. In addition to its hateful mission, the Klan was a clever money-making scheme, raking in millions of dollars for its organizers and officers. Henry decided that if the local Klavern was planning a big event, secret or otherwise, he wanted to get a look at it, both to know if they were up to anything in particular and to see if Tuttle had gotten involved.

~

Having neither seen nor heard anything about a Klan event, other than the vague reference by Jenkins, Henry decided to ask Calvin Birdsong if he had gotten wind of anything. He was the only person, other than Mary, whom he trusted, and he doubted she would know anything about it. Plus, he didn't want to worry her. Henry found the little man alone in one of the corrals with his team the next afternoon.

"Calvin," Henry said, after walking over to him as he was using a curry comb on one of his mules, "I've got a question for you. You got a minute?"

"Yes, sir, Mr. Henry, what is it?" Calvin asked. He stopped brushing.

"I hate to bring this up to you," Henry said, "'cause I know it's not pleasant to talk about, but I know you keep your ears open. I was wondering. When you've been out and about, or otherwise, have you heard anything about a big Ku Klux meeting about to happen somewhere around? I know there's a Klavern here now, and I'm curious to find out how far along they are and what they're up to. It's not likely to be anything good, leastwise far as I can see."

Calvin laid his curry comb on his mule's rump, took off his floppy hat, and ran his hand across his close-cropped salt-and-pepper hair. "Yes, sir, I heard something about it. It's kinda surprising what some white folks will say 'round us coloreds sometimes. Almost like they don't even see us. Not you, of course. I don't know what it is, but there's something supposed to happen Saturday night. Some kinda big meeting."

"Any idea where?"

"No, sir. But if I had to guess, I'd say out yonder off the Louann road about three miles. There's a logging road that turns off to the left as you go out. There ain't been no cutting out there lately and no drilling at all, but twice when I've been coming back to town real late, I've seen three or four cars turning in there. There ain't no houses or anything down there. Ain't none of my business, and I figured maybe they was going down there to drink or something. Could be they's doing something else, though. Like getting ready for something."

"You think maybe somebody's selling moonshine out there?" Henry asked.

"No, sir, Mr. Henry. I doubt that."

"I reckon you'd know, wouldn't you?"

"Yes, sir. I might."

Yep, Henry thought but didn't say, that's another conversation I want to have someday.

CHAPTER 40

Mary found Henry leaning against a brick wall in the vacant lot next to the American Theater. Out front, posters announced *A Connecticut Yankee in King Authur's Court* starring Harry C. Myers and his wife Rosemary Theby. A long line of folks stood waiting for the next showing. Henry had his back to the street and was holding his flat cap in one hand and using the thumb and first two fingers of the other to push against the area above his right eye.

"Are you okay?" Mary asked.

"Yeah," he said. "I just needed some fresh air." He waved his cap and forced a smile. "If you can call this stuff fresh."The breeze from the southeast, over Norphlet way, smelled worse than usual.

Mary and Henry both had on the same clothes, freshly laundered, that they wore to hear Billy Sunday. Henry had planned the evening as supper and a movie for Saturday night, but after talking with Al Jenkins and Calvin Birdsong earlier in the week, he had stopped by the drugstore and changed the outing to Friday. Unfortunately, Ralph's Café had been so crowded and noisy they couldn't carry on much of a conversation. And now this.

"I'm sorry I had to leave before it ended," Henry said. "You should have stayed with Jimmy."

"He's fine," Mary said. "It's almost over, and I told him we'd wait for him outside."

Henry glanced around to make sure they were out of earshot of passersby then said, "I should have known better. I read that book in college, and I knew Morgan and his men used Gatlin Guns to kill all those knights. I even knew there were land mines involved, but I didn't expect the movie to treat it like it was the Meuse-Argonne. What happened over there was too horrible to be in a movie that's being advertised as a comedy. Sometimes I can't stop thinking about it."

Mary put her hand on his shoulder but didn't say anything.

A few seconds later, Henry apologized again. "I really am sorry. I just wanted to be with you and Jimmy, and I was thinking more about that and about Mark Twain in general than about the story. Or about Jimmy losing his daddy in the National Guard. He's probably upset too."

"Andy was killed in a truck accident," Mary said. "Jimmy knows the difference. Besides, he's twelve. He knows what we were watching isn't real. Telephones, Gatlin guns, and motorcycles in the sixth century? He'll be fine." She let go of Henry's shoulder and squeezed his arm.

"Better than me, huh?" Henry said, smiling. He opened his arms, and Mary stepped into them. Each savored the nearness then stepped back when they heard the theater emptying.

"Tell you what," Mary said. "Why don't you come to supper with me and Jimmy on Sunday? We've only got one room, so it'll be crowded, but I make great omelets and hash brown potatoes."

The invitation surprised them both. Early on, Mary didn't know enough about Henry to feel safe telling him where she lived. Later, she had been ashamed to have him know how paltry her quarters were. Now, she was comfortable enough with him that none of that mattered. She only wanted to be with him. She didn't even care anymore if Eunice or some of her sewing customers found out and gossiped about her, a single woman, entertaining a single man in her home. Which she knew all except Mrs. Gordon would do, especially now that so many prostitutes were working out of rented rooms and houses all over town. Eunice and the gossips would leave out the part about Jimmy being with them, of course.

As Henry strode back to the mule yard after walking Mary and Jimmy to their door, he was already looking forward to seeing her again. He felt bad, though, about not having given her a reason for cancelling Saturday. He guessed politeness kept her from asking. He was glad she hadn't, though, because the only excuse he had come up with sounded not only lame, but also questionable. "I have a personal matter to take care of." At least he had the good sense not to tell her that.

~

Henry thought about renting a horse from Moss for Saturday night, or just borrowing one without saying anything, but he didn't want to take any risk, however small, of being found out. He set out on foot as soon as it was dark enough for cover. Keeping off the road, avoiding houses and other buildings, and tramping through brush and woods while keeping occasional sight of the road was both tiring and time consuming. By the time he got where he was going, however, he knew he had picked the right spot.

Henry saw the glow of lanterns and headlights through the trees before he heard the whine of automobile engines. He carried a small flashlight but dared not use it. Moving quietly, he skirted a large field where cars and trucks were arriving and parking along one edge. When he reached the opposite side, he found a spot that offered a good view from the cover of a thicket of netleaf leather flower vines under large pine trees. As he watched, scores of men, perhaps more than a hundred, wearing rope-belted white robes and pointed white hats arranged themselves into a large square with one side open. Each robe had a red circle stitched over the heart, and each hat had a shoulder-length apron-like piece hanging from the front and the back. The front aprons had holes cut out for the wearers' eyes. Henry couldn't see the details of the insignia, but he knew the circle contained a white cross in the center of which was a red apostrophe-like mark that represented blood Klansmen shed to preserve the white race.

Several men broke ranks and moved to the open side of the square where, using levers and ropes, they raised a wooden cross that was at least twenty feet tall and wrapped in burlap. Henry guessed the men that Calvin had seen driving out this way a few days before had built the thing and dug the hole for it. Most likely, some had remained on site until tonight to keep away intruders. Once the cross was upright, three other men brought a small podium from the parking area and set it near the center of the open end of the square. Two others brought an American flag and spread it over the podium.

A man Henry assumed was the leader took up a position behind the podium. Another man holding a lighted torch high overhead came and stood to his left, and a third came and stood to his right. This last one then stepped forward and spoke briefly. Henry strained to hear what the fellow was saying, but all he could pick up was "Grand Dragon." That was enough to tell him that this was no ordinary Klan meeting. Henry knew from newspapers that there was only one Grand Dragon in Arkansas, and that was James A. Comer, former head of the state Republican Party and now Exalted Cyclops of the Little Rock Klavern. And he was here.

After Comer spoke to the group, each man on the sides of the square leaned toward the man to the right of him as if speaking into his ear. Some sort of secret password or pledge Henry assumed. After that, some men broke from the sides of the square and formed a semi-circle in front of the podium. Then one of them led the whole bunch in singing "The Star-Spangled Banner" and "Blest Be the Tie That Binds." When that was done, Comer said something else Henry couldn't hear, and the man with the torch walked over to the cross, and set it on fire. It burned quickly, as if it had been soaked in kerosene.

Like he had done when the men first walked in from their parked vehicles, Henry watched them as closely as possible when the meeting broke up and they began leaving. He didn't see anyone who walked like Ed Tuttle, but that didn't necessarily mean that Tuttle wasn't a member. As Henry worked his way cautiously back to town, he wondered if the gathering this evening was the big event that the fellow who talked like Tuttle had mentioned to Al Jenkins, or if something else was afoot.

CHAPTER 41

In the dark outside Mary's shed, Henry hitched up his pants and cleaned the soles of his boots on the wooden scraper. He removed his flat cap, smoothed the front of his freshly laundered shirt, and rapped twice on the doorjamb. Warm light and the smell of fresh-cooked biscuits spilled out of the room as Jimmy opened the door and said something about coming inside. Henry caught the intent, though not the words, as his attention locked onto Mary standing in front of her wood-burning stove. She had on an apron that looked like a crazy quilt without batting and a blue, low-waisted dress he had seen her wearing once in the drugstore. She looked like the pictures of models that artists drew for mail-order catalogs.

"Hi, Henry," she said, glancing around between shuffling pans on the stove top. "Supper's almost ready. Just have to do the bacon."

"I brought some pear preserves," Henry said. He looked around the tiny room. "I hope they're good. I got them from a peddler out in one of the camps yesterday."

"Jimmy can set them on the table," Mary said. Bacon began sizzling in her iron skillet. "I'm afraid we only have two chairs, but Jimmy can sit on my sewing trunk. Go ahead and pull it over, Jimmy. And take Henry's cap and jacket and put them on your cot."

"I'll give you a hand, Jimmy," Henry said, aware now that he hadn't even said hello to the boy."

"Okay," Jimmy said, and together they lifted the trunk into place. "Momma keeps all her sewing stuff in here," he said. "She made that apron out of scraps. Ain't it pretty?"

Henry, still standing, wasn't sure what to do with himself or how to respond. When he was a boy Jimmy's age, he never paid any attention to such things. "You're pretty proud of your momma, aren't you?" he said.

"Yes, sir. She's real good at making stuff."

"Yeah, I can see that," Henry said. "And she's really pretty, too, don't you think?"

"Yes, sir, she is. You really like her, don't you? I know she likes you."

"Jimmy!" Mary exclaimed.

Startled, Henry and Mary looked from the boy to each other, trying to think what to say. Then both burst out laughing.

"Yes, Jimmy, I do," Henry said, looking at Mary instead of Jimmy, and winking. "Is that all right?"

"It's all right with me," Jimmy said.

"It's all right with me too," Mary said. "Now, both of you sit down at the table. Supper's ready."

Jimmy sat down, but Henry waited until Mary took off her apron, then he pulled out her chair for her before taking his seat.

Despite their chuckles over Jimmy's unrestrained enthusiasm, once Henry and Mary sat down, they found it harder to make conversation here, in her living quarters, than in a restaurant.

For twelve-year-old Jimmy, it was easier. After a few bites of biscuit and omelet, he said, "See that door over there." He pointed toward the wall space between his and his mother's cots. "That goes into the storeroom, then there's another door into the drugstore. Cousin Eunice don't like us using it, though, unless we're going to work in the store." When Mary thought Henry wasn't looking, she squinched her eyes at Jimmy and shook her head. Henry noticed, however.

Jimmy ignored his mother. "Where do you live, Henry?" the boy asked.

"That's 'Mr. Smith' to you, Jimmy," Mary said. "And you're not supposed to ask personal questions like that."

Henry looked at Mary to see how firm she was about the name business, but he couldn't tell. "It's okay," he said, chancing that Mary wouldn't object. "We're buddies."

"So, where do you live, Henry?" Jimmy asked again.

"Someplace not as nice as this, I'm afraid."

"Really?" Jimmy asked, surprise showing in his voice. Mary was taken aback too. Henry had never said where he lived, and despite wondering about it, she had been reluctant to ask.

"I live in the loft of a barn where I work," Henry said. Only Calvin Birdsong and some of the other mule skinners working for Moss knew. How many, Henry wasn't sure. He spread some preserves over the bottom half of a biscuit and said, "I like it 'cause it's private. I don't have any real walls or any furniture, except for a rickety old chair, but I've got my own little corner, and it's quiet and nobody bothers me."

"Cousin Eunice comes in here and bothers things when we ain't home," Jimmy said, and stuffed a forkful of omelet in his mouth.

"Jimmy!" Mary said, chagrined. She wanted to say that what happened with Eunice was none of Henry's business, but instead, she said, "Henry's not interested in hearing about Cousin Eunice."

Henry kept his eyes on his plate.

"Well, she does," Jimmy said. "She takes things too. She stole your mother's quilt, didn't she?" He put down his fork and looked at Henry. "I was afraid Momma would think I did it, but I didn't. I don't like Cousin Eunice. She's mean."

"Jimmy! That's enough!" Mary said. "I need you to be quiet now."

Silence settled over the room, as everyone busied themselves with their food. When Henry finally looked up, he saw that Mary's face had fallen, her earlier joy drained away.

"Maybe this wasn't a good idea," Henry said. "I think I'd better go."

"No, please don't," Mary said. She looked at her son. "Come here, Jimmy."

Jimmy slid off the trunk and stepped over to his mother. She put her arms around him and said, "It's okay, Jimmy. I'm sorry I yelled at you, and I think you were right to tell about the quilt. I think I need to talk about it." She looked at Henry, who now sat with his hands in his lap. He smiled at her, and she said, "Do you mind, Henry?"

"No," he said. "I'm a good listener."

Jimmy went back to his seat on the trunk and the rest of his food on the table. Mary pushed her plate back and Henry did as well. For the better part of hour, Mary told Henry about what it was like to work for Eunice and Grover and live on their property. She left out only the part about selling marijuana and Cresent City Powders. She also told Henry about Eunice stealing her mother's quilt, including how her mother had come to make it and what it looked like, including the clumsy corners.

~

All the way home to the mule yard, Henry played back the evening in his mind. He was so distracted that at the corner of Broadway and Fourth Street, he almost fell after stubbing his toe on something lying on the edge of the planks in front of the Upton Hotel. It looked like a book, but when he bent over to pick it up, he saw that it was a dirt-covered Sears, Roebuck catalog. Not the sort of thing the high-rolling lease hounds and other oil men in business suits who took rooms at the hotel and crowded into its lobby to trade stock and make deals every hour of every day would likely have been carrying. He looked around to see if there was anyone else nearby who might have dropped it, and seeing no one, he stuck it under his arm and continued north toward the mule yard. The outhouse needed a new supply of paper.

Henry was glad Mary had gotten comfortable enough with him to share the problems she was having with Eunice. If telling someone about them somehow provided a little relief, he was glad for that too. He almost wished, however, that Jimmy hadn't said anything about the quilt, even though it was probably better to have learned about it now rather than later. It was clearly the one Levi had found and Calvin had brought to the mule yard. Henry hadn't told Mary that he once had it in his grasp, and he didn't think he ever could. He feared that if he did, she could never forgive him. She would always know he hadn't considered it worth keeping, never mind that he gave it to someone he thought could make better use of it. He would know that, too, and he believed it would always be a wedge between them, even if unspoken.

Then there was Jimmy himself. Henry liked the boy. He was smart and had spunk. He had shown that with his newspaper selling, and with his oil-dipping escapade, the details of which Henry had gotten from Calvin who had heard them somewhere on his rounds. Henry guessed Mary never knew half the stuff Jimmy got into. Henry's own mother had certainly never known all the crazy things he'd done as a boy. He had loved her dearly, and still did, but she never treated him with the tenderness Mary showed Jimmy tonight after he did something else he shouldn't have. It was another thing Henry loved about Mary. But with Jimmy always around, how could he ever get any closer to Mary than he already was? The barriers between them seemed impassable.

CHAPTER 42

"You have to take the job, Amos. I can't find anybody else." Thaddeus Nalls, the thin, boyish-looking mayor of Berrytown, had resorted to pleading. "Bodies are still piling up down there at Randolph's place, and the oil companies and the preachers and church women are all complaining about the stink and the spectacle. He's got those petrified stiffs they keep pulling out of tank cars propped up on boards out back 'cause he doesn't have room for them inside. Leastwise, that's what he says. I think the perverted son-of-a-bitch likes looking at them. He says his building's full of ones getting shot in barrelhouses and whores' dens, and he puts those ones inside so people can come identify them. Anyway, that's not all. We've got hijackings happening all over the place in broad daylight now, anytime some lease hound or roughneck is fool enough to flash a roll of bills, not just nights."

"How many more times do I have to tell you I don't want to be no police chief?" the hefty township constable asked. "For one thing, I don't get around too good anymore, and for another one, some people, probably you being one of them, would expect me to stop drinking. That's something I ain't gon' do. I got to have an afternoon nip and a nap. Besides, I can't drive, and I'm too big to ride a horse. Same for getting in and out of a buggy all day long. There's got to be somebody else."

The two men were standing in the middle of the still largely unfurnished open room of the former township building on Fourth Street north of the railroad tracks. Little about it had changed since Henry had helped Burns bring Levi Birdsong there after a bunch of white men tried to hang him back in the summer. But now it was the town hall of newly incorporated Berrytown. Work was underway out back on a town jail, and inside, the newly elected mayor was trying to get the town government up and running.

Nalls took a handkerchief from his pants pocket and began wiping his glasses. "No, Amos, there's not. Everybody I've talked to is either too lazy or too scared or has something that pays more. If you take the job, we won't ask you to do any more than what you've been doing as a constable. We'll get you two or three officers and put them on horseback, and you can just boss them, walk around town some, and do the paperwork. I'll even help you with reports and stuff. Come on, what do you say? Doesn't 'Chief Burns' have a good ring to it?"

Burns stared out the window toward the street. Nalls could tell he was rethinking the matter.

"I bet you even know some fellows you could get to sign on with you," Nalls said.

"Well, I might know one, at least."

~

Preachers, church women, the incorporating committee, and Nalls were not the only people in Berrytown who were tired of crime and the general wide-open-anything-goes atmosphere in the community. Without waiting for Nalls and the new town government to do something about it, the other recently organized group of citizens had put together their own plan of action. They implemented it near dusk one weekday in early November.

Shopkeepers closing for the day and oil-field workers going to and from shifts saw them first. Fifty or sixty men, some leading the way on foot and some following on horseback came marching up Broadway from down near Fowler & Son Wagons. They were dressed in white robes and pointed hats with face coverings and were carrying shotguns and singing "Onward Christian Soldiers." About midway through the heart of town, near Seventh Street close to Hornbeck's Drugstore, they came to a halt and got quiet. From somewhere in the middle of the pack, a half dozen of them moved to the front, lit torches, and handed one to a man who came forward on a black horse. He rode well beyond the front of the column, raised his torch high over his head, and bellowed, "Whores, gamblers, and bootleggers! We are here to escort you out of Berrytown! Come out of your barrelhouses, gambling halls, and whoring dens and get on the road or a train now. If you don't come out, we'll burn you out!"

Everyone within earshot outdoors stopped where they were, and everyone within earshot indoors either came out or looked out to see what was happening. After a few moments, the man on the black horse signaled the column, and it moved up near El Dorado Avenue in front of the Upton Hotel, stopping short of the railroad tracks. There he repeated what he had said in front of Hornbeck's. After a few more minutes the robed ensemble moved across the tracks up to Second Street, where, except for one barrelhouse, only residences stood, and the leader delivered his message a third time. "Whores, gamblers, and bootleggers! We are here to escort you out of Berrytown! Come out of your barrelhouses, gambling halls, and whoring dens and get on the road or a train now. If you don't come out, we'll burn you out!"

When no one appeared on the streets with a suitcase or any other sort of baggage or gave any other appearance of leaving, the man on the black horse signaled to those on foot with torches. They walked over to a rooming house on the corner of Broadway and Second known to everyone as home to several prostitutes and set fire to it. Then they crossed to the other side of Broadway and set fire to the barrelhouse there. Both buildings were free standing and selected in part to avoid letting loose an inferno on the whole town, but their fiery demolition had the desired effect.

As the *Berrytown Journal* described the scene the following Friday, "The undesirable elements resembled a massive pack of rats into whose midst had been unleashed just the right number of experienced ratters."

~

At home the evening after the KKK march, Eunice Hornbeck set a pot of chicken soup on the table next to what was left of a day-old loaf of bread. Grover glanced at it, turned up his nose, and said, "I don't know what we're gon' do. Except for Big Sally and her girls, the Klan just ran off the bulk of our marijuana and Cresent City Powders business. The way you've been spending money on new clothes the last couple of weeks, we're ain't even gon' have soup to eat."

"First off," Eunice said, "we've still got money. Second, didn't you hear Floyd Roper today when he said a lot of those people would be back after a while and there's gon' be new ones coming as long as the oil lasts?" Eunice pulled out her chair, sat down across from her husband, and smoothed the skirt of her latest dress.

"That's another thing," Grover said. "Him showing up the day after like that. It's almost like he knew about it before it happened."

"That's silly, Grover. It's not likely anybody in the Klan would've told him about it ahead of time. Us and Sally are the only ones here that know him. Well, besides Mary. And she'd have been too scared to tell him even if she knew. And what would've been the point? It was a coincidence. That's all."

"Maybe, but I don't like the man," Grover said, filling his soup bowl. "Can't say he hasn't been good for us, though. And maybe he'll keep on being, if you stop spending so much and go back to putting our share of the proceeds into that special account you set up after we started selling his stuff."

"What you better be glad of is that I didn't let you go running into the street last night hollering, 'Don't shoot,' or something else stupid like that."

"I admit I was scared. And I'm still worried about that Treasury agent."

"You got any idea how many this makes, now?" Eunice asked.

"What are you talking about? How many what makes?"

"This is about the twentieth time you've brought that up and I've told you that the fellow in the brown suit is probably not an agent. And if he is, he's only coming around on some kind of routine schedule, not 'cause they suspect anything."

"I hope you're right about that, and I hope the town doesn't pass any drug ordinances we'll have to worry about either."

"Geez, Grover! Wasn't Roper right about our customers keeping their mouths shut about us? And far as the town's concerned, if they did pass any drug ordinances, whose fault would that be? You remember, I told you to keep off that incorporation committee. But no, you wouldn't listen. You ought to be worrying about some of those poor girls they ran out of town that don't have no other way to make a living. So, stop whining and eat your damn soup."

~

Mary shivered again as she put supper on the table for her and Jimmy. The two of them had watched the Klansmen through the drugstore windows last evening with Eunice and Grover. Jimmy had been helping Mary clean the soda fountain before closing. The Hornbecks didn't pay him for doing that occasionally, but they didn't object either, so long as he stayed out of Eunice's way.

All four of them had looked on in stunned silence as the Klansmen paraded up the street. By the time the adults found their voices, all three were thinking about how fast the customer base for the illegal drugs in the back of the store was shrinking right in front of them. They didn't say anything about that in front of Jimmy, of course. All they did was speculate about who the men under the hoods were. And hurry to get the store closed.

Later, when Mary and Jimmy had retreated to the shed, the only thing Jimmy said was that he wondered where all those people who had to leave would go. From hawking newspapers on street corners and overhearing adults talking about all manner of things, he knew far more about the world around him than the average twelve-year-old. Mary had been glad, on one hand, that he hadn't asked about a lot of things she would have to explain, but on the other, she wished he had. Talking to her son would have kept her from wondering if the Klansmen might come after Eunice, Grover, and her. She had slept little last night and worried about it all through today.

"Momma, are you sure you're all right?" Jimmy asked, pulling Mary back into the present as she sat down at their table.

"Yes, Jimmy," she said. "I'm okay. It's just a chill. I'm probably coming down with a cold."

CHAPTER 43

Henry turned up his jacket collar and watched his mules' breath form tiny clouds of mist in the early morning air. He was half an hour out of the Consolidated Oil Well Supply Company yard on Fourth Street, heading for Louann with a load of pipe collars, gate valves, and casing tongs.

When the front wheels of the wagon hit a crossing rut, a package wrapped in old newspapers slid from under the wagon seat into the foot well. Henry shoved it back with his heel. In it were two new blankets, the best he could find in Berrytown. Behind it, another package held an assortment of hard candies and jellybeans, plus several books he thought would be appropriate for kids the age of the Taylors'. He had bought the blankets at Bryant's General Store and the sweets and books at Compton's Drugs and Notions, avoiding Hornbeck's.

Two days ago, Henry had asked Moss to assign him to the next two-up job for Louann. When Moss asked why, Henry said only that he had a personal errand he would like to run over there, and it wouldn't take long. For a moment, Henry thought the old man was about to tell him to take care of his personal business on his own time. Moss pushed his derby back on his head, squinted at Henry, leaned over and let fly a mouthful of snuff-colored spittle, and said, "Henry, I've been watching you."

Henry couldn't imagine what was coming next, but he didn't figure on anything good. He wondered if Moss knew he had been snooping around the padlocked room in the front barn.

"I ain't one for wasting time telling somebody they're doing a good job," Moss said. "I just expect it. But you surprised me. I liked your cut first time I seen you, but I hired you mostly 'cause of Calvin. I didn't know if you'd last, but you ain't afraid of hard work. You're dependable and you take good care of your mules. I like that. So, yeah, you go on and do what you got to do. Just don't take any more time than you have to."

Henry hadn't cared much about what Moss thought about his work so long as he could keep his job and have a convenient place to stay while looking for Ed Tuttle, and lately while spending time with Mary Dutton. But he liked hearing Moss's words because he had come to like what he was doing. He didn't spend any time over the next two days thinking about that, however. He was too busy rehearsing what he was going to say to Sarah Taylor.

Honesty was the best approach, he decided. He planned to tell Sarah that the quilt had been given to him by someone whose relative had found it, that none of them had known at the time who made it or who owned it before, but he had learned recently not only who it had belonged to, but also that it had been stolen from her, and it would mean a great deal to her to get it back. He hoped Sarah would accept the two blankets and the gifts for Nell and Ruth in return for her understanding the situation and letting him have the quilt back.

Henry made his deliveries to several drilling sites, then drove out to the camp where the Taylors had set up their tent house. By the time he got there, long shadows from a sun sitting low on the horizon, together with recently added tents and tent houses belonging to new arrivals, made finding the Taylors' tent house harder than he expected.

Henry picked a place to stop his wagon and tether the mules on the edge of the camp. With his packages slung under one arm, he walked toward a woman taking clothes off a rope line next to an often-patched tent house that appeared to have been there for some time. Slight of build and clad in a dress and apron with no coat, she flinched when she heard him approaching. When she turned around and saw it was someone she didn't know, she stared at him without speaking—her mouth and eyes wide open and forehead furrowed. Two young children, a boy and a girl, appeared from behind the tent house and ran to her side, eager to see the strange man who had come to visit. The woman pulled them close behind her and looked right then left to see if anyone else was around.

"How do, ma'am," Henry said, removing his fedora, which still wore when working. "I didn't mean to startle you. I'm looking for Sarah and Cotton Taylor. I visited them out here several weeks back, and I can't remember where their tent house is. I wonder if you can help me."

The woman's features softened some, but she didn't move or say anything.

"They did me a kindness," Henry said, coloring his purpose a bit, trying to put the woman at ease, "and I brought them something in return."

The woman eyed his packages. "They don't live here anymore," she said. "Packed everything up and left 'bout three weeks ago."

Henry's shoulders slumped. "Did they say if they were going to Tonkawa, over in Oklahoma?"

The woman relaxed further when she saw Henry's reaction and heard "Tonkawa."

"They'd been talking 'bout that town," she said, "but the day they left, Sarah said she thought they might be going to someplace name of 'Burbank.' She said they wasn't for sure 'bout it, though. They was going to meet up with a friend of Cotton's in Ponca City first and figure out where to light. She didn't like not knowing right from the start, but Cotton's friend said there was enough work up there to last a long time and they could get them a real house. Sounds kinda peculiar to me. A bunch of Indians own all the land. Osages, I think she said they were. But the oil companies run things. Anyway, she said she'd write me when they got settled."

"Ma'am," Henry said, "if I give you an address and money for postage, would you write me and give me the Taylors' address if you hear from them? I would really appreciate it. Meantime, if you don't mind, for your trouble, I'd like you to have these things I brought for them. There's a couple of brand-new blankets here and a little something for the children."

"My name's Mrs. Clinkscale. Eliza Clinkscale," she said. "I guess I can do that. I may have to write Sarah back and ask her if it's okay first, though. And we don't want to take things you brought for her and her girls. Wouldn't be right."

"Please, you'd be doing me a huge favor. I'll make it up to the Taylors if I ever get a chance to see them again."

All the way back to Berrytown and well into the night, Henry thought about Sarah Taylor and Eliza Clinkscale, two women with little children trailing after husbands who were following oil from one place to the next. Despite the happiness he thought he had seen in the faces and behavior of the Taylors at dinner that Sunday noon, their lives seemed hard. And there was no joy at all in the face of Eliza Clinkscale. He remembered how the Taylors had all their worldly goods packed on the Model T stuck in the creek the day he met them. And the oil-soaked soil and foul-smelling air surrounding them where they lived. He wondered if they and other couples like them expected such when they fell in love and decided to get married.

But who was he to judge? Thanks to Ed Tuttle, instead of using his real name, "Henry Grant," he was going around calling himself "Henry Smith," and he no longer had any roots or any sort of life to offer a woman. Maybe it was just as well, for himself but especially for Mary Dutton, that there was little hope of finding the quilt.

When Henry got back to the mule yard, Moss was waiting for him.

"Amos Burns came by here a little while ago," Moss said. "Asked if you'd come back from your run yet. Said to tell you to come over to the town hall and see him when you got done, no matter what time it was. Wouldn't say what for. Just said it wasn't any kind of problem and he'd be waiting. You ain't got yourself in some kind of trouble, have you?"

"Not as far as I know," Henry said. He wondered for a moment if Moss might be worried that it had something to do with that back room. Then he thought, no, Burns wasn't likely interested in looking into any bootlegging. He was too fond of booze himself.

When Henry walked into the town hall a little later still puzzling over what Burns wanted, he found the constable straining a chair behind the once-lone desk in the back of the big room. Two smaller desks, a large table, and several other chairs were scattered about as if waiting for someone to choose permanent locations for them.

"Henry Smith," Burns said. "Just the man I want to see. Drag up a chair and have a seat. I got a question for you."

Henry selected a straight chair, straddled it backwards in front of Burns's desk, and rested his forearms across the back.

"You were in the war, wasn't you?" Burns asked.

"Is that your question?"

"You was an officer I'm guessing."

"Yeah," Henry said. "What's this about?"

"You ever thought about being a police officer?"

"Huh?"

"I'm offering you a job. I'm gon' be the new Berrytown chief of police. I get to hire three officers, and I'm asking you first. You interested?"

Had someone asked which surprised him most, Burns's announcement or his question, Henry would have been hard pressed to say. He stared at the constable for a moment and saw he was dead serious. Henry guessed the thing with Levi Birdsong a few months back had something to do with the offer, but what he couldn't grasp was why the mayor would appoint Burns to the chief's position, or why he would accept it, unless maybe there was something peculiar going on. He had to admit, though, that the man had gotten his attention. He wondered if this might help him somehow to find Ed Tuttle.

"Constable Burns," Henry began.

"Call me 'Amos.'"

"Okay, Amos. If you're figuring on running some kind of protection scheme with all the moonshiners, bootleggers, and barrelhouse operators so you can line your pockets and get all the free hooch you want, you can count me out."

"Boy, you get right to it, don't you?" Amos asked, unfazed by Henry's candor. "I don't mind, though. Everybody knows I like a nip or two every day and a nap. But no, this ain't nothing like you're thinking. I ain't looking to bother no little guys, specially them that've been living here all along, 'cause if you ask me, this Prohibition business is gon' be over pretty soon, and there ain't much way to enforce it anyhow. I'd like to stop outsiders who're bringing stuff in, though.

"But what I really want is to put a stop to all these hijackings and shootings going on all the time. I know the booze and whores cause a lot of it, but we can cut it way down if we put you and whoever else I get out there on the streets on horses where folks can see you. We do that and we stick a few hijackers and some of them jaybirds that want to fight all the time in the calaboose, and Berrytown will be a lot safer place."

"I expect you're right about that last part, anyway," Henry said. He looked down at the floor then back at the constable. "I don't know about the part that involves me, though, Amos. I'll have to think about it."

Chapter 44

Henry waited until all the other mule skinners had fed and rubbed down their teams and left the yard. He found Moss in the cluttered cubbyhole that passed for his office in the front barn. His door was open, and he was sitting at his rolltop desk shuffling through a stack of papers. He had not taken off his blacksmithing apron or derby hat, and he leaned sideways to spit into a Ball jar just as Henry was about to knock on the doorjamb.

"You got a minute?" Henry asked. He removed his fedora and held it in one hand at his side.

Moss looked down at the hat then up at Henry's face. He wasn't accustomed to men taking their hats off to talk to him. "I seen you pull in a while ago. Your rig looked all right. You ain't had no trouble, have you?"

"No trouble," Henry said. "Just need to tell you something and ask a favor."

Moss spit again and motioned Henry to an empty nail keg turned upside down with a box of wagon wheel hubs and flanges resting on top. Henry put the box on the floor and sat on the keg.

"Let me guess," Moss said. "You've got hives or something and you need to start late tomorrow so you can go to Hornbeck's first to get some medicine and see that pretty woman."

"No, nothing like that. You've been good to me and good to work for, but I've been offered another job I want to take, starting next week. And I'd like to stay on in the other barn back there till I can find someplace else. I'd expect to pay for it, of course."

"Well, I'll be damned," Moss said. He spit again and leaned back in his chair. "I sho' hate to lose you, Henry. What is it you gon' be doing?"

Henry put both hands on the brim of his hat and turned it around and around with his fingers. "I need to tell you first," he said, "that you don't have anything to worry about. I know you're bootlegging, and I'm not gon' tell anybody."

"Huh?" Moss exclaimed. He sat forward and grabbed both chair arms, squeezing them as his face turned red. "What makes you think that? Did Calvin tell you? And if I was to be doing it, what business would it be of yours?"

"Let's just say I think it because I keep my eyes open. The reason it's my business is I'm gon' be a Berrytown policeman. That's what Amos Burns wanted to see me about the other day."

"Well, I'll be John Brown!"

"But you don't need to worry. I don't care what you're doing, and neither does Amos. He's not much interested in moonshiners and bootleggers, only hijackers and thieves and such. And I'm okay with that. You've been good to me, and I don't want to mess things up for you."

Moss relaxed his grip on the chair arms and sat back. "Yeah," he said, "I reckon I know that. It's just that you come on me out of the blue with it. I guess I should've known a smart fellow like you'd catch onto the bootlegging, and I can sure see why Amos don't want to do anything about it, much as he drinks." Anyway, looks like I ain't got no choice but to trust you. It's hard to see, though, why you want to leave what you're doing here for something that's likely to get you shot, or worse. Like I've told you before, you're a good hand."

Henry nodded his agreement and appreciation, and neither man spoke for few moments, as each contemplated the changes taking place in their relationship.

"Yeah, sure," Moss finally said. "You can stay on in the barn. I won't even charge you. I'm thinking that having the law living right on top of me will keep anybody else from nosing around. But if anybody asks, you tell them you're paying me good money for letting out the space, and if they ask you how much, you tell them that's between the two of us."

"There's one more thing," Henry said.

"Yeah?"

"I'm gon' need a horse and saddle. I assume the town's gon' pay for it, but if they don't, I'm gon' need to rent one, or pay for it a little at a time. I know the one I'd like to have, and I'd appreciate it if you could see your way to work with me on that too."

"Probably. You got one in mind?"

"Yeah. That black mare you got off Otis Leatherwood."

~

Calvin Birdsong heard them first, then turned and saw them. Ghostly figures in white robes and hoods bursting out of the darkness riding galloping horses and carrying lighted torches held high. He had never been to Lone Star Hill before tonight and had come now only in search of his cousin Levi, who had gone missing after supper.

Unlike the two hundred or so Texans who made up the all-black community a little north of Berrytown over in southern Ouachita County, Levi and other local black men who helped dig oil storage pits all around the two-county area traveled back and forth each day from wherever they called home. Levi was still living with Calvin and his mother, and lately he had been talking about the hill almost constantly because he heard fresnos drivers with whom he worked joking and carrying on about the good times they were having in the barrelhouses there.

Both Calvin and Mrs. Birdsong had warned Levi to stay away from the place. Even though he had been a gofer on oil-pit construction sites for several months now, he still had headaches almost every day and confused white workmen with army officers. He also still wore his faded uniform jacket everywhere he went. White men and black alike made him the butt of jokes and pranks, but he seemed unaware that they were making fun of him. He became combative only when someone made derogatory remarks about his jacket. No one ever did that a second time, but Levi had come home bloodied more than once after bullies ganged up on him. Calvin knew that would almost certainly happen again if Levi went to a barrelhouse.

Since putting up the first huge cot house for its imported workers, the Texas-based pit-digging company had built two others. More workers had arrived from other places, and another barrelhouse, along with more lean-tos and tents, had sprung up alongside the first two and the small general store. Like those in the white communities, the barrelhouses offered all sorts of entertainment, but liquor and prostitutes were the main attractions.

Having walked several miles, Calvin was nearing the edge of Lone Star Hill when he heard the thunder of horses' hooves and turned to see the mounted men, dozens of them, coming around a curve on the road behind him. Hoping they had not already seen him, Calvin jumped a ditch on the near side of the road and crawled under the limbs of a downed tree. The horsemen roared past without a word. When the last of them cleared his hiding place, Calvin raced after them even though he was unarmed except for the bullwhip he always had tied around his waist. If the riders noticed him following, one of them could easily double back and dispatch him, but all he thought about was alerting the camp and saving Levi.

Calvin couldn't keep up with the horses, and when he tried shouting an alarm, no one heard him. Unlike when the Klansmen had paraded up Broadway in Berrytown and stopped three times to issue warnings, they paused in Lone Star Hill only long enough for two of the men to raise shotguns and fire four shots, after which, they all began yelling, "Niggers get out! Niggers get out! Niggers get out!" No one mistook their meaning. The riders were not only calling people out of the barrelhouses and other structures—they were ordering them back to Texas or wherever else they came from.

Calvin caught up in time to hear the warning yells and see torches hurled through doorways and onto canvas tent tops. Within seconds, everything was ablaze. People came running outside with only the clothes on their backs, and some not even that. Some screamed incoherently. Others cried, "No, no, please! Help me Lord! Momma! Momma!" Others yelled the names of friends but didn't pause for responses. They fled in all directions.

Thinking only of his cousin, Calvin raced into the melee calling, "Levi! Levi!" The Klansmen rode their horses into and over anyone too bewildered to run away. Calvin saw a burning barrelhouse shed fall on one man and another get kicked in the head by a rearing horse. Then he was knocked to the ground himself and stepped on. He managed to get up and dodge his way to the edge of the mob, then saw that no structure remained where Levi could have taken refuge and survived. Calvin could only hope his cousin had managed to make it into an adjoining field or woods. Seconds later, prodded by the butt end of a Klansman's shotgun, Calvin joined the exodus.

CHAPTER 45

Newspapers in Hot Springs, Arkadelphia, Pine Bluff, Little Rock, and elsewhere in Arkansas had reported the earlier Klan raid in Berrytown. But newspapers across the country, from Niagara Falls, New York, to Seattle, Washington, reported the raid on Lone Star Hill. Some saw it as another in a series of violent, racially motivated attacks like the ones that had left more than one hundred dead in Earle, Arkansas, three years earlier, and killed more than three dozen in Tulsa, Oklahoma, last year.

Six people died in the fires that swept Lone Star Hill off the map. Levi Birdsong was presumed one of them because he was never seen again after that night. Also, several near-melted army jacket buttons were found among unrecognizable human remains in the rubble of one of the barrelhouses.

For days after the second raid, many residents of Berrytown and the surrounding communities who decried the raucous side of boomtown life looked upon the attacks with favor. Never mind that most of the people chased out of Lone Star Hill were laborers, not barrelhouse owners, prostitutes, or gamblers. Some in Berrytown knew, and others suspected, that several of its leading citizens, including men they went to church with, had helped organize the Klan and the raids. Some also knew that the second raid, aimed almost solely at black people, represented the true Klan.

Henry fell into the second group. He had seen the Klan in action in Indiana. He took Levi Birdsong's death hard. Even though he barely knew the man, Henry appreciated how hard the soldiers in Levi's regiment had fought for their country in the Great War, and he understood how battle-ravaged the minds and bodies of soldiers lucky enough to survive the experience were.

Calvin Birdsong was devastated. He had come to regard Levi like a younger brother, one who needed looking after. It was a task he had taken on with increasing devotion, only, as he saw it, to fail. He came to work every day and did his job, but he no longer brought the joy he had once shown for it.

Henry empathized with him. It was not unlike when Henry returned from Europe and learned what Ed Tuttle had done to Helen and her unborn child. The more Henry watched Calvin struggle with his grief, the more Henry dwelled on why he had come to Berrytown. He thought about it while he drove his wagon during his last few days of working for Moss. While he brushed and fed Jake, Ben, Lon, and Sam every evening. While he ate supper in whichever café he wandered into afterward. And while he lay on his pallet in the barn at night.

He had allowed the difficulty of the task, as well as his desire to be with Mary, to keep him from correcting the legal system's failure to make Tuttle pay for the crimes he had committed. And for destroying the Grant family. He had been so worried about Tuttle getting wind of him and running away again that he had not only assumed the alias "Smith" and tried to hide his scar, but he had also held back potentially helpful inquiries that might have increased his chances of finding the murdering devil.

No longer, he decided. Now he would have greater mobility and a badge that would make searching easier. His legal reach extended only to the Berrytown corporate limits, but he would not let that hold him back. He would find reasons to link up with officers in neighboring jurisdictions. He had no authority to arrest Tuttle if he flushed him, but that didn't matter. Henry had in mind something of greater finality.

~

After spotting the drilling derrick rising on Isaiah Watson's farm that first time and getting so angry that he spilled most of the morning milk, Otis Leatherwood told himself he wouldn't track the progress of the spidery-looking contraption as it reached skyward. But he couldn't help himself. He peeked at it from his porch every day. It was close enough that he noticed when the drilling crew secured the crown block on the top. He recognized it by the boxy frame that stuck out over the sides of the tapered derrick. He didn't know exactly what function a crown block performed, but he knew it had something to do with raising and lowering the drilling equipment. Installation of it meant drilling would begin soon.

When it did, all the scraping, creaking, and banging would be another constant irritant. Like the pipeline crews tromping over his fields the past few weeks, and like the way they punctuated what he regarded as their "lawyered-up legal right to trespass" by blasting tree stumps over in the woods past his house. Except that the drilling would be going on non-stop twenty-four hours a day.

Otis had meant to do something more to fight back, beyond his newspaper ad and blowing up the first pipeline supplies dumped on his farm. He had way more than enough dynamite left to try again to get people's attention. So far, though, he had not come up with anything he thought he could pull off without hurting the land in the process. Blowing up a well, drilling site, storage tank, loaded tank car, or oil pit would only dump more oil into fields and streams. Those targets were all too heavily guarded anyway, as were oil-field supply yards. And blowing up a busy bridge or part of a rail line would harm a lot of people and businesses beyond those chasing oil money. Empty tank cars on a siding someplace or an unfinished pipeline somewhere other than on his farm, where round-the-clock guards were posted now for good reason, seemed like better targets.

In time, Otis settled on the tank cars. Twice he rode one of his mules into Berrytown and over to Louann to get a better feel for freight train schedules and to look at sidings and cleaning stations where the cars might sit empty at times. He concluded that his best chance of success lay with the cleaning station in Louann. It was smaller and more remote than the one in Berrytown, yet it was big enough that destroying it would foul up operations in Louann for some time. This might lead to a few more oil pits being dug, but it would at least slow things down. Maybe it would get more people thinking and possibly lead to some safer practices in the long run. Or maybe not. Maybe he would get away with it. Or maybe not. In either case, he would have done all that was within his power to do, and he was prepared for whatever consequences might come his way.

Otis was in Louann when he heard about the Klan raid on Lone Star Hill. He didn't hold much sympathy for the barrelhouse operators and prostitutes the masked riders ran off, but he hated that everyday working folks had also been targeted, and he figured that Isaiah and Luella Watson would be even more concerned about their own safety now, as well as that of their friends and members of Isaiah's congregation.

Otis loathed the thought of getting any closer than his own front porch to the drilling operation on Isaiah's farm, but the next morning he went over there nevertheless, taking the long way, on the road, to keep as far from the racket and commotion as possible.

As he walked, Otis noticed a stack of fresnos on the edge of one of Isaiah's fields and guessed the drillers were feeling pretty good about their prospects for success. Likely they had expected some of the men who had been run out of Lone Star Hill to operate them. The plight of the fresnos drivers together with the thought of an oil pit where tall rows of green corn once stood knotted Otis's stomach. Just this once, however, for the sake of Isaiah and his family, Otis hoped the drillers brought in a producing well so the Watsons could escape their own version of the madness here, and not have to stay on, with their farm ruined anyway and nothing at all to show for it.

Unlike when Otis usually came to the Watsons' house, Isaiah wasn't off somewhere else on the property doing chores. He and Luella were sitting on the front porch. At first, Otis thought they were watching what little of the drilling they could see from there, but then he saw that Isaiah was wearing a coat and tie.

Isaiah stood when Otis drew close. "Morning, Mr. Otis," he said.

"Morning, Isaiah. Morning Luella. You look like you're ready for church or something, Isaiah. I reckon I come at a bad time."

"No, sir," Isaiah said. "We was just sitting here talking a spell 'fore I go visit with some folks that's unsettled 'cause of that big fire up yonder at Lone Star Hill. You be welcome to come on up and join us."

Otis pushed his hat back on his head and ran a hand over the side of his face. "No, Isaiah, I don't want to hold you up. I just wanted to tell y'all that I'm sorry 'bout what happened up there. That was mighty sorry business. I reckon I understand better now why you and Luella want to go somewheres else. I know I've told you that before, but this here thing made it plainer than day. You know what I think about all this oil and such, but like I said before, I hope for y'all's sake this here well comes in. If it does, I'm sho' gon' miss y'all, though."

"Mr. Otis," Luella said, getting to her feet, "we sho' do appreciate that. We gon' miss you too. You been real good to us."

"I see the fresnos piled out there," Otis said. "The drillers must be pretty sure the well's coming in."

"Yes, sir, they are," Isaiah said. "It's looking so good, they already talking about drilling two more. If it's what they say, we're gon' leave right soon after. William and Samuel done making arrangements for us up in Chicago."

"This old world's a crazy place, Isaiah," Otis said, "but you're a good man, and you and Luella are lucky to have them three fine boys."

Isaiah nodded. "Yes, sir, Mr. Otis. The Lord's been good to us."

Otis stepped closer to the porch and put out his hand. Isaiah stepped down and took it, and the two men shook once, firmly. Otis looked over at Luella and nodded, glanced again at Isaiah, then turned and walked away. He waited until he was out of sight to brush the back of his hand across his eyes.

CHAPTER 46

The bullwhip popped like a firecracker, and the bearded roustabout squealed like a pig. He jerked his bleeding oil-stained hand high in the air, and his .38 revolver hit the ground with a thud. The slender man the roustabout was aiming to shoot took that as an opportunity to pull a wood chisel from his carpenter's apron and lunge at his would-be assailant. He managed only half a step before the whip sliced his knuckles with another loud pop.

"Goddamn!" he howled, as his chisel fell beside the gun.

"Don't even think about running," Henry commanded, as he dismounted Trixie, whip still in hand. He ordered the combatants onto their knees and the gawkers in front of Ralph's Café to go on about their business. Astonished more than angry, the pair did as they were told, and within minutes, Henry had them handcuffed together and walking ahead of him and Trixie up Broadway toward the now-completed Berrytown jail. Henry hadn't counted on his brief experience as a mule skinner coming in so handy, but he had gotten good with the whip and decided to carry it with him on duty, much as Calvin Birdsong walked around with one all the time.

People in line at the café, others trying to beat closing hours in stores, and still others heading to the American Theater stared at the new officer and his prisoners. A few applauded, appreciative of Mayor Nalls' efforts to make Berrytown's streets safer. Without looking around, Henry tipped an index finger to the brim of his Stetson, his only new attire other than the badge with the single word "Police" he wore pinned to his denim jacket. The town had so far been unable to get badges with its name on them, and this, as well as the lack of any sort of uniform, suited Henry perfectly. He could go anywhere in the two-county area with it and have people think he had authority there until they learned better.

This week, he was beginning to like being a police officer. Last week, though, he had doubted his decision to take the job. Mother Nature had picked Sunday night before his first day on duty to send southern Arkansas its biggest rainstorm in months. The deluge didn't stop for two days. Creeks overflowed their banks, bridges washed out, supply lines of all kinds shut down, and Berrytown streets swallowed up vehicles and draft animals near about whole. Everyone was in a foul temper.

Henry and the other two officers—Preston Briggs and Vernon Delcapp, cousins of the mayor, brought in from somewhere over near Texarkana, where they had been sheriff's deputies a short while—had met briefly with Amos Burns at Moss's mule yard on Sunday and spent time getting familiar with their horses, which the town was renting from Moss, along with tack. When Burns offered town-issued pistols, all three men said they preferred their own. Briggs and Delcapp had holsters, and Burns said he would order one for Henry. He said his pants pocket would suffice until it came.

Briggs and Delcapp, who were boarding with Nalls, arrived late at the mule yard on Monday morning, having already struggled to navigate the flooded streets. Things went downhill from there. All three officers spent the entire week working up and down Broadway and on side streets, often on foot, breaking up arguments and trying to help mule skinners and drivers get their wagons, animals, cars, and trucks out of the mud. Henry worried most about the horses, mules, and oxen that often bogged up to their bellies and had to be pulled out of the muck with ropes. During the day, he fought off memories of wounded mules and horses screaming on the battlefield in France, but at night they filled his dreams, and he awoke each morning with his head pounding.

The officers spent the second week almost entirely on horseback. They patrolled the streets and alleys, made themselves visible around the train depot, and rode along the train tracks within town limits. In the process, they stopped fist fights, arrested men for being drunk and disorderly, and caught four hijackers running away from shouting victims.

Chief Burns didn't venture far from the town hall and jail either week, but no one cared. The consensus around town was that crime, public brawling, and raucous behavior were all declining. No one knew how much of that to attribute to the new officers and how much to the demographic changes wrought earlier by the Klan. But nearly all who wanted the town cleaned up welcomed having policemen.

Henry passed by Hornbeck's several times on foot during the first week and several more times on horseback during the second but never stopped in or looked through the windows. Twice, however, he saw Jimmy on the corner selling newspapers before school and returned the boy's waves.

During the storm, when normal foot traffic dropped off in the businesses up and down Broadway, owners and clerks had plenty of time to observe the spectacle of mud and frustration. Mary spotted Henry the first afternoon. He was sloshing his way across the street toward a car bogged down in front of the store. His rain-soaked Stetson and the badge pinned to his drenched jacket came as a jolt. She had heard the town was hiring policemen, but she didn't know he was one of them.

She hadn't seen him since the evening he came to supper. At first, she had missed his company. More, in fact, than she would have believed if someone had told her then that they wouldn't be spending any more time together. Initially, she blamed herself. She figured she and Jimmy had scared him away with all their talk about their troubles with Eunice, things too personal and better kept to themselves. Then she grew angry that Henry had sat and listened to some of her innermost concerns and callously never said another word to her after that night. It was insensitive and humiliating.

In time, she wondered if Jimmy was also a problem for Henry. Maybe he didn't want to get further involved with a woman who had a half-grown son. She guessed she could understand that some, but still, it infuriated her. Jimmy missed seeing Henry, too, and that angered her more.

She was also mad at herself for being vulnerable. She had allowed herself to care deeply for a man for the first time since she lost her husband, and all she got from it was a bruised heart.

When she saw Henry crossing the street wearing a policeman's badge, however, her first thought wasn't anger. It was fear that he could be hurt or killed.

In the midst of the incorporation of Berrytown, the Ku Klux Klan raids, the rainstorm, and the creation of a new police force, oil continued to tighten its grip on the community. Leasing, drilling, producing, transporting, and polluting kept expanding. Despite the exodus of so many people the Klan and others considered undesirable, Berrytown, as well as nearby Louann and Norphlet, grew apace as more and more speculators, oil-field workers, tradesmen, and others flooded in. By late November, the population of Berrytown alone had swelled to almost twenty thousand. Mayor Nalls added two more law officers, both of them sons of distant cousins of Chief Burns and both thankfully more energetic. The added police presence kept street rowdiness, public drunkenness, and hijacking down, but new barrelhouses sprang up, new ladies of the evening came to the area, and illegal booze continued to flow.

Everyone expected the growth to continue as long as new wells kept coming in. They also knew it would stop when the oil quit flowing. The oil men, the gamblers, the prostitutes, and any businesses that depended exclusively on them would move on to wherever the big companies and the wildcatters found new pools of black gold.

Local businesspeople understood that dynamic, and it affected their thinking and planning, especially those who were breaking the law. Frightened as Grover Hornbeck was of getting caught selling illegal drugs, he and Eunice were earning as much money that way as otherwise. So, he reluctantly agreed with Eunice that they would keep at it and make all they could while they could. What came after, they would address then. That did not, however, keep Grover from continuing to aggravate Eunice by worrying out loud about going to jail.

Wilbur Moss took a different approach. His illegal enterprise—bootlegging—was only a sideline for him. It was also one he had been engaged in long before the first gusher blew in, albeit on a smaller scale with a different supplier. He had always been more concerned with his mule yard and freight business and was even more so now. It had continued to grow despite the big hauling outfit that had moved in from Missouri early on, and Moss was enjoying it. When Berrytown declined, as it inevitably would, and the Missourians bailed to the next big discovery area, Berrytown's population would still be larger than before the boom, and Moss would still have plenty of business. If he didn't get arrested first, something he only now began to think about.

With the new police officers around every day riding his horses out of his barns, the booze running he had been doing with Calvin Birdsong's help now seemed riskier. He didn't think he had anything to worry about from Amos Burns, or even from Henry Smith, if that was his real name—Moss had wondered about that from the outset—but the mayor and all those cousins were complete unknowns. Plus, there was the Klan to think about. Its leaders up in Little Rock were even organizing females. The Women of the Ku Klux Klan was the first statewide Klan auxiliary in the country, and it meant even more prying eyes.

Chiefly, though, Moss was tired of dealing with his source, Owen Sutro, who in Moss's view was getting too ambitious and too careless, a deadly combination that could soon bring the Treasury Department's Prohibition Unit down on the rascal and all associated with him. Sutro had arranged early on for the delivery of shine to Moss in wagonloads of hay in broad daylight on weekdays when all the mule skinners were out on runs, and now he was pushing Moss to add new drop-offs along his freight routes, which would mean more deliveries to the front barn and bringing at least one more mule skinner in on the operation.

Sutro was also the reason Moss couldn't figure a way out. The man stood well over six feet, was heavily muscled with thick black hair and glowering eyes, and always toted two pistols in heavily tooled leather holsters. He was also the sheriff of Ouachita County, head of the Camden Klavern of the KKK, and ran the biggest moonshine operation in all southern Arkansas. People were not known to say no to him and get away with it.

CHAPTER 47

After two weeks of working for Amos Burns, Henry was comfortable in his new role and confident that Burns didn't much care what he and the other officers did so long as they made enough arrests to keep the mayor happy. Nalls had set huge fines on even minor offenses and was raking a heap of money into the town coffers, supposedly to go with new tax monies to pay for improved public services. Henry had his doubts about all the fines ending up where they were supposed to, but he didn't say anything. He had no proof and didn't want to start something that might hamper his looking for Ed Tuttle.

One chilly morning the last week of November, Henry rode out southeast, near Norphlet, to where he had last talked with Al Jenkins, only to find that he had moved his peckerwood mill again the day before. Henry got directions from the farmer on whose land the mill had been operating and caught up with Jenkins a little before noon. The big man was standing with his hands on his hips directing installation of the circle saw when he looked up and saw Henry approaching on horseback. His jaw dropped when he saw the badge on Henry's jacket.

"Morning, Al," Henry said. He swung down, tied Trixie's reins to a wagon wheel, and walked up to the log carriage. "You got a minute?"

"Yeah, sure," Jenkins said, stepping around the saw. "What the Sam Hill's going on?"

"I've got a new job."

"I can see that. Why?"

"Thought I'd try something different. Stop being tied to somebody else's schedule."

"Looks to me like a good way to get shot at or something."

"Well, I've been shot at before," Henry said. He removed his hat and spun it once on his fingers. "I've got a question for you. Since I can get around a little easier now, I thought I might look up that fellow you said talks like me. I got to thinking about it, and he sounds kinda like somebody I might know from back home. You said you thought he was working in one of those barrelhouses over in Ouachita County. You got any idea which one it might be?"

Jenkins shifted his stance and scratched an itch. "I don't recall that he said exactly, except that it's in Blackjack Hill, sort of north of Standard Umpsted. You go over there, though, you better take off that badge. Some of them ole boys are liable to try to make you eat it."

"Yeah, I've heard talk about the place. I'm surprised the Klan didn't go in there the first night they rode."

"Don't you know why? It's 'cause Owen Sutro owns just about everything up there. He's the law and the Klan both. If you're gon' keep on being in the police, you better get a better handle on who's the crooks and who's the good guys."

"Yeah," Henry said, putting his hat back on. "I reckon I'll work on that." He remounted and, as he turned Trixie to leave, he added, "You keep on watching out for rattlers, now."

"Wait," Jenkins called. "What you just said about snakes. You recall I told you the guy was falling-down drunk when he was running on. You just made me remember he also said the only thing he didn't like about his job was 'the river and the goddamned snakes.' I don't know what that has to do with anything, but it was strange that he was talking about the barrelhouse one minute and the river and snakes the next. Might be connected someway or other."

"That one thing all he said about them?"

"Yeah. Leastways, it's all I understood of it."

"All right, thanks," Henry said. He tipped his hat to Jenkins and coaxed Trixie into an easy running walk. He was coming to really like her.

"You remember I told you, Alma," Otis Leatherwood asked, "I've been thinking a lot lately about that niece of mine, and her boy Jimmy?"

The sun was long down, and Otis had been sitting on his porch talking to his beloved Alma again since finishing his afternoon chores. He hadn't eaten and wasn't hungry. He didn't know if there was a heaven, but he believed that if one was up there somewhere, Alma was its prettiest angel. He knew he still felt her presence every time he sat out here where they had shared so many evenings over the years.

"Well, I've got a confession to make, and I hope you ain't gon' mind it. You know how all this time I've left everything in the house just the way you liked it, except for using some of them wrapping papers you saved and bringing our picture downstairs, and the thing I told you about the other day. Well, this morning I did something else. I got to studying on things, like the time I gave you my mother's cameo pin with all them little pearly-looking thingamajigs around it. And I decided

Mary ought to have it. Rebecca was her grandmother, too, just like she was Eunice's, but Eunice don't care nothing about family. Never has. Anyway, I went up and found that pin, and I'm gon' take it to town and give it to Mary. I'm gon' give Jimmy my daddy's pocketknife too. It's 'bout time he had one."

Otis reached over and patted the arm of Alma's rocking chair. "I knew you'd understand," he said. Then he smiled, leaned his head back, closed his eyes, and fell asleep, oblivious for once to the banging and clanging coming from the drilling over on the Watson farm.

~

Otis still had money from selling Trixie, and the next morning he rode one of his mules into town and tied him up in front of the newspaper office.

"I want to run my ad four more times," he told Nathan Collier when he went inside.

The editor had been tempted to hide in the back somewhere when he saw Otis coming. "Don't you know you're wasting your money?" he asked the old farmer. "And people are laughing at you, what with you asking them to give up good money just 'cause you've got a burr under your saddle about a little lost cropland and a few ruined trees?"

"Mr. Collier, you know blooming well there's more to it than that. But I ain't gon' argue with you 'bout it. I got the money right here. You gon' run it or not?"

"Yeah, I'll run it. I'm adding four more pages to the paper, and I can use the filler."

"All right," Otis said, handing over some bills. "I already counted this out. Do yourself and everybody else a favor and don't just run it. Read the damn thing and think about it, hard."

"You know I've already read it," Collier said, putting away the cash.

"Read it again," Otis said, going out. He slammed the door behind him.

~

Mary was dusting and straightening the newspaper and magazine rack when Otis entered Hornbeck's. Grover was behind the prescription counter in back fiddling with bottles. Eunice was nowhere around and there were no customers.

"Morning, Mary," Otis said quietly. "I had to come to town on an errand and I brought you something. I've got something for Jimmy, too, but I don't want Eunice to know anything about either one of them." He handed her a small bundle wrapped in more of the brown paper Alma had saved long ago.

Mary looked over her shoulder toward Grover then turned back and whispered, "Good morning to you too." She took the package, peeled off the paper, then smiled and looked up at him.

"The pocketknife belonged to my daddy, Jimmy's great-granddaddy," Otis said, before she could speak. "I want Jimmy to have it. He's way yonder old enough to have one of his own, and I happen to know he don't, lessen you give him once since he was out to the place last. If you don't want him to have it now, that's fine. Just hold onto it for him.

"The pin was your Grandmother Rebecca's. I believe she'd want you to have it. I know I do. Just don't wear it where Eunice can see it. She'll have a hissy fit, not 'cause she'd care anything about it, but 'cause I give it to you instead of her."

Mary took a moment to find her voice. "Uncle Otis, I love you, but I don't know about this. Are you sure? I mean, Eunice..."

"Shush, child. I know who's deserving and who's not, and I know what I want."

Mary threw her arms around her uncle's neck and kissed him on his cheek. Startled, he stepped back then grinned the way he had last night when he was talking to Alma. Mary squeezed his arm and, not trusting her voice, mouthed, "Thank you."

"Just keep on being the way you are, Mary," he said, "and take good care of Jimmy. He's a fine boy."

Mary watched as Otis strolled out and got on his mule. After she rolled the broach and the knife back into the brown paper and dropped the bundle into her apron pocket, she turned to see Grover staring at her. She wondered how long he had been watching and how much he had heard.

CHAPTER 48

There was no real hill to Blackjack Hill, only a gentle rise, like so many other so-called "hills" in the mostly flat countryside. When someone approached it, though, it seemed to spring up out of nowhere. And it couldn't have been uglier if that had been the aim of those who built on it. Three unpainted two-story frame buildings stood in haphazard array across from a stumpy field where a handful of grimy cot houses and a scattering of tents competed for space at the edge of a pine grove. Whatever other vegetation had once found a hold anywhere in the vicinity had long-since been stomped down. Only dirt, black with oil, remained.

Between the road and the three barrelhouses, thirty or more automobiles and two dozen or so wagons and buggies sat in haphazard array, their drivers having been too eager to get inside to bother about order. Two horses and a mule were tied up to a post set close to the first building apparently for that purpose. Dim light from the open front doors and few first-floor windows of the buildings fell across the vehicles and cast long, odd-shaped shadows broken every now and then by cigarettes fired up by men stepping outside to relieve themselves or head back to their places of abode, all their money gone to drink or to other men with better luck and greater skill with cards. Or to prostitutes. Like Big Sally's

Place in Berrytown, the upper floors of the buildings had no windows. They weren't needed in the narrow rooms where women known here as "oil-field doves" plied their trade.

This was the third time in the last five nights that Henry had come to the retail side of Sheriff Owen Sutro's illegal money machine. The first time, Henry had debated briefly about whether to wear his badge and gun openly on Blackjack Hill or carry them hidden. He didn't need long to decide on concealment. Some patrons might recognize him even without them, but he figured that if he didn't stand out, he would have a better chance of learning whether Ed Tuttle was anywhere around, or of finding out something that might lead to him.

The first two nights, wearing his fedora and carrying his pistol stuck in the back of his trousers under his jacket, Henry looked like any other roughneck or roustabout out to forget his daily grind. He divided his time among all three barrelhouses. As with the upstairs activities, the goings on downstairs were pretty much the same as at Big Sally's. Each building had a long bar on one side of the room and a few tables scattered around a dance floor. Music depended on piano, harmonica, and fiddle players whose talents resembled the drabness of the setting rather than the enticing outfits of Sutro's girls.

All three barrelhouses were so crowded that Henry had little trouble blending in, and no one recognized him. He watched the women stay busy by going back and forth upstairs with men who were either leaning on them for support or pawing at them in anticipation, and by keeping others busy buying drink after drink at the bar and tables. Henry also watched men working behind the bars make repeated trips to back rooms to bring more liquor up front. There was no pretense that any of it was smuggled Canadian or other branded booze. It was all moonshine in Ball jars.

Henry had seen no sign of Ed Tuttle on either of those first two nights. Nor, with one exception, had he overheard anything that might even be a reference to him. While sitting at the end of the bar in the first barrelhouse around twelve thirty on the second night, Henry heard one of the barmen standing in the doorway to the back room say, "Hey big man, bring in six more cases if you've got that many out there." Since no one brought more cases into the front room in the next little while, Henry assumed the barman was talking about cases being delivered to the back room. Maybe, if Al Jenkins was right and Tuttle worked up here somewhere, it wasn't as a barman or bouncer, or as anything else inside, but as someone transporting the moonshine from wherever it was being made. Maybe he was even helping make it. He certainly fit the description of a "big" man.

Tonight, on his third visit to Blackjack Hill, Henry didn't go inside the barrelhouses. As he had done the first two nights, he tied Trixie to the hitching post in front of the first building and loosened her saddle girth to make her more comfortable while she waited, and to eliminate the possibility that some drunk would try to mount her on a lark or a dare. Then he disappeared into the shadows of the vehicles and skirted around to the back of the buildings. He found a hiding place near a pile of unstacked firewood, where he had a good view of the back entrances to the first two structures. For what seemed longer than it was, he saw no sign of activity. Then around ten thirty, a Model T truck went past those two buildings and stopped, he thought, behind the third barrelhouse. About an hour later the same truck, or one like it, stopped behind the middle building.

Henry watched while a man got out, removed several boards from the bed, then unloaded twelve wooden boxes like those he had seen in Moss's locked room. Henry couldn't see the driver's face well, but even though the man was tall like Tuttle, he didn't come up on his toes when he walked. Oddly, he was wearing rubber boots.

If whoever was behind making the moonshine, most likely Sutro, had sent one truck to each of the first two barrelhouses, it stood to reason that a third would be along soon. Sure enough, around twelve thirty in the morning, a truck pulled up to the rear of the third barrelhouse, and the man driving it took boards from the bed and unloaded twelve crates and carried them inside, one at a time. He was wearing rubber boots like the driver of the second truck, but unlike him, this man came up on his toes when he walked. He struggled with the crates, which was surprising given his size. Henry got only a fleeting glimpse of his face, but no matter. It was Tuttle. Henry had spent too much time with him not to recognize him.

Henry's heart pounded and every muscle in his body tensed. He wanted to rush over and beat the murdering bastard to death on the spot with his bare hands. He had been obsessed with killing Tuttle for months, until he got distracted by Mary Dutton, and here at last was an opportunity. He couldn't be sure of finishing the job, though, before someone happened along. Moreover, if Tuttle cried out, someone was bound to come to his aid. Henry wanted certainty, and after going over all he knew while he sat waiting and watching, he believed there was another way of getting it. He kept rooted to his hiding spot until Tuttle finished his task and drove away.

Then Henry made his way around front to Trixie and headed back to Berrytown.

Mary didn't think Jimmy was too young to have a pocketknife. She simply hadn't been able to afford one for him. She wished he could have his daddy's, but Andy had taken it with him when he went to New Mexico with the National Guard, and it had not come home with his body.

All the rest of the day after Otis left the store, Mary looked forward to giving Jimmy the knife at supper. At the same time, she worried about the look she got from Grover. Mary didn't know how much, if anything, Grover had overheard, but she was sure he knew Otis had given her something he didn't want the Hornbecks to know about. She was also sure that Grover would tell Eunice the first chance he got.

Mary knew she could never wear the pin openly without getting into a fuss with Eunice. Nor could Mary hide it in the shed. Eunice would sneak in and paw through everything without even knowing what she was searching for. The thought of it turned Mary's stomach. She hadn't been able to figure a way to put padlocks on her two trunks, and she would have to keep the broach on her person somewhere every time she went out, even to work.

That is, unless she did something she now knew she should have done long before but was afraid to. Since Henry had stopped coming around, she had not only been fuming about having let her guard down with him, but also about allowing Eunice to push her around. If she feared being arrested for violating the Harrison Act by selling drugs, then Eunice must as well, at least to some degree, despite her bluster. Damn Henry Smith and damn Eunice Hornbeck.

In mid-afternoon, when there was a lull and Eunice was assisting the only customer in the store, Mary went over to them and said, "Eunice, I need to run an errand. I'll be back in a few minutes." Before Eunice could object, Mary walked outside and went up the street to a general store.

That night, after she gave Jimmy his great-grandfather Leatherwood's knife and cautioned him about its use while also celebrating the joy it brought him, she also gave him a key to the new padlock she had installed on the door connecting their living quarters to the back room of the drugstore.

"From now on," she said, "we will not be going through the workroom to get into the drugstore or go out anywhere. We will use the back door only. I'll have to walk around the building to get into the store. You already use the outside door when you go sell papers or go to school, so it's not gon' bother you. I want you to have this key, though, in case there's ever any sort of emergency in here and you can't get out the back door."

"But, Momma," Jimmy asked, "won't Cousin Eunice be mad?"

"Let her," Mary replied.

"What about the back door?" Jimmy asked. "Did you get a new lock for it?"

"Oh my! That's right," Mary said. "I was rushing around so this afternoon that I didn't think about Eunice having a key to that lock. I'll get a new one first chance I get."

~

"Well, darn it, what do you think it was?" Eunice asked Grover as they were getting ready for bed.

Grover wished he had told Eunice earlier what he had seen. Now, she would nag him until his nerves were so frayed he would never get to sleep.

"I told you, I don't know. Whatever it was, it was small enough to hold in one hand. It was probably just some money. He knows she doesn't have much."

"No. It couldn't have been money. He doesn't have any either. The old fool probably spent every nickel he could get his hands on going off up to Little Rock and taking out those stupid ads in the paper. I bet it was something that belonged to my mother. Something that's rightfully mine."

"Are you gon' ask Mary about it?"

Eunice crawled under the covers on her side of the bed. "You better believe I am," she said.

"What if she won't tell you?"

"Then first chance I get, I'll go look for it. You sure you didn't even get a peek at it?"

"I already told you. No, I didn't," Grover said. He kicked off his slippers and slid into bed.

"Grover," Eunice said, turning away from him, "sometimes I think you're totally useless. But that's all right. I'll find out one way or another. I'll throw her out if I have to."

"You do and she'll tell the authorities about us."

"Go to sleep!"

CHAPTER 49

"I'm gon' ask her now," Eunice told Grover in mid-morning. She closed the cash register at the pharmacy counter and headed up front as the last customer went out. The morning had been hectic until now with a steady stream of business and with Mary coming and going through the front instead of the back. Right after Grover opened, Mary had come in from the street and said Jimmy had come down with something, he was not going to school, and she would be back as soon as she got him settled. She left and came back the same way. By that time, Eunice had arrived. A little later, Mary had left through the front door again, and a few moments ago she had come back through it, this time with what Eunice assumed were copies of the *Arkansas Gazette* that had been dropped off outside somewhere for Jimmy to hawk. Eunice hated that she had ever agreed to let Mary put the boy's leftover papers in the magazine and newspaper stand for sale when the store's allotment ran out. Even with the 50 percent cut Eunice took, it wasn't worth the aggravation of keeping track.

As Eunice walked to the front, she saw Mary extend the newspapers toward the stand, then gasp and drop all but one. Seconds later, she let it fall to the floor, too, and turned toward the front window. "Damn him!" she hissed, and stomped her foot.

Annoyed by the mess but too startled by Mary's outburst to say anything to her, Eunice bent down to retrieve the papers and put them on the rack. Then she saw the headline: "Luther Pike Arrested for Fraud in Berrytown."

Grover had picked up the store's copies and put them out this morning, and Eunice had not seen them. "Oh, my God!" she shouted. "We're ruined!" She grabbed the top paper on the pile, scanned the opening paragraph, and turned to the rest of the story on the inside. Luther Pike and Company was only one of the entities for which Pike had been selling shares, and the slick-talking lease hound had pocketed almost all the money he had taken in. Most of the leases he claimed to have taken out on oil land did not even exist, and only a handful of the real ones ever produced oil. The certificates he gave to his investors were worthless.

Mary continued staring out the window as if she hadn't heard Eunice's shriek.

Grover came rushing from the back, his pharmacist's coat flapping against his legs. "Eunice, what on earth?" he asked, puffing from the exertion.

When Eunice kept reading without saying anything, Grover snatched a copy of the paper off the rack and ran his eyes over the front page until they landed on "Fraud in Berrytown." He opened his copy, and for several minutes husband and wife stood side by side, each absorbed in the story in different ways. Grover had seen the name Pike in advertisements but didn't recall ever seeing the man.

"You know this fellow, Eunice?" he asked his wife.

"Yes, I know him," Eunice snapped, already going on the defensive and directing her anger at her husband. She wadded the paper with both hands, hurled it at the soda fountain, pushed Grover aside, and started for the back.

Not as much a fool as Eunice thought, Grover called, "How much?"

Eunice ignored him and kept walking.

Grover hustled after her, holding the newspaper at his side. "How much?"

When she reached the back counter, Eunice turned around. "How much what?" she asked.

"How much of our money did you give this crook?" Grover asked, his voice rising.

"Come on, honey," Eunice said, forcing a smile and trying a different tactic. "Don't be mad. I was just trying to fix it so we could expand the store. Run that upstart Compton's out of business."

"How much?" Grover yelled, not so much because he was finding his backbone as because he was afraid of the answer.

"All we saved from the Crescent City Powders."

"Goddamnit, Eunice!" Grover started to strike his wife but slammed his hand against the pharmacy counter instead. Only, he missed the flat surface and struck the edge. Howling in agony, he snatched his arm back and saw his little finger and the one next to it sticking up at a peculiar angle.

"Goddamnit to you too, Grover!" Eunice yelled, then stormed into the back room.

Grover grasped his wounded hand with his good one and rushed up the center aisle and through the front door, thinking only about his throbbing pain and hoping old Doc Fuller was in his office down the street.

Mary, left alone to keep the store, thought about her daddy and his Pullman stock, and about her uncle Otis's warning about Pike. She had ignored both, and now almost all her little savings had disappeared in the dust of Pike's schemes. Her investment was based more on hope than on expectation, however, and she had known the risk she was taking and believed she had no other choice.

She took some consolation in seeing Eunice and Grover go at each other. She knew she was wrong to do that, but she couldn't help enjoying their discomfort, given the way they treated her. She doubted they were in danger of losing the store and leaving her without a place to live. She had overheard Grover saying long before that he had paid for it with money he inherited. Still, their loss would likely affect her because they would probably now look for ways to move even more illegal drugs for Roper and Arcadia Pharmaceuticals.

~

First, Otis heard his mules braying, then his pigs took to squealing and his milk cow began bawling. Having finished supper and taken to his front-porch rocking chair with a jar of shine, he started to get up and see if a varmint of some kind had spooked his animals. Then he felt the porch planks quiver under his feet and heard a low rumbling noise that sounded like a train coming, except that the nearest tracks were miles away. The rumbling grew louder and louder, like a score or more trains instead of one, and he knew then that the well on Isaiah's farm was coming in.

The underground pressure didn't blow out the drilling pipe or ruin the derrick, like often happened, but the well came roaring in with enough force to rain crude all over Isaiah's farm and Otis's too, blackening the land anew and coating buildings before the drilling crew got it under control a little before dawn. Otis reckoned with the oil now flowing into the completed pit in one of Isaiah's fields, money would soon be flowing into the Watsons' bank account, the oil company would be boring more holes over there, and Isaiah, Luella, and Robert would be on a train heading north.

Lease hounds, whether they had seen Otis's ad in the *Berrytown Journal* or not, would be pestering him once more. All except Luther Pike. Otis had heard what happened to him. At least that was some reason to smile—not because of what the crooked snake in the grass had done to people, but because he was getting the comeuppance he deserved.

With Isaiah's hopes met, Otis was ready to get on with what he had to do, and now he knew what he would go after once he blew up the tank cars on the siding in Louann. He didn't know much about how pipelines worked other than oil went in one end and came out the other, and they were built in sections. He figured an entire line didn't have to be finished for initial portions to go into use.

Otis knew from talking with Isaiah that oil discovered on the Watson farm would eventually flow from holding pits into the main line already snaking its way across his own farm from points south. So, he reckoned that anything he did to the line north of his farm wouldn't hurt Isaiah. It might not hurt any money-grubbing, big-shot oil men either, or change any other folks' minds about leasing, or prompt anyone else who was worried about the land to try to do anything about it. But it would at least nettle them some more.

CHAPTER 50

"I ain't got no idea where it is," Moss said, "and I couldn't tell you if I did." He and Henry were standing in the cubbyhole that passed for his office. Moss reached for his big Ball jar on the floor, spit his entire load of snuff into it, and set it on his open rolltop desk. "Damn, boy! You got some nerve asking me that after telling me you wasn't gon' do anything that'd mess into my business. Not to mention me letting you stay on in my barn."

After a light day of chasing pickpockets and breaking up fights on Berrytown streets, Henry had returned to the mule yard early, curried Trixie, and put her in her stall in the front barn with fresh hay and grain. Then he had gone looking for Moss, found him in a tact room, and asked him if they could talk in private. Once they walked up to the office and closed the door, Henry had gotten straight to the point and asked where Owen Sutro made his whiskey. Moss's reaction was milder than Henry expected.

"I don't intend to mess into your business," Henry said. "I told you that before. I'm not looking to get you into any trouble with Sutro or the law. I just need to know where his still is."

Moss shook his head. "What makes you think I know that?"

"Henry pushed his Stetson back. "Look" he said, "I know there're folks making shine all over the place. But they're small time. I hear Sutro's got the biggest operation anywhere around, and I believe it. I've been up to Blackjack Hill. I know who the man is, and I know what he is. He's not the sort to put up with competition. Has to be the big cheese. So, it stands to reason that anybody moving much shine around is getting it from him."

Moss pulled a rag out of his blacksmith apron, sat down in the desk chair, took off his derby hat, and wiped his head. He laid the rag on the desk beside the Ball jar and held out his hands, turning them and looking at them, almost like he couldn't believe they were his.

Henry stood waiting. Moss remained silent.

"A minute ago," Henry said, trying again, "you said you 'couldn't' tell me where Sutro's still is. You didn't say 'wouldn't.' I think you know and you're afraid to say."

Moss leaned back and held his breath for a couple of ticks. "No. I really don't know. But you're right about one thing. Anybody who knows that bastard and ain't at least some scared of him don't have their wagon hitched right. Truth is, he's squeezing me, and I'm past being tired of dealing with him. I wouldn't care if you busted up his place. But if this ain't about the law, then what business do you have with him?"

"It's not with him exactly, and it's personal."

"I might know how you can find out what you want, but you've got to level with me first."

Henry stared at the floor for a minute or two then straightened up. "I'll tell you this much. Sutro's got somebody working for him who's got a debt to pay. I came all the way down here from Indiana to collect it. I don't want anything from Sutro. I just want to find the bastard I've been looking for." He paused, then added, "Unless Sutro gets in my way."

"What kind of debt?"

"That's all I'm gon' tell you, Moss. Now, you and me both know something about the other one we don't want spread around. So, how about it? You gon' help me or not?"

Moss stood up and put his hat on. "Tell you what. You go watch for Calvin, and when he gets in, tell him I want to see him soon as he takes care of his team. Then you come on back without waiting for him. I don't want anybody thinking something's going on they might want to nose into. And don't tell him anything more than that. I'll do the rest."

~

When Calvin got to Moss's office, Henry was waiting for him with Moss. Henry hadn't told Calvin that he would be here, and he could see that Calvin was surprised.

"You wanted to see me, Mr. Moss, sir?" Calvin asked. He held his hat in one hand and tugged with the other on the rope holding his bullwhip, like it was knotting up his britches. He nodded at Henry, "Mr. Henry, sir."

"Calvin," Moss began, "Henry here knows about my little sideline, and I expect he knows a right smart, too, about what you have to do with it. He also knows you and me have worked together a lot of years. Right, Henry?"

"That's right," Henry replied.

Calvin's growing concern showed on his wrinkled forehead. He glanced at Henry.

"Now, there ain't nothing for you to worry about," Moss said. He's not looking to haul anybody off to the calaboose."

"Yes, sir."

"He wants to know where Sheriff Sutro makes his whiskey." Calvin stiffened when he heard that. "Henry says he ain't out to bust it up," Moss went on. "He just wants to find somebody he thinks is working there. Knowing how much you get around all over, 'mongst your people and mine, too, I thought you might have an idea about it. If you do, I'd be obliged if you'd tell us."

"I don't rightly know where it is" Calvin said. He rolled up his hat brim with both hands. "I swear to the Good Lord."

Moss and Henry waited while Calvin unrolled the hat brim then rolled it up again.

"I might have an idea 'bout it, though," he said. "Problem is, I'd be scared to say it. Y'all know what'd happen to me if I helped you, or to anybody that helped me do it, and the high sheriff found out? Mr. Henry, there, he done saved my cousin Levi from hanging, but he wouldn't be able to stop the law. Begging y'all's pardon for saying so, but I don't want to be strung up to no tree and have my manhood cut off. No, sir. I got to think about this."

"Calvin," Henry said, "why don't you think about what those Klansmen did to Levi? I'd bet about anything some of them were Sheriff Sutro's men. Wouldn't you like to get back at them? What if I found Sutro's still, and the fellow I'm looking for, and then I tipped off the Treasury agents and let them bust up the place? You and Mr. Moss would lose out some, but he's already told me he's getting tired of dealing with Sutro."

"Yes, sir," Calvin said. "Mr. Moss done told me he might have to quit sometime. I like the extra money, but the truth is, I don't mind if he quits, 'cause I'm getting a right smart scared of getting caught. They's too many new folks that don't know me and Mr. Moss. We make somebody mad, they might turn us in for spite." Calvin continued to fiddle with his hat brim. Like before, Henry and Moss waited.

"All right," Calvin said, finally. "I don't know where it is exactly, but it's way over southeast of here, 'round Huttig or Felsenthal somewhere, right on the Ouachita River. 'Bout forty miles, maybe a little more. They've got two stills paired up like a mule team, and they're all the time moving them from one slough to another one, so folks will think the smoke's from different hunting or logging camps and won't come snooping 'round."

That, Henry thought, would explain why Tuttle and the other driver he saw at Sutro's barrelhouses were wearing rubber boots.

"From what I hear," Calvin said, "the stills ain't something just throwed together, neither. They must have got a good coppersmith to make them somewhere else then brung them in. They're cooking with sugar instead of corn, I reckon 'cause they can't get enough corn. They get the sugar brought on riverboats from down in Louisiana. And they've got a big powerboat they use to take the whiskey up the river someplace where they can put it on trucks at night. Probably Calion Lake but maybe all the way up to some bayou or other close to Camden."

"Calvin," Moss asked, "how do you know all this, and how come you ain't never told it to me?"

"Well, sir, you ain't never asked me before now, and I guess I figured you knew it since you was buying from them."

"So, how do you know it?" Henry asked.

"I got relations living all back over in there. Some of them's got farms. Some of them work at that big lumber mill in Huttig. All of them hunt and fish. They see stuff and hear things. A lot like me."

"Do you think any of them would help me find the stills?" Henry asked. "Just kind of point me in the right direction?"

"I might be able to convince them. They's kind of worked up right now. Sheriff Sutro's men are ruining lots of good fishing places dumping spent mash and running that powerboat in sloughs that's barely deep enough."

Neither Henry nor Moss responded right away. Calvin unrolled his hat brim and rolled it up for the third time.

"Henry," Moss asked, "if Calvin was to get some of his kin to show you sort of where to look, how would you get in there by yourself? Ain't none of them fellows likely to go with you right up to where moonshiners are cooking. I've been over in there some myself, fishing. A man can get lost pretty damn quick. You'd have to use some kind of boat too. Can you handle one?"

"I was just thinking about that," Henry said. "I did some rowing when I was in school. And maybe I could hire a guide. Take two boats in. The guide could leave me there with one of them, and I could stay as long as I needed to."

"I got a cousin might be willing to do that," Calvin said. "He guides for some of the men that run the lumber mill.

CHAPTER 51

Henry took another bite of cold ham and two-day-old biscuit and scrunched sideways in the small boat to keep out of drizzling rain blowing in under the tarp he and Benoit Shavers had stretched overhead between cypress trees. Benoit, a stout, almond-colored fellow with a heavy beard, shifted on his seat, too, and reached into his rucksack for another biscuit.

"Good, huh," he said, holding it up and grinning.

Henry had told Amos Burns he needed a few days to take care of some personal business so important he would have to give up his badge if he couldn't take time off. Burns had said to go ahead. For the last two days, Henry and Benoit, whom sometimes Henry could hardly understand, had been paddling in and out of sloughs in a labyrinth of creeks and lakes on the west side of the meandering Ouachita River north of Felsenthal.

"If he tells you something you don't understand," Calvin had explained when he introduced them, "ask him again. He won't care. He knows he talks like a Cajun." Shaver's father was a widowed South Louisiana riverboat man who had stopped off at Felsenthal one day and taken up with one of Calvin's aunts. He sent for his two young boys, and they all kept pretty much to themselves afterwards, living off the land and coming out of the swamps only occasionally for Birdsong family gatherings.

"We can't tell what Benoit's saying half the time, but he knows what he's doing. He was raised back in there."

Henry and Benoit had pulled their two small craft out of a slough onto barely dry land after a second day of searching for the Sutro stills. Each man had a tarp when they set out the morning before, but it was Benoit's they were sitting under now. Henry's was floating rolled up somewhere back toward their jumping off place in another slough. He had thrust his paddle under it and hurled it out of his boat when a water moccasin dropped onto it from a tree. He made no effort to retrieve it.

Remembering the moccasins he had seen the day he went looking for a pipeline job near El Dorado, Henry had asked Calvin and Benoit earlier if they were likely to run into any here. Calvin said no, they would be hibernating by now. But Benoit said, "Unless they come out to sun themselves." Henry was relieved when the weather front moved in late the second afternoon and brought rain clouds, but he hoped they passed by morning. If they stalled over the river bottom, it would be difficult to spot smoke from the moonshiners' cooking fires. So far, they had seen only wisps, nothing big enough to suggest a sizeable cooking operation. They took that to mean the stills were on the move to a new location.

~

Otis fed his animals, did the evening milking, and ate a light supper of scrambled eggs and left-over biscuits with syrup from Isaiah Watson's last batch. Then he cleaned up the kitchen and took a half-drunk Ball jar of shine onto the front porch. Oil well noises from the Watson place were not as loud as the ones he had endured before Isaiah's well came in. Otis leaned against a support post for a few minutes and looked out over the parts of his fields visible from here and thought of them as they once had been—green and lush, corn tassels waving in a light breeze and cotton bolls white and ready for picking—not the shades of brown and black like now.

He sat down in his rocker and said, "Alma, it's been a long day, and I'm gon' have another nip. I know you don't approve, but there's times a man needs a little lightning down his gullet to settle his belly and straighten his backbone, and this here's one of them. I'm sorry for letting you down like this again, but I'm glad you've always loved me enough to forgive me." He took a long draw from the jar. "I have to tell you, too," he said, "that whoever makes this stuff I get from Wilbur Moss sho' does know what he's doing." He took another long drink, set the jar down beside his chair, and leaned his head back. He had a couple of hours before he needed to gather the last of his materials, plenty of time for a nap.

When he woke, he knew at once that he had slept longer than he planned and would now have to hurry. He left the Ball jar sitting on the porch and headed straight for the barn. He stopped at a fence post and took a leak then went in and put a scrubby saddle on his best mule. Having lined an ancient pair of saddle bags with burlap and straw, he went to place them up behind the saddle, then thought better of it. He would wait, fill them first, and then put them in front and tie them to the saddle horn. He had earlier placed fuse cord and detonator caps in another sack and a flashlight, matches, and ball of twine in a third and tied them off. Now he tied the ends of the binding strings on those two sacks together and lifted them over the back of the saddle.

"Come on, boy," he said, picking up the saddle bags and taking the reins of the mule to lead him out of the barn, "them tank cars are sitting over there waiting for us."The mule trailed obediently behind, as Otis walked the one hundred fifty or so yards back to the long-razed dwelling of some previous owner of the property. He had come here in the afternoon and moved the half cord of firewood off the cover of the old well. Now he tied the mule to the leaning orchard fence and walked over to the dry hole.

This time he removed all the covering boards except the one to which weeks earlier he had tied the top end of a rope that extended downward. He peered into the opening and, unable to see as much as he thought he would, he grumbled aloud about not having put his flashlight in an overalls pocket. He retrieved it from the bag on his mule, leaned over the well, and shined it toward the bottom. The lower end of the rope was still knotted around the handle of the padded oak basket holding the sticks of dynamite he saved the night he blew up Milo Yeager's pipe and other crap.

He moved the light beam around over the contents of the basket, looking for any signs the dynamite was sweating. If he saw drops of nitroglycerin, or even any dampness, he would leave the basket where it was. It would be too unstable to disturb. He planned on doing major damage at the rail siding; he didn't plan on blowing himself up in the process.

He had also not planned on getting his hands damp from dew while moving the boards. The moistness was so slight, he didn't feel it even when he took the flashlight out of the bag. He became aware of it only when the flashlight began to slip out of his hand over the hole. When he saw that he couldn't stop it, he swiped at it, hoping it would land in the dirt instead of hitting the basket.

The last thing Otis Leatherwood saw was wet burlap in the beam of the falling flashlight.

A little after nine o'clock the next morning, Police Chief Amos Burns came into Hornbeck's Drugstore unshaven and ashen looking. When he saw that Eunice, Grover, and Mary were all engaged with customers, he feigned interest in a display of pipes and tobacco. Mary came free first, went over, and asked if she could assist him.

The big man removed his hat and said, "No thank you, Mrs. Dutton. I was hoping I could talk to you and Mrs. Hornbeck for a minute." He looked around to see if Eunice was still occupied. Noting that she was completing a sale, he turned back to Mary. "I see she's 'bout done now. Could you walk to the back with me?" If he noticed the color drain from Mary's face, he didn't let on. By the time they reached the back counter, Grover had also finished with his customer at the pharmacy counter.

"Morning, Mrs. Hornbeck. Grover," Burns said, still holding his hat. "I'm glad y'all are all here. I'll get right to it. I'm pained to tell you that Otis was killed last night."

"Oh, no!" Mary cried. She gasped for breath, took in too much, and bent over coughing. She put her left hand over her mouth and held onto the edge of the pharmacy counter with her good arm.

"Huh," Eunice said. "What happened? He get in a fight with somebody? Be just like the blamed old cuss." She leaned back, folded her arms over her chest, and waited for Burns to continue. When he did, Eunice looked at Grover with eyebrows raised. She did not share what she was thinking.

Burns explained how Otis had died and said there was a huge mess to clean up, but he understood the house was little damaged except for broken windows. At least that was the assessment of the deputy sheriff summoned by the pipeline fellows who found Otis. Burns hadn't been out there himself. Officer Delcapp had, and the county man had sent him back to tell what they knew so far. Randolf Ingramhoff was on his way out to collect Otis's remains, and Isaiah Watson had volunteered to take care of the livestock until other arrangements could be made.

"Well, Amos, I mean Chief Burns, when do you think we'll be able to get in the house and see to things?" Eunice asked, emphasizing "Chief."

"I ain't sure exactly, but not till the sheriff officially determines there wasn't no foul play, and the county coroner signs off on the cause of death. Them's only formalities, but it may be a few days. The sheriff will send word."

"Oh, good," Eunice said. "Well, it was kind of you to come let us know." She turned toward Grover, motioned with her head for him to come around the counter, and took a step toward the front. "If you will excuse us now, Chief, we have a lot to think about."

When they had ushered Burns out the front door, Eunice said, "Mary, this is terribly distressing. I need some time to compose myself. Will you be a dear and look after things for a few minutes?" Without waiting for a reply, she tugged on Grover's sleeve, and he followed her into the back room, leaving Mary standing alone in the middle of the store.

When Eunice closed the storeroom door behind them, Grover, who had remained silent until now, said, "Just what we need. Another thing to worry with."

"No," Eunice said, smiling. "Don't you see? We're gon' be rich. They struck oil on that ole nigger Watson's farm, and that pretty much proves there's oil on Daddy's land too. Only it's gon' be ours now."

CHAPTER 52

Around noon on their third day out, Henry and Benoit spotted what they were looking for, a column of smoke that seemed too big for a hunting camp. Benoit said he had a good idea where it was coming from, a sweet gum brake off a place called Turtle Slough near the river but not directly accessible from it. Getting there required navigating another series of creeks and sloughs. All were deep enough to accommodate a power boat, another good sign. Benoit said he could guide Henry to a point from which they could reach the brake if they kept moving counterclockwise, turning left each time they came to the mouth of another creek or slough. Conversely, if Henry then retraced those steps, he should be able to get out easily enough without Benoit's help.

There was, however, risk in being seen approaching or leaving if any of the moonshiners themselves happened to be coming or going. Although Henry hadn't told Benoit he was looking for a man, or that he intended to kill him, he had said he didn't want to be seen coming up on the moonshiners' operation. Benoit didn't either, for that matter. Henry wasn't worried about what Benoit knew ever having any legal consequences; none of Tuttle's partners were likely to report a murder where they were cooking mash. And all Benoit could ever do, anyway, was confirm that Henry had snuck up on the site. The moonshiners telling Sutro about it was another thing entirely, but Henry had plans for avoiding or least responding to any comeback from the sheriff.

After moving as close as they dared during daylight, Henry and Benoit pulled their boats ashore again and waited until dusk to continue toward the brake. Henry worried all the while about water moccasins in the trees above him but didn't look up for fear of seeing them. He preferred pretending none was there.

Around midnight, at a small point of land, Benoit pointed Henry right onto a new stream, instead of keeping left on the main slough. When Henry pulled abreast of him, Benoit said this was the edge of the sweet gum brake and he was certain the moonshiners' camp was half a mile or so up the slough on the left. He said he remembered a place there that would be well suited for it, and he suggested Henry row fifty yards or so up the smaller stream on the right, hide his boat, and walk across the brake.

"You remember how to get back, Mr. Henry?" Benoit asked.

"Yeah," Henry said. "And I've got a compass in case I get lost."

"I ain't thinking that thing will do you much good out here," Benoit said, as he shoved off, heading back to where they had first put in the boats. "Ain't no straight lines to anywhere, land or water, except from right here to them shiners. Remember, when you head back from here, keep going clockwise."

Henry moved up the little stream as directed, secured his rowboat, put the army-surplus binoculars he had bought in Berrytown around his neck, slung the .30-caliber Springfield rifle he had purchased at the same place over his shoulder—for alligators he had told Calvin and Benoit—and set off walking. He wanted to be in place, quiet and hidden, when the sun came up.

He had no trouble finding the site or a hiding place with a good view of it through underbrush. What he saw when he settled in was more elaborate than he expected. Several small fires cast an eerie light over the camp. Apparently, the whiskey makers had started fermenting mash made of sugar, yeast, and water sometime the previous afternoon. They had twelve steel barrels, in two rows of six, sitting atop crude cast-iron racks that looked like giant kitchen trivets. Hot coals were banked under each, and two men were moving from barrel to barrel stirring each mixture with long wooden paddles to keep the temperature even and hasten fermentation. Squat wooden sleds stood between the barrels and the water's edge. Henry assumed that when time came to find another location, the shiners used them to move the barrels and other materials onto the flat barges moored at the shoreline.

Beyond the two rows of barrels, two large copper pots for cooking the mash after it had fermented for four or five days sat on small woodburning stoves. A copper coil stood next to each, ready to fit onto the pots and loop through a wooden barrel of cool water to condense the steamed mash after it was sufficiently heated. Crates of empty Ball jars waited next to the stills.

Several ratty tents set a few yards past the distilling pots, and various supplies, sugar and yeast among them Henry assumed, sat on other barges. The operation, though huge, was designed for mobility, but it looked clumsy. Henry thought federal revenue agents should easily be able to locate it and take it down. After all, he had found it. He guessed Sutro was paying off someone, but there were ways to get around it.

So far, Henry had spotted two men, neither of them Ed Tuttle. Henry figured others were either standing guard somewhere or asleep in the tents. It was now a matter of waiting. He hadn't decided exactly how he was going to kill Tuttle and get away, so he ran over the possibilities again as he watched. He had envisioned either catching Tuttle on the water somewhere and shooting him from a distance, or somehow grabbing him quietly when no one was with him and cutting his throat. In addition to the rifle, he had brought along a hunting knife in case Tuttle went into the woods to relieve himself or otherwise got off alone somewhere, maybe as a lookout.

After months of looking for the guy, Henry knew he had been fortunate to get this close so quickly in recent days, and he was prepared to wait as many more hours as necessary to do what he had come for. As he sat waiting for sunrise and the rest of the moonshiners to show themselves, he pictured himself pulling the trigger or slashing with the knife. During the war, Henry had seen enemy soldiers he shot fall dead, and he assumed others died from grenades he hurled blindly over the tops of trenches. He never heard any of those make a sound he knew came from them. But he had killed two Germans up close when they overran American barricades, and sometimes in his dreams he saw those men anew and heard them screaming. They came to him again now as he imagined killing Tuttle, and painful as those sounds had been to hear in France and were still, Henry wanted to hear Tuttle make them here as he felt his life slipping away at his brother-in-law's hand. Shooting him would be less satisfying than using a knife, but a rifle bullet would do if no other opportunity presented itself.

Getting here on the water had been tiring and sometimes nerve-wracking, but now the final minutes seemed longer than the hours of searching and rowing. Having visually examined all he could see of the camp from his present vantage point many times, Henry thought about moving to another one to get a different view. Then he decided that the risk of detection was too great. He had been lucky so far. No sense in pushing it.

He unbuttoned his jacket and shirt and pulled out the photograph taken of his family before he left for Wabash. He wiped his hand on his pants then carefully removed the oilcloth from the picture. He couldn't make out details in the darkness, but he didn't need to. The images traveled with him in his head everywhere he went, along with others never captured by a camera. He had brought the photograph along because he wanted a physical connection to his family when he avenged their deaths, especially Helen's rape and murder.

Henry pressed the photograph to his chest then re-wrapped it, put it back inside his shirt, and returned his gaze to the moonshiners' camp. What he mostly saw, though, was his twin sister's face, not only as it appeared in the photograph, but as it was when they played as children on the farm, when they shared meals with their parents, when they celebrated birthdays, and when she accepted her first teaching position—smiling, winking, teasing, full of life and joy.

Remembering those things made him recall when he first saw Mary in Hornbeck's, and how she had reminded him of Helen. Although the differences he came to see in them had soon far outweighed the similarities, he wondered now if each would see a little something of the other in themselves if they could meet. He wondered if they would like each other.

Thinking about Mary sparked a whole different set of emotions. He had held her in his arms only twice, once the night they returned from hearing Billy Sunday in El Dorado and once in the alley outside the American Theater, when scenes from *A Connecticut Yankee in King Arthur's Court* sent searing pain across his forehead and forced him to leave the movie house. And he had kissed her only the first of those times. He had longed for more than that, and sitting here now that yearning returned, even as he waited to do the thing that had turned it off before. The thing he had come to Berrytown to do. And the thing that would likely prevent his ever satisfying the newer craving.

When daylight began creeping in, Henry tried to push the thoughts and images of Helen and Mary aside and refocus his attention. Men other than those stirring the mash barrels began appearing. Henry watched for Tuttle, hoping he would show up and then separate from the others.

Minutes dragged on. One man started a cook fire. Another looked in the mash barrels and talked to one of the men stirring. Two others headed into the woods, already unbuckling their pants as they went. Then there he was—Ed Tuttle. Walking in from the other side of the camp, probably from lookout duty, coming up on his toes with each step.

Henry lifted his binoculars for a closer look, and gaining it, he saw not the virile, brash man he remembered, but one whose unwashed clothes hung loose on his frame and whose features were drawn and haggard, his face unshaven, his nose pushed permanently to one side from what must have been a painful blow. A man living in near-primitive conditions and, from what Al Jenkins had said, finding his pleasures with booze and prostitutes. He walked over to one of the cook fires, flopped onto an empty crate, fished into an overalls pocket, and brought out the makings for a cigarette. His hands shook as he rolled it.

Henry put the binoculars down and raised the Springfield with the ease and care of an experienced soldier, pointed it at Tuttle's head, and sighted along the barrel. An easy shot. A sure thing. And at this distance, ample time to get away while the sound of the exploding bullet rolled across the campsite, confusing everyone in it.

With his finger resting outside the trigger guard until he was ready to shoot, Henry watched now through his gun sights as Tuttle lit his crudely formed cigarette, took a long pull, and launched into a fit of coughing. Henry wondered if the convulsing man ever thought about what his laziness and unbridled anger had cost him. About what murdering Helen and her unborn child had brought him to. Or about what lay ahead for him.

CHAPTER 53

Hornbeck's Drugstore stood dark in the middle of the week, closed the day after Chief Burns brought the news of Otis Leatherwood's death. Black crepe paper framed the glass in the front door, and a hand-lettered sign dangled inside it on a string: "In Mourning. Re-opening Tomorrow."

Mary had told Jimmy about Uncle Gramps's passing the night before. They had hugged, cried, laughed, and shared memories. Now she sat alone in the shed room, still grieving over losing the only relative they had been at all close to for years.

At Mary's insistence, Jimmy had gone to school. "We will miss Uncle Gramps and pray for his soul," Mary had told him. "But he wouldn't want you to miss school on his account." She had no basis for believing that, but she didn't think it would do Jimmy any good to mope around with her all day.

Eunice and Grover didn't have an automobile, but Grover knew how to drive, and Eunice insisted he rent a car from Mac's Autos for their trip out to the farm that she knew would be hers as soon as all the necessary legalities were settled. "A buggy would be tacky," she had said. "We have appearances to keep up."

When they arrived, Eunice showed neither surprise about, nor interest in, the several automobiles and wagons parked in front of the house, or the two Union County sheriff's deputies she saw, along with several laborers, poking around the place, especially near the barn and back where the explosion had occurred. One of the deputies came over as Eunice and Grover were getting out of the car and told them they were welcome to walk about the yard and look, but they could not go into the house.

"Why not?" Eunice asked. "I'm his daughter. This place is gon' be mine."

"Not till all the paperwork is done," the deputy told her.

"Nonsense," Eunice said. "I'm going inside and check on his things, and you can't stop me."

The deputy looked at Grover, who only shrugged. "Oh, what the hell," the fellow said, throwing up his arms and walking away.

"Come on, Grover." Eunice yanked on his arm. He stood for a moment looking over the broken windows and run-down condition of the place and thinking about how much money it would take to fix it up. He guessed cost wouldn't matter if even one well came in on the property.

Once they were inside, where only she and Otis had set foot for years, Eunice took a quick glance into the downstairs rooms and said, as much to herself as to Grover, that her father was not only a "damned old fool but a pig to boot." Then she began going through every room in the house opening every door to every closet, cabinet, and piece of furniture and every lid to every box and every other container.

"What on earth are you looking for?" Grover asked her.

"The will, stupid," she said. "I want to know if he left a will. The legal stuff will be easier that way."

When they got to Otis's and Alma's bedroom, untouched since Alma's death except once when Otis retrieved the picture of them long ago and twice more in recent weeks, Eunice didn't notice the near-dust-free space on the bedside table. She did, however, see that the dust on the little cardboard box that held her mother's jewelry was smeared.

"Ah ha," Eunice said, raising the box lid. She reached inside, pulled out a piece of wrinkled brown wrapping paper that had been folded up like an envelope and had "Eunice" written on the top in pencil. She tossed the box lid onto the bed, unfolded the paper, read the few lines on it, then let it drop, grabbed the sides of her head with her hands, and screamed.

The men outside looked up at the house, waited a tick for anything more, then continued about their business. Grover picked up the paper and read it aloud: "Dear Eunice, if you are reading this, you are probably looking for my will. You can stop now because it is not here and I am not leaving you the farm. Otis Leatherwood."

~

After seeing the sign on the front door of Hornbeck's, Isaiah Watson walked around the corner to Seventh Street, turned left into the alley, and went to the cobbled door to the shed. He knew Mary Dutton lived here because Jimmy had told Robert about it. Isaiah took off his hat and knocked, hoping she was at home and would come to the door quickly. It was dangerous for a black man to be seen lurking around where a white woman lived.

Mary knew Isaiah from hearing Otis and Jimmy talk about him and from seeing him in the store a few times. After cracking the door and seeing who was there, she opened it.

Isaiah spoke first. "Begging your pardon, Miz Dutton, my name's Reverend Isaiah Watson. I'm your uncle's neighbor, and I'm bringing this for him. I apologize it's opened. He didn't say who it was for when he gave it to me. He said if anything happened to him, I was to open it, see whose name was on the inside, and take it to them."

He held out the envelope and Mary took it.

Before she could look at it, Isaiah said, "I heard the deputy sheriff say Mr. Burns was gon' tell you and Miz Hornbeck about what happened, so I reckoned it was all right to go ahead and bring this to you now. I sho' am sorry about Mr. Otis. He was a mighty good man." Eager to leave, Isaiah added quickly, "Don't you be worrying none about Mr. Otis's livestock. I'm gon' be looking after them till me and my family leave. We're going up to Chicago where our oldest boys are. Probably in 'bout three or four weeks."

Mary turned the envelope around. The printed return address read, "Franklin K. Davis, Attorney at Law, Broadway and Sumac Alley, Berrytown, Arkansas." That was the First Berrytown Bank building. There was no addressee.

When she started to open the flap, Isaiah said, "Begging your pardon again, Miz Dutton, if you don't mind, I got to get on."

"Yes, thank you, Isaiah," Mary said. "It was kind of you to bring this."

She closed the door, sat on the edge of her cot, and opened the envelope. The heading on the document inside read, "Last Will and Testament of Otis Leatherwood."

"Oh, my God!" she said when she got to the intent of it. "Eunice will kick us out." All she could think about next was what she and Jimmy would do.

The sun was sinking when Henry returned the Dodge truck he had rented from Mac's Autos and set out walking to the mule yard, rifle slung over his shoulder. It had taken him two days to find his way out of the river bottom and get to the remote spot where he and Benoit had left the vehicle. Benoit's boat was there, too, and Henry assumed that, as planned, the helpful fellow had walked the several miles to his closest relative's place and gotten a ride from there. Although Henry had smelled like rotting fish and decaying plants, he had driven south to Huttig, avoiding Felsenthal, where he was more likely to run into people with direct connections to the moonshiners and be taken for a revenue agent. He found a place to get something to eat then slept in the truck cab until he felt awake enough to drive back to Berrytown. On the way, he left the boats, borrowed from some other cousin of Calvin's, at Benoit's place without seeing him. Now Henry was looking forward to cleaning up in the makeshift shower he had rigged, then lying on his pallet in the barn loft and letting sleep wash over him.

He was striding through the front gate, past mule skinners and wagons coming off their runs when he heard Moss calling his name. Henry looked toward the front barn expecting to see his former boss in his derby hat and apron doing something with a horse, mule, or wagon. Instead, Moss was standing in the doorway, his right leg in a cast from the knee down, supporting himself on a pair of adjustable crutches like the kind invented a few years back for wounded soldiers returning from France.

"Hey, there," Moss said, when Henry walked over, "I was afraid you got yourself lost over yonder. Did you find the fellow you was looking for?"

"Yeah, I found him," Henry said. "What the blazes happened to you?"

Moss ignored the question. "Did you collect the debt he owed?"

"More or less. It wasn't anything I could put in my pocket."

"You found Sutro's stills then?" Moss asked, letting Henry's vague reply slide.

"Yeah, I found them. But I doubt he's gon' be in business much longer. You might as well get prepared for it."

"Did you do something to them?"

"No, not exactly."

"I don't understand what you mean by 'not exactly,'" Moss said, "but it don't matter none, 'cause that's what I want to talk to you about." He shifted his weight on the crutches. "You asked what happened to me. I fell out of the goddamned hay loft. And I've been thinking about that, and about Sutro, and a whole bunch of other stuff, and I've got a proposition to make you."

"Now?" Henry asked. He removed his hat and ran his hand through his dirty hair. "I'm about dead on my feet and I'm tired of smelling myself."

"Yeah, now. I've been near 'bout busting a gut for you to get back so I can see what you think about it."

CHAPTER 54

Franklin K. Davis's office was on the third floor of the new, red brick First Berrytown Bank building. While it was going up on the site of the old frame structure, the bank had operated out of another one they put up for a temporary home and afterward sold for a café. The directors were proud of their new quarters and had spared no expense on them.

Mary paused, looked at the attorney's name in gold letters on the door, and knocked. A tall, thin woman in a white blouse and black skirt that looked like some Mary made, came to the door and ushered her into Davis's office. It smelled new and looked like money—windows overlooking Broadway, shelves lined with books in pristine covers, polished oak flooring, a large oak desk with matching credenza behind it, a large table in one corner.

Davis, a well-turned-out man whose middle strained his suit vest, rose from the desk, and came around to the side. "Come in, Mrs. Dutton," he said, his bushy moustache turning up at the ends as he smiled. "Let me take your coat. I'm Franklin Davis, and I believe you know Mr. and Mrs. Hornbeck."

Eunice and Grover sat on chairs pulled up to the desk from the table. A third chair had been placed there for Mary. Neither Eunice nor Grover looked around or spoke. Mary said hello to Davis and let him help her off with her coat. She was wearing her blue blouse and black skirt. Davis handed the coat to his assistant, and as she was leaving the room with it, Mary sat down in the vacant chair, folded her hands in her lap, leaned over, and said, "Good morning, Eunice, Grover."

Eunice stiffened, ignoring the greeting. Grover bent forward, looked toward Mary, and nodded slightly. Eunice glanced at him and cleared her throat.

Davis, returning to his desk chair, noticed the tension. He picked up a sheaf of papers and skipped most of the legalese lawyers usually relied on when they were about to read wills to named parties.

He said only, "Mr. and Mrs. Hornbeck and Mrs. Dutton, I have here the last will and testament of Otis Leatherwood. He bequeaths to you, Mrs. Hornbeck, your mother's Bible, stating herein that although he was not a church-going man, he believes you can make good use of it. To you, Mrs. Dutton, he bequeaths all his remaining worldly possessions."

"Oh, no, that can't be right!" Eunice exclaimed, unwilling to believe what she heard, despite the note Otis had written. "I'm sure you misread."

"I assure you I did not," Davis said, reaching into his desk drawer. "Here is the Bible and here is a copy of the will. You and Mr. Hornbeck may go now, as I have other business to discuss with Mrs. Dutton."

"You can keep the damned Bible," Eunice sputtered, scrambling to her feet. "And you, you bitch," she said to Mary, "this won't stand. I'll not accept it. And don't bother coming back to the store. You and your snot-nosed kid are done there."

After Eunice stormed out, dragging a stunned Grover with her, Davis said, "You don't have anything to worry about, Mrs. Dutton. This is all perfectly legal, and there's nothing she can do about it."

Mary smiled and said, "Thank you," and while Davis went on about remaining details, she said a silent prayer of thanks for her Uncle Otis and another for Ozella Gordon.

Mary had hated going to Mrs. Gordon, but she knew Eunice would throw her and Jimmy out, and she couldn't think of anywhere else to turn for help. Otis's house was not ready for occupancy, and even if it were, she couldn't earn a living staying out there. She needed something in town, now. Hoping that Mrs. Gordon might have some suggestions or know someone, even someone who would take her on as housekeeper and cook in exchange for a roof over her and Jimmy's heads for a little while, Mary had steeled herself and sought her best sewing customer's help.

She had not expected Mrs. Gordon to open her own home to them. But she did exactly that, saying they should stay with her family while Mary settled things with the farm and found a place for the shingle she intended to hang out as a seamstress. The woman was a saint. She even had a room in which Mary could do sewing in the meantime. Jimmy wasn't fond of this idea, saying kids at school would rag him no end about Elizabeth. He knew, though, how much Mrs. Gordon's kindness meant to them.

Too, Jimmy liked what was happening while he was at school today and Mary was at the lawyer's office, at least the part she told him. Mrs. Gordon had helped Mary find someone to move their things, and last night, Mary had packed their few possessions. This morning, after she let the two moving men Mrs. Gordon arranged for into the shed through the cobbled back door, she hooked the shank of a new padlock into the door clasp and told them to lock up when they left. On her way out of the alley, she opened the outhouse door and tossed the old lock, the keys to the new one, and the keys to the lock on the storeroom door into one of the holes. This she didn't tell Jimmy.

"Mrs. Dutton?" Davis asked, sensing that Mary was no longer listening. "Are you all right?"

"Yes, sir. I'm sorry, what were you saying?"

"I was saying that when you get the final deed and are ready to start leasing for oil, I'll be happy to assist you with contracts and such."

"Thank you, Mr. Davis," Mary said, getting up to leave, "but there's no way I'm gon' allow drilling on that land. I'll starve first."

CHAPTER 55

The man behind the counter was busy with another customer. Impatient to read the headline story grabbing his attention at the rail station newsstand, Henry dropped a nickel on the counter and helped himself to a copy of the *Arkansas Gazette*.

Still disturbed about some of what he had learned in Oklahoma, he was happy to be back in Arkansas. A few days earlier, when he had gone once more to see Eliza Clinkscale, the former neighbor of Cotton and Sarah Taylor near Louann, she still had not heard from them. All she could tell him was what she said before. The Taylors were going to Ponca City in the former Indian Territory and would figure out a landing place from there.

Henry had taken a train to Little Rock and made several line changes to get to Ponca City, where he got a room in the Arcade Hotel on Grand Avenue. The aptly named street bustled with cars, trucks, and pedestrians, and he wondered if he was looking at some future version of Berrytown. Ponca City had been booming ever since E. W. Marland had brought in the area's first gusher less than ten years ago. Now, the streets were paved, and Marland lived in a huge mansion at one end of the avenue.

As the new owner of 25 percent of the renamed Moss & Grant Freight Company, Henry hoped Berrytown would follow a similar pattern. He had been flabbergasted when Moss offered him a partnership. Moss said it was partly a gift because he had some business ideas he couldn't go after without a younger partner. One who had some schooling and experience being in charge of things, like Henry in the army. And one who didn't go around with a mouthful of snuff. The rest was a buy-in Henry could pay off over time. Both men thought that would be easy if they borrowed money, added trucks, and expanded into other communities so they could keep growing even after the oil boom ended. If things went as they hoped, they would discuss a larger buy-in down the road. The more Henry looked at all the signs of progress in Ponca City, the more pleased he was with his good fortune. And with Moss, who, when Henry told him Smith wasn't his real name, had only said, "I thought so."

What bothered Henry about Ponca City was how all the oil was on Indian land leased to the oil companies, and how under federal law, the Indians, mostly Osage, had little or no control over it. Each had a trustee who parceled out earnings only after taking an exorbitant cut for himself. This began nagging at Henry as soon as he heard about it, and he couldn't shake it. He thought about the Susan Wallace book he'd told Mary about, and what the Spaniards had done to the Pueblo Indians and their land hundreds of years earlier. And that reminded him of Otis Leatherwood and his newspaper advertisement. Maybe, Henry thought, if he succeeded in Moss and Grant Freighting Company the way he pictured, he could help keep Otis's call for caution alive. How exactly, he didn't know, but he'd seen enough to share the old man's concerns.

It was Cotton Taylor who had told Henry about the Osage, after Henry found him and Sarah through a lot of looking and asking around. Despite Cotton's and Sarah's dislike for some of what was going on around them, Cotton was making good money. They were living in a frame house for the first time, and the children had a yard to play in. Cotton said the oil companies were still finding new pools west and southwest of Ponca City, and he expected to have work for years.

When Henry told Sarah about the quilt and asked if she would trade it for the two new blankets he had brought along, she was happy to do so. She said she could never enjoy it while knowing how much time and love Mary Dutton's mother had poured into it and what it meant to Mary.

After making the exchange, giving the Taylor children gifts of books and candy, and sharing a home-cooked meal with the family, Henry had rushed back to the Arcade to pack his things and get to the railway station in time to catch the next train out. In his haste he dropped the quilt while getting out of a taxi at the hotel. Before he could scoop it up, a truck ran over it, ripped away the newspaper pages in which Sarah had wrapped it, and dragged it along the street, leaving it torn and dirty.

Now, in Little Rock with the battered quilt re-bundled in the latest *Ponca City Courier* by a hotel bellhop and stuffed safely into his travel bag, Henry headed for the nearest bench to read the story in the *Gazette*. Before he even sat down and opened the paper, he thought he knew at least part of what he would find under the headline: "Treasury Agents Strike Twice in Union County."

Upon learning the extent of Sheriff Owen Sutro's crime ring, Henry had written to a man with whom he had served in the American Expeditionary Force. Henry didn't know if Captain Wesley Emerson had left the army after the war or stayed in. He did know, however, that in the waning weeks of the fighting, Emerson had been assigned temporarily to a new military police unit and discovered that not only did he have a talent for law enforcement, he also liked it. Although Henry and Emerson had not remained in touch, they had exchanged civilian addresses with the intent of doing so. Henry hoped that somehow his letter would reach Emerson wherever he was, and if it did, he would either have or find a contact in the Treasury Department's Prohibition Unit with whom to share the information.

After locating the stills over near the Ouachita River, Henry had written Emerson again. So far, Henry had not received a reply to either letter, but now it seemed likely that one or both had gotten through. The newspaper reported that large portable stills had been discovered and destroyed near Felsenthal in eastern Union County. Charges of violating the Volsted Act by making alcoholic beverages had been brought against individuals in both Union and Ouachita Counties. All were in jail awaiting trial. Owen Sutro wasn't among those identified in the article, and Henry guessed he had either bought his way out of it or the investigation was ongoing. In any case, there near the bottom of the list of those arrested was the name "Ed Tuttle."

The other item in the *Gazette* story was a shock. Pharmacist Grover Hornbeck and his wife, Eunice Hornbeck, had been arrested in Berrytown and charged with criminal violation of the Harrison Act by selling illegal drugs. Their store had been seized and they were in custody. The article said federal agents had been surveilling the pair's activities for months. It did not say whether anyone else was arrested or implicated in the crimes.

Henry laid the paper on the bench, picked up his travel bag, and ran his fingers over the latch. The quilt inside was as near as he could get to Mary Dutton at the moment. He wouldn't allow himself to believe that she had knowingly sold illegal drugs or been arrested. She must have been terrified, though. And this coming on the heels of losing her uncle. Henry wished now that he had gone to see her and offered condolences as soon as Moss told him about Otis. At the time he was still chagrinned about giving away the quilt, and he had told himself that his showing up would only sadden Mary more.

He left the newspaper where it lay, got up, and paced the station lobby and corridors until his train was called. Remembering then that he hadn't eaten for hours, he almost missed the connection while racing to grab a sandwich to take on board.

The ride to Berrytown seemed agonizingly slow. The cars were crowded, much the same as the first time he had made this journey, but not so much that he had to stand like before. Also, unlike before, Henry was not carrying his .45. It was locked away in the mule yard office, and he intended to leave it there. When the train finally screeched to a stop in the gray dusk of the late December day, Henry pushed his way through the crowd at the depot and rushed down Broadway to Hornbeck's, around the corner on Seventh Street, and up the alley to the shed in back. It was dark like the store, and padlocked on the outside. He doubted there could be anyone inside but he knocked and pounded on the door anyway.

He thought for a second about going back around to the street and asking passersby if they knew where the woman who once stayed in back of the store lived now. Then he thought, no, that would be demeaning to Mary, and there was a better way. He ran back up Broadway, dodging wagons, cars, and people on foot until he crossed El Dorado Avenue and the railroad tracks. From there he raced the short distance up the Camden highway to the mule yard, hoping Moss hadn't left for the evening. If he wasn't there or didn't know what had happened to Mary, maybe one of the police officers would be there tending to his mount and would know.

Henry found Moss in his little office in the front barn fiddling with papers.

"Hey, partner," Moss said, "I was beginning to think you wasn't coming back."

"Do you know where Mary Dutton is?" Henry asked, skipping any sort of greeting and failing to notice that Moss had gotten rid of most of the clutter that usually surrounded him.

"Ain't you even gon' say anything about my office?" Moss asked.

"Yeah, looks good," Henry said without taking his eyes off Moss. "Do you know where Mary Dutton is?"

"I heard her and that boy of hers are living over at the Methodist preacher's house."

Henry opened his travel bag and took out the quilt. He dropped the bag at Moss's feet, put the quilt under his arm, and dashed out the door.

Seconds later, he returned and asked, "Where's that preacher live?"

~

The two-story white frame house Moss described was three blocks south of Hornbeck's and four blocks east of Broadway. Far enough that Henry, tired from having run from the train station to the drugstore and back to the mule yard, could get there faster if he took Trixie. She was stabled only a few stalls down the center aisle from Moss's office.

Henry rode bareback, like he often had back in Indiana. When he got to the Gordon house, he leaped off Trixie, wrapped the reins around a gate post, and bounded up the front walkway and onto the wide porch, carrying the wrapped quilt under one arm. Curtains were drawn over the front windows, but a dim light shown through. Someone was home.

Henry paused to gather himself then knocked lightly on the frame of the screen door.

A slender woman with graying hair opened the interior door and peered over her glasses through the screen.

"I'm sorry to disturb you, ma'am," Henry said. "My name's Henry Smith, and I'm looking for…"

"Oh, my goodness," the woman interrupted, her hands flying to her mouth. "She's here. Wait right there and I'll get her."

"Thank you," Henry said, trying to assess Mrs. Gordon's reaction. He watched and listened through the screen as she walked into an adjoining room and told Mary there was someone at the door for her.

The night was so black, Mary couldn't see who was there until she reached the screen door.

"Henry!" she said, stepping to the side and pushing the door open. "What a pleasant surprise."

"Mary," he breathed, as he entered with his package. He wanted to tell her he was sorry about her losing her uncle, about what had happened at the drugstore, and about not coming to see her since the night she made supper for him. But all he could get out was, "Are you all right?"

"I'm fine. How are you?" she said, her eyes locking onto his.

"I brought you something," he said, holding out the quilt with one hand and yanking the newspaper off it with the other.

"My quilt," she said softly. "How did you…? Where?"

"It's a long story."

Mary ran her hands over the fabric, then let the quilt fall to the floor. She put her arms around Henry's waist and her head on his shoulder. "I've missed you so much," she said.

Henry wanted to lift her chin, touch his lips to hers and let them linger there, exploring, but he hesitated, fearful of embarrassing Mary if Mrs. Gordon was peeking. Instead, he squeezed Mary lightly and said, "I've missed you, too, and I have a lot to tell you."

"I have a lot to tell you too," Mary said. She leaned back, looked into his eyes again, and smiled.

Her dimples and mouth were so enticing Henry could barely think of anything else. Finally, he mumbled, "I'm sorry the quilt's all messed up. It got run over and two of those big corners are torn pretty bad."

"That's all right," Mary said, reaching up and brushing the back of her hand across his face, "I never liked them anyway. I'll just take the stuffing out and fix the holes."

Henry took her hand in his, held it to his lips, then released it, and put both of his behind her head and pulled her close.

Just before his mouth touched hers, she whispered, "I love you, Henry Smith."

"I love you too," he whispered back, "and my name's Grant, not Smith. But that's another long story."

"Tell me later," she said, pressing her lips to his.

AUTHOR'S NOTE

Look Unto the Land is a work of fiction. Through it, I wanted to tell an entertaining story, present a realistic picture of 1920s oil-field development, and help call attention to the history of racism in the United States and to the ever-present need to protect and conserve the natural environment.

The setting of the novel is based generally on the history, geography, and demographics of southern Arkansas. A real town inspired the story, but Berrytown is fictitious. All major aspects of national history, as well as that of the various states it encompasses, are rooted in fact, but I have taken minor liberties with the order of some historical events and activities. All real people and places are used fictitiously. Other names, places, characters, and events are products of the author's imagination, and any resemblance to actual events, places, or persons, living or dead, is entirely coincidental.

Although depicted fictitiously, the oil industry and the illegal drug and liquor activities in the novel are consistent with the history of the time and place. Oral histories and printed first-person recollections about drug trafficking in southern Arkansas during the boom are sparce, but illegal drug activities in the lower Mississippi Valley and Southwest regions, as well as in the rest of the country, at the time are well recorded and are depicted realistically in the story. Drug laws and mechanisms of enforcement in both the United States and Mexico are also realistically represented. The sale of marijuana was legal in Arkansas at the time but banned shortly after.

Much of the color and many of the events in the story were inspired by material in more than four hundred oral histories of 1920s oil-boom life collected by the Arkansas Museum of Natural Resources in Smackover, Union County, Arkansas.

For additional historical background information about the oil industry and boomtown life in southern Arkansas in the 1920s, I relied especially on: Mary L. Barrett, "The Oil Waste History of Smackover Field, Arkansas," *Environmental Geosciences*, 8, no. 4 (2001), 231-241; A.R. Buckalew and R.B. Buckalew, "The Discovery of Oil in South Arkansas," *Arkansas Historical Quarterly*, 33, no. 3 (1974), 195-238; Kenny A. Franks and Paul F. Lambert, *Early Louisiana and Arkansas Oil: A Photographic History, 1901-1946* (College Station: Texas A&M University Press, 1982); Phillip E. Norvell, "The History of Oil and Gas Conservation Legislation in Arkansas," *Arkansas Law Review*, 68, no. 2 (2015), 349-380; and Carl Coke Wister, *Oil! Titan of the Southwest* (Norman: University of Oklahoma Press, 1949). Other helpful volumes about everyday life in oil boomtowns in the Southwest included: Mody C. Boatwright and William A. Owens, *Tales from the Derrick Floor: A People's History of the Oil Industry* (Garden City, New York: Doubleday & Company, 1970); and Bobby D. Weaver, *Oilfield Trash: Life and Labor in the Oil Patch* (College Station: Texas A&M University Press, 2010).

For information about illegal drugs, alcohol, prohibition, and pharmacies in the 1920s, I consulted in particular: H. Carmen Boullosa and Mike Wallace: *A Narco History: How the United States and Mexico Jointly Created the "Mexican Drug War"* (New York: OR Books, 2016); Ben F. Johnson III, *John Barleycorn Must Die: The War Against Drink in Arkansas* (Fayetteville: University of Arkansas Press, 2005); Geogory J. Higby and Elaine C. Stroud, *American Pharmacy (1852-2002): A Collection of Historical Essays* (Madison, Wisconsin: American Institute of the History of Pharmacy, 2005); H. Wayne Morgan, *Drugs in America: A Social History, 1800-1980* (Syracuse: Syracuse University Press, 1981); and Louis Vyhnanek, "Muggles, Itchy, and Mud: Illegal Drugs in New Orleans during the 1920s," *Louisiana History*, 22, no. 3 (1981), 252-279.

For background related to the First World War, I relied in large part on: Kinshasha Holman Conwill, editor, *We Return Fighting: World War I and the Shaping of Modern Black Identity* (Washington: Smithsonian Books in association with the National Museum of African American History & Culture, 2019); Emmett M. Essin, *Shavetails and Bell Sharps: The History of the U.S. Army Mule* (Lincoln: University of Nebraska Press, 1997); and Wendy Holden, *Shell Shock: The Psychological Impact of War* (London: Channel 4 Books, 1998).

Helpful books about the Ku Klux Klan included: Charles C. Alexander, *The Ku Klux Klan in the Southwest* (Norman: University of Oklahoma Press, 1965); Linda Gordon, T*he Second Coming of the KKK: The Ku Klux Klan of the 1920s and the American Political Tradition* (New York, Liveright, 2017); and Felix Harcourt, *Ku Klux Kulture: America and the Klan in the 1920s* (Chicago: University of Chicago Press, 2017).

The following provided a thorough overview of evangelist Billy Sunday: Roger A. Burns, *Preacher: Billy Sunday and Big-Time Evangelism* (Urbana: University of Illinois Press, 1992);

W. A. Firstenberger, *In Rare Form: A Pictorial History of Baseball Evangelist Billy Sunday* (Iowa City, University of Iowa Press, 2005); and John R. Rice, comp. and ed., *The Best of Billy Sunday: 17 Burning Sermons from the Most Spectacular Evangelist the World Has Ever Known* (Murfreesboro, Tennessee, Sword of the Lord Publishers, 1965).

A word about style: Today, common practice calls for capitalizing the word "Black" when referring to African Americans. I adhere to that practice elsewhere in my writing, but I did not do so in the novel because that was not accepted style at the time when the story takes place.

I am indebted to many for invaluable assistance with *Look Unto the Land*. Samantha Bynum and Charles Liccardi of the Arkansas Museum of Natural Resources in Smackover, Arkansas, and Whitney Curry of the Barton Library in El Dorado, Arkansas, provided helpful access to unique local history collections. Lisa Feinstein, David Harris, Vanette Harris, Laura Sadowski, and Celeste Schantz read all or portions of the manuscript in various drafts and provided invaluable feedback, as did my quilting and novel-loving spouse, Diana Murphy Adams. Kelly Johnson provided essential help with various aspects of production. I appreciate the assistance of each of them.

Lastly, I am grateful to Diana and to our children Brady, Amy, and Amanda for their ongoing understanding and support of my writing.

If you enjoyed *Look Unto the Land*, please post a review, or simply rate it, on Amazon and Goodreads and help call it to the attention of other readers.

QUESTIONS FOR DISCUSSION

1. What did you think of Henry Grant? How would you characterize him? Was he a good man or a flawed man? As the story unfolded, did the way you regarded his reason for coming to Berrytown evolve or change?
2. Henry introduced his sister to Ed Tuttle and left home to join the army. Did either of those things make Henry responsible to any extent for what happened to the Grant family?
3. What do you think accounted for the decision Henry made when he was sitting alone in the river bottom near the end of the novel?
4. Did you like Mary Dutton, or did you see her as someone who could have done more to stand up to Eunice Hornbeck? Did any of Mary's actions surprise you?
5. What did you think of Eunice? Did you feel any sympathy for her?
6. As you came to know Otis Leatherwood in the story, did any of his actions or interactions surprise you? Do you think his attitudes and actions toward the oil industry were justified?

7. How did you feel about Otis Leatherwood's relationship with Eunice? Was one of them more responsible than the other for the nature of it?
8. Did the relationships between Otis Leatherwood and Isaiah Watson and between Jimmy Dutton and Robert Watson surprise you in any way? What about the relationship between Henry Grant and Calvin Birdsong? Did you regard these relationships as realistic?
9. In what ways did WWI and its aftermath affect the characters and arc of the story?
10. Many soldiers returned from WWI with "shell shock," generally known today as Post-Traumatic Stress Syndrome. What impact did that have on the actions of characters in the book? Based on what you have read or heard, or based on personal experiences or relationships, do you believe the United States has improved its recognition and treatment of these types of battlefield effects over time?
11. How does the historical character Billy Sunday compare to modern-day evangelists? Did he remind you of anyone or of any activities in recent or present-day America?
12. In what ways are 1922 and 2022 similar, for example, societal issues and changes in technology and culture? Did you think about those as you read the book? Do you think it is possible for Americans today to do a better job of not repeating darker aspects of the past?

Earlier works by George Rollie Adams:

Found in Pieces, a multi-award-winning novel

South of Little Rock, a multi-award-winning novel

General William S. Harney: Prince of Dragoons,
a biography

Ordinary People and Everyday Life: Perspectives on the New Social History, a book of essays,
edited with James B. Gardner

Nashville: A Pictorial History,
with Ralph Jerry Christian

The American Indian: Past and Present (first edition only),
a book of essays, edited with Roger L. Nichols

Awards for *South of Little Rock*

Winner, Next Generation Indie Book Award
for Regional Fiction

Winner, National Indie Excellence Award
for Regional Fiction

Silver Medal, Readers' Favorite Award
for Social Issues Fiction

Bronze Medal, Independent Publisher's Award
for Regional Fiction

Awards for *Found in Pieces*

Winner, National Indie Excellence Award
for Historical Fiction

Winner, National Indie Excellence Award
for Regional Fiction

Winner, Independent Press Award
for Race Relations

Gold Medal, Global Book Award
for Modern Historical Fiction

Silver Medal, Independent Publishers IPPY Award
for Regional Fiction

Silver Medal, Readers' Favorite Award
for Social Issues Fiction

ABOUT THE AUTHOR

George Rollie Adams is a native of southern Arkansas and a former teacher with graduate degrees in history and education. He is the author of *Found in Pieces*, which received six independent publishers' awards for historical, social issues, and race relations fiction; author of *South of Little Rock*, which received four independent publishers' awards for regional and social issues fiction; author of *General William S. Harney: Prince of Dragoons*, a finalist for the Army Historical Foundation's Distinguished Book Award; coauthor of *Nashville: A Pictorial History*; and coeditor of *Ordinary People and Everyday Life,* a book of essays on social history. Adams has served as a writer, editor, and program director for the American Association for State and Local History and as director of the Louisiana State Museum in New Orleans. He is president and CEO emeritus of the Strong National Museum of Play, where he founded the *American Journal of Play* and led the establishment of the International Center for the History of Electronic Games.

See the author's website and blog at
www.georgerollieadamsbooks.com